ALSO BY PHILLIP DEPOY

THE CHRISTOPHER MARLOWE SERIES

A Prisoner in Malta

The English Agent

THE FEVER DEVILIN SERIES

The Devil's Hearth

The Witch's Grave

A Minister's Ghost

A Widow's Curse

The Drifter's Wheel

A Corpse's Nightmare

December's Thorn

THE FLAP TUCKER SERIES

Easy

Too Easy

Easy as One-Two-Three

Dancing Made Easy

Dead Easy

THE FOGGY MOSCOWITZ SERIES

Cold Florida

Three Shot Burst

The King James Conspiracy

The E
Ag

The English Agent

Phillip DePoy

MINOTAUR BOOKS
NEW YORK

This is a work of fiction. All of the characters, organizations, and events portrayed in this novel are either products of the author's imagination or are used fictitiously.

Printed in the United States of America. For information, address St. Martin's Press, 175 Fifth Avenue, New York, N.Y. 10010.

www.minotaurbooks.com

Library of Congress Cataloging-in-Publication Data is available upon request.

ISBN 978-1-250-05843-0 (hardcover)
ISBN 978-1-4668-6259-3 (e-book)

First Edition: February 2017

10 9 8 7 6 5 4 3 2 1

Is it ridiculous that almost every dedication is to Lee, or do people find that romantic? After a relationship that's touched three decades, Lee, I can't help it if I'm still in love with you. Isn't that a Hank Williams song? Now I'm quoting Hank Williams? How will that play with the snooty theatre and academic types? Am I thinking about this too much? Am I over-worrying about a dedication that, let's face it, maybe seven people will read? Should it just say: TO LEE and let it go at that? If you're reading this, and have an opinion, tell me what it is. I really want to know: www.phillipdepoy.com.

ACKNOWLEDGMENTS

Thanks again to Anthony Burgess's book *Shakespeare*, not just for great insider information, but for its tone and humor.

I owe a debt to Thomas Dekker, especially his description of Elizabethan London street life, and to John Donne's satirical elucidations of the Elizabethan Court.

I also continue to acknowledge the debt I owe to Dr. Milton Goldberg who, at Antioch College in 1968, allowed me, as a freshman, to be in his upper-level Shakespeare class.

Finally, I'd have to acknowledge that reading John Fowles novels, especially *The Magus* and *A Maggot*, forced me to write a certain way.

The English Agent

†

PRELUDE

"William the Silent is dead." Walsingham let the words sink in.

The Queen's face remained unchanged, but her fist tightened.

"When?" she asked.

The small private chamber was silent, and a dozen candles failed to eliminate the gloom from Walsingham's pronouncement.

Elizabeth was seated next to a small desk upon which one of the candles suddenly sputtered.

"Three days from now," Walsingham answered at last, "if we do not dispatch our people to Delft today."

He stood silently, eyes fixed on his queen.

Her face at last betrayed her thoughts.

"You deliberately shocked me," she snapped. "To what purpose?"

"To convey the urgency of the matter."

She took a moment to control her ire.

"You have his imminent assassination on good authority?" she demanded.

"The plot is certain," he answered.

"It's clever," she sighed, "taking William out. He's the only man who could stand against the Spanish in the Netherlands."

"William is our ally," Walsingham agreed, "and were he gone, the Netherlands might be unstable enough to allow Spanish invasion forces to pass through to the coast. But it is not yet clear the intention of this assassination. It may well be a civil matter."

She nodded. "We must send someone to Delft at once to gather information, and to prevent William's assassination, if possible."

"First things first," Walsingham said firmly. "We need our people here in England, in case there is more to this business than meets the eye."

The Queen nodded. "You mean we must ascertain whether or not it has to do with us, with our person."

"Yes, Majesty," Walsingham confirmed.

"You have a devilishly suspicious nature, Francis," she said softly.

"Yes, Majesty," he repeated.

"Whom do you select for this investigation?" she asked.

"Beak," Walsingham sighed.

"Of course," Elizabeth responded softly. "But not alone."

"No." Walsingham folded his hands. "I would not allow Beak to do this alone."

The Queen stood and turned toward the door. Walsingham bowed. The Queen hesitated.

"I suppose I know whom you will associate with Beak," she said without looking back.

"Yes," Walsingham answered. "It's Marlowe."

ONE

1584, CAMBRIDGE, ENGLAND

Christopher Marlowe sat at his usual table near the fireplace in The Pickerel public house. By his side: the most irritating mentor with whom God had ever cursed a poet, or so Marlowe was thinking at that moment. Thomas Kyd, dressed in blue frills, the highest London fashion, was fat, drunken, lewd, and smoking. To make matters worse, the noise of the place was maddening. A makeshift stage in a corner of The Pickerel was colorful but, alas, not the liveliest nor even the loudest spot in the public house. In addition to being a place for students to gather, it was the second best brothel in Cambridge. The clientele were ale sodden, rude, and entirely unencumbered by social restraint—and that on an ordinary day. To make matters even worse, the riverside location assured the presence of sailing men, cutpurses, traveling criminals, and general miscreants in addition to the studious young men on their way from better places to a class at the college.

Still, Marlowe had always found the place comforting. The low ceiling and slanting afternoon sunlight gave a warmth to body and spirit, and the ale was flavored with rosemary. It was a home away from home—on most days. But this day, to everyone's dismay, there was also a play at hand.

There were actors on a stage, shouting to be heard.

"Did ever men see such a sudden storm?" one of the actors howled. "Or day so suddenly overcast?"

The audience shouted back. Louder. A man at the bar responded directly to the actor's questions.

"Did ever a man see such a sorry spectacle?" he hollered, "or a day so destroyed by a scabrous play?"

The second actor on stage did his best. "I think some fell Enchantress dwells here, that can dive into black tempests treasury as she means to mask the world with clouds."

A large man in a green tunic near the stage bellowed a more concise critique. "Shite!"

The general chaos of noise rose higher after that, pelting the actors with insults and laughter.

At his table by the fireplace, Kyd leaned close to Marlowe and whispered, "Generally I like a play that attracts audience attention, but is this quite what you had in mind?"

Marlowe, dressed entirely in black, turned to the older man and spoke very politely. "Find a raw carrot, lower your breeches, and shove it as far up your ass as you possibly can, do you mind?"

"Time enough for fun later, Kit," Kyd responded. "I thought you wanted me to watch your play."

"You're too drunk to watch your thumb," Marlowe answered. "I wanted Kyd the playwright, not Kyd the lout."

Kyd sat back. "Oh. Well. You should have told me that before I started drinking, don't you think?"

"You know I love you," Marlowe complained, "but I can barely stand to be around you."

Kyd dismissed that pronouncement with a flourish of his right hand. "All of my friends say that."

The young boy playing the part of Anna, on stage in an ill-fitting dress and terrible wig, seemed to have forgotten the next line. Prompted three times, he finally gave forth, in a high-pitched squeak, "In all my life I never knew the like, it hailed, it snowed, and lightning all at once!"

The place erupted in catcalls, howling, a general demand for the play to come to an end. Sooner than immediately.

The man who had yelled "shite" was on his feet.

"Come over here, sweetheart," he said to the boy playing Anna. "Give us a kiss."

He staggered toward the stage.

The other two actors moved instantly to protect the younger. One suddenly had a knife in his hand.

"Now it's getting interesting," Kyd slurred. "I really like it when the audience is a part of the play."

Marlowe ignored Kyd and bounded toward the stage.

"That's enough for one afternoon," he called out. "The play is ended."

The large drunk in green turned, slowing, in Marlowe's direction. His beard was alive with ale and saliva.

"That was a *play*?" he growled. "I thought my great ox had laid a pile of dung in that corner."

"Ah," Marlowe said quickly, "well I defer to your superior knowledge of an ox's ass."

A few in the room laughed.

"How's that?" the man asked more slowly.

"I say the play's over," Marlowe answered, as if the man were hard of hearing. "You can go back to buggering your ox."

More laughed.

"Right," the man bellowed, drawing a long knife of his own.

As he did he caught a nearby patron on the chin with his elbow. The patron objected loudly.

"Christ!" the patron complained.

That complainant drew a dagger of his own. His round, greasy face contorted in a grin.

The man in green turned and punched the complainant twice. The complainant fell backward onto the floor and stayed there, dagger still in hand, grin gone.

Then the man in green turned and lunged at Marlowe.

Without warning, Kyd was there, placing his considerable girth between Marlowe and the marauder.

"You're a very rude person," Kyd said to the green man.

Then Kyd, holding a tankard of ale in one hand and his pipe in the other, simply stepped aside, nudging Marlowe out of the way. The man in green went sprawling across the nearest table. The men at that table objected. They were on their feet in seconds, all with weapons in their hands: two knives and a rapier.

Marlowe drew his own rapier and stood next to Kyd, who took a sip of ale and then pulled hard on his pipe.

The man in green was struggling to rise; the other three were not certain who had offended them the most.

"Should we go on?" one of the actors called timidly.

"No," Marlowe answered before anyone else could. "Wait outside. I'll bring you your money."

"But we just started," the boy playing Anna complained.

"That's your play?" one of the three men asked.

Marlowe nodded once.

"Good enough for me," the man said, and charged.

The others followed.

Marlowe found himself attacked on three sides. Kyd stood firmly at Marlowe's back, tranquil as a summer's day.

Marlowe took the rapier first. He lunged forward, twirling his blade in small, wild circles. When he was close enough, he caught his opponent's rapier in the vortex and sent the other man's weapon flying. With one single, final sidestep, Marlowe stabbed that man in the forearm—his sword arm—and then kicked the man's knee so hard that everyone heard it crack.

Without stopping to think, Marlowe turned toward one of the knives. Before he could get his balance, the man rushed, snarling, blade forward, teeth bared.

Kyd did not appear to move of a purpose, but a single dance-like stumble thrust his pristine boot forward at the other man's ankle. As if by some odd spell, that man found himself facedown on the floor in the next instant.

Marlowe turned his attention to the last man.

That one stood, glancing around at the others groaning on the floor and blinking. He lowered his knife.

"So that's your play then, is it?" he said, only a slight quaver in his voice.

"It is," Marlowe responded, his rapier aimed directly at the man's throat.

"Well," the man said, as if it were a complete philosophy.

Kyd's voice boomed out generously. "Truer words were never spoken!"

Marlowe glanced at the stage. The actors were gone.

Then, out of the corner of his eye, he caught a glimpse of red, a slight furling of a crimson cloak—and the barrel of a pistol. That was, it seemed, what had actually stopped the brawl. The last man standing had seen the gun.

Marlowe realized that The Pickerel had fallen nearly silent, quieter than it had been in a decade.

Marlowe took a deep breath. "I thank one and all for your indulgence. I will continue to work on the piece."

"What's it called?" the last man standing asked quietly.

"*Dido*," Marlowe answered. "It's about a queen of Carthage."

The man nodded. He clearly had no idea what Marlowe was talking about.

Marlowe sheathed his rapier, took Kyd by the arm, and headed for the door.

"You should try your hand at a Hamlet play," Kyd said, sucking on his pipe. "Everyone's doing it."

Marlowe moved faster, nearly dragging Kyd along. "No," Marlowe complained, "*you've* done the definitive version of that story. Who would pay attention to any other?"

Kyd finished his ale and set his tankard down on one of the tables as he was being rushed out the door.

"True," he mused. "Why are you shoving me outside? I need more drink."

Once in the street, Kyd froze. He saw why Marlowe had rushed him out of the inn. In one of the shadows across the narrow dirt street there was a flair of red cloth, and a pair of familiar eyes.

"Oh." Kyd would not be moved further. "Dr. Lopez."

Rodrigo Lopez, Portuguese Jew, remorseless assassin, and

Queen Elizabeth's Royal Surgeon, was also Marlowe's boyhood tutor.

"What's he doing here?" Kyd whispered, unable to disguise the fear in his voice.

While most other men lived in terror of the doctor, Marlowe considered Lopez his only genuine friend.

"He's come to see me," Marlowe answered apologetically, then he glanced around. "My actors seem to have vanished."

"That's a shame," Kyd lamented absently. "I was hoping to get to know the one who played Anna a little better."

"Leave that one alone, Kyd," Marlowe warned. "He's barely twelve years old. And put out that pipe, it stinks."

Kyd sniffed, partially regaining his swagger. "How many times have I told you? Only a fool does not like tobacco and young boys. The former is good for the health, and the latter is superior for the spirit."

But Marlowe was already halfway across the street. Lopez did not move.

"Doctor," Marlowe said softly as he approached his old friend. "You didn't need to break up that brawl. Kyd and I would have handled it."

"Kyd is a brilliant tactician," Lopez agreed, stepping slightly into the slanting ray of golden light from the west. "I've never seen a greater adept at his style of combat."

Marlowe hesitated. "I can't tell if your intent is to praise him or to ridicule, but I assure you—"

"I am in earnest," Lopez interrupted. "I've seen Thomas Kyd's tactics before, in London. His ability to use force and intention against any opponent is unparalleled. I saw him best five men, barely laying a hand on a single one. He had no weapon and never spilled his drink. When his attackers tried to strike, he simply wasn't there."

Marlowe smiled. "Yes, he can get out of the way better than any man in England."

Lopez remained cold. "And: he's not a bad playwright, as I understand it."

"That man," Marlowe nodded, glancing in Kyd's direction, "despite some very obvious difficulties, is one of the finest poets I know, and the greatest playwright in the world. Our age will be remembered for its female monarch and the plays of Thomas Kyd."

Kyd had found a convenient barrel outside the inn and was seated filling his pipe. Grinning and singing to himself, he looked very much like the village idiot.

"Your Queen requires you," Lopez said.

"I know." Marlowe's voice betraying a certain wariness. "Why else would you have come unannounced? What has happened?"

"An assassination of worldwide consequence," Lopez said with a dead voice.

"Who has been murdered?" Marlowe swallowed. He had rarely seen Lopez in so strange a mood.

Lopez leaned close to Marlowe's ear.

"William the Silent," he whispered to Marlowe, "is dead."

TWO

William the Silent could not be dead. He was too important to England.

When William was eleven he became Prince of Orange under the condition that he be given a Catholic education. By the time William was in his thirties he stood by the side of the gout-ridden King of Spain, Charles, who abdicated his throne in favor of son Philip. But William began almost immediately to criticize Philip's campaign against non-Catholics. His famous quote, repeated across Europe, was, "I cannot approve of monarchs who want to rule over the conscience of the people, and take away their freedom of choice and religion."

He eventually aligned himself with the French Huguenots, most especially by marrying one. William was subsequently declared an outlaw by the Spanish king in 1580, making William an ally to England, albeit surreptitiously. William's knowledge of the inner workings of the Spanish court—and its secret plans to invade England—could not be replaced.

Kyd called out from across the road. "Do you know why they call him *Silent*? He wouldn't talk about Protestants during a stag hunt."

"No," Marlowe said without turning to face Kyd, "it's because he refused to discuss the Inquisition. If only you would be *Kyd the Silent*."

"Oh, yes, I shouldn't be talking about this so loudly," Kyd looked around at the rabble in the streets. "There could be Spanish spies."

Lopez growled his disapproval. "Thomas Kyd, you must leave us now. Back to London. Drink until you cannot remember this meeting. If I hear that you have recounted what has been said here, you will find yourself in the Tower. Do you understand?"

Kyd stood at once.

"I understand completely," he said. "I have to return to London anyway, they're doing my new play in Shoreditch. In fact, there's an excellent chance that I was never in Cambridge at all this week."

Kyd's face had drained of blood, and his hands were shaking. In the next second he was gone, vanished around the next corner.

"Was that necessary?" Marlowe sighed. "Despite his braggadocio, he is an easily frightened man."

"*Braggadocio*?"

"Ah," Marlowe answered, "it's from a character that Sydney is trying to work out for a poem. I think he's calling it *The Faerie Queene*—terrible title. But that word, *braggadocio,* is the name of an Italianate braggart who—"

"Marlowe, stop talking." Lopez took Marlowe's arm and dragged him into the shadows.

Marlowe nodded gravely. "I may be a bit in my cups. My play is terrible, you understand, and I drank too much, so I'll need an hour or two—"

"No time." Lopez dragged Marlowe around the corner where two horses stood ready. "We are to meet with Walsingham's agent in Buntingford before sundown."

"Yes," Marlowe said hesitantly, "perhaps just a bit of cold water in the face or a—a very brief nap."

Lopez spun around, his face only inches from Marlowe's.

"Philip Sydney has taken your Penelope to bed," Lopez snarled.

They were only a few words, but no curse or spell could have worked any better to silence Marlowe, or to sober him.

The ride to Buntingford worked to further rouse Marlowe. Lopez did not keep to any road or path, so the riding was difficult and took concentration. There was no opportunity for idle conversation, so Marlowe had time to think about Philip Sydney in bed with his beloved Penelope Devereux. And the journey took four hours, more than enough time for any Englishman to recover from a little ale.

Buntingford, on the River Rib, had little to recommend it save for the Bell Inn. Surrounded by lovely open meadows and abundant barns, room enough for lofts to house grooms and smiths, the inn was the perfect place for changing horses on the journey from London to Cambridge. Indeed, Her Majesty had stayed at the Bell several times. Its hospitality was widely known.

The sun was near setting when the meadows came in sight. The evening was warm and the summer day was so long that it could well have been past nine o'clock. Everything was green, and there were brindled cows in the fields walking slowly toward the buildings. Sunlight was amber and gold in long low beams. Someone in a field, out of sight, was singing "The White Hare of Howden" and, after a moment, others joined in.

Lopez slowed his horse and Marlowe rode alongside him.

"The man we are to meet is called Beak," Lopez said softly, his eyes on the public entrance to the inn in the distance. "He's been told to expect me. Only me. You'll go into the room first, take a table, order something, and wait. I'll enter. He is to recognize my manner of dress. He'll approach me. Watch to see if anyone else in the room takes notice. Do you understand?"

"We don't trust this *Beak*," Marlowe answered.

Lopez smiled but did not look Marlowe's way. "We don't trust anyone."

"Agreed." Marlowe nodded.

The inn was plain, two stories, lots of windows. As they approached, a boy of twelve or so appeared.

"Shall I take the horses?" he suggested expressionlessly.

"Where would you take them?" Lopez asked.

"Stables," the boy answered, looking over his shoulder toward the closest barn.

"I'll go with you," Lopez said, sliding down from his horse.

"I'll go in," Marlowe said softly.

Lopez nodded, handed the reins of both horses to the boy, and walked by his side toward the barn.

Marlowe rubbed his face, took a few deep breaths, and then ambled into the Bell.

The place was quiet, a sedate, distant cousin to The Pickerel. The ceilings were high, and the room seemed large because of it. There were ten or twelve tables, neatly arranged, a wide stone hearth, and the floors were wooden. Windows faced west, so the setting sunlight was nearly blinding as it poured in. There was a bar set with several kegs, a rack of dishes, and a small door behind the bar which would lead to a kitchen.

A well-dressed older man at the bar and a primly adorned younger woman were obviously employees of the place. Only five customers were in evidence: three men at separate tables and a well-to-do couple in the corner having a quiet, wordless meal. Marlowe eliminated the couple instantly and concentrated on the solitaries.

One man, very large, sat by the fire, clay pipe in hand. By his clothes Marlowe guessed he might be a baker: powdery flour on his cuffs and at his ample belly.

Another man, older, was asleep in his chair, and had the look of Protestant clergy, though he wore no such identifying collar. His thick black beard and bushy eyebrows were almost a cliché.

The third was young, nervous, looking all about, dressed in rough clothing, had the look of an apprentice of some sort. His hair was tousled and his cheeks were ruddy. He was drinking a large tankard of something or other.

Marlowe might have ventured to guess that the third man was Beak, but recent experience had taught him that anyone in the room could be Walsingham's agent.

Marlowe took the empty table nearest the door, back to the wall and windows, momentarily hidden by the door to anyone who entered the room. It was a perfect vantage point.

The serving girl headed his way. Her expression was only a little haughty, but enough to fend off initial warmth. Dressed in a plain green dress, allowed both upper and lower classes by the Sumptuary laws, she might have been the owner's daughter, or wife. Her entire manner was meant to explain to the casual visitor that she was a proper young woman, no common tavern lackey.

Without thinking, Marlowe began speaking before she arrived at the table—in French.

"*Bonsoir, mademoiselle. De vin. Le mieux.*"

She stopped short. "*Dire: 's'il vous plaît.'*"

Marlowe tried not to smile. "*S'il vous plaît.*"

"Your manners are as bad as your accent," she scolded, turning away.

"And your education is better than your circumstance," he countered.

That stopped her, but she did not turn around.

"I have no idea why I spoke to you in French," Marlowe continued. "Maybe I wanted to seem exotic. I suppose I wanted to distinguish myself."

She glanced over her left shoulder. "With poor behavior and a student's charm?"

"Tell me your name."

She was gone in a flash, without another word.

A moment later Lopez appeared in the doorway, backlit by the setting sun. His entrance was, Marlowe thought, very theatrical. Apparently everyone else in the place agreed: a momentary silence reigned.

Marlowe glanced carefully about the room, trying to discern the slightest clue as to Walsingham's man. Lopez's appearance affected each man differently. The one with the pipe seemed offended. The nervous young man wore a clear expression of fear. Only the clergyman seemed unconcerned; he merely opened his eyes.

There, Marlowe thought, that's our man, that's Beak.

Lopez strode into the bar as if he might be about to repossess it, or rob it. The owner reached behind the bar for something, obviously a weapon. The serving girl, her face grim, moved toward the doctor with easy grace.

"Sir?" she said simply.

"I'm famished. I have been riding all day without a bite to eat. What might I have to break my fast?"

"I prefer the boiled rabbit," she answered, "and there's a muddle of goose blood that most of our visitors admire."

He nodded. "I'll have both, please, and sack, if it's good."

"Best this side of London," she assured him, and vanished into what must have been the kitchen.

Lopez sat at the bar, his back to everyone except the man standing behind it. Lopez stared at the man; the man stared back. After a moment Lopez whispered something and the man behind the bar laughed, though softly. He relaxed, and both of his hands became visible once more—visible and empty.

The clergyman smiled, which told Marlowe he might have overhead what Lopez had said to the barman.

A moment later the girl appeared again with the sack and set it down in front of Lopez.

"Muddle's ready," she said. "Rabbit's on the plate, with turnips."

Lopez nodded, took the sack in his left hand and drained the cup in seconds.

The girl appeared to be waiting for Lopez's opinion of the drink, staring at him with funereal scrutiny.

That's when Marlowe noticed the knife in the clergyman's hand. The blade was in the man's lap, but it was clear that the clergyman was assessing his target, preparing to throw the dagger.

Realizing that he wouldn't have time to stop the blade, or to warn Lopez, Marlowe let his reflexes take over. He leaned back in his chair, got his foot just right on the underside to the table in front of him, and kicked with all his strength.

The table flew through the air, crashed into the clergyman, knocked him off his chair and onto the floor.

Grunting and cursing the man tried to get to his feet, but Marlowe was already standing in front of him, rapier drawn, the point in the man's face.

"Think you can do anything with that dagger," Marlowe asked

softly, "before I shove this rapier through your eye and into your brain?"

The man exhaled. "We might both act at the same instant," he answered, his strangely accented voice high and mincing. "I'd throw my blade and be dead, but so would the Jew."

Marlowe didn't bother to look in Lopez's direction. "Think so? Have a look."

The man looked. Lopez had vanished, along with the serving girl and the barman.

"So you'd be dead for nothing, really," Marlowe continued.

Without another word, Marlowe kicked the man under his jaw, heard the jaw snap, saw the man drop his blade and fall back onto the floor. At the same time he sheathed his rapier and looked to the couple in the corner.

"Apologies," he said to them. "This man has no manners and is, apparently, religiously intolerant."

Marlowe picked up the man's dagger and slipped it into his belt.

There was a moment of silence, and then the couple continued eating as if nothing had happened.

The nervous boy was glued to his table, a look of abject terror on his face. The baker, if baker he was, smiled.

"And I cannot abide a clergyman so quick to throw a knife," the baker said to Marlowe. "Makes you wonder what's become of religion in our modern age."

"Indeed," Marlowe agreed affably.

With that the barman appeared once more; he had been hiding behind the bar. Marlowe glanced his way. Only the man's eyes moved, but they indicated where Lopez had gone: into the kitchen.

"Now," the barman said softly.

Marlowe nodded and headed that way.

"I wonder what's keeping my supper," he said as he rounded the bar.

The kitchen was small, hot, and well-occupied. An older woman stood over a cauldron cooking a lamb stew. The smell of it was intoxicating: rosemary, thyme, cinnamon, and cherries. Marlowe had never smelled anything like it, and was momentarily distracted. Then he noticed the serving girl standing in a far corner. Lopez was in front of her, red cloak tossed back over his shoulders.

When Marlowe looked their way, the girl stepped around Lopez and narrowed her eyes.

"If you've broken one of our tables," she complained, "you'll be paying for it."

Marlowe ignored her. "We've been betrayed by Walsingham's man," he said to Lopez. "He tried to kill you. There was a knife in his hand."

Lopez lowered his rapier.

"Mrs. Pennington," the girl said to the cook, "would you be so good as to help my father tidy up the public room? This ruffian has thrown one of our tables at a guest."

The cook shook her head. "The youth of today," she mumbled.

"I saved the doctor's life!" Marlowe protested.

The cook headed for the door. "We can always get another doctor," she said, looking at no one, "but the man is dead who made those tables, and we'll not see his like again."

With that she was gone.

Lopez almost laughed, a rare phenomenon.

"That assassin was not our contact, Chris," he said. "Allow me to introduce Leonora Beak, Her Majesty's eighth cousin."

Unable to hide his surprise, Marlowe glared. "This girl is Walsingham's man?"

"I saw the assassin get out his dagger," she said sternly. "There was no need to toss our furniture about—but no matter. My father and Mrs. Pennington will take care of him. How much do you know?"

"I know nothing," Marlowe admitted hopelessly. "Obviously."

"We understand only that William the Silent is dead," Lopez intoned solemnly.

"Ah, well," she responded quickly, "that is the rumor, but the *fact* is that there has been a threat on his life. London fears that William soon *will* be dead."

Lopez frowned. "But then I am not certain. . . ."

"Why there has been such urgency to Walsingham's summons? It is precisely because of the nature of William's current work and the very believable plot to take his life."

"Still," Lopez shifted uncomfortably in his seat. It was obvious that he hated being excluded from the inner circle of facts.

"You may know that William married—for the fourth time—this April past. His wife is Louise de Coligny, a French Huguenot, the daughter of Gaspard de Coligny."

"Of course," Lopez interrupted impatiently.

"William is currently at his home in Delft," asserted Leonora Beak. "Or at least he will be there on the tenth day of July, the day after tomorrow, in order to dine with his guest, Rombertus van Uylenburgh. They are to discuss matters concerning the Frisian state."

Marlowe felt certain he understood what that meant. Frisia alone in Europe had managed to escape all feudal structure introduced by Charlemagne and established throughout the western world since that time, in one way or another. "Frisian Freedom" had become, in the current century, a common phrase, though somewhat coded. It was a call to arms among certain philosophical elements—students, peasants, pirates—to rid the world of the so-called ruling classes.

Almost entirely to see how Leonora Beak would react, Marlowe said, simply, "Pier Gerlofs Donia."

Pier Gerlofs, folk hero, the last Frisian rebel, had fought and won many a battle to maintain his nation's famous freedoms, but could not withstand the constant forces of Burgundy. His battles ended in 1519, he died in his bed in 1520—what life does a rebel have outside of his cause?

"*Bûter, brea, en griene tsiis,*" Leonora responded.

Marlowe smiled. "*Butter, bread, and green cheese,*" he said. "If you couldn't pronounce those words properly, Pier would know that you were a German spy, and no true Frisian."

"Our nation stands at a precipice," Leonora snapped, "and you're talking about the history of pirates."

"What is it that our Queen would have us do?" Lopez said coldly, his eyes piercing hers.

Marlowe had been the recipient of that gaze from the doctor. He knew its effect.

She reached down behind the kitchen table and retrieved a small parcel wrapped in plain brown cloth. She handed it to Lopez.

Lopez unwrapped it to discover a small, familiar-looking golden cylinder: Walsingham's device for secret communiqués.

Marlowe stood so that he might better see what was written on the thin, rolled paper which Lopez was drawing from the cylinder.

An instant later, a short burst of laughter was torn from his throat.

The missive began: *Bûter, brea, en griene tsiis.*

Lopez shook his head. "Is it possible that Walsingham is a seer?"

Marlowe contained himself. "Well, there are certainly those enemies of our nation who believe that he is in league with the devil."

Leonora wore a look of desperate curiosity. Marlowe interpreted it to mean that she had often sat in meetings of this sort. How many times had she been so close to momentous information, yet excluded from its revelation? He sensed her anger, and her yearning.

Knowing that Lopez might object, and realizing it was a breach of protocol, Marlowe nevertheless told Leonora, "This note begins with the very words we just quoted from Pier Gerlofs, green cheese and all."

Lopez seemed not to hear. His eyes were fixed on the rest of the letter from Walsingham. Leonora Beak's face contorted in a rushing sequence of reactions so demonstrative that Marlowe immediately wished he might capture them in some net of words. An entire play was offered by that face, and in the span of several seconds.

But she did not say a word.

Lopez, however, exclaimed, under his breath, in Portuguese.

"It seems, my friend," he said to Marlowe, "that you are to go to Delft and prevent the death of William the Silent."

"You're not going with me?" Marlowe asked. "I'm supposed to go alone to prevent the death of a man who is already dead, by most accounts?"

"No," Lopez said softly, "you will not go alone. This woman is to be your companion."

Marlowe and Leonora both spoke, at the same time, a single word: "No."

"The dictum is clear," Lopez told them. "It says, 'The woman who proffered this note, one L.B., will accompany M. on his journey. When they arrive in Delft, they are to say to W. the words with which this missive begins: *Bûter, brea, en griene tsiis.*' "

Lopez looked up, then, at Leonora Beak. "And then there is a phrase written here, the words which you have been instructed to say to me, in proof of your identity."

"How do we know she hasn't read Walsingham's note already?" Marlowe complained.

Lopez shook his head. "I watched her. She was clearly surprised by the contents in this letter. She has not read it." He looked into Leonora's eyes. "So. What are the words you are told to say to me?"

Leonora glanced once at Marlowe, then sighed.

"I am to say, 'Hail, snow, and lightning all at once.' "

Marlowe had no time to consider his response. He simply gasped.

Lopez shook his head. "This is a line from your very bad play," he said. "How would Walsingham—"

"I have no idea," Marlowe whispered. "That sad spectacle in The Pickerel was the only time it's been read aloud."

"Then how could these words be contained in this missive?" Lopez turned to Leonora. "Who told you to say them?"

"The man who delivered this cylinder," she answered hesitantly.

"Perhaps Walsingham does, indeed, have some mystic power," Marlowe said.

"I—I took it to mean," Leonora intervened, not at all timidly, "that the current state of affairs is so grave—a tempest of horrible proportions. Is that not—"

"I take it to mean," Lopez countered, "that Walsingham has spies who spy on spies. That he somehow harvested a phrase from our young poet's work that only he would know."

"Except that you knew it as well," Leonora corrected.

"Fortune placed me there," he answered. "The phrase was meant for Marlowe."

"Why," Marlowe managed to say, "would he want this woman to go with me to Delft?"

"I am well-trained," she answered testily.

"A well-trained barmaid is hardly a match for Her Majesty's agent!"

Leonora produced a knife from somewhere under her dress, turned around once, and was suddenly behind Marlowe's chair, the blade of her knife at his gullet.

"Have a care what you say to me," she concluded.

Marlowe smiled. "I might say the same to you."

She felt a slight pinch in her belly, looked down, and found Marlowe's dagger poised to stab her.

"I don't know who trained you," he said, "but I learned from Dr. Lopez. He is the world's finest physician, because he knows every way, in heaven or hell, to kill a man."

"As luck would have it," she said softly, "I am no man."

Her blade was gone in the next instant. Marlowe found himself tantalized by the thought of where she might have it hidden.

"Are you both finished?" Lopez sighed. "There is a final item in Walsingham's note."

Leonora sat. Marlowe put away his blade.

" 'We are certain,' " Lopez read, " 'that foreign agents follow you, bent on preventing you from protecting William. If possible, dispatch these agents.' "

"The clergyman," Marlowe said. "Done."

Lopez rolled the letter in his hands. "I wonder."

"Yes," Leonora agreed, "that was very—obvious. And very easy."

"What about the nervous boy in the corner?" Marlowe ventured.

Leonora sighed. "That's Davey. He's come every day this month to ask for my hand in marriage. He seems not to understand the word *never.*"

"He works in the stables, does he not?" Lopez asked.

"How did you know?" She stared.

"His dress," Marlowe answered, "his hands, and—well, his smell."

"Indeed," she sighed again.

"The man with the pipe," Marlowe went on, "the baker, my surmise is that he is a baker."

"He is," Leonora answered. "He's a fine, gentle man, sweet humored, without enemy. He's not our man."

"Then the clergyman is our only foe," Marlowe insisted, "and he's done."

"He's not dead, is he?" Lopez asked.

"I think not," Marlowe answered. "But he's in no shape to cause any trouble at this point."

"You've forgotten the traveling couple, the two dining in the far corner," Leonora pointed out.

"Those two?" Marlowe laughed.

"I've seen them here before," she went on, "and they were watching everything you did from the moment you came in."

Marlowe paused to think.

As he did, he took an extra moment for a first real look at Leonora Beak. Her hair, slightly red, was pulled back severely. Her face was stern, but her dark eyes were lively. Her green dress was well laundered and her hands, though small, were not delicate. She was short, and could not have weighed much. Still, Marlowe had the impression that, when cornered, ferocity would make up for size. Walsingham had chosen her. There was clearly something to the girl.

"Staring at me," Leonora said suddenly to Marlowe, "will not help you to determine anything about that couple in the other room."

"Well." Marlowe stood. "Let's go ask them, then."

Leonora smiled. "Yes. Let's."

"Marlowe, would you precede us," Lopez directed. "I need to

hear the final instruction from Walsingham, the verbal message our hostess is to impart. For my ears only."

"Ah, yes," she said. "Mr. Marlowe, would you mind?"

Without another word, Marlowe left the kitchen.

He discovered a nightmare on the other side of the door.

The old woman cook, Mrs. Pennington, lay lifeless on the floor, her face and clothing soaked in blood. The barman, Leonora's father, was in the corner, trying to sit up, gasping. Davey, the sad stable boy, was seated sedately at his table, eyes wide, his forearm slit and pouring blood like a fountain.

The clergyman, the couple, and the baker were all gone.

"Lopez!" Marlowe howled.

The doctor appeared in the doorway an instant later. He surveyed the bloody scene. Leonora burst through the door and shoved past Marlowe, flying to her father. The doctor followed, bending over the wounded man.

"He's alive," Lopez assured her softly.

"They've killed Mrs. Pennington," the father moaned. "And Davey too!"

"Hush, father," Leonora implored him. "Let the doctor do his work."

Lopez turned toward Marlowe.

"They can't have gone far, whoever did this," Lopez snapped. "After them!"

Marlowe leapt forward at once, over Mrs. Pennington's dead body, and burst through the front door of the Bell.

The sun was nearly gone; the horizon was red. He looked first left, then right, but the road was empty, but the mud to the left of the door marked the direction of the tracks.

"Horses!" Leonora shrieked from right behind Marlowe.

She raced toward the barn, hiking her skirt up to reveal leather breeches and knee-high boots, and a small pouch at her waist.

Marlowe ran after her.

The boy who had taken the horses was standing in front of the barn. He had a look of utter madness on his face.

"They took them," he squeaked. "Your horses. Gone."

Marlowe was nearly at the boy's side before he saw the spot of blood on the boy's shoulder.

"Are you wounded?" he asked the boy.

The boy looked down at his shirt. "That woman stabbed me," he said in shocked wonder. "For no reason."

"Can you make it to the inn?" Marlowe asked

He nodded, face still contorted in pain.

"There's a doctor there," Marlowe went on. "Go now. Show him your wound. You'll be fine."

The boy nodded but didn't move.

"Which one of them stabbed you?" Leonora demanded.

"The woman," he answered, mystified. "With a tiny rapier no bigger than a fire poker."

"Go!" Marlowe commanded.

This time the boy agreed, and stumbled toward the Bell.

Leonora was already in the stable.

"Damn!" she growled. "Your horses are gone, yours and the doctor's!"

"You have other horses, surely," Marlowe snapped. "This is a changing station."

"Yes." She glanced across the fields in the darkening landscape. "There!"

Marlowe could barely make out another barn nearly hidden by large trees.

"Good," he said.

Minutes later they had two horses out of the barn, into the evening air.

"But which way?" Leonora asked as they neared the road.

"I saw the hoofprints," Marlowe answered, heading east. "They're making for the sea."

Marlowe slowed his horse for an instant, considering that he ought to be off to Delft instead of chasing after these phantasms. But Leonora was already down the road, on fire, and nothing could turn her back.

THREE

Past midnight, Marlowe spotted a small fire not a hundred yards down the road in front of him. It was a well-traveled thoroughfare, lined with trees and shrubs. On either side there were wide-ranging fields, some wild, others filled with wheat, oats, barley. But the night was so dark that it was impossible to see very far. The second Marlowe noticed the flame, he encouraged his horse to flank Leonora's and then touched her arm.

"There," he said as softly as he could. "Fire."

She slowed her horse.

"Might not be our assassins," Marlowe allowed, "but the better effort lies in caution."

Leonora actually growled, but she seemed to agree and stopped her horse completely. Marlowe slowed his horse and dismounted, dagger in hand.

There was only the sliver of a moon, and an intermittent shadow of clouds moved constantly overhead, obscuring most of the stars.

"I don't know why we're stopping," Leonora complained. "The assassins would not have stopped by the side of the road over a cooking fire!"

"Sh," Marlowe insisted. "What if they've left behind the clergyman or the baker to stop anyone who might pursue them?"

"Not the baker, I'd vouch for him with my life," she answered, "but the man you refer to as a clergyman is a stranger to me."

"The high-born couple?" he mumbled. "You think they're the Spanish agents? And they were sent to murder the doctor and me?"

"Or me and my father." Her voice betrayed a tension.

Marlowe took in a short breath. “Do not worry about your father. I know that Dr. Lopez will mend him.”

“Yes, better to spend my efforts on the vermin ahead,” she told him, “rather than the worry behind.”

“So. I’ll go see whose fire that is.” Marlowe headed out.

An instant later he found that Leonora was right beside him.

“I was thinking that you’d wait with the horses,” he said very softly.

“And I was thinking that you need my help more than the horses do.” She moved ahead.

Moments later they were crouched behind a hawthorn bush, straining to see who was gathered around the fire only ten yards away. Even in the light of the dancing flames, it was nearly impossible to discern any recognizable face.

“Looks like the couple,” Leonora whispered, her lips touching Marlowe’s ear. “That doesn’t make sense.”

Trying not to react to the touch of her lips, Marlowe squinted, straining to see faces. He failed—at both efforts.

“Let’s find out for certain,” he said after a moment.

With that he stood, holding his dagger in front of him, and walked quickly toward the fire.

“A very good even friends,” he cried out, adopting a somewhat foppish, drunken manner of speech, “and well met!”

All faces looked his way. They were, it appeared, a young family: father, mother, and boy child. The man was wrapped in a tattered rustic cloak. The woman clutched a thick shawl around her shoulders. The boy, not more than seven or eight years old, shivered in rags. Their faces were ruddy and the woman had been crying.

As Marlowe drew nearer he could see a small cart close by, and realized by the decoration on it that these were Traveling People, most likely from lowland Scotland by the look of their clothing.

The man said something to the woman in a language Marlowe didn’t recognize, though it was vaguely Pictish, or Erse. Then he looked directly at Marlowe, his face hard.

"We've naught to share, and less to steal," he said in a coarse accent. "You'd best be off."

From the other side of them, Leonora spoke up. "We may have something to offer you, then."

The man was startled. The woman cried out and clutched the child. Marlowe had no idea how she'd managed to get into her position, but it did seem clever, made the family feel surrounded.

"You're free born of the Traveling People, am I correct?" Leonora went on.

The man nodded once.

"Then you see things that other people do not." Leonora took a step closer.

The man raised his arm. Marlowe moved faster, and tossed his knife, hilt first. He knocked a short dagger out of the Gypsy's hand. Before the man could recover, Marlowe had his rapier out and was closing in on the family. The woman shrieked.

"Stop!" Leonora commanded.

Everyone froze.

"I say we have something we would like to give you," she repeated to the Gypsies softly, "in return for your observations."

"What would you give us?" the man asked defiantly.

Leonora kept a steady bead on the man. "You have no horse to draw your cart; someone has taken it. That makes for difficult traveling. I'll give you mine."

The Gypsy and Marlowe asked the same question at the same time.

"What?"

Leonora remained steady. "I said you have no horse now, but you did have until recently. We're looking for the people who took it."

The man looked back at Marlowe. "Is she mad or a witch?"

"Are those my only two choices?" Marlowe asked in return.

"Someone took your horse," Leonora insisted loudly. "I'm offering to give you one. Do you want it or not?"

"What's the price?" the Gypsy asked.

"I've already told you," she answered. "Either you are ignorant, in which case my friend will just kill you, or you're deliberately playing at ignorance, in which case my friend will kill your wife and child, and then kill you. Which is it? Quickly!"

Marlowe took his cue, moved forward, the point of his rapier near the woman's heart. She began to sob.

"Two well-born and another," the Gypsy answered loudly. "They held us at pistol point and took horse and food, left us here."

"How long ago?"

"Not the half of an hour," he lamented. "I wanted to give chase, but . . ."

The man slowly opened his cloak to reveal a deep wound in his right thigh.

"Ah." Leonora moved so quickly that everyone was startled.

She flew to the man's side, retrieved several vials of liquid from the pouch at her waist and went immediately to work on the man's wound. The first she poured caused him to wince and twitch.

"Hold still!" she commanded.

"A witch, then," he said to Marlowe, eyes rolling.

Without a word, Leonora then sprinkled a bit of powder on the wound. Then she produced a long scrap of white linen and bound the wound.

The entire ministration took fewer than sixty seconds.

The man exhaled. "Well. That—that's much better."

The woman said something in the other language, and the man nodded.

"Thanks be to you, ma'am," she said to Leonora, her accent so heavy it was difficult to understand her.

"Now." Leonora stood. "My horse."

"Wait," Marlowe intervened.

"There were three, he said," Leonora told Marlowe impatiently. "That would be the couple and the so-called clergyman whom you wounded."

"Yes, but," Marlowe began.

"They only stole two horses from the Bell," she interrupted, "so they've obviously been riding double—the couple I assume. They had to take the horse from these people to move more quickly."

"So why give away your horse now?" Marlowe complained.

Leonora looked down at the family.

"I shall give you my horse on the condition that you take it up the road to the Bell Inn, do you know it?"

The man nodded.

"My father owns it. He'll recognize the horse. You'll tell him I sent you, Leonora Beak sent you, and you'll be taken care of. Do you understand?"

"No," the man admitted. "I don't."

"I have heard that the Traveling People of the Scottish lowlands abhor a debt," she said.

"It's true," he admitted skeptically.

"And if I give you my horse," she went on, "and my father takes care of you and your family until you are well enough to move on, you'll be mightily in my debt, is this not so?"

"Aye," he sighed. "It would be a fearsome burden to me."

"And that's the price," she said, a bit triumphantly. "You'll be in my debt and you'll come to my aide for as long as I say until I release you."

The man looked at Marlowe, then back at Leonora. "I don't know. What is it you're likely to be wanting of me?"

"We are bound for the Netherlands," she said plainly, "where there is an abundance of Travelers similar to you and your family, like-minded cousins, shall we say, who are sometime known at *Egyptians* or *Heidens*. Am I correct?"

The man paused, then nodded once, uncertain what Leonora was getting at.

"And they are often accused of being spies for the Turks," she continued, "and therefore hounded by those in authority, generally treated poorly."

"Aye," the man assented, albeit warily.

"Then this is what I ask: that you establish for us, me and my friend, a network of support and communication in that other country, and in this one." She lowered her voice. "I know you can do this. News and gossip move faster through your camps than a peregrine falcon can fly."

"It's true," he said, grudgingly, "but you ask for too much. We keep to ourselves, the Traveling People."

Leonora shook her head. "I'm not asking for anything but eyes and ears. No action on anyone's part. It's not very much payment for the lives of you and your family."

"And a very nice horse," Marlowe added, grumbling.

At that Leonora made a clicking noise, something not quite human, and her horse trotted quickly to her side.

"This is Bess. She's tired. Let her rest. Take her to the Bell Inn at dawn. There will be food, warmth, and a doctor."

"The alternative is that we leave you as we found you," Marlowe said. "Traveling People without horse, food, or weapon. What do you think your chances are there?"

The woman said something. The man nodded, then stood.

"We are in your debt," he said stiffly. "My name is Gelis. Might I know yours?"

"I am Leonora Beak," she answered, "and my friend is—"

"Robert Greene," Marlowe interrupted quickly.

Whatever else Marlowe had learned from Walsingham, he knew better than to give out his true name to strangers. He was surprised that Leonora had done so.

Gelis nodded in an imitation of subservience.

"Good, then," Leonora said briskly.

"What can you tell us about the people who attacked you?" Marlowe asked immediately.

"As I say," Gelis began, "two men and a woman, and the woman was the worst. Had a pistol. She's what shot me."

"What kind of pistol?" Marlowe asked.

"Wheel-lock," he answered.

Not the latest model, but spectacularly effective at close range, a wheel-lock worked by spinning a spring-loaded steel wheel against a piece of pyrite to produce the spark that would ignite the gunpowder and fire the shot. It was a weapon that could be ready in an instant and fired with one hand. It was also an expensive weapon, implying that its owner would be wealthy. Marlowe felt quite pleased with himself that he had discovered a great deal about the trio he and Leonora were perusing simply by asking the right question.

Leonora preferred a more direct interrogation.

"Did they say anything important to our pursuit?" she asked.

Gelis took a breath. "The gentleman who appeared to be her husband said not to bother with me and the missus because they had to be in Maldon before dawn."

"Maldon," she repeated.

Marlowe's eyes narrowed. "They're on their way to kill William. They'll find a ship in Maldon that will take them to Delft."

Leonora's face darkened. "I fear you are correct. We must be on our way at once."

Marlowe glared at Gelis and his family.

"I take you on your honor," he said harshly. "You will send out word; your brethren will come to our aid. And you will make no mention of this to anyone. Or when I'm done with my business, I'll see to you."

Gelis smiled. "If you can find me."

"I take you at your word without threats," Leonora intervened. "You will help us and keep silent because I have given you a horse and shelter, and because that is the sort of man you are."

Gelis looked down. "Alas, yes."

His wife said something again, and he looked at her and smiled.

"And I am reminded," he said, "to be grateful when a stranger does me a good turn."

Leonora smiled. "We'll be off, then."

She took her horse, Bess, by the reins and patted her once on the neck. Gelis took the reins from her, and she hurried toward Marlowe.

"Now." She brushed past him running toward his horse.

"Wait," Marlowe called out.

But Leonora was already mounted and shaking the reins impatiently.

"We have no time to lose," she muttered. "We can't let them get on that ship."

"I agree," he sighed, "but you've hampered our ability in that regard by giving away your horse."

"It was a good decision," she said sternly.

"Well at the very least, slide back," he insisted. "I'll be in the saddle."

She shook her head. "I know the way to Maldon better than you."

"It's my horse," he countered.

"In point of fact," she snapped, "this horse belongs to my father. The assassins stole your horse."

"You gave away the horse you were riding on," Marlowe said, his voice louder, "so get off or slide back!"

"Are we seriously going to argue about this while the villains gain advantage?" Her voice was also louder, and becoming shrill.

"Are you seriously going to let them go just because you want to ride in front?"

"Yes!" Leonora screamed so violently that the horse reared up, nearly tossing her onto the ground.

"You see?" Marlowe yelled. "Even the animal wants you to move!"

Without further discourse, Marlowe shoved his left boot into the empty stirrup and threw himself upward, into the saddle. The combination of the horse's motion and Marlowe's bulk forced Leonora out of the saddle and onto the horse's backside.

In the next second Marlowe had slapped the reins and the horse took off down the road in the direction of Maldon.

"You'll kill us both," Leonora shouted.

"Why in the name of Christ did you give your horse to that man?" Marlowe demanded.

"Now we have eyes and ears in the Netherlands!" she answered.

"The *Heidens*? Are you seriously suggesting—?"

"Go faster," she interrupted again. "We can't let them get on that ship!"

"Hold onto something, then," Marlowe warned.

He leaned forward, tapped the horse's side with the heel of his boot, and the horse responded perfectly, nearly doubling his speed.

Leonora's reflex was to throw her arms around Marlowe's chest and press her body to his back.

FOUR

All of Maldon was asleep by the time Christopher Marlowe and Leonora Beak caught first sight of it from the road. Not a single light could be seen, and the night air had acquired a slight chill.

As they drew close to the few streets of the town, they could see the church built on the highest part of the hill. Once on the High Street, they could see down to the docks. Marlowe slowed the horse to a walk.

"We've missed them," Marlowe swore. "The ship's gone."

"What makes you say that?" Leonora asked, staring toward the water.

"Do you see any light down there?" he complained. "Their ship would have running lights for going down the river to the sea."

"Not if they were trying to go unnoticed."

"We wouldn't have missed them," Marlowe snapped, "if you hadn't given your horse away."

"Would you stop going on about the horse," she railed.

"Sh!" Marlowe commanded.

Some faint sound could be heard coming from below, around a corner, close to the black waterside. The sound of people whispering echoed in the night air on the water.

Leonora put her lips on Marlowe's ear.

"Turn left at the church," she breathed, "and into the first side street. Stables are there."

Marlowe nodded. Of course she would know where the stables of Maldon were located; they would be sister to the ones she and her father managed on the road. Without a sound Marlowe encouraged his horse in that direction.

The Maldon stables were small and unattended. Marlowe dismounted and reached his hand up to help Leonora down, but she slid off with an agile grace, and without his aid.

The inside of the barn was unusually clean for a travel stable. The two-story building, about a quarter the size of an estate stable, held ten stalls below and a hayloft above. The wood beams and stall dividers seemed relatively new. The smell of the place was uncommonly pleasant. Hay on the floor helped, but as Marlowe cast his eyes upward he could see that the rafters were hung with huge sheaves of lavender and rosemary, another touch not ordinarily found in public barns.

Marlowe only spent another moment looking before he saw, in the nearest stalls, the horses that he and Lopez had ridden. They were still saddled, and quite wet. There was also, in the back of the barn, a third animal he presumed to be the one stolen from the Traveling family.

Cursing under his breath he went to them immediately and began to tend one of the animals.

"What are you doing?" Leonora asked softly. "We have to go down to the water."

"Not until these horses are taken care of," he answered. "We won't get very far if the horses fall sick."

"We're not going to ride them across the ocean," she groused. "We need a ship, not a horse!"

"I'll take these two," Marlowe said, ignoring her objection. "You see to the others. They all need care."

She only paused for an instant before she nodded and went to work.

Quiet as they were, their ministrations did not go undetected. Just as Marlowe had finished wiping down the second horse in his care, a man the size of a boulder rolled around a dark corner of the barn with a very serious pitchfork in his hands. The fact that he was only wearing a nightshirt did not diminish the obvious threat.

"Leave off them beasties, my lad," he growled, jabbing at Marlowe with the tines.

Leonora appeared beside Marlowe instantly and brushed the offending implement aside.

"Edwin!" she cried.

"Leonora?" he responded, clearly surprised.

"Since when do you put up animals like this?" she demanded of him. "Just you wait until I inform the other ostlers!"

Edwin lowered his pitchfork.

"Hang on a minute." Edwin looked around. "Where'd all these horses come from?"

"Well, that's done it," Marlowe railed. "If we've not awakened half the town, at least the villains have heard us now!"

Before anyone could respond, a knife blade seared past Marlowe and stuck hard into the supporting beam beside him.

Instantly Marlowe had his rapier and dagger out, and Leonora had ducked into a stall. Only Edwin seemed unable to move, which was unfortunate. A second knife hit him in his left side and down he went, howling.

From the shadows two figures emerged, the couple from the Bell Inn, both armed. The man had a pistol in one hand and a claymore in the other; the woman had two daggers in one hand and some sort of iron rod in the other.

Disarm the pistol first, Marlowe thought. Without another thought he lunged forward as if he were trying to stab the woman in the belly, but at the last second Marlowe dropped to the hay-strewn floor of the barn, rolled, and ended up jabbing his rapier into the man's knee.

The man stumbled; Marlowe rose. On his feet once more, he jumped quickly to one side. In a lightning pirouette he knocked the iron rod out of the woman's hand and held his dagger to her throat.

At that same moment Leonora reappeared with her hands clenched tightly in fists, as if she were going to thrash her attackers bare-knuckled.

The man with the pistol took aim. Marlowe was faster, and

flicked out the point of his rapier, slicing the back of the man's hand. The pistol dropped, uncocked.

Unfortunately, that slight distraction allowed the well-dressed woman to elbow Marlowe in the chest as she turned back and away from the knife at her neck. Marlowe, the breath momentarily knocked out of him, stumbled backward toward the wall.

The woman got her balance, raised her arm, and threw one of her daggers into Marlowe's sword arm.

Or so it seemed, but Marlowe smiled. The knife had cut the loose fabric of his doublet and shirt, only grazed the flesh of his arm.

Just as he was about to right himself and use his own dagger, Leonora came between him and the woman. With startling speed Leonora opened her fist and blew a fine dust from her hand directly into the woman's face. The woman seemed, at first, only irritated, then surprised—but after a heartbeat or two, her eyes widened and her mouth contorted. She gasped, gargled, and began to stumble.

Not waiting for any further effect, Leonora danced lightly around the woman and cast the powder in her other fist directly into their other assailant's open mouth, just as if she were flinging a handful of ashes.

The man gasped, choked, dropped his claymore, and began to foam at the mouth.

Marlowe blinked.

At the same time the woman fell down, shaking her head violently as if trying not to pass out.

"Curious," Leonora said primly. "She should already be dead by now."

Leonora strode to the woman on her knees and grabbed her by the hair.

"Why aren't you dead yet?" she asked the poor woman.

The woman responded by producing another dagger from the folds of her dress and swiping it at Leonora. But Leonora was too quick. She jumped back. When she did, the woman's hair came off in Leonora's hand.

The woman looked up and Marlowe tilted his head.

Even in the dim, flickering torch light it was obvious: the woman was a man.

What was more, Marlowe knew the face, it was familiar to him somehow. Leonora examined the wig.

At length the boy in the dress fell backward, panting and gasping.

"Well, that's why you aren't dead," Leonora scolded, stepping over to look down at the person. "You were pretending to be a woman so I gave you a lesser application. Now you're suffering. It's your own fault. And, incidentally, did you kill Mrs. Pennington back at the Inn?"

The boy croaked.

Marlowe stepped in.

"Is there any possibility," he said calmly, "that I might question this person before he dies? If these are William's assassins, then our job is done. Or at the very least this person could tell us where the third member of their alliance might be hiding."

"The *clergyman*, as you call him," Leonora answered. "Yes, well."

From a pocket in her boot Leonora produced a stone vial with a cork stuck in it.

"What's that?" Marlowe asked, only idly curious.

"Never carry a poison without its antidote," she told him. "That's a lesson I learned the hard way."

She pulled out the cork, stood over the dying boy in the dress, and spoke as if to a troublesome child.

"Open your mouth if you want to live," she said, staring directly into the boy's eyes. "It's of no consequence to me either way, but my friend would like to chat."

Gasping, beginning to convulse, the boy in the dress leaned forward and opened his mouth. It was a grotesque imitation of a baby bird wanting to be fed.

"This should do the trick," Leonora mumbled.

She poured a thimbleful of viscous liquid into that maw, and the boy in the dress began to cough. He coughed for a full minute. Then he vomited so violently that he seemed in danger of losing internal organs.

"Although," Leonora confided to Marlowe, "some will tell you that the cure is worse than the poison."

"What in God's name did you give the boy?" Marlowe asked.

"Bark of mulberry boiled in vinegar, and rancid oil," she responded happily.

She reached into her pocket and produced a sturdy tin vial.

"Take this," she said, holding it out. "Never know when you might need it—for yourself or someone else."

Marlowe accepted the strange gift silently, and then turned his attention to the heaving actor at his feet.

By the time the barn was silent once more, Leonora had tended to Edwin's wound and verified that the man with the claymore was dead.

Marlowe stood over the boy in the dress.

"How are you feeling?" he asked without emotion.

"Get," the boy rasped, gasping to breathe, "stuffed."

"Good, then answer me this," Marlowe continued briskly, "where is the other man, the one who was with you at the Bell Inn?"

"Maybe," the boy answered, still struggling, "you should look up your ass."

"Well," Marlowe opined good-naturedly, "I would, but I have no reflecting glass, and, you understand, without one—"

Without warning Leonora slid up beside the boy in the dress and brought down an iron rod on his back. The thud was bad, the crack was worse. The boy in the dress howled, vomited again, and began to cry.

"I don't have any idea what you want from me," he sobbed. "I don't."

"We want," Leonora began, "your cooperation."

"Did you break one of the bones in his back?" Marlowe asked.

"Did sound like it," she acquiesced.

"Listen, friend," Marlowe said to the boy in the dress, "I'm not used to this sort of thing. I'm a student, you understand. But this woman here? She has killed a dozen men since breakfast, and without so much a loss of breath or a quickened heart. So. Please tell us where the other man is."

"Docks," the boy whimpered. "Waiting for our boat."

"Where were you bound?" Leonora asked, pitching her voice to match the lies that Marlowe had just told about her.

The boy was still sobbing. "Netherlands. I think my back is broke."

Marlowe studied the dress he was wearing. "Exactly where did you get that dress? And whose idea was it that you should wear it?"

"Done it before," the boy said, breathing with difficulty. "Theatre."

Marlowe's head snapped back a bit. "I thought I recognized you! You aren't Ned Blank."

"I am," the boy said, even managing a bit of pride at being recognized.

Marlowe turned to Leonora. "This is Ned Blank!"

"So he says," she responded, utterly unimpressed.

"No," Marlowe went on with growing enthusiasm. "This boy was, only a short time ago, the greatest actor of female roles in all of London theatre!"

Leonora stared down at the wreckage groveling on the floor of the barn. "This?"

"I saw you play Ophelia," Marlowe said to Ned, "in Kyd's *Hamlet;* you were spectacular."

He turned to Leonora.

"In the scene after Hamlet rapes Ophelia," he said in hushed tones, "Ned, here, was able to make every single person in the audience weep, myself included."

The boy sat up straighter. "I did get good notices for that one."

"What the hell are you doing with these murderers?" Leonora demanded angrily.

"Murderers?" Ned asked, blinking. "They said they was spies."

"What the hell are you doing with these spies, then?" Leonora asked immediately.

"Oh." Ned's head drooped a bit. "Well. Money."

"Money?" she snapped. "You don't get paid to be an actor?"

He sighed heavily. "Not any more. I'm getting older. My voice is about to change, and my looks are—well, as you see."

"You can't get the young female parts anymore," Marlowe said sympathetically.

"You have no idea how hard it is for an aging actress," he complained. "All the roles are for nine-year-olds."

"And yet he's still too young for any of the male roles," Marlowe lamented. "It's truly a tragedy."

"If we might," Leonora interrupted in clipped tones, "return to our business at hand!"

"Ah, yes." Marlowe offered Ned a hand. "Well, you're working for us now, Ned. Take off that dress."

FIVE

Edwin's quarters were small but pleasant for a stable master's, tucked between the barn and the building next to it. It was only two rooms, but they were tidy. In the first room: table and chairs, several lamps, and a window that looked out on the alleyway behind the barn. The other room held only a bed, but a nice wooden one, with a full, stuffed mattress—evidence of the kind of money Edwin made.

Despite the fact that Leonora put him into the very nice bed, he was up almost at once, offering food and drink despite his wounds. He seemed to relish the role of host, and he was rabidly curious about his visitors.

Ned had taken off his dress and was shivering in a thin undershirt and poorly maintained wool breeches. He downed the drink that Edwin had given him without asking what it was, and held out his cup for a second dose. By his third cup he seemed to have collected himself, acquired a cheerful glow, and was willing to be questioned.

"Have a seat," Marlowe instructed him, "and tell me how you came to be in such disreputable company."

"Well," Ned allowed, "there's a tale. I was in Shoreditch, wallowing along in some pig swill idiocy penned by one Robert Greene—a play with the terrible title of *The Honorable History of Friar Bacon and Friar Bungay*. I played Margaret, the Fair Maid of Fressingfield, what Prince Edward intends to have in his bed with the help of the questionable Friar Bacon, a necromancer of sorts."

"Ned," Marlowe interrupted.

"Right, sorry. To the point. The play wasn't actually finished, it was just something Greene was trying out, and one of the backers, the man what's killed in that barn just now, he approached me."

"In what way?" Leonora asked.

"The usual: offered me a drink. It's one of three kinds that offers a person such as myself a drink. You've got your admirers, what only wants to tell you how good you was in the play. Then there's the bollocks boys with bulging codpieces and a bit of drool on the chin. And finally it's the best of all: the ones with an offer of employment. Our dead man was of this third sort."

"How old are you?" Leonora asked. Her voice managed to sound at once sympathetic and disapproving.

"Couldn't say for certain," Ned said loudly, as if he were bragging. "But the general consensus is thirteen. And there's my trouble. The voice. It's about to drop. It already cracks. What's an actor to do?"

"Ned," Marlowe sighed again, "we're after the details of your employment with these persons."

"Ah," he agreed, "of course. They wanted me as both maid and man, as it were. I was to accompany the gentleman as his wife, a prim and somewhat sickly creature, mostly to throw off suspicion, he said—though suspicion of what he never said. We was bound for the Netherlands. That was a bit of enticement for me. Never been to another country. Once on that distant shore, I was to play the part of his son, a lonely boy whose mother had just died. I was really looking forward to that. My first role without a dress."

"What about the third man, the other man you were traveling with?"

"We just met up with him in the inn," Ned answered a bit more somberly. "No idea what the hell happened there. That man, he's the one what killed the cook; killed her as soon as she come out of the kitchen. And he would have caused more havoc except that the main man, my husband, cursed him and shoved him out the door, dragging me along, all at sea."

"He's playing the innocent," Leonora snapped, then leaned her face close to Ned's and addressed him directly. "You're playing the innocent, but you shot a man on the road with a wheel-lock pistol and you took his horse!"

Ned pulled back, and his face lost its pleasant glow.

"They was going to leave me behind," Ned said, his voice gone cold. "The third man, the murderer that's met at the inn? He was bargaining with the people we met on the road, those filthy Heidens. Said I was a bond servant. He was trying to sell me to them. So, yes, I took the pistol from his saddle bag and shot the road rat. Nobody sells Ned Blank. My husband was then in a better position to convince the other man to stick with the original plan. The other gent agreed, I took the family's horse, and here we are."

"Which returns us to my question," Marlowe insisted. "Where is the third man?"

"Docks," Ned mumbled.

"You already said that," Leonora growled impatiently. "He's waiting for your ship. But if we just go wandering down to the waterside, I fear we will encounter his pistol, the same you used to steal a horse."

"Not if you stay to the shadows," Ned answered darkly, "and give out the sign."

"Sign?" she asked angrily.

"Three or four short whistles, pining, like a chiffchaff."

"A birdcall?" she sneered. "By the waterside in a port town?"

"I didn't invent it," the boy objected angrily. "That's what he told me when we—you know we heard you come into town, don't you? You was rowdy as a dozen drunkards."

"Hardly," Leonora snipped.

But Marlowe shot her a glance that said *I told you.*

"You wait here," Leonora told Ned, ignoring Marlowe. "I mean it."

"Where would I go?" he asked, still shivering a little.

"Edwin will be watching over you," she answered.

Edwin nodded. It was evident from his face that the events of the evening were the most exciting in his life.

"He'll not get away from me," Edwin swore.

"A chiffchaff sounds like this," Marlowe said as he headed for the door to the alleyway.

He gave first three, then four drifting trills.

"No," Leonora corrected, "it's more like this."

She softly whistled her own interpretation of the bird.

Two minutes later they were silent, crouching behind a rain barrel at the end of the long street that ended in the docks. The harbor, such as it was, seemed vacant. There were two small boats dragged onto land from the River Blackwater, but otherwise there was no evidence of any navigable craft whatsoever, let alone one that could cross the ocean to the Netherlands.

The Blackwater had been a source of fish and oysters for the town of Maldon since Roman occupation. In AD 991, Viking invaders were defeated very close to where Marlowe and Leonora were crouched, in the fierce Battle of Maldon. Salt panned from the river sat on finer tables all over England. Eastward from Maldon the river emptied into the Blackwater Estuary that met the North Sea at Mersea Island. From there it was short sailing slightly northward to the Netherlands and eight-or-so miles inland to Delft.

"He's not here," Leonora whispered into Marlowe's ear from her position slightly behind him.

"I've only given the sign twice," he grumbled without turning around.

"Well what are you waiting for? Give it again."

Marlowe sighed, sipped a breath, and gave out once more with the sweet, staccato "chip-chip-chip" he had heard as a boy, the chiffchaff singing to attract a mate.

The call was met with silence.

"He's not *here,*" Leonora whispered again.

Marlowe did his best to ignore her lips on his ear.

"Give him a second to respond, would you?" he answered her.

"There's no boat," she began, failing to keep her voice down, "no answer to the sign, and no evidence whatsoever—"

But her complaint was interrupted when someone grabbed her by the neck, choking her, pulling her backward and up.

Marlowe felt more than heard the trouble and whirled around, dagger in hand.

He found himself face to face with the "clergyman," who had the muzzle of a wheel-lock pistol pressed against Leonora's temple. His arm was wrapped entirely around her throat, his thick black beard obscuring the side of her face.

"What did you think you were doing whistling like that?" the man asked. Unlike the few words he had spoken at the Bell Inn, this time he failed to hide a heavy French accent. "You made it so easy."

"The sign," Marlowe began foolishly, realizing as he said it that Ned had lied.

"First I will kill this girl," the Frenchman said "and then I will kill you."

Marlowe didn't move, but he spoke in a voice filled with confidence.

"That would be a neat trick," he said calmly. "If you shoot her, I'll cut out your heart and liver before you have time to reload that ridiculous pistol."

"I don't need to shoot her," the man said, grinning, displaying a row of crusty teeth.

He began to tighten his arm around Leonora's throat, and as she began to gasp for breath, he pointed the ridiculous pistol directly at Marlowe's face.

"I can kill you both at the same time." He pushed the gun closer to Marlowe's left eye. "I've done it before, many times: this two at once."

Leonora sputtered and Marlowe glanced at her. Unbelievably, she winked, and somehow Marlowe read her mind.

With a sudden sweep Marlowe brushed the gun away from his face at the exact moment that Leonora dug her dagger into the assailant's knee cap. The gun went off, the man went down, and Leonora rolled away from him, all in a single instant.

Marlowe drew his rapier then and thrust toward the man's heart.

"No!" Leonora croaked.

At the last atom of an instant, Marlowe twisted his wrist and stabbed the man in his shoulder.

The man made no sound.

"Your compatriots are dead," Marlowe told him. "The man with the claymore and the boy he had dressed up like a woman."

The man remained silent.

"All right," Marlowe continued. "Stand up."

The man nodded, appearing weakened. He leaned forward, groaning, obviously having a bit of difficulty standing. Marlowe lowered his rapier. Leonora cleared her throat and rubbed her neck. The man had nearly crushed her windpipe. She was still having difficulty breathing.

Without warning the man was up. He jumped backward like a spider, another pistol in his hand. He did not hesitate. He shot Marlowe.

Marlowe grabbed his side and dropped his rapier.

The man picked up his other pistol and bowed very theatrically.

"I wish I had time to stay and kill you both, for certain," he began, "but I am called hence. I *will* see you again."

Only then did Leonora notice a small dingy moored to a large rock just beyond the other two boats on the shore, almost impossible to see in the darkness. Before she could manage to cry out, the assassin was away, reloading his pistol and dashing toward the craft.

Leonora, still gasping for breath, stumbled to Marlowe's side.

"He's getting away," Marlowe rasped, trying to clear the pain from his mind.

"Shut it," Leonora commanded. "You've been shot and I can't breathe!"

"Go after him!"

"If I go after him now," she snarled, "he'll shoot me, and then who would save your life?"

They could hear the noise of the small boat being scraped across the beach.

"Save my life?" Marlowe suddenly felt very cold. "Is it that bad?"

"I'm afraid it's a very bad pistol shot wound, yes," Leonora said. "I can't stop the bleeding."

"I see," Marlowe mumbled.

She held both hands tightly on his side. "I'm afraid you're dying, Marlowe."

"Oh," he whispered.

The last thing he heard was the sound of the murderer's oars in the water, and suddenly he was back home, in the Stour River, drowning in black water.

SIX

Marlowe woke up with a start. He was in a strange bed in a cold place. He reached for his dagger, but it was not there—and neither were his clothes. As his mind cleared he realized that he was in the stable master's bed, naked, and dying of thirst. On the table beside him there was a taper with only a half an inch left. Most of the light seemed to be coming from outside the barn: day was breaking.

He sat up.

Leonora sat sleeping in a chair close by.

Marlowe pulled back the covers to examine his wound. It was angry, red, and burned like a hot poker, but not nearly as bad as he'd expected. It was stitched with a fine strong string, possibly catgut, and had been rubbed with a cream-white salve.

Casting his eye about, he found his clothing folded on the floor near the bed. The doublet was crisp with dried blood but the breeches were relatively clean. He leaned toward them and was surprised that his wound did not torture him.

"Lie back down," Leonora commanded sleepily, head still down, eyes still closed.

"Is this your work?" he asked, staring at the wound once more. "It's remarkable."

She sat up, stretched, rubbing her eyes. "I took out the pistol shot," she told him, "cleaned the wound. You'll be fine in a week or two."

"A week?" He sat up and reached for his clothes. "We haven't got an hour. I assume the assassin got away."

"He did," she said. "And there's more."

"More?" Marlowe held his breeches in his hand.

"The stable master, Edwin, is dead," she said, "and your Ned has gone with two of the horses."

"Two?" Marlowe wasn't certain he'd heard her correctly.

"The body of the man who had the claymore, that's gone as well."

"Ned's betrayed us," Marlowe acknowledged.

"He's more a part of the larger plot than he let on."

"The larger plot to kill William?" Marlowe shook his head. "Not likely. He's an actor. He doesn't care about politics in the Netherlands."

"Lie back down, I said." She stood.

"Look," Marlowe countered, "I'm going to put on my breeches now. Would you mind leaving, or at least turning around?"

She sighed. "You understand that I took those breeches off. It's not likely that I'll see anything this morning that I did not see last night."

Marlowe looked away. "Yes. Well. Things are a bit—different this morning."

She crossed her arms. "No."

"I—it's a bit—look. Last night I was unconscious. Asleep. *Lying down.*"

"Yes. I lugged your guts back here myself, without help from you."

"No, my point is," Marlowe insisted, "that this morning—this morning I am a bit—at attention."

He glanced downward.

It took Leonora a moment to realize what Marlowe was saying. When she did, her face turned vermillion, and she instantly quit the room.

With some doing Marlowe wrestled his breeches on, then his stockings and boots, his undershirt and soiled doublet. As he was beginning the buttons he called out.

"I'm thirstier than I've ever been in my life. Is there any ale about, do you think?"

"Are you dressed?" she asked angrily.

"Yes."

She appeared in the doorway with a tankard. "I knew you'd be parched. You lost a great deal of blood. You should eat something."

"Possibly I should," he agreed, "but wouldn't it be more in keeping with our appointed task if we found out what happened to the man who tried to kill me?"

"Oh," she answered, "you mean the man who rowed his small boat down the river just far enough to meet a ship in the channel? A ship out of the line of sight from this town's harbor area? That man?"

"How do you know—you followed him?"

"I saw to it that you'd not bleed to death and then, yes, I scurried down to the waterside just in time to see that ship was headed far off down the river, running lights on at last."

"He left without a thought of his compatriots," Marlowe said slowly, "and his accent was decidedly French. We know Ned is a Londoner, and we might assume that the dead man in the barn is a Scot"

"Owing simply to his claymore?" Leonora shook her head.

Marlowe nodded.

"Just a guess, of course," he answered, "but my point is this: it was an odd crew. It's entirely unclear to me what, exactly, happened at your inn. They met there, Ned told us."

"The couple," she began slowly, "I mean the man with the claymore and Ned dressed as a woman, they were meeting the Frenchman at the Bell. They weren't there to kill Lopez or even to stop me from delivering Walsingham's message to you."

"Agreed," Marlowe nodded. "I wonder if they even knew we'd be there at all."

"My recollection," she mused, her eyes far away, "is that they hadn't spoken to each other at all before you and the doctor came in. They had only just arrived themselves. Maybe one was waiting for some sort of sign from the other."

"And we merely happened in." Marlowe shook his head. "Is that too much a coincidence?"

"Judging by the chaos that our trio left in their wake," Leonora answered, "and the unanswered questions about Ned's part in all this, I'd say that none of this went as planned—nothing like a plan emerges at all, under examination."

"Yes." Marlowe was working to ignore the pain in his side. "The Bell Inn is, after all, the primary horse-changing station in this part of the world. It would not be out of the question that they would meet there in order to—but that's just it: in order to do what?"

Leonora bit her upper lip, staring out the small window of dead Edwin's bedroom.

After a moment she responded. "We might answer that question if we followed after Ned, back to the Bell. We could make certain my father is all right. But—"

"Very likely that Dr. Lopez has done his magic and all is well on that account. And Lopez will be gone by now." Marlowe sucked in a deep breath. "Do you know where?"

She avoided his gaze. "I'm afraid I cannot say."

"Right." Marlowe sighed. "Well, our aim is to see to it that William the Silent is not murdered. And the man who means to kill him is on the North Sea by now. We have no time to lose."

Marlowe headed out the door, angling for the river.

Leonora sighed heavily. "You won't make it out of this barn," she called after him, "let alone across the ocean."

"I have faith in your ministrations."

"Marlowe," she began.

"Are you coming?" He stepped into the dawn-lit alleyway, looking both ways. "I think it'll be easier to get to a ship if an attractive woman does the asking."

She shook her head. "Yes, but where could we find an attractive woman at this hour?"

"Well," Marlowe allowed, not looking back, "with Ned gone, you'll have to do."

Marlowe eased into the street. The sun was just barely over the horizon. A shot of golden light blasted the street, blinding, obscuring the path and making dark places darker. Dust motes from hay and animals and the ordinary refuse of the street floated in that light, turning like dancing atoms, spinning the night into morning.

Marlowe kept close to the buildings, partly because it was difficult to see with the sun in his eyes, partly in order not to be seen by anyone standing in the shadows. Leonora caught up with him, fell silent, and stole behind him toward the waterside.

There were several men going about morning rituals: grumbling, laughing, spitting. One of them walked to a boat that had been pulled up onto the shore and began to drag it back toward the black water.

Marlowe took a breath and then strode very deliberately toward the man.

"A very good morning to you," he called out.

The man looked up, startled.

"I was just wondering," Marlowe continued in a very jaunty manner, "how I might gain passage on some ship or other bound for the Netherlands. Today."

The man straightened up and glowered at Marlowe. He was old and thin; his beard was patchy and his eyes were red. His brown clothes had not been washed in a year.

"Today?" He squinted. "For the Netherlands?"

Marlowe nodded enthusiastically.

"Well that's what you might call a coincidence," the old man mused. "You see, just such a ship sat in the river only last night. But it's away. It left during the night, which is curious. They don't sail much at night, these big ships. You might, if you had a good horse and a bit of luck, catch it at the end of the river, at Mersea Island, just before she slips out onto the ocean."

"You think a horse could beat that ship?" Marlowe asked.

"Well," the old man said, scratching the back of his neck, "the river wanders, narrows, and generally impedes a craft that large."

"You saw the ship in the river? Last night?"

The man nodded.

"What manner of ship was it?"

"Was a Dutch caravel, it was," he answered. "Sleek."

"What makes you think it was Dutch?"

"Well," the man answered lazily, "there was the matter of the Dutch flag. That was my first hint."

Marlowe smiled. "I see. And you saw it leave?"

"Leave? No. I just happened to be on my way home from the public house, when I saw the man who shot you climbing aboard."

Marlowe blinked. Leonora appeared beside him.

"This is a nice quiet town," the old man went on. "Not much happens, but when it does, I know about it."

"You saw our encounter with the man who got on the ship?" Leonora asked.

"I did. I'm the oldest member of our Night's Watch here in Maldon."

"You *watched* as this man was shot," Leonora asked accusingly, taking a step in the old man's direction, "and did nothing?"

The man squinted.

"I *watched* as you tended his wounds like a doctor," he replied very steadily, "and I *watched* as you dragged him back up to Edwin's barn." He sniffed, staring Leonora in the eye. "And then I got in my little boat, here, and rowed myself very delicately out to the Dutch ship, tied a tricky line about the rudder, just enough to make the whipstaff hard to work."

Marlowe smiled. "Just enough to slow them down, but not enough to make them stop until morning."

He smiled back. "And now it's morning. I was about to nip down the river myself to report your murder to the authorities. But seeing as you're not quite dead, you might consider this: get you on a fast horse, hie you to Mersea Island, and catch the bastard yourself."

"Excellent suggestion." Marlowe took Leonora's elbow. "Come on."

"But," Leonora protested, "there's something very strange about all this."

"I agree," Marlowe whispered. "But our better course lies in stopping a killer. Time enough for other mysteries when that's done."

Leonora begrudgingly agreed with a small but explosive sigh, and began to run toward the barn. Marlowe barely kept apace, but they were into the stables in no time.

"If we ride fast enough," Leonora said, "can we really catch the ship before it sets to sea?"

"I think I understand what our night watchman has done," Marlowe answered, breathing heavily. "He's hampered the rudder, which means the ship cannot possibly sail true. Especially as dark as it was last night. The ship might easily have run afoul of the shallows, on either side of the river, perhaps even nudging the shore a time or two."

"Which would slow it down considerably." She nodded. "But I'm concerned about your wound."

"That's very touching," Marlowe grinned.

"If you tear the stitching I've done to your side, you'll be useless. I could kill the Frenchman myself, but I'd have difficulty getting his body onto a horse and taking him back to the inn."

Marlowe stared. "Why would you want to do that?"

"Identify the man," she said as if it were obvious. "Walsingham will be able to find out who he is. Then we'd have a key to the entire plot."

"Plot?"

Leonora began to saddle one of the horses. "There is more to this than the assassination of a Dutch leader who is moderately favorable to the Crown of England. Surely you can see that."

Marlowe swallowed. She was right, of course.

"Walsingham would not have sent Lopez to fetch me," he said, mostly to himself, "unless there was more at stake than the—this actually *is* a part of a larger scheme against the Queen."

Leonora finished tightening the saddle around the first horse and turned to face Marlowe.

"Yes," she said simply. "I have been assured that you would not have been *activated* otherwise. Despite our differences, I concede that Walsingham has a nearly supernatural belief in your abilities to solve a murder or, in this case, to prevent one. That is your primary duty on Her Majesty's secret service, is it not?"

Marlowe did his best to make his face a blank, give nothing away. He was uncomfortable knowing that this very odd person understood so much of his relationship with the Crown.

"I think we had better saddle the other horse," he answered, not looking her in the eye, "and ride as fast as we possibly can, for the sea."

SEVEN

MERSEA

Not many hours later, Marlowe stood in the sand at the edge of the North Sea, watching the waves roll away. Leonora had taken the horses to the stable and then gone to fetch a bite of food. She hadn't been gone for half an hour when Marlowe saw, crashing through the water in slow but wild zigzags down the River Blackwater, a Dutch caravel, the vessel that he was certain held the French assassin.

Marlowe smiled to think what a dreadful journey the wretch had endured, owing to the Maldon night watchman's sabotage.

This should be an easy matter, he thought. Simply wait for the ship to dock for repair, board the scow, and apprehend the bruised and shaken murderer.

He headed for the dock area. He was delighted to see Leonora already there, a small parcel in her hand. Marlowe's stomach began to growl and his side suddenly ached worse.

"Oatcakes," she called out, "and boiled eggs."

To Marlowe those words were a call to banquet.

"Why am I so hungry?" he asked her as she drew nearer.

He wondered at the way her green dress and leather breeches seemed none the worse for recent adventures, while his own clothing looked as if it had been worn by angry badgers.

He also spent a moment too long lingering on her eyes. When he realized he was staring, he began to cough. The coughing hurt his side, and that made him gasp.

Leonora rushed to him.

"You got out of bed so soon," she chided. "Let me look at the binding."

"No," Marlowe snapped. "Just let me eat fifty or sixty oatcakes and I'll be fine."

She glared. "Well. I suppose it's good sign that you're hungry."

He reached for the parcel she had in her hands.

"Then it's a very good sign." He reached in and grabbed. "I'm beyond starving!"

Leonora kept her eyes on the approaching ship.

"Here comes our man," she said softly. "He'll be the worse for wear."

"I was just thinking that." Marlowe swallowed an oatcake whole. "We'll just meet him when the ship docks, should be easy to take him then."

She smiled as the ship jolted against the bank, righted itself, and then tilted with the rushing current.

Ten minutes later they stood at the only real dock on the East Mersea shore. The vessel was having difficulty making its way the last hundred feet or so. A man who looked as if he'd been shaken in a giant tumbler of dice, face white, head bruised, leaned over the side and shouted to Marlowe.

"For the love of God catch this rope and secure it, man," he wailed. "We'll haul ourselves in."

Without waiting for an answer, the man tossed a thick roll of rope toward the shore. It unwound neatly, but landed ten feet short, in the drink.

"Go on," the man yelled. "Dive in and get it!"

Marlowe smiled. "Can't swim," he lied.

Leonora cast her eye about, saw a fishing net nearby, hanging on several pylons, fetched it, and brought it to Marlowe.

"Use this," she commanded. "You can snare the rope and pull it our way."

Marlowe shook his head. "I'm enjoying this."

"Oh for God's sake," she whispered.

Without another word she tossed the net wide, holding onto a single round at the rim, and the long drawstring with her other hand. The net landed expertly across the slowly sinking rope. She jerked the drawstring, and in seconds the rope was headed toward the dock.

"Nicely done," Marlowe said teasingly.

"Shut up," she answered.

Marlowe reached down, with some difficulty, and retrieved the rope from the water, tied it to the closest post, and stood back.

"There," he shouted to the ship.

The man didn't answer. He only set to work, with other members of the crew, to the slow task of hauling themselves to haven.

When, at last, they were secured, and the plank was lowered, Marlowe drew his rapier. Leonora took a few steps back and produced two wicked-looking daggers.

"You have a Frenchman onboard," Marlowe said calmly. "He killed a friend of ours and we're going to take him."

The man who'd spoken to them was wheezing and bent over. He was dressed in a drenched brown coat and pants, no shoes, a kerchief tied around his head. He was, perhaps, forty years old, plump, and milk-eyed.

He only managed to say, "Got off."

Marlowe took a quick step toward him, halfway up the plank, the point of his rapier headed directly for the man's ample midsection.

"He got off the ship!" the man repeated louder—and angrier. "When he saw we'd been scuttled, he put a pistol to my head and made me ram the shore. Me! The captain! He jumped ship, I'm saying. Most likely got a horse and arrived here at Mersea Island before morning. *Christ* what a rotten night I've had!"

"Damn it," Leonora swore softly.

"Is there another ship he might have caught here," Marlowe asked the poor captain. "You were taking him to the Netherlands."

"How should I know?" the captain raged. "Ask Willie!"

"Willie?" Marlowe repeated.

"Harbormaster," the captain said, "now kill me or get out of my way, I don't much care which."

Marlowe whirled about. "Harbormaster."

It took the better part of an hour to find Willie the Harbormaster. He was asleep on the floor of a nameless public house close to the docks. He was wrapped in a worn blue cape, a once fine item of clothing that had seen the dirt of too many barroom floors. Rousted, he complained with an assortment of the rudest curses Marlowe had ever heard, and then demanded rum.

That secured, he was willing to be questioned. The three of them sat at a table not big enough for one in a room barely large enough for three.

"Was there a ship here last night that departed for the Netherlands before this morning?" Marlowe asked harshly.

"Aye," Willie growled, and then he drank deeply.

"Why?" Leonora asked. "One's just come in this morning bound that way."

"There's always a ship or two here," Willie answered. "We're a busy little place. I works like an ass, and paid about the same."

"There was a ship here last night that just happened to be bound for the Netherlands?" Marlowe demanded.

"No," Willie complained. "Christ. It was the *Orion* bound straight for Domburg, like always. Waiting for first light. But up comes a bleeding Frenchie what wants to go to Delft, he says. Wants to leave by the light of the moon, he says. And when I tells him no, he give me this!"

Willie tilted his head toward Leonora and showed a bloody wound across his forehead.

"Then he cuts the captain of the *Orion,*" Willie went on, "and then, nice as you please, gives him a purse of gold fat enough to sink the ship."

Marlowe nodded. "At what hour?"

"Hour?" Willie snarled. "No idea. Between midnight and dawn's all I could tell you, and that's the truth."

He finished his rum and held out the cup.

Marlowe stood.

"I really hate to suggest this," he said to Leonora as he headed for the door, "but I think we're going to have to ask a favor of that fat little captain whose life I just threatened."

Leonora was right beside him. "As soon as you fix his ship."

After a bit of snarling negotiation with the fat captain, Marlowe spent a soggy hour untying the devilish knot attached to the ship's rudder. The Maldon night watchman had done a superb job. The rudder would work, but only enough to keep the craft from crashing into the shore or turning sideways. It would have been impossible for the whipstaff up on deck to make any subtle navigational choices.

"Thought you couldn't swim," the captain called down for a second time.

"I'm wading, not swimming," Marlowe answered, shivering in the water. "What's the name of this boat I'm saving for you?"

"Told you," the captain sniffed. "*My Beauty.*"

Marlowe took a moment to examine the scow. All its paint was gone, if ever it had been properly painted. It stank of tar patches and sweat. It was too small for the North Sea crossing, with questionable accommodations below deck and a filthy crew of five—not enough men.

"*My Beauty,* indeed," Marlowe mumbled.

The last knot finally succumbed to Marlowe's combination of cursing and tugging, and the rudder was free, little the worse for wear.

Dragging himself out of the drink, Marlowe shook off and trudged up the bank, across the dock, and onto the gangplank beside Leonora.

All he said was, "I'll pay the same as the Frenchman, to go to the same place he wanted to go."

Captain Darling—the man's name was Jacob Darling, further exacerbating Marlowe's sense of the ironic—seemed only too glad to have Marlowe's money. But he balked at the mere idea of taking a woman onboard.

"Jonah, I calls it!" And he spat. "No!"

"Ah, I see the problem," Marlowe answered before Leonora could object. "You think this person is a woman. Well. Between you and me, this is Ned Blank, the famous actor—plays women's roles in the London theatres."

Captain Darling glared. "No."

"Test me," Leonora snapped defiantly, taking Marlowe's cue, doing her best to sound like a young man.

"How do you mean, test you?" Darling asked thickly.

"Who's your best fighter?" Marlowe responded. "On your crew, who's the best?"

"Oh." Darling looked around. "That would be the Scot, Duncan."

With that a monster the size of three men lumbered forward: shirtless, hair dripping with greasy sweat, face a mass of stubble and pimples, and muscles like boulders.

"Fine," Leonora said matter-of-factly, her hands jammed down into the pockets of her dress.

Darling grinned. "Duncan?"

"What?" the great ape growled.

"Toss that woman in the river, there's a good boy."

Duncan scowled, momentarily trying to decide what some of those words meant, it appeared. Then he set his sights on Leonora, nodded, and stomped his way across the deck and down the gangplank toward her.

Leonora did not move. She smiled.

Duncan was nearly on top of her when she pulled her hands out of her pockets and blew a yellow dust into the big boy's face.

Inertia kept Duncan moving forward, but he began to cough and gasp.

Leonora stepped aside neatly, as if it were an act of manners, and allowed Duncan to lumber forward, tilting, until he reached the dock and fell down face-first, so hard that it cracked the boards beneath him. He lay very still.

"What the hell?" Darling began.

"Next!" Leonora called out.

"What?" Darling muttered.

"Too easy," Leonora shouted. "The monkey was too easy. Give me someone who's a challenge."

With that she pulled her dagger, hiked up her dress so that everyone could see her leather breeches and riding boots, and took a very fearsome stance blocking any exit from the ship.

"You'd better send someone his way," Marlowe urged Darling. "You don't want to make Ned mad. He'll kill half your crew before I can stop him, and then where will you be?"

"Christ!" Darling howled. "Everything happens to me!"

Leonora began a kind of low rumble. She strode up the plank directly toward Darling.

"Ned, no!" Marlowe called out in mock panic.

Before anyone knew what was happening, Leonora had cut Darling's ear, arm, and leg. Then, in a single move that looked more like a dance than a fight, she cut the captain's suspenders. His trousers dropped immediately, and lay in a puddle-like heap around his feet.

Dagger still very visible, Leonora asked, "Now, are you taking us to Delft or not?"

"Some of you go get Duncan, if he's alive," the captain sighed, pulling up his pants, "and then make ready to sail; we're away within the hour."

EIGHT

MONSTER, THE NETHERLANDS

The next day, shortly after noon, the coast of the Netherlands appeared on the horizon over the bow of *My Beauty.* Two hours later the ship set in at Monster, some ten miles or so from Delft. Not a single word had passed between crew, captain, or passengers. Leonora slept most of the time. Marlowe slept, ate, stretched to test his wound, and slept again.

And when the dock was bumped and the gangplank was lowered, Marlowe and Leonora were first to disembark.

Just as Leonora's foot hit the dock, the captain called out, "Why do you do it?"

Marlowe turned. Leonora stopped, but did not look back.

"Why do I do *what*?" Marlowe asked.

"Not you," Captain Darling rumbled. "Him. Why does he dress up like a woman?"

Marlowe grinned. "I told you. Theatre."

"No," the captain objected, "but I mean, now. Why is he dressed up as a woman *now*? This ain't a theatre. It's bleeding Holland!"

That provoked Leonora to turn and face Captain Darling.

"All the world is my theatre, Captain," she told him. "You—you and your crew, you're merely players. That's all."

With that she strode, in a very manly fashion, away from the ship and off the dock.

Marlowe followed silently. But when he caught up with her he could not help but exclaim, "You're a poet, Miss Beak. A philosopher. That was brilliant."

"It's not original to me," she chided. "You've heard that before."

"Never." Marlowe held his breath for a moment. "But I think I'll use it in a play."

"Horses," she responded. "That's what we need. Delft is at least ten miles away, and time is clearly of the essence."

"We don't know the Frenchman's plans," Marlowe agreed, "but we really ought to assume that he'll try to kill William as soon as he can."

"Exactly."

"I don't suppose you have any more stable contacts up your sleeve."

"No," she admitted, "but I might mention the Bell Inn. It's quite well known."

"And as to finding a stable," Marlowe said, sniffing, "I need only follow my nose."

In no time they had located a stable, close to a church—one of the largest churches Marlowe had ever seen.

"I think that's how this town got its name," he mused as they entered the stable.

"What?" Leonora asked vaguely, looking around for the stable master.

"*Monster* in Dutch means *big church,*" he told her. "As in the Latin *monstrum.*"

"What are you—why are you telling me this?"

"Thought you'd be interested," Marlowe sighed. "I'm just about to achieve my degree from Corpus Christi, and I know things, you see."

"We need horses!" she snapped.

On cue a very thin young man appeared out of the shadows. His drab clothes were dotted here and there with hay but they were neatly appointed and relatively clean. His boots looked new. He was smiling, jabbering happily and incoherently in Dutch.

"What's he saying?" Leonora asked Marlowe.

"Not a clue," Marlowe admitted, then he turned to the young man and said, crisply, "*Spreekt u engels?*"

He lit up.

"Ah! The English! Yes. Most apology. Of course I speak it."

Marlowe turned to Leonora. "There."

She sighed, then turned to the young man. "Have you two horses we might use?"

"Ah. Well. You must buy. Not to use." He smiled.

"Of course," she agreed. "How much?"

He shook his head, and turned to Marlowe.

"Most apology," he told Marlowe, his brow furrowed.

"*Hoeveel kost het?*" Marlowe said, smiling.

"Yes, yes. The cost. Ten."

"Ten?" Leonora turned to Marlowe. "Ten what?"

"English," the thin man said quickly. "You are English, pay in English. Ten pounds."

"Ten pounds?" Marlowe roared.

"Each," the man said, still smiling.

"Are they made out of gold?" Marlowe asked loudly.

"Sorry?" the man asked, head cocked.

Using her hands as puppets, Leonora mimed as she spoke. "If we bring the horses back here when we're finished, in a day or two, could we get our money back?"

The man looked down, slowly translating, it seemed, and then he nodded.

"Yes," he said. "I keep one pound, give back nine."

Marlowe was about to continue his objections, and then decided on another approach.

"Is that what you made the Frenchman pay?" he asked. "*Fransman*?"

"*Fransman,* yes." He lost his smile. "Not good. He is not good."

"Did he have to pay ten?" Marlowe asked sternly.

The young man looked away. "No."

"He threatened you," Marlowe continued. "*Bedreiging.*"

"For someone who doesn't speak Dutch," Leonora interrupted, "you know a lot of Dutch words."

"Sh!" Marlowe commanded.

"*Fransman,* yes. He told he would kill me. *Moord.*"

“Murder,” Marlowe translated for Leonora.

“That word I got all on my own,” she told him.

“Look,” Marlowe said to the stable keeper, “Ten for both. Not each. And you keep one when we bring them back. But we also want food. *Eten*.”

He hesitated, took in a deep breath, and then nodded his head. “Cheese? Bread—brood?”

“And ale?” Marlowe ventured.

The man regained his smile. “Ale? Best in the world. Make myself.”

NINE

DELFT, THE NETHERLANDS

Twenty minutes later Leonora and Marlowe were galloping out of Monster on the road to Delft. Marlowe was still eating bread and cheese. His side burned.

The landscape flew past, a blur of trees and fields. In the distance the occasional windmill beckoned, but the ribbon of road held strong, and the horses, surprisingly swift, raced toward the home of William, Prince of Orange, often called William the Silent, leader of the Dutch revolt against the Spanish. That revolt made Delft, more or less, the capital of the newly independent Netherlands.

William's home in that city was, by all reports, a comfortable residence: gardens, a good kitchen, less stately than many princely apartments.

With luck, Marlowe thought, they might arrive at dinner time.

Even though he was bleeding a little, his spirits had been bolstered by Dutch ale—and his conviction that they would see William and warn him of the plot on his life, thus saving his life. A good day's work that would surely be rewarded by a great evening's meal, not to mention rendering remarkably speedy service to the Queen.

By the time the spires of the old church in Delft came into view, and then the lesser buildings, Marlowe's self-satisfaction was complete.

The horses slowed, Marlowe and Leonora relaxed, and the sun began to sink low in the western sky.

"I think the house is just over there to the right," Leonora said softly, tilting her head. "There, behind the church, do you see it?"

Marlowe nodded. "How do you know that's the house?"

"It was described to me in a part of Walsingham's missive," she answered absently.

Marlowe stared at her. Walsingham trusted this person with all manner of knowledge. Who was she? What was she to Walsingham? More than an eighth cousin to the Queen, certainly.

Leonora sipped a breath. "But now that we're here, what, exactly, are we doing?"

She sounded exhausted, and her voice reminded Marlowe that he, too, was not at his physical best, despite high spirits. It had been a long ride.

"Occam's Razor," Marlowe mused. "We do the simplest thing: ask to see the prince, tell him there's a plot against his life, from a French assassin, gather his guard around him, and then have a very nice dinner."

Leonora laughed, leaning forward onto her horse's neck. "Honestly? That's your plan?"

"Unless I've added up my hours incorrectly," Marlowe responded, irritated by her tone of voice, "Prince William is, this night, hosting Rombertus van Uylenburgh. They are to discuss matters concerning the Frisian state. Do you not recall?"

"I do," she sighed, then lowered her voice. "And we are to say the Dutch words—butter and green bread. . . ."

"*Bûter, brea, en griene tsiis,*" Marlowe corrected, "Butter, bread, and green *cheese*."

Leonora rolled her eyes. "Men make up the most ridiculous codes."

Marlowe ignored her.

The streets were moderately crowded, the last of the day's business coming to a close. Though Marlowe and Leonora might have provided a bit of interest to the populace, so obviously foreigners, Delft was a very cosmopolitan city, and most citizens of the residents were happily inured to strangers from nearly everywhere.

Stone and brick buildings rose several stories on both sides of the street leading to the church, and then, around to the right and behind, one might just make out the front gardens of Prince William's house.

As they drew nearer, they could see nearly every window in the place was filled with light. Candles and lamps had been lit, apparently, all over the house, to suggest a kind of opulence ordinarily reserved for guests.

"Do you suppose that William's dinner companion has already arrived?" Marlowe asked, almost to himself.

"A bit early for dinner, isn't it?" Leonora scanned the sides of the house, looking for signs of a carriage or stable activity that might indicate a recent arrival.

Unsure of the proper protocol for such a circumstance, Marlowe made bold to ride his horse through the front garden and up to the main entrance of the house. The building was lovely, smaller and more comforting than most royal apartments. The gardens were well-tended but not fussy; nature's hand was more evident than any gardener's.

Marlowe dismounted, patted his horse, adjusted his soiled black doublet, and stood waiting for Leonora to join him.

She stayed on her horse.

"Are we certain that barging in the front door is the proper behavior?" she whispered. "Aren't we supposed to be spies?"

"You're a spy," Marlowe corrected. "I'm an investigator in the service of the Queen. At this moment I am attempting to prevent a murder, international mayhem, and the ruination of civilization as we know it—in that order. Care to join me? Here on the ground?"

Sighing heavily, Leonora dismounted.

Without further discussion, Marlowe strode to the front door and banged loudly.

After a moment the door cracked slightly and the thin face of a very irritated servant appeared.

"*Nr,*" was all he said.

"He says, 'No.'" Marlowe took a step forward. "*Ik wens te zie* William."

"*Nr,*" the man repeated, and made as to close the door.

"*Bûter, brea, en griene tsiis,*" Marlowe intoned.

The man laughed, but it was not a pleasant sound. "*We hebben geen eten voor u.*"

Marlowe turned to Leonora.

"He says he has no food for us," he translated.

"Well tell him what the problem is," she scolded, "and stop trying to be subtle."

Marlowe turned to the man and squinted.

"*William in gevaar is,*" Marlowe told him, raising his voice.

"*Weg!*" the man shouted.

Marlowe turned back to Leonora.

"He's just told us to go away."

"Christ," she muttered.

Reaching into a fold in her dress she produced a small leather pouch, one that Marlowe had seen before. She dipped her hand into it and stepped toward the door, smiling sweetly.

"Look here," she said to the man in the doorway, smiling.

Then she blew an orange powder into the man's face. He jerked his head back and seemed just about to rail angrily, when his eyes rolled and he collapsed onto the floor, allowing the door to open a few more inches.

"Shall we?" she asked, inclining her head toward the inside of the front room.

"Eventually you're going to have to tell me how you do that, all those powders." Marlowe stared through the doorway at the motionless servant. "Is he dead?"

"Of course not," she said, pushing the door inward. "But he won't awake for a while."

The man's body was preventing the door from opening completely, so they were forced to scrape their way inside, careful not to step on the man.

Once in, Marlowe took the servant's arms and dragged him inward. Alas, before he got very far, another man appeared. This one was more in the line of a guard. He had a weapon drawn, a riding sword with its slightly wider blade gleaming in the light from the chandelier in the front entranceway.

Marlowe held his hands out to assure the man he had no weapons of his own in them.

"*Wij zijn hier voor willem op zaken van de koningin van Engeland,*" Marlowe pronounced very carefully.

"English?" the man asked, cocking his head.

"Yes," Marlowe said.

"Your Dutch is not good." He glanced down at the unconscious servant. "Did you kill Hans?"

"Of course not." Marlowe dropped his hands. "He fainted when I told him why I'm here. I'm on urgent business of the Queen of England. William is in grave danger."

The man smiled. He pointed his sword directly at Marlowe's face.

"I think not," he said, his eyes shooting to Leonora.

The man wore a tunic over what appeared to be light armor. He was, by appearance, a knight. The crest on his tunic was a red shield with a standing, golden lion on it. The lion held a sword, its claws and tongue were blue—the coat of arms of the Dutch Republic.

"Someone is coming to murder William," Marlowe said quickly. "I think he should know about that."

"The prince is currently dining with Rombertus van Uylenburgh," the man sniffed, "and after dinner he must attend to a small matter, a passport for one Francis Guion, of Lyons. Possibly when that matter is concluded—"

"*Bûter, brea, en griene tsiis!*" Marlowe shouted. "Say that to William!"

"Ah!" the man snapped. "All you want is *food*?"

"We are on the Queen's business," Marlowe began, his voice even louder. "I must insist that you tell Prince William—"

"And I must insist that you wait outside!" the man interrupted, matching Marlowe's volume. "There are wooden benches at the door."

Without another word he turned and walked away very calmly.

Stunned, Marlowe watched the man retreat.

"It's a nice evening," Leonora offered. "Maybe we should just wait outside until the prince has finished his dinner. He's obviously well-protected here."

"Did you hear what that man said?" Marlowe howled. "There's a Frenchman wanting a passport. *That's* our man! He's already in this building!"

Leonora turned and opened the front door. "I have grave doubts about that. Why would he be asking the prince for a passport?"

"It's a ruse!" Marlowe told her. "Christ! Am I the only thinking person in this city?"

"Well, you're certainly the only one who thinks the way you do." Leonora opened the front door. "Shall we?"

"I may lose my mind." Marlowe brushed past her, fuming.

Leonora followed. "The prince is dining. There are guards. This man, this Rombertus van Uylenburgh is with him. All is well."

"All is shite," Marlowe countered. "No one seems to know the—what would you call the secret words, the passwords? This feels wrong."

The evening air was cool. Marlowe sat, vigorously attempting to display his ire.

"Christ, calm down," Leonora said softly as she sat beside him. "Everything has happened at such a pace—let us sit a moment, take time to survey the larger situation."

"All right," Marlowe agreed grudgingly. "Then tell me when did you receive the message from Walsingham?"

"Hm?" She sat beside him. "The day before yesterday, in the morning. It came by special courier."

"The courier was a man you'd seen before?"

"No, but that's not unusual. It's a different man every time."

Marlowe shook his head. "As I sit here, I can't make the sequence of events fit right. Do you recall the passwords you were to tell us?"

"The bit about the storm? 'Hail, snow, and lightning all at once.'"

"That's from a play of mine," Marlowe whispered. "Not a very good one, at present. It's only been performed once—not even fully. And that was the morning that Dr. Lopez came to fetch me in Cambridge with the news that William the Silent was dead."

She started to speak, then held her breath.

"Yes," Marlowe went on. "You see the problem. How could those words have gotten into the missive from Walsingham?"

"Is it possible that someone read the manuscript some days earlier?"

"Possible," he admitted, "but not likely. Only one or two others have ever seen the lines."

"Then—what?"

"I don't know, that's just it." Marlowe stood and began to pace. "None of this is right: the Traveling Scots we met on the road, the fact that Ned Blank, one of our premiere London actors, is somehow involved, the murder of your cook back at the Bell. It's all too sloppy. Deliberately so."

"*Deliberately?* You mean that someone is trying to obscure the waters of the larger plot."

"Yes." Marlowe took in a short breath. "I'm beginning to agree that there is more to all this than an assassination of this Dutch prince. He isn't to be murdered in order to make it easier for Spanish invasion troops to assemble. They're already gathered, waiting. Someone wanted us to be distracted from that."

"And when you say *us,* you mean?"

"Lopez, me, you, Walsingham, the Queen."

"Well if you're right," she said, "we're not just distracted. They wanted us out of the country. Out of England."

"This is all a ruse!" Marlowe's voice rose. "There is no plot on William's life! We have to get back to England!"

At that exact moment three pistol shots rang out from inside the prince's home.

Shock seized Marlowe, but it did not prevent him from drawing his rapier and barging into the home. He could smell the gunpowder, and hear voices shouting, crying.

He rushed toward the noise, Leonora running at his side. They quickly found a glut of men and women gathered at the bottom of the stairs. In the middle lay a dead man, blood bubbling from two holes in his chest. On the stairway wall, just above, he saw two smoking holes that could only have come from gunshot.

"God in Heaven," Marlowe swore.

The man in the lion tunic stood over the corpse, weeping. He looked up at Marlowe.

"William the Silent is dead." His voice grated.

The prince lay in a woman's arms. Her face was covered in tears.

"Where is the assassin?" Marlowe demanded.

Five or six arms raised, fingers all pointing in the same direction, toward the back of the house.

Without another word, Marlowe raced in that direction, drawing his dagger in addition to the rapier in his right hand. He could hear Leonora behind him as she knelt beside the dead man, muttering some words of comfort and asking several questions. But a moment later he was out of earshot and his own heart's blood was pounding in his ears.

Around a corner and past several rooms, a door to the outside stood open.

Marlowe raged through it, growling. He did not bother to look which way the murderer had run. He knew it would be toward the more populated streets of the city, toward the church.

As he barged down a narrow way he suddenly caught sight of the villain up ahead, running toward the ramparts. With a start Marlowe noticed a pig's bladder around the assassin's waist. The man was going to ascend the ramparts and plunge into the moat, using the bladder as a float.

Gasping for breath, his lungs burning, his side screaming, Marlowe began to gain on the man. Several pounding heartbeats later, the man flung himself forward. Marlowe thought he was attempting to leap onto the ramparts.

A moment later it was clear that the murderer had stumbled over a rubbish heap and had crashed to the ground.

Marlowe sheathed his rapier and was on top of the man at once. He grabbed the man by the throat and held the point of his knife at the man's left eye.

"Traitor," Marlowe snarled. "Coward."

"I am no traitor, Monsieur," he gasped, "I am a patriot."

"A *patriot*?"

"In the service of my master, the King of Spain!"

An instant later several other men appeared. Screaming, they tore the assassin from Marlowe's grasp and began beating him. Fists, boots, the butt of a sword, all rained down on the demon. Marlowe swallowed, catching his breath, and was about to question the killer. But the gang began to drag the Frenchman back toward the house, still beating him mercilessly.

"Wait," Marlowe called. "I need to question that man!"

Perhaps they did not hear him for all their shouted curses, perhaps they did not understand English; they may have simply ignored him in the rage of the moment.

It didn't really matter. William the Silent was dead. Marlowe had failed.

The assassin's name was Balthasar Gérard. Soon after Marlowe's repeated attempts to question him were ignored, city magistrates appeared. They began a feverish examination, more inquisition than trial.

Gérard, unrepentant, almost glowing, oiled each response.

"I have been planning this holy act since March," he concluded. "I, like David, have slain Goliath!"

Obviously mad, the Frenchman went on: singing snatches of old tunes, as one incapable of knowing his own distress.

Stopping the assassin in the middle of a sentence, a little man in grand purple, a hat that cost more than everyone else's boots, and a belly like a pregnant sow, shot up. Pointing his finger at the Frenchman he declared: "Balthasar Gérard, you shall be taken out of this house and tortured for two days. Then you shall be brought into a public place where your right hand, that which slew our great prince, will be burned off with a red-hot iron. Then flesh will be ripped from your bones with pincers, after which your limbs will be torn from your body, all four. You will be disemboweled alive and live as long as you may in that condition. Thereafter, before you are dead, your heart will be gouged from your chest and flung into your face, and your head will be cut of and served to dogs."

Gérard nodded. That was all.

Marlowe kept insisting, in the Queen's name, that he be allowed to question Gérard. It was clear to Marlowe that William's murder had been a planned distraction, something to confuse Walsingham, to misdirect his attentions. It seemed almost as certain that the missive delivered to Leonora Beak had not come from Walsingham. Aside from being a blow to Dutch support for the Crown, William's murder would be an incitement to greater horrors on the world stage, fomented by the Spanish, with whom Gérard was admittedly in league. It was also therefore likely that Gérard knew something about the greater plot.

Every fiber of Marlowe's intuition told him that the murder of William the Silent was a stepping-stone on a path to killing the Queen.

After hours of pleading Marlowe secured, at last, a moment with Gérard in the condemned man's cell, a dank room in a government house not two blocks from William's modest palace. When he arrived he found the wretch hanging by his elbows from a low pole.

The cell was a gray stone, windowless room. There was a menacing fire going in one corner, and blood on the floor. The smell of the place was vicious: excrement, urine, terror.

Having been lashed mercilessly with a whip, it appeared that honey had been smeared into Gérard's wounds. The guards, one man told Marlowe, had sent for a goat to lick the honey.

Marlowe stood before the living corpse.

"You deserve this," Marlowe said softly.

"Soon, I will go to God, who will elevate me above his angels for what I have done."

"Soon I will return to England and stop the rest of your plan." Marlowe knelt and looked into the Frenchman's eyes. "All you've done is murder a man. Nothing else. You've broken a commandment. How do you suppose God feels about men who break his laws?"

Gérard was having difficulty breathing, but he managed a short laugh.

"What would you know about God's laws, you English pig?"

Marlowe leaned close to the man's ear. "I don't like to mention it, but I am, myself, a Catholic. I believe I would know as much as you do about the church."

Gérard grinned, a monstrous grimace. "Then you will be happy to learn that you will soon have a Catholic Queen on the throne of England. And there is nothing anyone can do about it."

"Not even for *Bûter, brea, en griene tsiis*?" Marlowe ventured.

Gérard's eyes flashed. "Yes," he muttered. "Say those words to Sir Anthony Babington. He is here, in Delft, staying at William's home."

Marlowe did his best not to react, but all fears had been confirmed. Alas, before he could press the matter with the assassin, several guards returned.

They brushed Marlowe aside. Having failed to find a goat, they wrapped Gérard in a shirt soaked in alcohol. The Frenchman screamed until his throat gave out. Then, casually, one of the guards sauntered to the fire in the corner. Using long tongs, he picked up an iron pail that smelled like burning bacon fat. He called out a warning, instructing everyone to step away from the prisoner, and then slowly poured the searing fat over Gérard's head and back. The Frenchman tried again to scream, but only air escaped his mouth.

Marlowe turned away. He would glean no more information from the man. That man was already dead.

Winding his way upward, through several guarded hallways, Marlowe came to the front door of the government house. He burst through it, into the evening air. Taking several deep breaths, he rubbed his eyes and shook his head.

Leonora was there, pacing impatiently.

"We've been duped, both of us." Marlowe stared at Leonora.

"You've told me your theories," she sighed wearily. "The message I received was false, we were drawn out of the country of a purpose—"

"We must go to William's home immediately!" Marlowe interrupted.

"Why?" she asked, startled.

"There is a man there," Marlowe snapped, beginning to run toward William's palace.

Moments later Marlowe and Leonora stood at the front door of William's home pounding on it, once more, to be admitted.

"Are you absolutely certain of what you've just told me?" Marlowe asked Leonora.

"Certain? No." She shook her head. "But I *think* one of the men who stood around William's dead body in the stairway was Anthony Babington. I've only seen him twice, both times at the Bell. But the man in the black cloak with the green hat? He did *look* like Babington."

"I know the one you mean; I picture his face."

Then Marlowe pounded on the door again, and kicked it twice.

At last the knight who had refused them admittance came to the door.

"What in God's name do you want?" he rumbled in a voice rife with pain.

"Let us in," Marlowe snapped impatiently. "There is a man in his place with whom I mean to speak."

"Go away," the knight sighed wearily. "Go home. There is no one here."

"The last time you refused to let me in," Marlowe seethed, "the result was the death of the man you were supposed to protect."

"Marlowe," Leonora began.

"Yes." The knight's eyes were dead. "But that assassin has been apprehended."

"By me!" Marlowe growled. "While you stood here with your thumb in your ass and the same drooling expression you wear now!"

"Marlowe, stop it," Leonora insisted.

Ignoring her, Marlowe took a single step back and drew his rapier. "Step aside or go to hell," he snarled at the knight.

The rapier snapped through the air and its point stopped right between the knight's eyes.

"We only wish to talk with a guest of the house," Leonora intervened quickly. "A countryman of ours. Sir Anthony Babington."

"No. I said. He is not here." The knight's eyes never changed. "He's gone. No one is here. This place is empty. All gone."

"Gone?" Marlowe shouted. "Where?"

"Back to England, I suppose." The guard closed his eyes. "God."

"Let it go, Marlowe," Leonora said softly.

Marlowe hesitated, suddenly realizing that his anger was as much at himself as at the desolate knight. He sheathed his blade in a single arc.

Leaning forward so that his face nearly touched the knight's, he whispered harshly, "The fault is yours!"

The knight didn't open his eyes. "I know."

Marlowe turned to Leonora. "We must return to England at once."

"You're exhausted and wounded," Leonora objected. "You won't make it to your horse, let alone back to England."

"Gérard was working for Philip," Marlowe said softly, headed toward his mount. "Philip is working to free Mary. Mary is somehow in contact with Babington. The end of their vile efforts would see Mary on the throne of our country—and Elizabeth dead. I have to make it back to England."

Without another word, Marlowe threw himself onto his horse. Sweating, dizzy, and in pain, he urged his mount forward, toward the coast.

TEN

LONDON

Marlowe sat in a completely uncomfortable chair in a very dark room in a nearly airless corner of Hampton Court. The room was small, made of stone, furnished only with the chair in which Marlowe had been told to sit, and a small desk behind which sat the only other chair. Nothing hung on the walls, and the sole light in the gloom issued from a single candle on the desk.

He had been waiting for more than an hour. He knew that he was a shambles: hair a wild tangle, clothes caked with grime, face unwashed and unshaven. The journey from Delft to London was a blur in his mind. Leonora Beak had mostly been in charge. A combination of fatigue, blood loss, hunger, anger, and shame had rendered Marlowe all but comatose.

At Buntingford he and Leonora learned that her father was alive—though barely—Lopez was missing, and the Traveling People whom she had helped on the road had stayed for only a day at the changing station, thereafter vanishing into the woods.

Too weak to ride at that point, Marlowe had been placed in a coach that Leonora managed to acquire. For most of the bumpy ride from Buntingford to Hampton Court Marlowe had slept, all the while being tossed like dice in a cup.

Just as his head was drooping, the only door to the room burst open and Lord Walsingham glided in, followed by two guards. He was dressed in dark gray, including his cap, and his beard was not as neatly trimmed as it usually was. His eyes were bleary, and he moved across the floor with a slight limp.

Marlowe struggled to his feet.

"No!" Walsingham barked. "Sit!"

Marlowe did exactly that.

"This," Walsingham said, flourishing a single page of paper, "is what I have been waiting for."

He dropped into his chair behind the desk.

"My Lord," Marlowe began, "I have urgent news of—"

"I know most of it already," Walsingham assured him briskly.

"William the Silent . . ."

". . . is truly gone," Walsingham interrupted. "Yes."

"I—I failed in my task. Utterly. If you—do you require my dismissal from your service? Or—am I to be detained—I have no idea what I'm to do, but—"

"Marlowe," Walsingham snapped. "Gather yourself. You did not save William. Neither did his guard, his household, or his country. I'm encouraged to believe that you have vital intelligence in this affair which affects Her Majesty, is that so?

"Yes, sir, but, let me see—where to begin?" Marlowe said. "Leonora Beak received a missive which we thought was from you but which I now believe was entirely false, or at least altered, and that missive lured us to the Netherlands when we should have remained here in England."

Walsingham nodded. "When Lopez told me about the message, I was alarmed. As you have correctly ascertained, it was not mine. Which is why we hold you blameless in your failure to save William's life. That was not your assignment."

"Lopez is safe?" Marlowe could not hide the relief in his voice.

"He has been dispatched to another part of the world at the moment." Walsingham looked down. "But continue."

Marlowe related his entire adventure, careful to omit no detail, as Lopez had taught him. Even the Traveling family, the odd presence of the actor Ned Blank, the strange night watchman who disabled the ship in Maldon—anything might contain some important bit of information that only Walsingham's mind could detect and decipher.

And then Marlowe offered his conclusion.

"The last words the assassin Gérard said to me indicate a greater plot," he said, leaning forward, "than the death of our Dutch ally. I believe that the murder of William was one link in a chain of events that would see Mary on the throne, and our true Queen dead. And then he told me to seek out Sir Anthony Babington."

Walsingham nodded. His demeanor was unusually reserved, cold.

"With our Dutch forces in doubt," he said deliberately, "we must go to the source of this plot, and stop it before it gains strength. The loss of William is a blow to our cause. Let it not be any more significant than the wound in your own side: difficult, but not deadly."

"Agreed," said Marlowe, ignoring the burning pain in his side. "But as to Babington?"

"Tell me," Walsingham went on, more softly, "why do you suppose that the assassin Gérard confided such a key element of the larger scheme to you? Was it the torture?"

"No," Marlowe said quickly, "I had no part in that. But. I may have encouraged him to believe that I am more Catholic than I actually am."

"I suspected as much." Walsingham nodded. "Good. It is to our advantage that some believe you to be a secret Catholic, although I know that your true church is England."

"My true church is theatre," Marlowe corrected. "Beyond that, I have no religious affiliation whatsoever, if I may be permitted complete honesty."

Walsingham leaned back. "I see. That is why it has not yet occurred to you who sent the false message, the one alleged to be from me."

Marlowe's attention focused. "What are you talking about?"

"I have read this forged missive," he said, "and have surmised the identity of the only person who could possibly have known the words included in it, the words from your new play. But your affiliation with the theatre prevents you from naming him."

The impact of Marlowe's sudden realization was as substantive as a blow to the head. He sipped in a violent breath, and shivered.

"Kyd," he rasped.

"Alas," Walsingham confirmed, shrugging.

"No." Marlowe stood. "Why would Thomas Kyd betray me?"

"You misunderstand," Walsingham answered calmly. "Thomas Kyd betrayed England. You were merely in his line of fire."

"Why would our greatest playwright betray his country?" Marlowe demanded, something like anger growing in his brain.

"Thomas Kyd has—proclivities." Walsingham appeared to think better of continuing, for the moment.

Marlowe exhaled. "'He is a fool who likes not tobacco and young boys.' I've heard him say it a thousand times. But the things he says, they are largely in jest. He is rarely of a serious mind, and most of what he says is intended as humor. Not to mention that his belly may be the largest single repository of finer ale on this continent."

"And in moments of excess," Walsingham sighed, "a man may agree to do things that his better, more sober self might not."

"He's been blackmailed, then," Marlowe assumed, "because of his public statements. He's agreed to help—not the Spanish. Certainly."

"No, of course not. He's not valuable to Spaniards."

"Then to whom has he succumbed?"

"That we do not know. But you must find out."

"Of course. I know how to find him."

"No," Walsingham said, "you must not find him. He must find you. But not now. Now you must go directly to Mary. You must confirm what we suspect about Babington, and the scheme he has engendered. Mary is under strictest confinement at Chartley Hall, though few know it—I have let it be known that she will not be there until Christmas, but she is there now."

"That way," Marlowe assumed, "the only people who would know about her imprisonment there would be your inner circle, or conspirators."

"Yes," Walsingham confirmed. "She is quite guarded. Sir Amias Paulet is her keeper. He is a Puritan, and hates Mary. Among other punishments, Mary is forbidden any correspondence with the outside world. But we have reason to believe that she has subverted that condition."

"She has communicated with Babington," Marlowe concluded.

"Yes." Walsingham held out a single sheet. "Here is one such missive. Study it. You may have need to recognize his handwriting."

Marlowe took the letter and stared at it.

"You must go to Mary as a secret Catholic ally," Walsingham went on. "Under the guise of confederacy, you will agree to transport her secret letters for her. Those letters, I believe, will contain the final elements of her downfall, and her death."

"I am to do this alone? Without Lopez or—"

"Not exactly alone." Walsingham held aloft the piece of paper which he had flourished upon entering the room. "This document is your companion, and your weapon."

Marlowe stared at the paper and thought, for a moment, he might be in a dream.

"What is that page?"

"It is the newly signed Act for the Surety of the Queen's Person," Walsingham answered confidently. "It is a law which permits the bearer great latitude in pursuit of *anyone* who would plot against the Queen of England. And there is no doubt that Mary is at the center of this plot. Your evidence from the mouth of the assassin Gérard permits us to take Mary, but we—that is, our Queen desires more tangible proof. She remains loath to condemn Mary. You must obtain something substantial."

"I—yes, but—" Marlowe stammered.

"There are other assurances in this document," Walsingham continued, "that may aid you in all of your continuing pursuits as an investigator for us. For instance, you are allowed to use any and all means to secure your ends with complete impunity."

Walsingham inclined his head toward Marlowe.

Marlowe shook his head. "I'm not certain I understand."

Walsingham held out the paper, offering it to Marlowe, insisting that he take it.

"Under this law, you will not be held liable for any illegal activity employed during the course of your investigations," he told Marlowe. "Including murder. You are given license to kill."

Marlowe stared at the paper, then took it delicately, as if it might explode in his hand.

Then Walsingham heaved a sigh so filled with emotion that Marlowe gasped.

"Sir?" he said to Walsingham.

"There is another matter." Walsingham closed his eyes. The old man was in great distress, Marlowe read it on his face.

Without a word Walsingham held up one of the golden cylinders used for the transportation of secrets. He removed the end of the cylinder and extracted the rolled up message. He stared at it, pinched his lips, and then looked up at Marlowe.

"Something has transpired which—I—one of our agents—forgive me, I don't have the words."

The old man was clearly shaken. He leaned forward heavily on the desk.

Marlowe stared at Walsingham. "What has happened?"

"There has been another murder, one of a more personal nature," Walsingham said softly. "Leonora Beak is dead."

For a moment the words weren't real. Marlowe was certain he'd heard incorrectly.

"No." Marlowe shook his head. "That's wrong. She's not dead. I just saw her, left her tending to her father at the Bell Inn."

Walsingham locked eyes with Marlowe.

"She lies dead in Buntingford." Walsingham's voice strained to betray no emotion, but his eyes brimmed with great intensity. "A rider arrived an hour before your coach did. With this message."

"No!" Marlowe insisted. "It's wrong. You have been misinformed!"

"Marlowe!" the old man roared.

"Who?" Marlowe demanded. "Who killed her?"

"That is not known."

"Well it will be soon! I'm going to Buntingford, I'll find the villain, and I'll kill him!"

"I—no, Marlowe," Walsingham began.

Marlowe stood. "Do not dissuade me!"

But Marlowe's legs gave out, and he nearly fell. His side was bleeding again, and his head pounded so hideously that he found it hard to see the room around him.

"Sit down!" Walsingham commanded.

"I'm going to—to the Bell," Marlowe offered weakly.

"Yes, Marlowe," Walsingham responded, his voice was iron. "That is your assignment. Now be silent."

"Sir," Marlowe objected, at last collapsing back into his chair, "I have not impressed upon you the greatness of this woman's character, or her bravery, or—"

"You will go to the Bell and discover the identity of the murderer! You have three days. Then you go to Chartley. No matter what. Whatever she may be, Leonora Beak is not more important than our Queen."

"I'll need more than three days," Marlowe pleaded. "You have other agents at Chartley, but there is only one man in England with a reason for finding Leonora's killer. You did not know her as I did."

"I realize that she was your companion, and that you grew to care for her," Walsingham began again, remaining calm only with great difficulty.

"I cared for her more than you can possibly imagine," Marlowe interrupted.

"I think not, young man!" Walsingham suddenly raged. "Leonora Beak was my daughter!"

The moment of silence that followed was absolute.

Then, in a voice surprised by tenderness, Walsingham said, "No one knew it—not even she."

Marlowe saw the aura of suffering that surrounded the old man, an odd glow, a vapor.

"Then let me find the man who killed her," he said at last.

Walsingham closed his eyes. His head was quivering.

"Yes," he said to Marlowe in a voice so soft it was nearly impossible to hear. "You have three days. Then to Chartley. It is a command. You know what's at stake, Marlowe. Now go."

ELEVEN

Marlowe stood outside in the warm air, a half-moon sailing above in the sky. How could she be dead? How did she die? Where? Did Kyd have anything to do with it? Where was Lopez?

Dizzy with such questions, Marlowe staggered to a small wooden bench and sat down. Several guards stood close by.

Marlowe sat; the moon sailed. Then, no telling how much later, the young boy who had delivered the news of Leonora's death came silently to Marlowe's side. After a moment, he sat down next to Marlowe.

"I'm to tell you there is a carriage prepared to take you to the Buntingford changing station," the boy said plainly. "You're to wait here for it."

Marlowe looked at the boy, all of nine years old, relatively clean, dressed in adult clothing that had been tailored to fit him: a pale shirt, gray pantaloons, and very expensive boots. He was the son or nephew or cousin of someone in court, someone known to the Queen, in the queen's favor.

And to have a job of such importance meant that he was also, in some way or other, exceptional—exceptionally intelligent or remarkably slow-witted. Either would do for a messenger, though the latter was preferred.

"What is your name?" Marlowe asked him.

"Leviticus."

Marlowe smiled. "Your parents were cruel."

"My parents were Protestants," he said immediately.

"That explains it."

"I have not made up my mind, as of yet," the boy went on.

"About what?"

"I can't decide if our Anglican communion has gone far enough in its efforts to rid us of the tyranny of the Pope in Rome."

Marlowe examined the boy more closely. "When I was your age," he said, mostly to see the boy's reaction, "I did as my parents told me to do."

Leviticus looked up. "That was a wiser path than mine, Master Marlowe. I find that I am in desperate trouble most of the time because my brain will not allow me to do as anyone tells me to do."

"Alas," Marlowe commiserated, "I understand that ethos all too well. Do you mind my asking what is your age?"

"My body is eleven years old," he answered, "but my mind is at least eighty, or so I have been told."

"And who has told you that?"

"Lord Walsingham," the boy sighed.

"He would know. He knows everything."

The boy looked down. "He did not know that Leonora Beak would be killed."

"No." Marlowe closed his eyes, and in his mind he could see her standing over him, tending his wound. "Did you know her? The sound of your voice tells me that you may have."

"I did. She was kind."

Marlowe opened his eyes. "No more? That is all you will say?"

The boy stood. "I have been trained to say nothing, and I have ignored that training enough for the moment. I have delivered my message. I bid you good night."

He began to walk away.

"You said your parents *were* Protestants," Marlowe called softly.

The boy stopped. "My parents are dead."

"And how did you come to your present position?"

The boy did not move.

"You are related to someone at court," Marlowe surmised.

"I would imagine," the boy acknowledged, "though the identity of my kin or benefactor is unknown to me. I may even be related so someone of very high degree. But no one will answer my questions. No one."

"You are curious about the subject."

The boy turned to face Marlowe. "Some days, I can think of little else."

Marlowe stood, but did not approach the boy. "I shall find out for you."

"You shall not," the boy countered, "because the answer is unknown."

Marlowe shook his head. "Any question devised by the mind of man has, as a matter of definition, an answer. That is to say: the human mind is incapable of conceiving any question which has no answer. You might as well say to someone, 'Think of something that you can't think of.' The moment you think of it, the original statement is rendered meaningless because, you see, you have thought of it."

"It's a tricky bit of philosophy, isn't it?" The boy squinted. "Lord Walsingham says that you are clever, so you may be correct. But why would you do this thing for me?"

"You are suspicious of me."

"I am."

"That is what a life in court does for you," Marlowe mumbled. "But good. You *should* question my motives. So I will tell you: if I find out what you want to know, you will owe me a favor, will you not?"

The boy made no reply.

"Before your suspicions get the better of you," Marlowe went on, "I can tell you that I am more loyal to Walsingham, and our Queen, than any man alive, and I would never ask you to betray a confidence or a royal trust."

Still the boy hesitated.

"The thing is," Marlowe sighed, "I would like to know the answer myself. I see wheels within wheels here at Hampton."

"Yes." That was all the boy would say, it appeared.

"I will say this: I have not done well, of late." Marlowe observed that his voice sounded sick. "I have failed in my attempt to prevent a murder of national importance; I have lost a true and good companion to a second murder; my greatest theatrical mentor may well be a traitor to our country; and my greatest friend is missing—only God knows where he is. I have no idea why my intuition tells me that you know much more about all of that than you will tell me at the moment. But if I discover your heritage, you will answer my questions."

"I hope you will have a safe journey to Buntingford," the boy said, his voice cold. "Your carriage is to leave at dawn."

With that he turned and vanished into the shadows on the dark side of the building.

Before Marlowe could think what to do, a familiar form appeared in the moonlight, emerging from a door near the garden.

"Is that John Bull?" Marlowe called out.

The man hesitated, found the source of the question, and sighed.

"Marlowe," he said. "What in God's name are you doing here at this time of night?"

"I might ask you the same question."

Bull walked toward Marlowe. He was dressed in silver and black, a crisp new doublet, scrubbed boots, no weapon at his waist. He was a hale sort, ruddy but mannered, and in perfect health despite his prodigious consumption of French wines.

"Me?" he said, nearing Marlowe's bench. "I've got a commission. Real money."

"To write music for the Queen," Marlowe surmised. Why else would he be so clean, and parading about without a sword or knife?

"I cannot say." Bull looked down at Marlowe. "You're a mess, Marlowe. You'd best clean up before you go to see anyone in there."

Bull tilted his head toward Walsingham's private door.

"Good advice," Marlowe said. "Listen, you wouldn't happen to know where Kyd is at the moment. You know how it is: he owes me a tidy sum, and I need the money."

"You need a new doublet," Bull agreed. "I think he's over at The

Curtain Theatre, rehearsing his new—whatever he's working on now. Are you going that way? I'll walk with you."

"No," Marlowe demurred, "I have a few things to do before I see him. Congratulations on your commission, though."

"Thanks," said Bull. "I'm in your boat: could really use the money."

Too soon, the morning came, and Marlowe found himself falling asleep in a coach on the ragged road back to the Buntingford changing station. Alas, a deadly mixture of dreams, rage, and self-doubt prevented all semblance of proper slumber, so he sat up and stared out the window of the coach.

Trying to piece together the tatters of the previous few days, all he could see clearly was that he—and Lopez and Leonora Beak—had been deliberately led astray. The false message alleged to be from Walsingham could only have come from Kyd, or with Kyd's aid. No one else could possibly have known the line from Marlowe's play that was supposed to have been Leonora's countersign. And now that she was dead, there was no way to question her more about the man who delivered the false message.

At the first stop, a short bit of water for the horses, one of the two coachmen, a young boy in a woven hat, appeared in the window of the coach. He offered Marlowe a drink from a gourd.

"You look like you could use a week's rest," the boy said, "if you don't mind my saying so."

Marlowe nodded, took the gourd, drank it all, and said, "I can't sleep."

"Well," the boy said, taking the gourd, "you've got a lot on your mind, then, I'd imagine."

Marlowe closed his eyes once more and the coach took off.

Possibly Leonora's father might know something about the false message, but Marlowe was uncomfortable with the notion of questioning a wounded man whose daughter had just been murdered.

There was also the question of sending Marlowe and Leonora to

Delft in the first place. What if they had succeeded in preventing William's death? That would have strengthened England's position against the Spanish king, as well as providing more defense against any attempt to place Mary on Elizabeth's throne. So much of the plot was confusing to Marlowe.

"If I were writing this," he thought to himself, "I would simplify the story. In general, audiences prefer not to be confused. The details of this current plot: obviously the work of an amateur."

And then he fell asleep again, and dreamed of Leonora Beak.

She and Marlowe were swimming together in the ocean, near the beach. Lopez, a black horse, the Traveling family, Thomas Kyd, and Balthasar Gérard were all standing on the beach singing "The White Hare of Howden."

TWELVE

Marlowe awoke with a start.

Disoriented, he reached for his dagger without thinking. The coach had stopped. There were voices. Then, without warning, a door flew open and an arm reached in.

Marlowe thrashed, but he found that his dagger was gone and someone had thrown a sack over his head. Dragged by his ankles from the coach, he hit his head on the step and landed on the flat of his back, on the ground.

More indecipherable words were whispered, and the coach took off.

As the noise of its equipage faded off toward Buntingford, Marlowe's hands were tied. Then he was hoisted onto the back of a horse. The reins were put into his hands.

Then a woman's voice from below him, on the ground, said, very gently, "There now. You're safe."

Taking that pronouncement for a threat, Marlowe kicked out in the direction of the voice, but his boot found only air.

"Let's get off the road, then," said another voice, gruff, masculine.

Seconds later Marlowe was riding. There were at least three other horses around him. They rode fast. Marlowe had to concentrate in order to stay on his horse. Only then did it occur to him that the water he'd taken from the boy at the watering stop had been laced with something. That would explain the odd dream, the inability to defend himself, and his trouble steadying himself on top of a horse.

"Have I been poisoned?" he called out.

A man laughed.

A woman's voice, the same that had spoken before, said, "After a fashion."

There was more laughter.

Marlowe struggled to remember what Lopez had taught him about just such a situation.

First: pain. Marlowe twisted his wrists against the binding that held them together, and winced. He twisted harder. He could feel blood on his hands. Good.

Second: breath. He concentrated, partly thanks to the searing pain in his wrists, on steadying his breathing, and slowing it down. The heart pumped the poisoning of the blood, the breath pumped the bellows of the heart. Slow the heart and slow the poison. He took in long steady breaths, counting to seven each time, holding it for a moment, then exhaling for another count of seven. His body relaxed. His mind cleared.

Third: action.

Without another thought, Marlowe let go of the reins, took one foot out of its stirrup, and launched himself backward, off his horse and onto the ground. He landed on his back again, but he was prepared. He rolled, somersaulted twice, and came up on his feet. With his tied hands he plucked the sack from his head.

For a split second the riders up ahead seemed not to understand what had happened. Good. Marlowe reached down into his boot and retrieved his other dagger. They'd not found that. With three deft moves he sliced the leather strap around his wrists just enough to weaken it. Twisting, sending more blistering pain up his arms, he snapped the bonds.

To his right there were thick woods, too thick for horses, but also difficult for any living thing. To his left there was a small stream, and across it more woods, but an easier way. Just as the riders stopped and began to turn around, Marlowe caught sight of something in the corner of his right eye. A white hare slipped into the thicket and vanished.

Marlowe followed.

It was a tunnel too small for a man, but Marlowe's desperation ploughed through, and his dagger sliced and snapped the worst of the vines and branches. The rabbit was long gone, but Marlowe was able to claw and crawl his way out and up until he found himself on the other side of the thicket. Bruised, scratched, and light-headed, he stood. He could hear the others, only yards away, shouting and hacking at the tangled hedges and brambles. Taking a very deep breath, Marlowe turned and ran as fast as he could in the direction opposite that noise.

He picked up his pace, his chest pounding and his eyes blurred, until the sounds behind him faded. He came to a relative clearing and stopped to catch his breath, and to think.

Four: water.

Lopez had told him that if he were ever poisoned, Marlowe should drink water in big gulps, very fast, and then try to vomit. Glancing around, he took a moment to regret not having run toward the stream. Then he set off again, a bit slower.

The woods were pleasant enough. The morning was headed toward the midday hour, and linnet song filled the warm air. The trees were not so thick, and he could see a cloudless sky. There was moss below his boots, which he took as a sign that there was water somewhere near. Scanning the area all around him, he spotted several gray boulders, and headed for them.

As he drew nearer, he thought he could hear the sound of splashing water. Unfortunately, his feet were made of lead, and his body longed for the moss below them. His eyes closed. He forced them open. They closed again.

The last thing he knew, he was on the ground, thankful for the soft moss, and the lovely bit of sunshine on his face.

Marlowe sat up with a start.

He was sitting beside a small cooking fire. The sun was easing toward the western horizon. There were several wagons, dozens of horses, and children playing nearby. His hands were not tied. It took him a moment to clear his head, but he was forced to admit that he had not died.

He was in an encampment of Traveling People.

"Look who's up," said a voice from behind in a thick Scots accent.

Marlowe turned. His eyes adjusted. He blinked.

"Is it," he began hesitantly, "did I meet you on the roadside? Is it *Gelis*?"

"It is indeed," the man said, smiling. "And you told me that your name was Robert Greene, although it is not."

"No," Marlowe agreed, "it is not."

Gelis sat down beside Marlowe, still wrapped in his tattered cloak, and handed over a plate of food. Marlowe took it but only stared.

"It's good," Gelis assured him. "Good food."

"As good as the water I drank at the rest stop?" Marlowe asked, slowly inching his hand down toward his boot, and the hidden dagger. "The boy who gave it to me was one of your lot."

"Well, yes, in truth," Gelis admitted. "But that was for your own good, you see. You were meant to fall asleep and wake up here."

"You poisoned me!" Marlowe set down the plate and reached for his blade.

"It was a sleeping potion," Gelis complained. "Nothing more."

Marlowe realized at that moment that his dagger was gone.

A second later Gelis smiled and held it up. "Looking for this?"

"See here," Marlowe began, standing up.

Instantly five or six men appeared, all armed. They were dressed oddly, some in ribbons, almost like Morris Dancers. But their dark faces were hard, not built for revelry.

Gelis had not risen. "This is exactly why we slipped you the sleeping potion," he rumbled. "You're a hothead, and you're good with a blade. I know that from experience with you, but we've also been warned."

"Warned?"

"Your friend the doctor told us you'd be trouble."

"You've spoken with Dr. Lopez?" Marlowe looked down at Gelis, not certain that the man was telling the truth.

"Sit down. I don't feel like standing, and this hurts my neck."

Another quick review of the several men standing around forced Marlowe to accede to that request. He sat.

"The doctor told us to give you something that would make you sleep," Gelis went on, "so that we could get you here, away from prying eyes and ears, and tell you what's happened since last we met."

Gelis turned then and said something in a language Marlowe didn't know. The other men vanished behind carts.

"I assume you know," Gelis continued, his voice grave, "that Leonora Beak is dead."

Marlowe nodded. He discovered that he could not speak for a moment.

Then Gelis offered Marlowe back his dagger.

"She's the reason you're here and not dead on the roadside," Gelis went on. "I think you'll listen to me now—now that you know I am bound to help you because of her that helped me."

Marlowe nodded once more, taking the dagger and sliding it back into its hidden sheath in his boot.

"Good," Gelis said softly. "And now I shall tell you what has happened, and how you come to be at the finest encampment of Traveling People in all of England."

According to Gelis, after Marlowe and Leonora rode off toward Maldon, Gelis and his family took Leonora's horse and hitched it to their wagon home. They went directly to the Buntingford changing station, and the Bell Inn.

When they pulled up in front of the inn, a very angry stable boy raced their way, shouting.

Seconds later, a man dressed in red appeared, rapier in hand, and told Gelis in no uncertain terms that everyone on the cart was going to die.

The wife screamed. The son was struck dumb. Gelis, at least by his own report, remained calm.

"What have we done," he asked the Spaniard, "to provoke such a harsh welcome to this place?"

"That's Miss Beak's horse!" the stable boy screamed. "These bleeding Egyptians have killed her!"

Gelis was careful not to move. The man in red was at his side, and the point of the rapier was touching Gelis's Adam's apple.

"The very kind lady, Leonora Beak by name," Gelis began, not looking anywhere in particular, "gave us this horse and told us to return it here. Then she and Mr. Greene rode away, toward Maldon."

"Why?" the man in red demanded to know. "Why would she give you her horse?"

"Ours had been stolen from us," Gelis answered, still frozen, "by them that Miss Beak and Mr. Greene was chasing. This ungodly trio, two men and a very vicious girl, they menaced us, and took our Primrose. That's our horse's name. Primrose. And, you see, Miss Beak is, it would seem, a kind soul. She seen what devastation is wrought on a Traveling family that cannot travel, and took pity. She give us her own Bess. That is what she called this one here. Bess."

"He's lying!" the stable boy screamed, his face red, tears in his eyes. "They've killed her and taken Bess. They're all villains, these cur dog Egyptians!"

But the man in red lowered his blade.

"How would he know the horse's name?" he asked.

"That's right," Gelis said, failing to hide the relief in his voice. "Miss Beak, she called this here horse by name of Bess."

"Anything else?" the man in red asked, sheathing his weapon.

"She said," Gelis answered, "that there was a doctor here present."

"Yes?" the man in red locked eyes with Gelis.

"Well," he began, and pulled aside the blanket on his lap, "I've been shot, you see, and she mentioned that there might be a doctor hereabouts."

The man in red smiled. "She did, did she?"

"Aye." Gelis nodded. "You'd be the doctor, then."

Gelis's wife whispered something.

"And," Gelis went on, "we've not eat in now these three days."

The man in red turned to the stable boy.

"Take Bess to her place," he told the boy.

Still certain of the treachery of the Travelers, the boy began to unhitch Bess from the cart.

"Come inside," the man in red said.

That was all. He turned and entered the inn.

Gelis climbed down, steering clear of the stable boy, and helped his wife and child down. They moved warily toward the entrance to the inn. Gelis opened the door.

There was blood everywhere. Tables and chairs were overturned. The place was empty save for the man in red.

"Take a seat," he told Gelis.

Gelis found a chair and sat. The wife and child stood so close they were touching him.

"Please tell your wife that she may avail herself of what food she may find in the kitchen room," the man in red announced, taking off his cloak and his rapier.

With that he approached with a cup in one hand and a dagger in the other.

"You'll need to drink this," he told Gelis, "and then I'll dig out the shot in your leg."

The boy began to cry. The wife's eyes were so wide they threatened to explode.

Gelis told them, in the family language, to go into the backroom and find food. They didn't move. Gelis insisted. The man in red stood his ground.

At length wife and child quit the public room in favor of the kitchen, and the doctor knelt beside Gelis.

Gelis, primarily to distract himself after drinking from the cup given to him by the doctor, looked around the room and observed, "Looks like there was a war in here."

The doctor nodded. "The three people who attacked you killed a woman and a young boy here, and may have murdered the landlord of this place; he has not yet recovered."

"That would be Miss Beak's father, I'd imagine," Gelis said absently, staring at the blood on the floor, "from what she said."

Without a warning, the doctor tipped the point of his dagger into the wound on Gelis's thigh.

Gelis grunted and stared down at the mess. The drink the doctor had given him had taken hold of his brain, and he thought to himself that his wound looked like a rose blooming out of his flesh, a red, bleeding rose.

The doctor nosed the dagger deeper, and in some remote part of his brain Gelis knew that he ought to care, but he did not. Then he abandoned all thought, took a deep breath, and fell fast asleep where he was, sitting in the chair.

"That doctor's a wonder, I'll tell you that," Gelis concluded.

Marlowe moved a little closer to the fire. It was a fine warm evening, but the flames were comforting.

"So you stayed on at the Bell?" he asked after a moment.

"Aye," Gelis answered.

"There's more to the story, though," Marlowe said. "I was told you'd stolen horses and run away."

"There's more to the story," Gelis acknowledged.

In the background, behind one of the wagons, there were children playing. Someone on the other side of the small camp was playing a highland harp. Marlowe could tell the difference between the sound of fingernails on wire strings and fingertips on gut.

"But Mr. Beak, the landlord," Marlowe went on after a moment, "is still alive?"

"He is."

Marlowe stared into the fire. "Good."

Gelis reached behind himself and produced a jug and two cups.

"Have you ever had the Water of Life?" he asked Marlowe.

"Sorry?" Marlowe looked up at Gelis.

Gelis poured. "Take it slow. It's not ale. You've got to sup it. And if you've not had it, ever, it'll skin your tongue at first. But as surely as God is in heaven, the pure joy of the world is in this jug."

He held out a cup and Marlowe took it. Gelis set down the jug and saluted with his cup.

Marlowe sipped. Fire tore through his mouth, seared his throat, and attacked his gut with the fury of a berserk avenger.

"Christ," Marlowe rasped.

"Aye," Gelis answered, grinning. "Take another sup right now!"

Marlowe obeyed. The second taste was warm, filled with oak fire and a vague sweetness near the end.

"What in God's name is this stuff?" Marlowe managed to say.

"Water of Life." Gelis downed his cup. "Make it myself. All it takes is a copper kettle, a coil, a wood fire—and patience."

"Fire and coil." Marlowe stared at the liquid fire in his cup. "You've distilled something. Possibly the devil's backside."

Gelis exploded with laughter.

"That's it exactly!" he coughed as soon as he collected himself. "You might well think we've boiled down the devil's rump. But by the time you get to the bottom of the cup, you'll be asking me if we made it from an angel's wing. Anyway, doesn't taste like that warm piss you folk in London town call ale, now does it?"

"It does not." Marlowe took a bigger gulp. "And you're right: it does get better with every taste."

"Good." Gelis licked his lips, and his face went dark. "Now."

Marlowe understood that the man had something serious to say. He finished his cup, squinting against the pain of the swallow. The brew was already making the world a softer place, and a kinder one.

"Sometime early last night, while Leonora Beak was in attendance at her father's bedside, as she had been nearly every second after she returned from your adventures," Gelis said briskly, "a villain stole into the room and strangled her from behind while her father slept."

"You know she was strangled?"

"Aye. You could see by her neck: purple as a sunset. And it was a wide swath, like someone had come up behind her, locked an arm around her throat, and held tight until she was gone."

"No other evidence?"

"No other *what?*" Gelis asked.

"I need to see the room," Marlowe told him. "I may be able to ascertain something about the murderer from the lay of the room."

"I don't see how," Gelis began.

"Who found her?" Marlowe interrupted.

"My boy," Gelis answered. "The wife had found a bit of lamb stew in the kitchen, something from the cook that was killed."

"Mrs. Pennington," Marlowe affirmed.

"Aye," Gelis went on. "She took it up for Miss Beak to eat, and a short while later the boy went to fetch the bowl. He found it on the floor, stew spilled everywhere. He called to Miss Beak, then shook her, then he seen her neck. He come running to me."

"The chair was not overturned?"

"No."

"Her father saw nothing?"

"No, he's never woke up," Gelis said. "Still."

"Who was staying at the inn?"

"None but us," Gelis answered. "The doctor departed as soon as he was certain that I won't bleed to death."

"You and your family," Marlowe said, leaning forward. "None of the rest of your fellow Travelers were at the inn?"

"Them lot?" he laughed. "No. They don't generally care to stay indoors for much of anything. They've been camped here, waiting to meet up with us."

"And why did you take me from the Queen's coach," Marlowe asked, his voice a little louder. "Why did you bring me here instead of letting me go to the Bell?"

Gelis screwed up his face, not quite understanding the question.

"I owe a debt to you and to Miss Beak," he answered. "I was never going to let you go to the Bell Inn and get yourself killed as well as herself. I did it to save you."

"You did it to save me," Marlowe repeated.

Marlowe looked around. The serene world of the Travelers' camp belied everything he had ever heard about the people. There was absolutely no telling, in his mind, whether or not to trust this man.

"First things first," Gelis went on, seemingly unaware of Marlowe's suspicions. "Did you catch them that assaulted me and mine?"

How best to respond? Marlowe wondered. He didn't want to give anything away. On the other hand, the facts were the facts, and easy enough to ascertain, especially if the stories about "Gypsy gossip" were true.

"One's dead in Maldon," Marlowe said harshly, "another is dead in Delft, and the woman who shot you is, in actuality, a man. He's escaped."

Gelis smiled. "Good. It's good to tell the truth."

Marlowe took that in. "You already knew those facts."

"Aye," Gelis admitted, looking into the fire. "But I didn't know what kind of man you were. Mr. *Greene*."

"You want to know my real name."

"I do."

"Then let me see what sort of a man *you* are. Who killed Leonora Beak?"

Gelis looked up, his expression gone to darkness. "If I knew that, I'd have that man in front of me now, instead of you."

"Where did you get the horse that's pulling your wagon now?"

Gelis winked. "Made a bargain with that stable boy at the Bell."

"What sort of bargain?"

"Promised to take him with us on our travels," Gelis locked eyes with Marlowe, but called over his shoulder. "Toby!"

From behind one of the nearby wagons, the stable boy appeared.

"Yes?" he answered, striding toward the fire.

Then he saw Marlowe, and froze.

"It's all right, boyo," Gelis assured him. "Mr. Greene, here, is helping us find him that murdered your mistress."

"We don't need help from the likes of him," the boy snapped, his face flamed red. "He abandoned Leonora and went off to London!"

"What is this boy doing here?" Marlowe asked Gelis.

"Tell Mr. Greene what you told me, Toby," Gelis insisted calmly.

"Why?" he wanted to know, somewhat belligerently.

"Because Mr. Greene has been seen with the Queen," Gelis answered in bizarre singsong.

Toby went slack-jawed. "The Queen?" he muttered.

"Have you not?" Gelis asked Marlowe.

"I have not," Marlowe answered honestly, "at least not in some time."

"But you are about her business," Gelis prompted.

"Possibly." Marlowe turned to Toby. "What is it that you told Gelis? Tell me now."

Toby bit his upper lip, thinking, the process of which seemed extremely painful for him.

"I am looking for the woman I love," he answered a length, with the sort of fervency only youth could muster.

Marlowe turned to Gelis, at a loss.

"Our boy here," Gelis said, clearly trying not to display amusement, "is smitten by the woman what was in the Bell with them other two, them that robbed me and mine."

"What?" Marlowe blinked once.

"She is in trouble," the boy said desperately. "I know it. She touched my hand when she took the horses from the barn. She smiled at me. No woman ever looked at me before that moment, not in the eye. She has feeling for me, I know that. And so I must help her. The others, the men she was with, they've captured her. Forced her to go along with them. I'm certain of that. And so I have to help her!"

Marlowe did his best not to show amazement. "What on earth does this unfortunate, melancholy fantasy have to do with—?"

"Let him finish," Gelis encouraged. "Go on, Toby."

"I saw it in her eyes," Toby continued, his voice growing in volume and intensity. "She wanted me to help her. That's why I'm going to London with these Travelers. As she was getting on the horse, I saw a bit of paper in her boot. The top part stuck out and I read it."

"You can read?" Marlowe interrupted.

The boy looked down. "Miss Beak taught me."

"Ah." Marlowe sighed.

"Tell him, then," Gelis nudged. "Tell him what you read."

"It was a handbill of some sort. It said 'Curtain Road, Shoreditch.' And I reckon that's a place to start. See what I might find out about her, and the villains that took her away from there."

Marlowe sat up straighter. "Curtain Road."

"Thank you, Toby," Gelis said. "Time to bed down the horses."

"Yes." Toby looked momentarily confused, and then he turned and vanished behind the wagon whence he'd come.

Marlowe waited for a moment, then, lowering his voice, said to Gelis, "He doesn't know that the woman he loves does not exist?"

"He does not know that the woman he loves is a man," Gelis said plainly. "Nor did I until you told me. He'd be desolated by such news. And, too, he'd not be quite so willing to help us to find the person in question."

"Well, yes." Marlowe got to his feet. "You know what's in Shoreditch, at Curtain Road, don't you?"

"A house of entertainment called *The Theatre*," Gelis said. "Know it well. We all do."

"Yes, well, that's the place where Ned Blank works."

"Who?"

"Ned Blank," Marlowe repeated. "The *woman* who has stolen Toby's heart."

"You know him?"

"Not only is he the greatest actor of female parts in London," Marlowe answered, "but he may—I say he *may*—be the person who murdered Leonora."

Gelis shook his head. "No," he said emphatically, "we would have seen—even Toby would have spotted that *woman* at the inn."

"Except if that *woman* were dressed as himself, as a man," Marlowe rejoined.

"No," Gelis insisted. "We—there were no strangers at all, no newcomers at the inn for as long as we stayed there. It was all Travelers. I'm telling you: we would have seen them."

"Except for the fact that you did *not*, in fact, see the murderer."

Gelis looked down into his empty cup. "Aye."

"So." Marlowe got to his feet. "While I appreciate your care for me, kidnapping me as you did to save my life, I must go to the Bell Inn. I must go to the scene of my comrade's murder, and to watch and pray, see to her burial if need be. That is my task, a dismal one from which no effort, not even your good care, may prevent me."

"But," Gelis began to protest.

"You must realize," Marlowe interrupted, "that Leonora's death is a thread in the larger fabric of betrayal. Someone killed her for a reason. And that reason has to do with a great threat to our nation, and to our Queen."

Gelis nodded sagely. "I see. What would you have me do, then?"

"Exactly what you were planning to do: go to London, enjoy a bit of theatre, and try to find that phantasm with whom young Toby has fallen in love. I may join you thereafter in London when I have finished my investigation at the Bell Inn."

Gelis stood, a bit clumsily, and offered his hand.

"Done," he said. "Poor Toby. Though, if I may say, all men fall in love with the woman they invent from their own desires and not the actual woman in question. It is a fearsome combination of longing and hope—and the image of a certain face."

Marlowe took Gelis's hand. "Are all Travelers like you?"

"How do you mean?"

"Are you all philosopher poets?"

"If all life is a journey," Gelis answered, "who would know it better than the man who never leaves the road? Mr. Greene."

"It's Marlowe, actually," he answered softly. "Christopher Marlowe."

"At last," Gelis sighed. "It's good to tell the truth. Mr. Marlowe."

THIRTEEN

The Bell Inn appeared deserted when Marlowe arrived. The night was nearly moonless and there were no lamps lit inside. He went around the inn and across the yard as quietly as he could to stable the horse Gelis had given him, a sturdy, if elderly, animal. Then he made his way back to the inn's front door without a sound.

He stood for a moment, listening. Somewhere in the distance a dog barked, but then was stilled. Owls called to one another. Stars blinked. The world was, in general, at peace.

Judging the place to be safe, Marlowe opened the front door and slipped into the public room. His eyes adjusted to the darkness within, but it was still impossible to see anything clearly. He felt his way along table tops, bumping into chairs, until he reached the bar. After several clumsy minutes, he found tapers in a case on the floor. Lighting two from the embers in the fireplace, he set one on the bar in a small tabletop pricket and carried the other one before him. He took a few steps toward the kitchen.

He could see, then, that the place was in pristine order, cleaned beyond mere tidiness. Who would have done that? It was a far different place from the one he had left only days before: a place soiled with blood, wrecked by brawling, and cursed with a corpse. Leonora might possibly have performed that task when she returned, but if she had spent most of her time attending to her father, as Gelis had said, could she have been so thorough?

The most logical explanation was that Gelis's wife had taken it upon herself to so stringently clean. But the place had a more military order, nothing like the relaxed environment of the Travelers' camp.

Lost in such thought, Marlowe almost missed the noise on the stairs. Shaken from his concentration, he realized that someone was creeping down the stairs from the upper rooms.

The stairway was close to the end of the bar, opposite where Marlowe stood. As he had never been upstairs, he could only assume that the sleeping quarters were up there.

He blew out the taper in his hand, but the one atop the bar was out of reach, and the footsteps were down the stairs.

"Who's there?" a brutal male voice demanded.

Marlowe dropped down, placing the bulk of the bar in between himself and the hulk descending the staircase. Marlowe thought he could make out a wooden club in the man's hand.

The man hit the bottom of the stairs and roared.

"Who's there, I say? Who's lit this candle?"

Marlowe stood slowly, dagger in hand. In the dappling of the candle's flame he thought he recognized the man. Racking his brain, it finally came to him.

"You're the baker," Marlowe said. "You were in here the day of all the trouble."

The man's head jutted forward as he tried to make out the speaker in the shadows. He took a step forward, and then Marlowe could see that he was holding a rolling pin in his hand.

"I was here that day too, with my friend the doctor," Marlowe said, lowering his blade and stepping into better light.

"Yes," the man said slowly, squinting to see Marlowe's face. "You were. What be your business here now? The doctor's gone."

Marlowe sheathed his dagger.

"In short, I'm here to find the person who killed Leonora Beak." He exhaled, feeling how difficult it had been to say those last few words.

"Why?" the baker asked, clearly suspicious.

"Because she was my comrade," Marlowe explained, "as fine a

traveling and fighting companion as I have ever known. And because I have been commanded to do so."

"Commanded?" the baker asked, his jaw jutting forward. "To find Leonora's murderer? Who *commanded* you to do that?"

"Are you the one who's cleaned up and kept this place in order," Marlowe asked, ignoring the baker's question.

"I'm asking you a question!"

"And I'm not answering you." Marlowe stepped from around the bar. "How fares Leonora's father, our innkeeper?"

"Why is that any of your—"

"I have been told," Marlowe interrupted, "by the very doctor who saved the innkeeper's life, that even in a deep sleep a man may hear and know certain things that have happened around him. I wish to speak to Mr. Beak to see what he knows that he does not know he knows."

"To see what he—look here, London Boy," the baker sneered, "I'm guarding the innkeeper from the very likes of you. And I'll not move from that task until he's up and about on his own. Now show yourself out like a good lad, or I'll be forced to bash your brains, teach you a bit of country courtesy."

The baker took a few quick steps down the stairs. They were intended as a threatening move.

Marlowe didn't move, didn't blink, didn't breathe.

"I said—" the baker began.

"Please be reasonable," Marlowe suggested steadily. "I have no quarrel with you, or desire to injure you. In fact, I'm grateful that you've taken such care with the inn."

"Boy," the baker growled, lowering his head and raising his rolling pin.

The baker, nearly twice Marlowe's size, raged forward.

Marlowe planted his body firmly in the path of the oncoming juggernaut, and then, at the last possible second, merely stepped sideways and behind the bar—Kyd's tactic. The baker lumbered on, losing his balance, and crashed headfirst into the wall.

Groggy but not fallen, he spun about.

"We can go on like this if you insist," Marlowe told him calmly, "but it's really a waste of time and you'll only end up with bruises—which you'll have given to yourself."

Unwilling to hear such a reasonable assessment of the situation, the baker attacked again, snarling. Marlowe placed one hand on the bar and vaulted over it, landed, drew his rapier. He thrashed that blade across the baker's forearm, the arm that held the rolling pin; down it clattered onto the floor. The baker, alas, kept moving, and flew into the bar, midsection first. The breath knocked out of him, he tried to stand, failed, and landed flat on his back with a thud to wake the dead.

Sheathing his rapier, Marlowe knelt beside the baker.

"I really am here to help. I'm going to find out who killed Leonora. And I'm going to punish that person in a very severe way. In front of witnesses."

The baker stared up at the ceiling.

"I—I'd like to be one," he gasped.

"You'd like to be one *what*?" Marlowe asked.

"Witness," he managed to say, and then passed out.

Marlowe smiled and stood.

Taking the taper on the bar, pricket and all, he ventured up the stairway, his other hand on his rapier's hilt.

As he reached the top of the stairs he could see, down the narrow hallway, under a low ceiling, six doors. One was open, and a bit of candlelight flickered there.

He moved carefully toward it. The entire inn was very quiet: no talking, no snoring, no groaning of dreams.

He reached the lit doorway, peered in, and there lay the innkeeper, eyes wide.

"Mr. Beak," Marlowe said gently.

Beak turned toward the sound of Marlowe's voice, a little alarmed. When he saw Marlowe standing in the doorway, he exhaled noisily.

"I heard all the trouble downstairs," he said hoarsely, "and I thought there were assassins in my inn once more."

"Just the baker," Marlowe told him, "and me."

"Well." Beak closed his eyes. "At least it's an assassin for the Queen."

Marlowe looked around the room. It was a simple one: a bed, a table, a taper, a washbowl, a chamberpot. A single window looked toward the stable. The bed was finely made, and the covers were clean. As Marlowe stepped lightly toward the innkeeper, the boards underfoot made very little sound. The inn was as well constructed as the innkeeper's bed.

"I am grieving for the loss of Leonora," Marlowe told the older man.

Beak sucked in a sudden breath, or a sob, and nodded, eyes still closed.

"I'm going to find her killer," Marlowe said.

Beak nodded again, only once.

"There was a chair in this room until recently," Marlowe began.

Beak opened his eyes. "Yes. Someone told you that my daughter was sitting here with me whilst I slept."

"Someone did," Marlowe confirmed, "but there are also scrape marks in the wood on the floor here."

He pointed.

Beak twisted his head and glared down. "I see."

"You were asleep when Leonora—when the killer came into the room," Marlowe went on.

"I was."

"Were you dreaming?"

"How's that?" Beak asked, raising his head ever so slightly.

"Can you recall," Marlowe insisted, "if you were dreaming."

"I—no, I cannot. What sort of a question is that?"

"It is a question I have learned to ask," Marlowe explained. "Dr. Lopez was my great teacher, and several of his lessons concerned the sleeping mind. While you are asleep, you may hear or even see things that happen around you in the waking world. Sometimes those things are translated into dreams. You may have knowledge of your daughter's murderer locked in your brain."

"Well I can't recall a dream," Beak huffed.

"Close your eyes."

"I've spent enough time with my eyes closed," Beak protested.

"Please, Mr. Beak," Marlowe said a little louder. "We may, together, discover some small matter that would aid me in finding the killer. And if not, what is the harm? I'm only asking you to close your eyes."

"Christ," Beak muttered. But he closed his eyes.

"Now," Marlowe began, as Lopez had taught him, "breathe in on a slow count of seven, hold for one, breathe out on a count of seven, and then don't breathe."

Beak, somewhat reluctantly, did as he'd been told.

"Again," Marlowe encouraged.

Again.

"Good," Marlowe said, softer than before, "keep going."

As Beak continued to breathe, Marlowe began to hum a single, low note. When Beak's breathing became slower and softer, Marlowe decreased the volume of his humming and then stopped, matching his breathing pattern with Beak's.

"Leonora is in a chair, beside you," he said in low tones.

"Holding my hand," Beak answered, as if in a dream.

"Someone comes into the room."

"Yes." Beak breathed out. "I hear it. Leonora does not. She's fallen asleep. I try to open my eyes, but a moment later, there are gurgling noises, and loud, heavy breathing. Leonora kicked my bed. Then the other one left again, dragging his foot out the door."

Marlowe didn't move. "He was dragging his foot?"

"Step. Drag. Step. Drag. Very laboriously." Beak fell silent.

Marlowe began humming again, then louder and louder.

At length he stopped suddenly and said, very pointedly, in a loud, clear voice, "Mr. Beak?"

Beak's eyes snapped open.

"Christ. Her killer. He walked with a limp!" he cried.

"Yes," Marlowe affirmed.

Beak twisted toward Marlowe.

"It's witchery, what you just did!" he said.

"No," Marlowe assured the man, "it's ancient knowledge from the Far East. Dr. Lopez is a well-traveled man and has acquired certain abilities. He taught me a few of them."

"So the villain is a cripple," Beak sighed. "That's something to go on."

"Possibly," Marlowe answered carefully, "but I believe that he is momentarily wounded and will recover, thus losing the limp. A man who is permanently lame has found a way to walk that, to him, is normal. He does not move, as you put it, *laboriously.*"

"Which means?" Beak asked.

"I've got to find him quickly," Marlowe answered. "Not give him time to heal."

Just as Beak was about to respond, the baker crashed into the room, staggering toward Marlowe with a monstrous kitchen knife in his hand.

"Get away from him or I'll kill you where you stand," the baker hissed.

"John!" Beak shouted. "No!"

Beak managed to sit up, but the baker was enraged, and paid no attention to him.

Marlowe glanced at Beak. "I don't want to hurt him, but I've already wasted time dealing with him."

Beak strained forward, coughed, and shouted, again, "John!"

The baker raised the knife and threw himself forward onto Marlowe. The sheer size and weight of the man knocked Marlowe against the wall. Searing pain from his unhealed gunshot wound momentarily distracted him, and the baker stabbed at Marlowe's shoulder, cutting through his black doublet. Unable to move his arms under the mass of his attacker, Marlowe kicked at the baker's ankles with such force that he heard bones crack. He raised his knee into the man's crotch as hard as he could, and the baker howled.

With all his might Marlowe pushed against the wall with his elbows, sending him forward against the baker. The baker dropped the knife he'd been wielding. It clattered to the floor, and seconds later, so did the baker. He was writhing in pain, doubled over.

Marlowe's dagger was in his hand and he leapt onto the unfortunate baker. He held his blade to the man's throat.

"Mr. Marlowe," Beak called out desperately. "John is not himself. Please do not harm him. He was in love with Leonora. He's destroyed by grief."

Marlowe kept his blade at the man's gullet and leaned close, his mouth almost on the man's ear.

"My grief is equal to yours," Marlowe rasped, "I can assure you of that. The difference is, I'm going to find her killer, and you're going to stay out of my way. Is that clear?"

The man cried out, a half-animal sound.

"If you come at me again," Marlowe assured the man, "I will kill you and think nothing of it. Do you understand?"

"John," Beak implored, "Mr. Marlowe is here to help us. He's here to find our Leonora's killer. You must understand that!"

The big man would not stop struggling, and did not appear to hear Marlowe or Beak.

"Unless," Marlowe went on, "John is, himself, the killer, and only wants to prevent me from discovering that."

John went silent. All strength seemed to leave his body, and he stared up at the ceiling.

"What?" he asked, barely comprehending what was happening. "You think that I would kill Leonora?"

Then he began to sob as a child would.

Marlowe exhaled, stood, and examined his shoulder. There was blood, and his doublet was cut. But the doublet was black, the better for hiding blood, as Lopez often said.

"You can't think that John is the killer," Beak gasped.

"Unlikely," Marlowe admitted. "You would have known it was him, even in your sleep; also: he has no limp and his affection for

Leonora is genuine. I believe, however, that she did not reciprocate that love."

"She didn't even know," John sighed, lying back down.

"Well." Marlowe put away his dagger. "Is there anyone else staying here at the inn now?"

"John's helped keep the changing station open," Beak answered, "but without Mrs. Pennington or Leonora, we could not accept lodgers."

"Of course." Marlowe turned to Beak. "You've suffered a great loss, and you have done so in service to the Queen."

"Why would anyone take Leonora's life?" John moaned.

"Why?" Beak echoed, weaker.

"Knowing the answer to that question may well point me in the direction of her murderer." Marlowe steeled himself. "And I swear to you that I will find the person who killed her."

"That won't bring her back," John snapped bitterly, still lying flat on the floor.

"Where is her body," Marlowe asked softly. "I should examine it."

"It's all in vain," Beak lamented, losing strength. "All that effort, that chasing about, and Leonora told me that you were unable to save the life of William the Silent."

"Yes." Marlowe looked out the window toward the stables. "But that death was only the beginning of a larger threat. And those responsible for this greater plot doubtless passed through this changing station in the past several days. I'm certain that they are to blame for the death of Leonora Beak."

FOURTEEN

Marlowe sat at the table nearest the fireplace in the Bell Inn. The sun had set and it was dark inside, save for the embers. He stared into empty space, deep in concentration.

Further examination of the innkeeper's room had revealed various small items which Marlowe examined with great interest. Stains on the floor were significant. There was recently dried food, possibly from the plate or bowl carried by Gelis's son when he found the dead body. There were flat, curved slices of horse dung, which meant that someone, possibly the killer, had come directly from the stables into the room. There were traces of horsehair to add to that theory. Both Beak and John claimed that they hadn't been in the stables for weeks, and the size and shape of the dung slices were clearly from a boot larger than those Leonora wore. Finally and most significantly: Marlowe found drops of dried blood, several near where the chair had been, several more by the door. Had Leonora managed to injure her assailant? She had certainly been capable of it.

Her body, laid out in the kitchen, gave up few clues. Only marks on her neck that confirmed Marlowe's suspicion that the murderer was able to sneak up from behind. Leonora had been asleep at the time. Awake she would never have been taken by surprise.

So, Marlowe wondered, why kill Leonora at all? She was no threat. She was clearly tending to her ailing father. Why would anyone go out of his way to come to the closed inn, steal up the stairs, see that Leonora was asleep—or wait for her to fall asleep—and then strangle her? *Why* was just as important a question as *Who.*

And though Marlowe was nearly certain that her death was directly connected to the assassination of William the Silent—and whatever subsequent plot was afoot—he had to admit that he might be wrong. He had failed enough in recent days to shake his confidence. So many doubts clouded his mind.

Were there other Spanish agents? Had Gérard somehow been able to communicate with others, alerting them that he was being followed by Marlowe and Leonora?

Worse: was it possible that Gelis, or other Travelers, were not as they seemed? Could they, in fact, have been in league with Gérard and the assassins all along? Kidnapping Marlowe on the way to the Bell was quite suspicious. Although, on the other hand, no one in the camp had tried to stop him when he left to go to the inn.

Was there any advantage in finding out more about the third man, the portly gent who had played the part of Ned Blank's husband—the one whom Leonora had poisoned in the barn in Maldon? Would finding out who he was be of help? Perhaps he had associates or even family who could shed some sort of light.

Just then John came lumbering down the steps carrying a tray.

"You want a bit of light down here," he grumbled.

Setting the tray on the bar, he took the small candle from the tray and lit the taper on the bar, the one Marlowe had placed in the iron pricket.

It did not illuminate so much as emphasize the growing darkness.

"John," Marlowe began, "might I have a word?"

"A word?" he asked, a bit belligerently. "All you want to do is sit and talk instead of getting out and finding the villain that murdered our Leonora?"

"I'm collecting information," Marlowe answered, "that will help me to do just that. Sit with me for just a moment."

John rolled his head, but after a moment's hesitation he came to Marlowe's table and sat.

"Recall the moment that the doctor and I arrived," Marlowe began. "You were seated there. The unfortunate boy who died, he was in the corner. The clergyman was at the table next to us, and the well-dressed couple was there against the wall next to the kitchen door."

John only nodded once.

"I want to know if that couple seemed familiar to you. Leonora told me that she had seen them before."

John grunted. "Once before. Two days earlier, I'd say, on the coach from London. Same dress, same comportment: haughty. Didn't say much. Ate and looked around, like they might want to buy the place, it seemed to me."

"Odd."

John shrugged. "Who knows what the rich are up to?"

Marlowe leaned forward. "Can you give me anything else?"

"Such as?"

"Did you overhear anything they said? Anything at all."

John's lower lip pursed and he shook his head. "Not that I recall."

Marlowe sat back. "I see."

"Except that the gent told his wife not to talk so much."

"What?"

"The wife," John went on, "she was babbling, like reciting with her eyes closed. Like she was trying to remember—I don't know. Something."

"I don't understand," Marlowe told John. "What was she saying? Can you remember any of the words at all?"

John closed his eyes. "It was quite odd, I thought at the time, which is why I remember it. It was so strange, in fact, that I mentioned it to the doctor while he was attending to Leonora's father."

"What was it?" Marlowe insisted.

"She said, I think I've got this right, 'Hang Balthazar about Chimera's neck, and let him there bewail his bloody love.' "

Marlowe's head snapped back. "No!"

John, startled by Marlowe's reaction, opened his eyes.

"I—I think I've got that right," he stammered, "only there might be a word or two that I . . ."

His voice trailed off as he stared at Marlowe's face. It had gone sheet white.

"I don't know what this means," Marlowe mumbled, obviously disturbed.

"But you know those words." John stared. "I can see that. Is it some sort of code?"

Marlowe shook his head. "They're words from a play, not yet finished. They're from a speech by a ghost in a play called *The Spanish Tragedy*. It's by a man named Thomas Kyd."

"Someone you know?" John asked.

"Alas," Marlowe answered.

"And this man, he has something to do with Leonora's death?"

"Possibly. Indirectly. Without his knowledge."

John sat at Marlowe's table.

"We seldom know the damage we do," he told Marlowe softly. "An oak doesn't mean to let go a leaf, the leaf doesn't mean to ripple the pond; the ripple has no intention of breaking open the eggs of a frog. But the tadpoles are no less dead."

Marlowe smiled, though he didn't look at John. "An admirably observed philosophy of the blameless quality of nature. But this murder was not a natural act."

"Unless someone was deliberately chopping down the mighty oak."

That forced Marlowe to look into the baker's eyes.

John stared back. "I am not a well-educated man, Mr. Marlowe, but I am also not an idiot. You, the doctor, Leonora—there must be some matter of great import afoot here, or you would not be haunting this inn, and our dear girl would not be gone. You said as much: there is a greater plot."

Marlowe nodded.

"I cannot tell you what is transpiring, John," Marlowe allowed, "except to lament that I have said too much, and that you have rightly assessed the situation."

"Then why are you sitting here, sulking in the dark," John asked, "instead of being about your business? Do something!"

Marlowe returned his gaze to the empty space in front of him. "I don't know what to do."

It was the first time in his life that Marlowe had ever said those words.

Dawn woke Marlowe. He had fallen asleep at the table. There was noise in the kitchen and it drew Marlowe up. Hand on the hilt of his dagger, he stole toward the kitchen door.

As he came near, he could tell that the noise was, in fact, someone crying softly. Marlowe nudged the door open and found John staring down at Leonora's dead body, laid out on the kitchen table.

John looked up and saw Marlowe standing in the doorway. He quickly wiped his sleeve across his cheeks and sniffed.

"There you are," he said. "There's our Leonora. I'm afraid that I suffer your malady: I don't know what's to be done."

"Done?"

"We've not the money to see her buried in the church," John lamented, "and her father cannot bear the idea of putting her into the ground near the inn. Says he'd be daily reminded. I am at a loss for what to do."

Marlowe forced himself to look at her face.

"She's not for the earth," he said, his voice thick. "She was a gallant companion and a fierce warrior. She must be given a wilder end than tame mewing and graveside chatter."

"Aye," was all that John could say.

"The River Rib is not quite wide enough," Marlowe said, mostly to himself, "but it will have to do."

Some hours later John and Marlowe stood on the banks of the River Rib, Mr. Beak seated on a chair between them. Each held a burning candle. It had taken a while to make a small raft of broken limbs and dry hay from the stables. They had dressed Leonora in a simple black gown and folded her hands across her heart holding a simple cross of willow woven around her dagger. The raft was held to the bank, against the river's gentle current, by a horse's bridle in Mr. Beak's hand.

"I would like to say about Leonora," John began softly.

"No words about her!" Mr. Beak interrupted. "What good are

words? They cannot hope to contain my grief, or my love. And death comes to everyone."

"All live to die," Marlowe agreed. "The stars move still, time runs, the clock will strike. Let my actions henceforth justify her death."

With that Mr. Beak let go the horse's bridle. Marlowe tossed his candle onto the raft. John and Beak did likewise. In moments the dry hay was ablaze. The river carried the burning barge slowly away.

Before it was out of sight, Marlowe had gone.

FIFTEEN

As Marlowe rode toward the Travelers' encampment, his mind pieced together a small puzzle. It was small because it consisted of few parts, and only some of them were missing.

Ned Blank was the only suspect in Marlowe's mind. Ned lied in Maldon, killed the stable master, and then returned to the Bell. Why? The Bell was his contact point. He had been there before; he went back and waited for a sign, or instructions. There he witnessed Leonora's return. Fearing detection, he stole into her father's room and strangled her.

His part in the assassination of William was unclear, but earlier at the Bell he had rehearsed lines from Kyd's play, one that was soon to be mounted at Burbage's playhouse in Shoreditch called The Theatre. Ned was associated with the Earl of Leicester's Men, a troupe that also included the renowned comic actor Will Kemp, with whom Marlowe was passingly acquainted and from whom intelligence might be obtained.

A complication: Robert Dudley, the Earl of Leicester and founder of the acting company, was Philip Sidney's uncle. Philip Sidney was in love with Penelope Devereux, an object of Marlowe's affection. Penelope had, only the year before, played a part in a plot to assassinate the Queen. She had done so to free herself from marriage to Sir Robert Rich in the hope of marrying Philip. Philip was, however, newly married to Frances Walsingham, with whom Marlowe was also severely smitten.

In short, a trip to London, and The Theatre, was fraught with more complicated and emotional drama than any single stage could hold.

Still, the way seemed clear: go to Shoreditch, speak with Kemp or otherwise find Ned; get Ned to confess to Leonora's murder. He only had two days in which to do it. As the encampment came into view, under the noonday sun, Marlowe's mind was made up, and speed was of the essence.

Gelis stood up as soon as he saw Marlowe coming.

"You're back sooner than expected," he allowed. "Have you solved the murder?"

"Possibly," Marlowe answered as his horse walked into the middle of the encampment.

Three large covered carts and several other smaller wagons were strewn carelessly about the open plot in the woods. One large fire was relatively central. Children were running back and forth playing tag; a woman was singing as she stood near the fire, skinning a rabbit.

"Well it didn't take you long," Gelis said. "Who did it?

Marlowe stopped his horse and slid to the ground.

"I'll tell you when I'm certain; my mind is still clouded," Marlowe said.

"Clouded?" Gelis asked, taking the reins to the horse.

"I've been shot and stabbed," Marlowe began, "I've traveled to a foreign land, I've failed to prevent two murders, and then I've lost a good and true companion. I am not entirely in my right mind."

"But you know who did it," Gelis goaded. "I can tell."

Marlowe nodded reluctantly

"Who is the villain?" Gelis asked, his voice hushed and menacing.

"An actor," Marlowe whispered back.

"My God." Understanding dawned across Gelis's face.

Unbidden, Toby appeared and Gelis did not speak further. Toby glared at Marlowe and took the horse.

"You're back, then," he said, sulking.

"I am, and it's good news for you," Marlowe answered. "We're going to London to find your heart's desire."

Toby's face brightened. "London?"

"We'll leave within the hour," Gelis assured him decisively. "You'd best prepare yourself, young Toby. London's not a place for man that does not have complete command of his faculties."

"London," Toby muttered again as he led the horse away.

"Sad to say," Gelis went on as soon as Toby was out of sight, "that the boy's heart's desire is also your quarry. This female-playing-actor killed our Leonora?"

"I believe so. I should have known it sooner. I was blinded by exhaustion and grief."

"And theatre," Gelis added.

"Sorry?" Marlowe inclined his head toward Gelis.

"If someone has stolen a horse from me," Gelis began, "I look first to the local gentry and criminal class, not to the fellows of my own camp."

Marlowe considered the wisdom of that pronouncement, especially as it so closely resembled Walsingham's admonition on the matter.

"Agreed," he confirmed at length. "Add to that concept the fact that another of the players in this grotesque pageant is a mentor of mine."

"So much the worse," Gelis commiserated.

Torches were burning in The Theatre, and Thomas Kyd was lying on his back in the middle of the stage.

"No! Christ on a carrot!" he bellowed.

He sat up and glared at the Ghost.

"If you hope to play this part by week's end, boy," he railed, "you'll have to know at least a few of the words I've written. You are to say, 'Then, sweet Revenge, do this at my request: let the lovers's endless pains now cease, Juno forget old wrath and grant him ease; Hang Balthazar about Chimera's neck, and let him there bewail his bloody love!' "

"I know the words," Ned growled, "you dank, cavernous tooth-hole. I'm buggered and bunged, is all. That bitch broke my back!"

"You let a woman beat you." Kyd coughed up his laughter from the center of his belly. "And now you walk like a clown."

Ned stood sweating in his white powder and long black cape. His legs ached, his back burned, and his eyes were rimmed in red. The Theatre was vacant save for the portly playwright and his tortured player.

"It's your fault," Ned swore bitterly. "I wouldn't be in this condition if I hadn't listened to you."

"You wouldn't be in this play if you hadn't listened to me," Kyd corrected. "You can't play the girls' roles any more. What was left but street whoring and cutting the occasional purse?"

Ned glanced down at Kyd's pants.

"The next time I'm down there," Ned said calmly, "I'm going to bite off your bollocks. I'm known amongst Leicester's Men. Kemp says I'm ready for Lyly's new play about the Italian lovers."

"John Lyly," Kyd snapped disdainfully, "is shite. What's this new play?"

"It is taken, I have been told," Ned answered, enjoying the upper hand, "from William Painter's book, *Palace of Pleasure*. As are several of your efforts, Tommy-boy."

Kyd sat up. "Painter's book? Which story?"

"It is the Lamentable History of *Romeus and Juliet*," Ned said grandly. "I am to play the very *male* role of this dick Romeus, what falls in love with a girl he should not."

"Blast God's Teeth!" Kyd snarled, scrambling to his feet. "I'm working on that story!"

"I know." Ned grinned. "But Lyly has finished his work and the play is to be presented. So give me the rest of the night off, let me soothe my back, or shove your ghost up the River Bum-whip and I shall take my services elsewhere."

"You ungrateful badger's colon," Kyd howled. "I saved you!"

"You embroiled me in the worst stew of my life, you great mound of pig guts!"

Kyd fell silent for an instant. When he spoke again, his voice was greatly changed.

"I know, Ned," he murmured. "I'm sorry. I had no choice."

Marlowe sat beside Gelis in a clanking, rattling cart. It was painted red and white, decorated with astrological designs, and the spokes of each wheel were alternately painted yellow and blue. The sun was going down and Marlowe slumped down, trying to sleep.

"I approve of this speedy travel," Marlowe mumbled, "but if I'm to be in a Gypsy cart, why can't I lie down in the back and get some sleep?"

"First of all," Gelis answered, "we don't generally respond to the word *Gypsy*, and second of all, I would not have you lie with my wife."

"I wouldn't be doing anything," Marlowe assured Gelis. "I'd be sleeping."

"Yes but it ain't you I'd be worried about," said Gelis. "You lying there beside my wife? Might put ideas into her head. She's a young woman, and I've seen the way she looks at you."

"The only look I've seen on her face," Marlowe responded, "is an expression of abject fear."

"Maybe she's afraid of her feelings for you," he suggested.

"Gelis," Marlowe began, but his objection was not completed.

A musket shot rang out, and in the next instant the roof of the cart cracked, showering bits of wood and sawdust downward.

Gelis dropped low and pulled the reins tightly.

Marlowe was out of the cart with his rapier in his hand, scanning the woods for a puff of smoke in the dim starlight.

Another shot splatted against the side of the cart. From inside Gelis's wife squeaked once.

Silver against a line of elm trees, Marlowe saw a small white cloud drifting off toward the west. He lowered his head and ran toward the spot whence the smoke had come. Was this a single assailant or were there several?

Marlowe stooped as he ran and scooped up a small branch, then tossed it as hard as he could to his left. The branch clattered across the forest floor, and sounded like half a dozen clumsy men in the relative quiet of the night.

A third shot rang out. Not enough time to reload; there were at least two assailants. But the smoke came from the same location as before; at least they were not scattered out.

"You three go that way!" Marlowe called out in a guttural voice. "Get around behind our attackers!"

Then he tore away to his right as silently as he could.

He could hear scrambling in the darkened woods. Someone tripped over a root, fell hard on the ground, cursing.

Picking out a large oak, Marlowe hid, listening, holding his breath.

Hearing nothing, he peered slowly around the tree. No movement, no clue, no one was in the woods anywhere near him. But it was unlikely that the attackers had given up. They weren't highwaymen. Robbers had better sense than to attack a Travelers' caravan—there was little worth stealing.

Just as that thought occurred to him, Gelis called out like a town crier.

"It's nothing, Mr. Greene!" he shouted. "Come back to the cart. We'll be on our way once more, then!"

Not knowing what to make of that, Marlowe carefully made his way back to Gelis's wagon. As he approached he saw that Gelis was not alone on the bench seat. A ragged scarecrow of a man sat beside him, grinning like an idiot. He was dressed in black, but hundreds of knots had been tied into the fabric of his shirt and pants, and each knot held a flower, an herb, or a small bauble of some sort. His boots were spotless, as if they had never touched the ground. His head was shaved, like a monk's.

Marlowe slowed his pace and kept his rapier up.

"This is Belpathian Grem," Gelis told Marlowe matter-of-factly, "lately of the Netherlands. He and his fellows have been tracking us since we broke camp. They saw you sitting beside me and thought I might be your prisoner or captive. I have assured him that we are all friends."

"*Vriend,*" the odd scarecrow said, still smiling ear to ear.

"*Wie bent u?*" Marlowe asked cautiously.

"Belpathian Grem," the man repeated.

"No," Marlowe demurred, stopping short of the cart. "You're speaking Dutch but that's not a Dutch name—that's not any kind of name I know."

"Mr. Grem is of the Weird Folk," Gelis answered. "He speaks twenty languages, knows medicine and witchery, and they say he's three hundred years old."

"The Weird Folk," Marlowe said, a faint smile touching his lips. "That's a children's story."

"A story I have heard for years, all over Europe," Gelis answered excitedly. "And I've seen him before. The stories are quite real."

"I can see that," Marlowe said, doing his best to hide derision, "but what is he doing in my seat?"

"As I say," Gelis answered, "he's been following us. He has intelligence from Delft. Leonora enjoined me to alert my network of Traveling brethren, and that has proved a worthwhile endeavor. Mr. Grem has news."

Marlowe didn't move. "I don't see how, unless his witchery allows him to bend the rules of time. He could not possibly have heard from you, gathered information, and delivered himself to us in so short a time. William has only been dead for—God, for the life of me I can't calculate how long he's been dead. Is it just two days? At any rate, not long enough for all that travel."

"That's where the birds come in," Gelis allowed. "I keep a dole of doves for communication, you see. Mr. Grem is one of the homes. He heard from me before you and Leonora was even arrived at the Netherlands. Though I must admit that his appearance here on the road is a bit of a surprise."

"He thought you were my prisoner?" Marlowe asked. "Was he trying to shoot me?"

"Yes," Gelis admitted.

Marlowe looked into the woods. "Then I'm glad he's not much of a shot."

"It's my brother's youngest son," the odd man said in English, without a trace of any accent except for a slight Yorkshire tang. "He's only nine. I took the gun away from him after the second shot."

Marlowe stared at the mystifying Mr. Grem.

"Gelis has told you about Leonora Beak and me," Marlowe began, "so now that you know who I am, will you tell me your news?"

"I can tell you what I can tell you," he said. "The rest is for other ears."

"I have no idea what that means," Marlowe said, his rapier still out.

"Spanish forces are gathered in Zutphen," Mr. Grem said, making an effort to sound ominous. "But there is more—something odd, in light of William's recent demise."

"And what would that be?" Marlowe asked, squinting. "This *something odd.*"

"In brief," Mr. Grem began, "The Spanish king Philip has a nephew, King Rudolf of Hungary, Bohemia, and Austria, the so-called Holy Roman Emperor. Rudolf has given me charge of a certain manuscript, written in what he called the *Enochian* language, that I am to deliver to John Dee, mathematician, astronomer, astrologer, occult philosopher—and advisor to your Queen Elizabeth."

Marlowe's rapier lowered, but only owing to his amazement.

"You are carrying a missive from Rudolf, the Spanish king's nephew," Marlowe asked softly, "to John Dee, Her Majesty's advisor?"

"No. John Dee has purchased a manuscript from Rudolf, and I am delivering same. It is not a communiqué of any sort."

"Let me see it," Marlowe insisted, taking a step toward the odd man.

"Of course not," he answered, producing a pistol.

Marlowe stopped, but he smiled.

"If you didn't kill me just now under cover of wood and the

approaching night," Marlowe said, "you won't shoot me in front of Gelis now."

Gelis shifted in his seat, leaned to his left, and suddenly held a knife to Mr. Grem's throat.

"I'm afraid he's right, Mr. Grem," Gelis announced. "I owe a large debt of conscience to this man and his deceased companion, and I would very much prefer you did not kill him."

"No intention of killing him." Grem smiled. "I just can't let him see the manuscript."

"Where's the harm?" Gelis asked reasonably. "You say it's written in the Enochian language—who can read that?"

"No one," Marlowe sighed, "because it doesn't exist. It's a fanciful invention."

"You don't believe in the Language of Angels?" Grem asked.

"I believe in coded messages between my country's enemies," Marlowe answered, "and my country's traitors."

Grem laughed, though it sounded more like a cry of pain.

"This manuscript I possess," he said, "is hundreds, or perhaps even thousands of years old. It transcends your ridiculous contemporaneous suspicions."

"I'm certain people tell you all the time," Marlowe countered, "that you have an odd way of talking."

But he sheathed his rapier; Grem lowered his pistol.

"There," Marlowe went on, "my weapon is laid to rest. Set aside yours, and let us be on our way to London. I'm in a hurry."

Grem stared unblinkingly. "Just like that?"

"I have urgent business," Marlowe told him.

Grem turned to Gelis. "Do I trust him?"

Gelis withdrew his knife from Grem's throat and turned to face the road ahead.

"You trust him," Gelis answered, "as much as he trusts you. But I will say that Mr. Greene, here, is an honorable man, as far as I can tell, and he needs my help."

"And you owe him a debt of conscience," Grem said.

Gelis nodded once.

Grem whistled then, and a boy on horseback appeared out of the darkness.

"You ride with Gelis, Mr. Greene," Grem said. "I'm on my horse with my young nephew."

Moments later they were on their way, Marlowe once again riding in the Travelers' cart.

All he could think about then was John Dee, Elizabeth's most mysterious confidante. An alchemist and Hermetic philosopher, Dee possessed the greatest library in England. Chief among the Queen's scholars, he had occasionally tutored Her Majesty, and enjoyed a close relationship with Sir Francis Walsingham. His allegiance was beyond question, or so everyone thought.

But if Dee was, in fact, receiving coded messages from Philip through Rudolf, the result would be devastating.

More troubling still was the fact that Dee was currently occupied as the chief tutor of Philip Sidney, and his uncle, Robert Dudley, 1st Earl of Leicester. The coincidence was too much for Marlowe. The connection between Ned, Dudley's acting troupe, Philip Sidney, and the assassination of William the Silent was not remotely clear, but Marlowe was certain that it existed.

Trying to piece together that puzzle occupied Marlowe until Gelis cleared his throat.

"You're deep in thought," he observed.

Marlowe nodded.

"I have no wish to compromise your relationship, whatever it may be, with this man Grem," he whispered, "but I must have a look at the manuscript he is carrying."

Gelis looked around. No sign of Grem in sight. Gelis leaned against Marlowe and whispered into his ear.

"Do you mean," he asked Marlowe, "this manuscript?"

He produced a volume, some two hundred and fifty pages of bound vellum, with illustrations on nearly every page.

"Took it from his person," Gelis went on, "whilst I had my knife at his throat. Thought you might want to have a look. Don't think he noticed. Could be wrong."

Marlowe stared at the volume. Of all things, his first thought was of Leonora.

“Miss Beak was right about you,” Marlowe told Gelis. “She had an instinct that you were a man of value. And you are.”

Gelis looked away.

Marlowe took the manuscript and spent the next two hours looking over the pages by the light of the lamp on the side of the cart, absorbed by the manuscript’s contents.

SIXTEEN

The work was divided into several sections. The first was occupied by botanical drawings, but Marlowe failed to recognize a single plant. The next set of pages had astrological sketches, star charts in radiating circles, with signs of the Zodiac. The third was a bizarre biological chapter filled with drawings of tiny female nudes, most of them pregnant and wading in green pools connected by tubes. He examined the rest only cursorily: a presenting of cosmological medallions; what appeared to be medicinal drawings of plants and roots in jars, and lastly endless pages of text. All baffling owing to the fact that it was written in a language that did not exist. Some letters and all numbers were familiar, but not a single word resembled any that Marlowe knew.

"I speak seven languages," he mumbled to Gelis, "read and write twelve more, and am, in all honesty, remarkably adept at breaking codes. But I can make no sense of this thing. It may be the most bizarre object I have ever seen."

"Wrong," Gelis assured him. "Belpathian Grem is the strangest thing you've ever seen. What you have there? It's just a book. Life is infinitely stranger than literature."

Marlowe looked up. "And again I marvel at your philosophical bent."

"Rather marvel at yonder sight," he responded, lifting his chin.

Against the retreating night sky, opposite the gold of a rising sun, the city of London came into view.

"London," Gelis went on, "where all our answers lie."

An hour later, Gelis and Marlowe left the carts camped in the green fields just outside the city, under the "mystical protection" of Belpathian Grem. Grem appeared content to cook eggs and tell jokes under an elm while Marlowe explored the Curtain Road in Shoreditch headed toward The Theatre.

When plague savaged London ten years earlier, the mayor banished all plays and players from the city as a measure to stop the spread of the disease. The Theatre was built in 1576 by James Burbage in Shoreditch, beyond the northern boundary of the city—outside the reach of the authorities. The area was a sanctuary for brothels, gaming houses, cutpurses, murderers, and actors. The streets, mostly mud and dung, were crowded with vermin of every kind, human and rodent. Laughing women in torn dresses, stumbling men covered in blood and ale, children with vacant eyes, dogs, chickens, flags, food, and knives—all studiously avoided contact with the Traveler at Marlowe's side. Offend a Gypsy in the morning, end up dead by noon.

The Theatre was good for plays and perfect for bearbaiting: a wooden polygon with three galleries around a cobbled open yard. On one side of the polygon there was a thrust stage. Standing room cost a penny, seats in the gallery cost three, and certain parts of the gallery were sectioned off for wealthy patrons, slumming.

It was, Marlowe informed Gelis, the primary venue for Leicester's Men, the acting company of Robert Dudley, 1st Earl of Leicester, of which James Burbage was a member.

That information brought forward motion to a halt.

"Wait just a moment," he said to Marlowe. "Some earl owns a company of actors? For what purpose?"

"Leicester is a patron of the arts," Marlowe answered, "because his nephew, Philip Sidney, is a poet. Of sorts. Here's a line of his: 'Of touch they are that without touch doth touch.'"

"What?" Gelis asked. "What does that mean?"

"No idea," Marlowe affirmed, resuming his journey toward The Theatre.

"So this uncle, this earl," Gelis went on, catching up with Marlowe, "he's forced to support the lame clink?"

"Well," Marlowe hedged, "the lame clink is also a member of Parliament. But he doesn't get along with the Queen. He won't be at court very long, I think."

The street narrowed and veered a bit to the left, and there was The Theatre.

"Ah," Gelis said, "now I remember this place. Saw a bear rip off some drunken sod's arm one afternoon. Great sport."

Without answering Marlowe charged through the door into the open yard, headed toward the stage.

At first sight there was pile of soiled clothing in the center of the platform. But as they drew nearer, the rags began to quake, and up sat Thomas Kyd.

"Marlowe!" he shouted, and then began to cough uncontrollably.

Marlowe picked up his pace, drew his dagger, and bounded onto the stage with a single leap. Before Kyd could get to his feet, Marlowe's knife point was inches from his left eye.

"Where is Ned Blank?" Marlowe asked softly. "Tell me now, or lose an eye."

"Marlowe," Kyd whimpered, "what are you doing?"

"I'm confronting a drunken tub of guts," Marlowe answered, "who has betrayed his country and killed a superior woman."

Kyd did his best to stay very still.

"I have killed no one," Kyd asserted fervently, "and I have betrayed no one but myself. Though *that* I have done most savagely."

"You are in league with assassins," Marlowe said, his anger growing, "who have murdered three: William the Silent, a stable master in Maldon, and one of the finest companions I have ever known! And all in service to a larger plan to kill our Queen!"

Kyd's eyes widened. "What? I never. No. You've lost your mind!"

"Ned Blank!" Marlowe roared, his rage getting the better of him.

"Yes," Kyd howled, "I set in on a—I introduced him to some men, because he needed money, and I was—I was forced to.

Marlowe, you have to believe me. I had no choice in the matter. I was done for."

"Tell me," Marlowe hissed, "and very quickly."

Kyd looked down, avoiding Marlowe's eyes. "I said something to a boy I—I got from the streets. You know me. I only wanted to impress him. I told him that—I told him that Jesus used St. John the Evangelist as did the sinners of Sodom. He laughed. It was all in fun. But then he told someone who told someone and several days later there I was: do what we tell you to, or the Privy Council hears what the boy has to say."

"You were blackmailed on the word of a single street boy?" Marlowe's voice betrayed doubt.

"The boy found papers in my rooms," Kyd went on miserably, "when I was asleep. After. I may—I may have actually written down some of my more—objectionable observations regarding Christ and religion in general."

Marlowe lowered his knife. "Why in God's name would you ever have written such things down?"

"Drink, humor, bravado, arrogance, and rancor," Kyd answered, "in that order. I'm an idiot, I know."

Marlowe shook his head slowly. "You have no idea of the damage you've done."

"I don't understand." Kyd finally looked up into Marlowe's eyes.

Marlowe let go a heavy sigh.

"No," he said. "You really don't understand, do you? Let me explain. Because of your desire to protect such a paltry thing as your reputation, you've betrayed your country, and you've been a companion to bloody murder."

From behind Marlowe heard Gelis's admonition.

"I'd go ahead kill him now," he urged. "I can see just by looking at him that he'd do it all again. He's that sort."

"On my life," Kyd whispered solemnly, "I would never."

"You probably would," Marlowe said, sheathing his dagger, "but I find that I cannot kill you now. Not this morning, at least."

"Why not?" Gelis objected. "Do you want me to do it?"

Marlowe turned around and looked down at Gelis.

"For one, everything I know about the theatre," Marlowe answered, "I learned from this fat drunken man. I may have lost my love for him, but not the debt I owe to him."

Gelis rolled his eyes. "What about your debt to Leonora? And mine?"

"Yes, that is the second reason I won't kill you this morning," Marlowe said, whirling back to face Kyd once more. "I have need of you. As I was saying: Ned Blank. Tell me how to find him, or lose an eye—is that about where we were?"

Kyd blinked, staring down the shaft of the blade.

Then, drawing in a great breath, he hollered to wake the dead.

Marlowe stood over the unconscious Ned Blank, dagger in hand, watching him sleep.

"He does look like a girl," Gelis whispered, "I'll give him that."

Ned was snoring on top of a pile of costumes in a backroom at The Theatre, lit only by the little sun that forced its way through cracks in the poorly constructed eastern wall. He was dressed in his ghost costume, and the white powder from his face was smeared on his chin by the drool from his gaping maw.

"A disgusting girl," Gelis added.

"Ned!" Marlowe shouted.

Ned sat bolt upright, eyes wide, scrambling.

Marlowe held the point of his dagger against Ned's cheek.

"From here to the eye," Marlowe said calmly. "A single cut: you're defaced and half-blind. So don't move."

"Pissing Jesus Bunghole!" Ned shrieked, and as he did, his voice broke.

"Ah, there's the pathos," Marlowe went on. "Your voice is changing. You'll never play Ophelia again."

"Mr. Marlowe," Ned began, sweat glistening at his hairline. "This is quite a surprise. Thought you was in the Netherlands."

Marlowe smiled. "And you've given yourself away again. I never told you my name."

Ned blinked. "You did."

Marlowe shook his head. "Most actors have a better memory than that."

"What do we care," Gelis interrupted, "about his acting? Slice him up!"

"What?" Ned jumped. "Why would you want to do that?"

"You killed Leonora," Gelis answered.

"I killed *who*?" Ned asked, twitching.

"The woman who was with me in Maldon," Marlowe answered.

"How could I kill her?" Ned asked, his voice higher. "She left with you, down to the docks to search out that bleeding French foin-a-scab."

"You killed her when she came back," Marlowe answered, his anger getting the better of him. "You waited at the Bell Inn and you stole up behind her, a coward's attack."

"God is my only judge," Ned swore fervently, "the second you left I bashed that stable master in the gob and tore out for London. I had a job! With Thomas Kyd!"

"Not really," Gelis objected.

"Easy enough to confirm," Marlowe said. "Kyd?"

Thomas Kyd staggered from the shadows, hands tied in front of him.

"It must be true," Kyd whimpered. "He returned to London on the day after he left. The next day, late."

"If that's true," Marlowe said carefully, "then Ned was back in London before Leonora returned to the Bell."

"But he limps," Gelis objected. "You told me that Leonora's murderer had a limp, and this boy walks like a leper."

"That woman broke my back!" Ned interjected.

"Don't talk," Marlowe warned Ned. "I'm still in the mood to kill you."

"If you're looking for someone to blame for murder," Ned went on, "you'd best seek out that French capon. He's a killer all right."

"Yes," Marlowe agreed at once. "But he was dead before we came back to England."

"Well we've got to kill *somebody* for Leonora," Gelis observed calmly.

"I can't make this all fit together," Marlowe said, rubbing his temples. "I have an abundance of pieces but no picture."

"Well," Kyd ventured cautiously, "perhaps I could help. I seem to have, inadvertently, caused you great distress. The least I can do is figure out what's going on. I'm very good at plots."

Marlowe turned to Gelis.

"He is that," Marlowe allowed.

Kyd sat down, nodding.

"Good," said Kyd. "Tell me everything."

SEVENTEEN

Marlowe stood in Walsingham's study, staring at the rows and rows of books. An hour had gone by. Shifting from one leg to the other, he knew better than to sit. There was no telling who might suddenly appear, including the royal personage. And so he stood.

With no warning, one of the bookcases grumbled, scraped, and opened like a door. Walsingham burst in, all in gray, head uncovered, growling low, or humming. Three armed men followed after him.

"You have Leonora's killer," Walsingham said without greeting or introduction, staring down at papers on his desk. "That is the message I was given."

"Yes."

"Where is he?"

"I have infiltrated a camp of Traveling People," Marlowe answered. "They owe a debt to Leonora Beak, and so have agreed to keep the murderer secreted away."

Walsingham looked up, glaring at Marlowe.

"Why have you done this?" he asked Marlowe. "The villain should be in the Tower."

"The villain, sir, is a part of the larger plot against our Queen. The Traveling People have methods of questioning that would horrify the worst interrogator of the Inquisition. They will glean information needed to hang Mary, as you have suggested."

Walsingham's eyes narrowed.

Marlowe went on. "You have instructed me to convince Mary that I am sympathetic to her Catholic cause. If I know key elements of her latest plot, I will have a greater advantage. If she knew that Leonora's murderer was in the Tower, which she would certainly learn almost as soon as he was shoved into his cell, she would also suspect that details of her plot would be in your possession, and suspect anyone who came to her with that information. But if she believes that this one conspirator is still at large, she will be less likely to suspect me. Do you not agree?"

Walsingham sucked in a breath and was about to speak, but thought better of it, and only inclined his head.

"Good," Marlowe continued further, "then tell me how you propose to get me into Chartley Hall, where Paulet is keeping her—as you have told me."

Walsingham shook his head.

"You surprise me, Marlowe," he said softly. "And I am so rarely surprised. Will you tell me, at least, the killer's name?"

"He is an actor," Marlowe answered, "by the name of Ned Blank."

"Ah," Walsingham sighed, "the Thomas Kyd connection."

"Exactly."

"Well, let us say, for the moment, that I believe you. That being the case, I agree with this course of action. You must proceed immediately to Staffordshire, and Chartley Hall. Mary is somehow communicating with the outside world, obviously. You must learn how it's been done, intercept some communication, and report back to me *immediately*. Do you understand?"

"Yes." Marlowe grimaced. "But please, no coaches. Let me ride a horse—and go alone. I've had enough of companions for a while."

"Agreed. That boy you like, the one called Leviticus, will bring you a mount and instructions within the hour, out in the courtyard."

"Leviticus?" Marlowe asked, attempting to sound confused.

"The one with whom you made a pact," Walsingham answered calmly. "You told him that you would discover his benefactor in court, and he promised to answer certain questions for you. How has your investigation in that matter gone thus far, I wonder?"

Marlowe shook his head. "When will I realize that you know everything?"

"The sooner you do," Walsingham confirmed, "the better for our mutual business."

"In fact I have done nothing as regards the matter of young Leviticus," Marlowe confessed.

"When would you have had the time?" Walsingham agreed. "Why not tell the boy that you suspect his mother is Jane Fromond?"

"I don't know that name," Marlowe said hesitantly.

"She is the new wife of John Dee," Walsingham answered. "He is not the father."

Marlowe froze. Was Walsingham testing him? Did he know about the manuscript sent to Dee from Rudolf? Better to say nothing; wait until the manuscript was decoded.

"John Dee the scholar?" Marlowe asked innocently.

Walsingham nodded. "She is thirty years his junior, and one hears the occasional rumor."

"Meaning that Leviticus might have heard the rumors."

"Yes," Walsingham said, "so it will have the ring of confirmation when you tell him that she is his mother. And then you can ask him about me. That is why you have created this strange bond, is it not? To have a secret ear in court, and in my chambers?"

Marlowe stood straight. "Yes, but since you know that, perhaps I ought to just ask you what I want to know."

"Ask."

"Where is Lopez?"

"No." Walsingham shook his head. "Ask something else."

"Where is your daughter Frances, then?" Marlowe asked, looking down.

"You know that she is married, Marlowe," the old man groaned. "She's not for you."

"Yes." He looked up. "I know she's married. That's not what I asked."

"You must stay to the task at hand. Go to Chartley. Now that you have solved the murder of Leonora Beak, you must find out how Mary is communicating with her cohorts. Get me evidence of her treason. There is no time to waste."

Marlowe heard urgency in the old man's voice.

"Something more has happened?" he asked carefully.

"William's death set certain wheels in motion," Walsingham affirmed. "This plot which Mary has concocted with Philip has cast shadows everywhere. You absolutely must discover how they are communicating. Without exaggeration I say that the stability of our nation is in peril."

One of the armed men moved toward Walsingham then and whispered.

"Very well," Walsingham said, retrieving something from his desk. "Go now, out to the garden. There you will be given your necessary papers. I remind you of the Act for the Surety of the Queen's Person. You are to stop at nothing in pursuit of your goal. Is that understood?"

Not waiting for an answer, Walsingham turned and was gone, once again through the bookcase-door. A single guard remained. He strode past Marlowe, not looking at him, and opened the outer door.

The garden was quiet and Marlowe had a moment to sit and reflect on his dangerous path. Lying to Walsingham was a terrible idea, but if it led to a greater truth, it would be excused. Or so he hoped.

And Walsingham had lied as well: why invent this poor young girl, Dee's wife, as mother to the lost, strange boy at court? What was the connection between Dee, the esoteric text that Gelis had taken from Grem, and the plot against the Queen? They were connected, only it was impossible to see how.

It was Kyd's idea to tell Walsingham the myth of Ned-as-murderer. Safe in the Travelers' camp, Ned would not only be free from harm, at least for a while, he could also be kept out of further mischief.

And assuring Walsingham that Leonora's killer had been caught would allow Marlowe greater latitude: he could ferret out the larger plot and in doing so discover Leonora's true assailant.

Or so Kyd had convinced him, after two hours of labyrinthine discussion.

There was the trouble: everything depended on Kyd, and Kyd was not dependable.

Lost in such doubts, Marlowe failed to hear Leviticus approach, and so was startled when the boy sat down beside him.

"Chartley used to be a real castle," the boy began, holding out a familiar-looking golden cylinder. "Over five hundred years ago. Then it was abandoned. Then the Devereux family got hold of it and built a moated mansion. That's where you're going."

"You know your history." Marlowe took the cylinder. "You're a very strange boy."

"Yes," he sighed.

"I meant it as a compliment," Marlowe went on. "And I have a bit of information, for your ears only."

The boy looked up, then around the garden, making certain they were alone.

"I now believe," Marlowe said very softly, "that your mother is none other than Jane Fromond."

Leviticus stood up, eyes wide. "What?"

"John Dee's new wife," Marlowe confirmed, and then improvised. "She had you when she was but thirteen, and you were given into other care, for the sake of her youth. She has seen to it that you are educated and looked after. But she dare not reveal your identity to anyone."

"Because John Dee is a magician," Leviticus whispered breathlessly. "Everyone says. There is no telling what he might do."

Marlowe smiled. "Let me tell you what magic is," he said. "Magic is a moment when a ghost appears on the stage, and everyone in the audience knows that ghost is an actor, and then, after another moment, in a hushed gallery, everyone forgets the actor, and there is actually a ghost on stage."

"Magic is belief," the boy said slowly.

"What a bizarrely intelligent person you are," Marlowe observed. "How old did you say you were?"

“Eleven,” the boy lamented. “Too old for a boy, and not yet a man.”

“I know a hundred men who don’t have half your wit,” Marlowe told him. “But what do you make of this news about your mother?”

“It’s puzzling,” he answered. “I thought I would be elated, or at the least relieved. But now I find that I only have more questions.”

“The curse of an eager mind,” Marlowe said sympathetically. “Every answer only engenders more questions.”

“You suffer from such a curse,” the boy said.

It wasn’t a question.

Marlowe stood. “I’m off to the Chartley, to wrestle more puzzles.”

The boy nodded. “And I may as well tell you that I’m off to Walsingham’s offices to report this conversation. I tell him everything.”

“I have just learned that,” Marlowe answered, “but don’t forget: you now owe me a debt of information.”

“The next time we meet,” the boy vowed, “I will tell you secrets that will boil your ears.”

“But not now.”

“Not now,” he said, turning to leave. “Now you must leave with great haste, on the Queen’s business.”

Without looking back, the boy strode away toward the side door whence he doubtless had come.

Marlowe opened the cylinder and withdrew several pages from it.

One was a copy of the Surety Act with Marlowe’s name on it, his permission to murder in the name of the Crown. One was a plan for his mission at Chartley. The last was the strangest; it was a set of drawings: strange letters or symbols, but not from any language Marlowe knew.

Inside a poorly lit room in Hampton Court, not a thousand yards from where Marlowe stood, Walsingham read aloud.

“ ‘Madimi is a pretty girl of seven or nine years of age, half angel and half elfin,’ ”

The old man looked up. “That is Dee’s first mention of the spirit.

She has instructed Dee in her own Angelic language, which Dee names *Enochian*. But later she has changed. He says, 'She openeth all her apparel and showeth herself all naked.'"

The Queen sat in Walsingham's chair, leaning forward on his desk.

"Has my scientific advisor gone mad?" she asked. "Is that what you are saying?"

"He is in pursuit of the Impossible." Walsingham shrugged, setting down the pages he'd just read.

"We know that he met with Rudolf last year," the Queen mused, somewhat stiffly.

"Yes," Walsingham answered carefully, "but though Rudolf is by designation the Holy Roman Emperor—"

"And by blood the cousin of Philip," the Queen interrupted.

". . . he is also, by nature, an idiot," Walsingham concluded. "He has always been more interested in esoteric fantasies than in guiding the ship of state."

"You mean that his mind is weak and his will is lazy, and I agree." She stood.

"I also mean that Dee is in pursuit of knowledge, not power," Walsingham said.

"Then why send Marlowe his way?"

Walsingham lifted his shoulders. "I could be wrong."

"Marlowe knows all about this, you realize," the Queen said. "He knows that you're leading him to Dee on purpose, with your gambit about Dee's wife. And that odd little boy. Marlowe has guessed it all."

"He probably has," Walsingham agreed.

"And why is he lying about the murderer of our agent Beak? She was never killed by that actor."

"Marlowe has a plan," was Walsingham's answer. "I would like to see how it works out."

"You have a plan, Philip has a plan, Marlowe has a plan," Her Majesty listed softly, "and no one knows where the wheel stops spinning; whose plan will win out in the end."

"As to John Dee," Walsingham said, deliberately changing direction, "I believe that he is genuinely attempting to converse with Angels for the primary benefit of your safety."

The Queen did not look back as she left the room, but she said, softly, over her shoulder, "Then let him work faster. I am in need of Angels just now."

Marlowe made his way down the narrow streets toward Shoreditch, leading the horse he'd been given, completely absorbed by his thoughts. He had hidden the cylinder in his boot and kept the odd manuscript at his waist, superstitiously afraid to put them side by side. The strange page from the cylinder was clearly an alphabetical key to the manuscript stolen from Grem. The manuscript was code; Dee had the key. Dee was in league with Rudolf, nephew to the King of Spain, the man working with Mary to destroy England, or at least the England Marlowe knew. But if Walsingham was aware of Dee's treachery, why not arrest Dee and have done with it?

Walsingham was truly depending on Marlowe to infiltrate Mary's confidence and ferret out the entirety of the conspiracy. Marlowe saw the wisdom of that. If they were going to destroy the tree of deceit, better to pull up all the roots than merely to hack off a few of the limbs.

So. Was the manuscript a necessary clue or a tangential distraction? To answer that, Marlowe needed a conversation with the very odd Belpathian Grem. Since a quick stop at the Travelers' encampment was in order anyway, on the road to Chartley, it seemed an easy task to accomplish.

An instant later that task became unnecessary: Belpathian Grem leapt upon him from a darkened alley, a slim silver dagger in his hand.

They tumbled into the street. Passersby looked the other way, walked around. Street brawls were common. And these men had knives. Best to ignore them.

After a few dozen yards, Grem ended up on top of Marlowe, with the point of his blade tickling Marlowe's throat.

"You have my book," Grem said plainly.

"No," Marlowe began.

The point of Grem's blade drew a small point of blood.

"You do," Grem said, smiling. "You have taken it from me as others have tried to do. You intend to sell it yourself."

"No, it is a communication from enemies of our Queen," Marlowe whispered. "You must not deliver it to John Dee!"

"In fact I must," Grem countered. "He's paid for it."

"It's treason!"

"No, it's five thousand pounds," Grem corrected, "and my word of honor that I would deliver it. I am unconcerned with the political constructs of your world, Kit Marlowe."

Marlowe blinked. "What did you call me?"

"*Kit Marlowe*," Grem whispered, "same as does your father, and a certain lady of whom you are lately enamored. I know secrets within secrets. I am, as Gelis told you, King of the Weird Folk."

For effect, Grem widened his eyes and began to drool.

"Ah." Marlowe relaxed. "There it is; you've gone a beat too far. I know theatre when I see it. You play a part. You are a fictional character. Let me up."

Grem hesitated. That was his peril. In that moment of hesitation, Marlowe drew his own blade, rolled to dislodge Grem, and came to his feet, dagger in hand.

Grem scrambled backward, grinning more manically.

"Nicely done," he snarled. "Say good-bye to Ned for me."

"What?" Marlowe asked, taken off guard.

"I said, 'Catch this!' "

In the next second Marlowe saw Grem's silver dagger hurling toward his head, hilt first, and then it bashed him right between the eyes.

Marlowe sank to his knees, his world gone black.

EIGHTEEN

Ned Blank lay sleeping in the noonday sun. In slumber, he looked like a child of seven or eight years. There was still a bit of rouge and powder on his face, and he was dressed in a ragged doublet and trousers too big for his underfed frame.

He awoke with a start when a shadow fell across his face.

"I'm the only reason you're here," Marlowe told him, "and not in the Tower. Do you understand that?"

"Tower?" Ned mumbled.

"You're the accused murderer of Leonora Beak."

Ned sat up. "That again? You know I didn't do it."

"Then who did?"

Ned rubbed his eyes. He was hemmed in on all sides. Gelis stood next to Marlowe. Both men looked unhappy.

"Who killed that lady?" Ned blinked. "How would I know?"

"You know more than you say," Marlowe answered.

Ned yawned. "Always."

"But now it's time to tell everything." Marlowe took a step closer.

"Everything?" Ned stretched. "That would take a good bit of time."

"Then let's begin."

Marlowe sat down on a three-legged stool next to Ned. Gelis's wife sat nearby, stirring a pot over coals, doing her best to ignore the men. The sun was warm. Ned began to sweat.

"Who is Belpathian Grem?" Marlowe asked.

Gelis's wife lifted her head at the mention of that name.

Ned looked at the ground. "Who?"

"You know very well *who,*" Gelis snapped. "The King of the Weird Folk!"

Ned shook his head, smiling. "The *Weird Folk.* That's a children's story, isn't it?"

"Ned," Marlowe said calmly, "I think you know the man. I think you have worked with him."

"No," Ned responded, but a little too quickly.

"He told me to say good-bye to you," Marlowe pressed.

"Good-bye? Where's he going?"

"In the short term, he intends to deliver a certain manuscript to John Dee," Marlowe answered. "Gelis stole it from him and gave it to me. Grem stole it back again, and left me in the street. But in the long term, I have no idea where he's going. I was hoping you'd tell me."

"Just take Ned to the Tower, Marlowe," Gelis muttered. "Have done with him."

"Wait," Ned said quickly.

Marlowe looked up at Gelis. "Or I could cut out his tongue. Put an end to his livelihood."

Gelis's wife stood and glanced once, in disgust, at the men, then returned to her cart.

"I could not be certain, of course, but I might know the man you mean," Ned said at once. "Under all that hair and madness, I may have detected one Robert Armin. And if that is true, he would be going anywhere that would pay him. He's more mercenary than actor, in my opinion."

Marlowe's head flew back. "I knew it!"

"Who is Robert Armin?" Gelis asked.

"He was, until recently, apprentice to a goldsmith," Marlowe answered. "But Tarlton himself has taken Robert under his wing."

"The very man," Ned affirmed.

"I don't understand," Gelis said. "Are you talking about the clown Richard Tarlton, the Queen's favorite jester?"

"Yes," Marlowe told him, "and this man Robert Armin is now Tarlton's protégé. I have heard gossip of it. He's an actor, not a king."

"But the stories about him," Gelis protested. "I heard them in the Netherlands, in Higher Germany; all over France."

"And have you heard tales of The Queen's Men in such places as well?" Ned asked.

"I believe what Ned is trying to say," Marlowe announced, "is exactly what I suspect: these so-called Weird Folk are, in fact, a traveling company of actors. A troupe whose metaphysical realities confound and baffle everyone everywhere."

"Aye," Ned confirmed. "And Robert Armin is better than most at delivering the eeriest of goods."

"Except that I have seen Robert Armin perform," Marlowe demurred, "and that man Grem is not at all like the clown I saw."

"He's well costumed and wigged," Ned objected.

"Or," Marlowe offered, "you could be lying."

"That's what actors do for a living, isn't it?" Gelis asked.

"I would argue the contrary: theirs is the only profession that requires absolute honesty," Marlowe countered, "but not everyone agrees with me."

Gelis took in a deep breath and gazed at the green fields all around, bathed in golden sunlight.

"What is real, and what is theatre?" he asked.

"I seldom tell the difference betwixt the two," Ned confessed.

"But to what purpose?" Marlowe asked. "Why would Ned lie about this?"

"And what could be the aim of such odd behavior on the part of the alleged Belpathian Grem?" Gelis added.

"These are only a few of the questions I mean to answer," vowed Marlowe, striding toward the horse given to him at Hampton Court, "before this week is done."

Every fiber of his being told Marlowe to find the imaginary King Belpathian Grem. But he knew what Walsingham would say: that the delivery of a manuscript to John Dee would not take precedent over the urgency of Chartley Manor. His first duty was to ingratiate himself to the false Queen Mary.

Imaginary King, False Queen—what odd characters we have in this play, Marlowe thought as his horse galloped northwest toward Stafford.

It would be a good day's ride; he'd not see the manor house until the next morning if he alternated between trotting and walking his horse. The packet Walsingham had given him would see to his bed and board, but gaining Mary's confidence would be a strange bit of theatre. It would require a good story. And since the best stories were the truest, in some fashion or other, Marlowe began to concoct a narrative out of his experience in Delft, and his encounter with the assassin Gérard, whose first name was Balthazar, and so might be linked to Kyd.

Then, without any warning, Marlowe suddenly knew who had killed Leonora.

Antony Babington had been in Delft, was probably in league with Gérard and Mary, and had returned to England around the same time that Leonora and Marlowe had come home. Had Babington gotten word of Leonora's involvement in Delft, and knowledge of Gérard and the greater plot against the Queen? And if he had, might that have led him to murder Leonora before returning to London—or to Chartley?

Babington killed Leonora.

That would have a kind of horrible clarity. It would also mean that Babington would be waiting to kill Marlowe too. So if Babington had gone to Chartley, the waters there would be even more difficult to navigate.

A little like having an incapacitated rudder, Marlowe thought.

Gain Mary's confidence without revealing himself to Babington. That would take some doing.

Or, if Babington walked with a limp, perhaps the path would be clear: strangle the man as he had done Leonora.

But that could not be done before evidence of his complicity with Mary had been obtained, if such evidence existed.

How to proceed?

Day declined, and wore on into evening. The moon rose and the stars winked; Marlowe rested and watered his horse, ate several oatcakes, and tried not to let himself be overcome by the impulse to revenge. It proved a difficult battle.

Riding on until dawn, the landscape turned hilly; here and there the trees betrayed a leaf or two of red or gold. It would be an early autumn, and a hard winter. Deer began to appear among the bracken and birch. Nightjar, brambling, yellowhammer, and bullfinch all crowded the trees, announcing the rising of the sun.

As he slowed his horse again, thinking to take a moment's rest, he saw three young girls picking lingonberries, a certain sign of the early fall season.

"Hello," he called out genially.

They all stopped what they were doing and looked up.

"Would you know how much farther it is to Chartley Manor from here?" he asked.

One of the girls giggled, but another took a bold step in Marlowe's direction.

"You're on your way to that cursed castle, then?" she asked, lifting her chin in his direction.

Her plain brown dress was pulled tightly around her slender waist, and her red hair was alive in the morning breeze.

"It's cursed?" Marlowe asked, smiling.

"For these three hundred years," she assured him. "It was in the month of May, and Robert de Ferrers, who lived in that castle, was losing the battle of Chesterfield. A black calf was born at Chartley then, and from that day to this, whenever there's a black calf born there, evil follows in its wake."

"I see," Marlowe said, failing to keep the amusement from his voice.

"You don't believe me," the girl said defiantly. "But heed this list: the 7th Earl of Ferrers, the Countess de Ferrers, their son, Viscount Tamworth, his daughter, Lady Frances Shirley, and his second wife. They *all* died following the birth of a black calf on the property. Why do you think the castle was abandoned?"

Then Marlowe recalled what Leviticus had said: "Chartley used to be a real castle. Then it was abandoned."

"As luck would have it," Marlowe told the girl, "my name is not de Ferrers. But I can see that you are a true and honest woman, and I do not doubt your word."

That seemed to satisfy her. She held out her hand.

"Lingonberries?" she asked.

"I think I'll break my fast at Chartley," he answered.

"You won't be there 'til afternoon," she warned.

"I won't be hungry for a while now," he assured her, leaning forward on his horse, "because I'll be well-fed by the memory of your red hair."

With that he was off, but the girl stared at his receding image until he had vanished over the hill and far away.

NINETEEN

Hours later, Chartley came into view, and Marlowe saw why it had been chosen for Mary's prison. In addition to the fact that its current owner, Robert Devereux, was a trusted friend to Elizabeth, the place did, indeed, have a moat. That would serve many purposes. It would be harder to get in except by the front gate. The royal laundry could be done without anyone leaving the grounds (eliminating serving women as couriers). Most devious of all: Mary hated the damp—a widely known but odd trait in a Scots woman—and the moat would insure seeping gloom, moss on the walls, and a generally soggy atmosphere. Walsingham was not above petty torment.

Marlowe found himself likewise tormented by thoughts of Penelope Devereux, Robert's sister, and one of the most beautiful women in England. She was unhappily married to Robert Rich, in love with the poet Philip Sidney, and occasionally amenable to the attentions of one Christopher Marlowe, who perennially longed to see her, despite her part in an attempt on the Queen's life only a year earlier.

She had lived at Chartley, but Marlowe knew she would not be there now. His heart quickened all the same. Strange, he thought, that when you loved someone, you also loved the places they had been, the objects they had touched.

Upon reflection he realized that if he truly loved her, he must therefore love all things, because it was quite possible that she had touched that blade of grass, or this stone on the road—that she had walked through all the fields one day. That, in turn, meant that she was everywhere, so he would, after all, see her there, if only in his mind's eye.

These thoughts were doubly painful for Marlowe because Philip Sidney was married to the other woman whom Marlowe loved most, Frances Walsingham. And everything about Sidney was irritating: he'd gotten both the women Marlowe wanted, he was widely regarded as the model of a courtly gentleman, and his renown as a poet was unsurpassed. It would be very easy to hate Philip Sidney.

Distracted by such thoughts, Marlowe nearly forgot the part he was to play at Chartley. As he ascended the hill toward the manor house and moat, he went over Walsingham's strategy once more in his mind.

He was to be a messenger from Anthony Paulet, Lieutenant Governor of Jersey and son of Sir Amias Paulet, Mary's harsh jailor. The message was simple: the son needed the father. As planned by Walsingham, Sir Amias would leave the manor house, though not for Jersey as he would tell everyone. He would only travel twelve miles down the road, to sequester himself at Tutbury Castle, Mary's previous prison.

Left relatively alone, Marlowe would reveal himself as Mary's secret ally, offering to aid her in whatever way she saw fit—possibly to communicate with her supporters in France or Spain.

It would have to be done subtly, and quickly. Mary was not a fool. But she was a captive: miserable, desperate, and damp. The plan might work.

In no time Marlowe's horse was approaching the bridge across the moat. To his left he was surprised to see empty ale barrels stacked neatly in a frame. Perhaps Sir Amias Paulet was not so strictly Puritanical as his reputation would suggest.

Marlowe was admitted to Chartley brusquely, and was taken in silence to Paulet's office. It was lit by a single taper and empty save for a tall wooden desk behind which the man stood.

"Ah," was all that Paulet would say as Marlowe was ushered in.

He was an austere presence in a barren room. A severe black cap covered his close-cut hair, but a thick full blond mustache occupied the majority of his face. He wore around his neck a blue sash from which hung a bobble of some significance unknown to Marlowe.

"Sir Amias," Marlowe began.

"Hush," Paulet commanded.

Marlowe knew that the man was a fanatical Puritan. Apparently his general demeanor was equally stern.

"Walsingham's plan is clear," he told Marlowe in clipped tones. "There is no need to gild the lily."

Marlowe stifled a smile. Paulet, though he probably didn't know it, was misquoting a line from Thomas Kyd.

"The deception might be aided," Marlowe suggested, "if you ushered me into Mary's presence yourself, allowing your disdain to show itself."

Paulet glared. "Do you imagine that I have not displayed my disdain for this woman in our every encounter?"

"I meant, sir," Marlowe answered, avoiding eye contact and stifling a grin, "your disdain for me—or for the character I am to play in this matter."

Paulet coughed once. "That, sir, will be very easy to do. I am not in favor of these stratagems, to be frank. I loathe the theatre in any form, but most especially when it is applied to real life. I would rather cut off Mary's hands. That way she could write no more letters, and she would be encouraged to tell us all of her vile secrets."

"I fear that Her Majesty Queen Elizabeth would not think well of mutilating her own cousin," Marlowe said calmly. "Mary is a member of the royal family. The sort of extreme measure you suggest sets a bad precedent for the family, don't you think?"

Paulet gave out with a low, guttural growl, but said nothing.

"Shall we, then?" Marlowe continued.

Without a word Paulet snatched a taper from his desk, strode to the door, and threw it open.

"Guards!" he bellowed.

Two men, swords in hand, appeared instantly.

Paulet turned his head but did not look at Marlowe.

"This way," he muttered.

Marlowe followed him, and the guards, down a narrow stone hallway. There were no torches, and Paulet's taper did little to illuminate the gloom. Water seeped from the stones, moss grew, and rats did not bother to scurry away.

At length they arrived at an iron door. Marlowe was surprised that no guards stood by. He soon learned why.

Paulet produced three keys. The first was thrust into an opening in the middle of the door which made a series of clanking noises before opening. The lock was an intricate system of gears, something that could not be picked. And when it opened, another door was revealed, this one made of iron bars set so closely together that it would be difficult to slide a piece of paper between them. The second key unlocked that door, which slid upward into its recess in the gray stone ceiling. Once it was gone, and the taper held up, Marlowe was baffled. There was nothing but a stone wall in front of them.

Paulet turned to Marlowe.

"As I took Mary into this place, I showed her these three doors." Paulet smiled, revealing black and yellow teeth. "And I made a great show, with much noise, of closing them and locking them when I left her. In this manner, I robbed her of all hope."

With that Paulet's third key, a wide metal paddle, was inserted between two stones in the wall. That wall began to rumble. Then it opened, very slowly, inward, moving on hidden, rusted iron hinges. Mary's rooms were revealed.

The first room was a kind of sitting room, windowless and fetid. There was a fireplace, but no fire. The damp cold assaulted Marlowe; he felt it seep past his clothes, onto his skin, and into his bones.

Mary sat in a stern wooden chair, all square angles devoid of comfort. She was trying not to show it, but she had rushed to the chair when she'd heard the first door open. She wanted to appear calm and royal when the men entered. It was a brave, sad attempt: she only seemed weak and desperate.

Her blue dress was a little too big for her frame, and her eyes were a bit hollow, which told Marlowe that she had not been eating. Whether this was Paulet's design or her choice did not matter; she was sallow and thin.

"Madame," Paulet snorted, mustering a full measure of contempt, "my son is in need of my aid in Jersey. This *person*, who brought me my son's message, is to be in charge of your keep while I am gone. Oh, his name is Marlowe and he is Walsingham's man. As such he will torment you with tricks and schemes designed to gather evidence of your plot against our Queen. You are a vile creature. I hope you succumb to his wiles."

With that Paulet turned on one heel and headed toward the door.

Marlowe cursed under his breath. Paulet, vexed by Walsingham's plan, had deliberately sabotaged it by exposing it to Mary. This way he could report to the Queen that Marlowe—and Walsingham—had failed, and that further such theatrics were useless.

Marlowe momentarily considered taking a knife to Paulet. It would be easy. The two guards would be no problem, they would never expect Marlowe to attack in such a situation. But before he could decide exactly what to do, he was distracted by Mary's voice.

"Tell me your name," she said, her voice gravelly and low.

"It is, indeed, Christopher Marlowe, your majesty," he answered softly.

"Ah," was her only response.

Paulet stood impatiently at the door.

"Come along, sir," he said to Marlowe. "I must attend to my son, and you must not speak with this woman."

Marlowe hesitated. If he killed Paulet in front of Mary, she would be more inclined to trust him. And it would be very satisfying to kill the man and report his treachery to Walsingham.

But just at that instant, Paulet locked eyes with Marlowe, and Marlowe saw something in the man's demeanor that gave him pause.

"If you do not come away this instant," Paulet insisted, "I shall lock you in this room along with my captive! Then you may speak with her as long as you like!"

Confused by what he'd seen in Paulet's eyes, Marlowe stepped toward the door.

The guards stood by as Marlowe went out, back into the black hall. Moments later he was following them, and Paulet, back to the spare office. As they approached it, Paulet turned to the guards.

"Take our guest to his quarters," he told them, and then addressed Marlowe. "I have arranged for food and a bath, if you are so inclined."

"You told Mary our plan," Marlowe said.

"Yes," Paulet answered. "That should speed things along."

Marlowe tilted his head.

"I have been told," Paulet went on, his patience once again wearing thin, "that you are something of a swordsman. Are you unfamiliar with a simple feint within a feint?"

Thunderstruck, Marlowe realized what Paulet had done. Mary would have ways of finding out about Marlowe. She had been able to smuggle missives in and out of her prison. She would learn that Marlowe might be Walsingham's man. Paulet's gambit could actually assure Marlowe of greater trust: he would only have to tread carefully and admit to things that were true. His father had been a Catholic. He had been recruited by Walsingham. The trick of being a double agent is convincing the prey that some truths are lies, and all lies are true.

"You might have warned me what you were going to say," Marlowe said.

"No," Paulet answered. "The look on your face when I told Mary the truth? That look gave her something to think about. You would not have achieved that degree of surprise had I told you the idea beforehand."

"You have little faith in my abilities as an actor," Marlowe told him.

"What need for theatre," Paulet rejoined, "when we have true life?"

Marlowe thought of a dozen answers, and said none out loud.

Paulet handed Marlowe the keys to Mary's rooms.

"I won't stay away long," Paulet warned as he vanished into his office. "Be about your business quickly."

The door was shut.

Marlowe glanced at the guards.

"There was mention of food?" he said to them.

An hour later Marlowe was in his room, fed, bathed, and exhausted. He fell into a fitful sleep, a candle still burning on the table beside his bed.

Over and over in half-dreams he saw the River Rib and Leonora dressed in a black gown, her hands folded across her heart. He saw the raft against the opposite bank, and the fire rising higher around her body.

At length he threw himself out of bed and was happy to find pen and paper on a shelf in his room. He began to write.

> I walked along a stream, for pureness rare,
> Brighter than sun-shine; for it did acquaint
> The dullest sight with all the glorious prey
> That in the pebble-paved channel lay.

TWENTY

The rising sun the next day found Marlowe exploring the manor house. Every room was as sterile as Paulet's office. The kitchen, Marlowe's goal, was occupied by a single worker kneading bread. He was a gaunt, spider-like man in a spotless brown apron.

Never trust a thin cook, Marlowe thought.

"Morning," he mumbled to the man.

The man looked up from his work.

"Aye," he replied, "that it is."

"I wonder if I might find a boiled egg or an oatcake," Marlowe suggested.

The man stopped his work.

"Your name is Christopher Marlowe?" the man asked.

"Aye," Marlowe answered, smiling, "that it is."

"Your breakfast has been prepared."

With that the man turned and headed toward another door. Marlowe followed.

The door opened into a small dining room, possibly intended for servants. The table was set for one, but might have held a crowded ten. The ceiling was high and the timbers were entirely exposed. The walls were naked stone, further evidence that it was a room for servants, not guests.

"Ale?" the man asked.

"Yes, I saw all the empty barrels across the moat," Marlowe answered. "You have more?"

"Delivered every morning," the man said. "Shall I?"

"Yes, please," Marlowe answered, staring at the plate that had been set at the head of the table. It was heaped with what Marlowe considered a solid country breakfast: a large bowl of some sort of pudding, manchet with butter, and a plateful of boiled eggs.

"Is that goose blood pudding?" he asked, glancing down at the bowl.

At that the man's face brightened, but only slightly.

"Aye."

"I can guess the ingredients by the delectable smell," Marlowe boasted. "You strained the goose blood, mixed it with oats and warm milk. Then: pepper, nutmeg, sugar, salt, rosewater, and—coriander seeds. Beat in eggs, boil in cloth, and here we are."

"How does a London gentleman know the makings of a goose blood pudding?" the man asked, almost smiling.

"I wouldn't have any idea what a London gentleman knows," Marlowe answered, "I hail from Canterbury, son of a bootmaker."

"Well, you didn't name the suet, but otherwise you got it right, sir."

"Tell me your name," Marlowe said.

"It's Drake, sir."

"Well, Drake," Marlowe answered, taking his seat, "would you join me at the table?"

The man stood frozen for a moment.

"Never been asked to sit at table with a gentleman. Wouldn't know what to do."

"You could try eating," Marlowe suggested, picking up his spoon. "That's what I'm going to do."

"Oh I et my cakes three hours ago, sir. And served Her Majesty after that. I'm already on to making the rest of the daily fare."

"Of course," Marlowe responded, his mouth full. "This pudding is the best I've ever eaten."

"Well." Drake looked down. "Never been handed an affirmation such as that neither. This is a festival day."

At that Marlowe thought he heard something in the man's voice, a hidden irony or even a hint of defiance.

"I'll wager," Marlowe went on casually, "that Queen Mary herself did not have this fine a morning meal."

"Same as you exactly," Drake said at once.

Am I being too suspicious, Marlowe wondered, or did Drake answer me a beat too quickly?

"Well I know she welcomed this pudding," Marlowe went on. "Her rooms are a bit cold and this is very warming. It's a little early in the year to be so chilly in here, don't you think? It's really remarkable how you've kept my pudding this warm for three hours."

"Made her batch separate," Drake answered, and then winced.

He hadn't meant to say that.

"That explains it," Marlowe said, eyes on his plate.

"You'll excuse me, sir," Drake said quickly, "I'd best return to my labors."

"Of course. And many thanks. This is superior."

Drake vanished quickly back into the kitchen.

Marlowe's mind was racing as he wolfed down his food. His suspicions were absurd, and yet they stabbed at his brain like tiny knives.

As he was lifting his spoon to his mouth, he inhaled the faint scent of the rosewater in the pudding, and he froze. In that instant he was overtaken by a memory from childhood.

"Use one part white lead," Dr. Lopez said softly, "one part litharge, one tenth part oleander leaf, and one tenth part of black hellebore, cook the ingredients with sesame oil and rosewater. This mixture will be fatal in but a single day."

"This is about my father," the fourteen-year-old Marlowe said.

They stood in the Marlowe kitchen in Canterbury. It was after midnight, and everyone else in the house was asleep. Lopez had doffed his red cloak. Marlowe was in his nightshirt.

The kitchen was cozy, warm; it smelled of cinnamon. Marlowe and Lopez had been at this particular lesson since supper time.

"Yes." Lopez stretched. "Your father has been poisoned three times in the past five years. You need to learn poison from the inside. If you can kill a man with poison, you can save a man from its treachery. I teach you about poison in order to save your life. I won't always be here when it happens. And it will happen again. You must learn poison."

"No," Marlowe objected. "The cure is mostly the same: boil bark from a mulberry tree or some such in vinegar, then make the victim eat butter. He will vomit out the poison thereafter. That's not so much a cure—or a salvation—as it is a recantation, the way some sinners confess their indiscretions."

Lopez sighed. "You are too intelligent, and too Catholic. Both will prove to be obstacles for you in this world. Rid yourself of them if you can."

"I have rid myself of Catholicism by law," Marlowe answered, "but my brain will not seem to obey any equally urgent censure."

"Then you must learn poison to protect yourself," Lopez insisted. "Either way: these are lessons you will need. Now tell me, what is the most essential ingredient in the poison I have just mentioned?"

"Simple," Marlowe answered. "Rosewater."

"Why do you say that? Rosewater has no lethal properties."

"Its smell *hides* the lethal properties," Marlowe answered. "Treachery is the easiest thing in the world. It's keeping the poison hidden that's the trick."

Lopez leaned back in his chair. "There, do you see? You have a remarkable brain. It will cause you trouble all your life."

"Yours is the voice of experience in this matter, I presume."

Lopez smiled, a rare phenomenon.

"I can only hope that my own son, whom I may never see again," Lopez said softly, "has a mind like yours."

It was the moment Marlowe realized that he loved Lopez as much as he loved his own father.

"At any rate," Lopez said sternly, returning to his usual stern demeanor, "tomorrow night I will teach you how to detect a poison in food without having to taste it. For now: off to bed."

Marlowe stared down at his spoonful of goose blood pudding and felt a sudden churning in his stomach. He knew it was not caused by a lethal ingredient in his food, but rather by the poison of doubt.

Had Drake poisoned Queen Mary? Had Paulet instructed him to do so? It would be an excellent gambit: Paulet was gone; Marlowe had access to the royal cousin. Paulet's fanatical hatred of Mary would find its fruition in her murder, and Marlowe would be to blame.

He set down his spoon, rose from the table, and flew to his quarters to fetch the keys to Mary's rooms. Careful to avoid alerting guards or servants, he stole down the cold black hallway to the iron gate. First one key and then another failed to open it. Marlowe had a sudden fear that Paulet had deliberately given him the wrong keys until he realized that his own eagerness was to blame. He tried the first key again, only slowly, and the lock clicked at once.

A few moments later the final stone wall slid aside, and there sat Mary, at her dining table, attended by two serving women.

Marlowe stood at the door, staring.

"Mr. Marlowe?" Mary said.

"Your Majesty," he answered, "I pray you will forgive my clumsy entrance, unannounced, but I fear for your safety."

Mary stared at Marlowe for a moment, and then glanced sideways at the servants. They nodded and vanished.

"Approach," she told him.

Marlowe strode toward her, not bothering to close the barriers behind him.

"Have you finished your breakfast?" he asked as he drew near.

"No." Her face betrayed indignance.

"Good," he said quickly, "I fear you have been poisoned."

Her eyes widened. "Indeed?"

"May I examine your goose blood pudding?"

"Paulet would never dare assassinate me."

"He might," Marlowe said, "if he had me to blame for it. He is gone, and I am charged with your keep."

"Ah." Mary sat back and glanced at her bowl. "In truth, breathing is a bit difficult, but that may simply be indigestion. I do not care for this pudding, and the cook knows it."

Marlowe took the bowl and smelled it. The scent of rosewater was strong. He stuck his finger into the center of the mush and tasted it. He recognized the faint trace of oleander and hellebore. Grateful for the lessons learned from Lopez, he knew the poison at once.

He drew from his pocket a sturdy tin vial he'd guarded more as a keepsake than a tool. He wiped the spoon clean and poured it full from the vial.

"You must drink this at once," he said to Mary, "and then you may wish to excuse yourself. The effect is nearly immediate, and quite unpleasant, but it will save your life. I must tell you that this is a gift from a woman named Leonora Beak. It is she who saves your life. Quickly, now."

Mary stared at the spoon, then at Marlowe.

"How can I be certain of what is in that spoon?" she asked. "A clever man might invent a poisoned bowl as inducement to willingly taste his own venom. And you, Christopher Marlowe, are a very clever man indeed, as I have learned."

Ignoring the fact that Mary had somehow learned, perhaps, too much about him, Marlowe leaned closer to her.

"Bide awhile, then," he suggested. "You will soon begin to perspire, and to feel pains in your joints. Breathing will become much more difficult. Alas, by the time you realize that I am true in my effort to save you, it may be too late. The poison takes a day to kill, but past a certain point it is no longer in your stomach, but in your blood."

"I do not care for the manner in which you speak of the royal personage," Mary snapped.

"There will *be* no royal personage if you don't heed my advice within the next few moments!"

Mary shook her head. "I think not. Why would my jailor, and Walsingham's man to boot, want to save my life?"

Marlowe stiffened, and saw an opportunity.

"I am Walsingham's man in service to you, Your Majesty," he

whispered. "If you have learned anything about me and my family, you have discovered that we are Catholic, and secretly working in your cause."

Mary's eyes narrowed. "Indeed."

"I met, by night, with Babington in Delft, very recently. I am aware of your plans, and I have already been of some service to you. A certain manuscript, written in perfect code, has been delivered to John Dee."

Marlowe stared directly into Mary's eyes, giving support to his lie.

"I do not know of any such manuscript," Mary demurred.

"It comes from Rudolf, Philip's nephew," Marlowe answered, "and I think you do know of it."

Quite suddenly Mary twitched forward, and her face contorted.

"Ah," said Marlowe grimly, "the first torment of the poison."

Mary nodded.

Marlowe offered the spoonful of purgative once more.

"You may wish to be in your—in a more private chamber, Your Majesty," Marlowe warned.

Mary made it to her feet and took the vial from Marlowe's hand, careful not to spill the viscous liquid.

"You are not excused," she muttered as she exited the room, not looking back.

An instant later the servants appeared and cleared the dining table.

Two hours later Mary emerged from some other room. Her face was pale. She had changed her dress, and wrapped herself in a thick cloak.

"The cure may be worse than the poison," she said hoarsely.

"I thought just that the last time I saw it at work," Marlowe agreed.

"You have saved my life," Mary said emotionlessly, collapsing onto a cushioned seat.

"I'm glad you believed me," Marlowe rejoined.

"I did not believe you," she said. "I fed the pudding to one of the servants. When she sickened quickly, I believed the evidence. I'm afraid we've drained your vial dry."

She held the empty vessel out.

Marlowe was momentarily at a loss for words.

"Who is Leonora Beak?" the Queen of Scots asked. "You said her name."

"I said that this vial was hers," Marlowe answered, taking it from the royal hand. "She was a fierce companion, and an adept in the art of poisons."

"You must thank her for me," Mary said, closing her eyes and leaning back.

"She is dead."

"Well, then. To business: I know you are Catholic, and that you were in Delft. What do you imagine you might do for me now?"

Marlowe pocketed Leonora's vial.

"I can smuggle messages out of this prison," Marlowe told her. "And get messages to you from the outside."

She shook her head. "Been tried. Only succeeded once, and was discovered by Paulet. That is why I am no longer permitted visitors."

"I have a plan."

"And what, pray, is your plan, Mr. Marlowe?" she sighed wearily.

"I plan to drink ale."

Mary glared. "I fear my purge has adversely affected my hearing."

"I could not help but notice," Marlowe continued, "a preponderance of empty casks on the banks of the moat just before I crossed the bridge into this manor house."

"I find that ale warms me," Mary responded, "and the water here is foul."

"Yes. As you have discovered, any person might be searched as they leave this house, but few would think to break open an empty cask of ale."

"Insert my missives into one of them." Mary smiled.

"Mark it with a certain sign." Marlowe nodded. "Babington

already knows the sign. As arranged, his men come to collect the casks tonight, and answer on the morrow."

"That quickly?" she mused.

"They bring ale every day." Marlowe suggested. "And time is of the essence, is it not?"

"It might work." Mary closed her eyes.

Marlowe watched her face; saw the various considerations play across her features.

"Agnes!" she bellowed suddenly.

One of the serving girls appeared at once, presumably not the one who had been poisoned. She was smiling.

"Pen and paper," the Queen commanded.

Agnes flew away.

Within the hour several empty casks from Mary's rooms were delivered to the kitchen for disposal, and Marlowe had taken leave of the Queen of Scots.

He wended his way down dark corridors to the kitchen, hoping to see the casks delivered to the other side of the moat; and thinking he might observe Drake's response to the news that the Queen was alive, and in good health.

The kitchen was filled with the sweet smell of roasted onions, and Drake was lolling in a chair at the kitchen table when Marlowe sauntered in.

"Ah," he said, "Drake. Just the man I want to see."

Drake scrambled to his feet.

"Sir," he said stiffly.

"I was wondering if there was any blood pudding left," Marlowe began. "Couldn't get enough of it."

"Your batch is all et," Drake said, avoiding eye contact.

Marlowe leaned in and said, confidentially, "I wonder if there's any left from the first batch, the one you made for the Queen."

Drake took any a deep breath. "You don't want any of that, sir. It's invented for the royal palate, as it were."

"Yes," said Marlowe, backing away. "I know it was."

And Marlowe produced his knife.

"You thought to poison Queen Mary and blame her death on me," Marlowe said, half-grinning, "or more correctly, you were instructed by Paulet to do it."

"Aye," Drake answered calmly. "I was instructed by Sir Amias, but not to kill a queen. It was done at his behest in order that you might gain the confidence of the vile creature."

Drake turned a gaze upon Marlowe that was twice as intelligent as his demeanor would suggest.

"You're Walsingham's man," Marlowe guessed, still holding his dagger.

Drake nodded. "But my instruction is to watch Sir Amias, not Queen Mary."

"Paulet suggested that you poison Mary's breakfast?"

Drake nodded again, and failed to hide the hint of a smile.

"The idea was—what? To make me suspicious, hope that I got to her in time, and—are you insane? Any one of a hundred things might have gone wrong with this plan!"

"Aye," Drake admitted. "If things had not gone as planned, you would be a sacrificial lamb to Sir Amias Paulet's ambition. He would have used the event to embarrass Walsingham, and to consolidate his own position at court. And if things had gone well, as they appear to have done, he would be credited with a brilliant ploy that enabled Walsingham's plan for you."

"Oh." Marlowe lowered his weapon. "Good plan."

"Sir Amias has a certain guile that might rival Walsingham's," Drake said, "on a good day."

Marlowe glanced around. There were no ale casks in evidence.

"I was hoping for a spot of ale to go with my pudding," Marlowe offered casually, "but as I am suddenly put off that dish, I would settle for a drop of ale."

Drake moved at last.

"Just getting in a fresh supply," he said amiably. "Sent the empties out a moment ago, the new blood should be here tomorrow."

Marlowe sheathed his knife.

"Excellent," he said, smiling.

No point in telling Drake more than he needed to know, Walsingham's man or not.

Very early the next morning, Marlowe stood yawning in the empty kitchen watching the sun rise over the eastern moat. Two men in a cart rode up and began unloading casks of ale on the far bank. Marlowe grabbed a boiled egg and headed out the kitchen door, only momentarily regretting not having put on his rapier.

The morning air was crisp and a bit chilly for late summer. The men at the gate nodded to him as he strolled by.

"Thought I might slip out for a fresh bit of ale for myself," he said. "If I keep a cask in my room, I won't have to bother anyone else about it."

One of the guards smiled and nodded.

Marlowe ambled toward the men unloading the casks, heedless of the fact that he was not wearing his rapier. As soon as he was close he called out, "Morning!"

Both men jumped.

One of the men was standing on the cart. He turned toward Marlowe and sniffed. "What do you want?"

"Ale," Marlowe answered.

The man on the cart looked down. "Are you a servant of the house?"

Marlowe smiled. "I am in charge of the house, charge given me by Sir Amias, who is away for the moment. And who might you be?"

The man turned away, suddenly trying to hide his face. Only then did Marlowe realize that the man looked familiar. Where had he seen this man?

"I might be the man who makes this ale," he said, face averted.

"You might be," Marlowe said, "but you're not. You've been too busy in Delft."

The man lost his balance and nearly fell over, grabbing one of the barrels close by. The other man glared at Marlowe. The man on the cart turned around. There was a pistol in his hand. He hadn't fallen, he'd gone to retrieve his gun.

"I really wouldn't shoot me so close to the house," Marlowe admonished. "And if you hadn't reacted so severely I might not have realized that you were Sir Anthony Babington. But your lack of composure has given you away."

Babington smiled. "Here's your problem: I shoot you now, we load you onto the cart behind some barrels before anyone comes to see what the noise could have been. You're dead on a cart and I'm gone home to bed."

"I suppose." Marlowe shrugged. "But then how would Mary get her message from you?"

Babington lowered his pistol slightly. "What?"

"I am, you see, the clever person who invented the idea," Marlowe said, as if Babington were an idiot.

Babington only stared.

A quick study of the barrels revealed the one with Mary's mark. Marlowe pulled that one from the frame.

"This barrel," he said. "This message."

"I—I have no idea what you're talking about," Babington sputtered.

"You were a page boy in the Earl of Shrewsbury's household when it was Mary's jail. You have been her devoted servant since that time. I know this because my very Catholic father told me, and he never lies about such matters. Now get down off that cart; I have a few things to tell you and I don't want to shout."

Babington, momentarily at a loss, put away his pistol.

"I saw you in Delft," Marlowe went on. "I know you were there. And I know that you stopped by the Bell Inn on your way back to London after that."

Why not lunge boldly? Babington was slow. He'd been taken off guard. He suffered from the same malady as most aristocrats: arrogant ignorance. Was he simply too stupid to realize that his mere presence on the cart was evidence of his part in the plot against Elizabeth? And if he was that witless, he might betray his role as Leonora's murderer.

Babington at last descended from the cart and stood before Marlowe.

He stared Marlowe in the eye and said, "Good plan, hiding the messages in that barrel. Why are you doing this?"

Marlowe smiled back. "To see the rightful queen on the throne of England."

The best lies, he recalled Lopez saying, are the ones that are also true.

"And you intend to deliver this—this barrel to Mary," Babington went on.

"I do," Marlowe affirmed.

Babington, his eyes still locked with Marlowe's, smiled back. "Then I suppose you'd better be off with it. I didn't go to the Bell after I left the Netherlands, incidentally. I sailed from Monster directly to London. Why did you think I'd gone to the inn?"

But the other man who had come with Babington could not remain silent.

"Sir," he objected, "is this wise, letting this person take the barrel? Kill this gob, I say, and leave all them barrels for Drake like always. He'll see to it that Mary gets the right one."

Marlowe's smile grew. He turned to the man, a stocky tough in his mid-twenties, dressed mostly in leather.

"You're an idiot," Marlowe said, "and Drake is Walsingham's man. Honestly, you'll ruin this thing yet."

"I'm an idiot?" the man snarled.

With that he drew his rapier and swiped it through the air directly at Marlowe's head. Marlowe bent over, barely ducking under the blade. He appeared to collapse onto the ground. The tough leapt forward; Marlowe rolled. But as he did, he kicked his attacker at the knee, dislocating it. Then, in one continuous move, he got to his feet and threw his bulk against the attacker, shoulder first, knocking the man to the ground.

Marlowe stepped on the man's rapier. The man groaned, his left hand going to his wounded knee.

"You broke my bones!" he said.

"Your problem was that you *said* you wanted to kill me." Marlowe shrugged. "You should never announce that sort of thing. If you want to kill me, just do it, don't talk to me about it."

"Christ, my knee!" the man roared.

Marlowe glanced at Babington. "Do you want me to kill this man, or will you take care of him?"

Babington sighed. "Riley, do get on the cart."

The man passed out.

Marlowe shook his head.

"I do hope we shall meet again," Babington said. "Did you tell me your name?"

"I did not," Marlowe answered.

Without another word, Marlowe hoisted the message barrel onto his shoulder, and ambled back into the manor house. No need for anything further with Babington. He had doomed himself, he'd be dead soon enough. And Marlowe saw that he was telling the truth, saw it in the man's eyes: he hadn't gone to the Bell; he was not Leonora's killer.

Up in his room, Marlowe found his way into the false bottom of the keg where, as he had expected, there was a note.

The code was simple enough, and Marlowe broke it in under an hour. When he did, the letter read:

> First, assuring of invasion: Sufficient strength in the invader from the Netherlands, now that Wm. is dead. Ports to arrive at appointed, with a strong party at every place to join them within the week. Second, the deliverance of your Majesty: my own men will take Paulet's, and assure deliverance two days hence. Third, the dispatch of the usurping Competitor: only C.P knows the identity of the chosen assassin, but assurances are certain that he is someone at court, and close to the Royal Person. For the rest, rely upon my service. Your Lieutenants are in the

> Counties of Lancaster, Derby and Stafford: all fidelities taken in your Majesty's name.

Marlowe stared at the note as if it were a poisonous viper, and knew it must be seen by Walsingham with all haste. It confirmed an invasion through the Netherlands, making clear the reason for William's death. It assured Babington's role as key conspirator, the coordinator of the crime: it was written in his hand.

Two vital questions had to be answered. Who was C. P., the only man who knew the identity of the appointed assassin? And who were the lieutenants in Lancaster, Derby, and Stafford?

Marlowe lay the letter on his desk and set to work: copying Babington's hand and composing a substitute note for Mary's eyes. Something close enough to the truth to reassure her.

> First, as to invasion: Gérard has been eliminated, may have revealed our plans. Second, the deliverance of your Majesty must bide a while, Paulet's men are redoubled. Third, the dispatch of the usurping Competitor: only C.P knows the identity of the chosen assassin, but assurances are certain that he is close to the Crown. For the rest, rely upon my service. Another message, same method, anon.

That should further dampen her spirits, Marlowe thought.

He placed the new note into the false bottom of the cask and took it once again on his shoulder. Down the dark hallways and narrow stone corridors he arrived at Mary's prison rooms.

Locks clicked, doors opened, and at the last one Mary stood waiting, dressed in a thick green robe with gold brocade.

"I dared not hope for response so soon," she whispered, "but I can only assume you bring me a—a new cask of ale."

Marlowe nodded, setting the keg on the damp stone floor.

"I do," he assured her. "There is your mark."

She glanced at it.

"What does the note tell me?" she asked.

"No idea," Marlowe said, locking eyes with Mary. "I only know that the empty cask was taken last night, and returned full this morning. There may not be a note in it at all."

Mary held Marlowe's gaze for a moment too long, and then sucked in a breath.

"Agnes!" she snapped.

The girl appeared at once.

"There." Mary pointed at the cask.

The girl knew what to do. She took it up and disappeared into another room.

"Shall I wait?" Marlowe asked.

"I believe I would prefer my privacy," she answered. "You will return in two hours."

Marlowe nodded and backed away.

"Two hours, Your Majesty," he said, lowering his head.

Doors closed, locks ticked, and Marlowe was gone, nearly running down the halls toward the kitchen.

There he loaded a small pouch with a bladder of ale, half a dozen oatcakes, three boiled eggs, and an entire loaf of manchet, relieved that Drake was nowhere in evidence. He slipped the keys back on the servant's hook.

With that he was out the kitchen door and striding toward the stables. He would be in London by nightfall.

Mary sat in a hard wooden chair, holding the note high enough to catch a ray of morning sunlight from a window too high in the wall. She read it for the third time, and shivered.

A cup of ale sat untouched on the table beside her. Agnes stood nearby.

"I must have a fire," Mary said softly.

"Yes, Your Majesty," Agnes said slowly, "but if we burn our allotment now, there will be less this evening, and the nights are getting colder."

"I know." Mary's voice was hollow. "But I must have a bit of cheer and warmth just now. I'll take to my bed early, and add an extra blanket tonight."

Agnes curtsied and left the room, silently thanking God for the kitchen fire.

Another night sleeping on the kitchen table and breathing in the smoke, she thought, but at least it's better than freezing to death in my room.

As she lifted three meager logs from the small stack by the servant's quarters, she heard a sound so rare that it made her pause in her work. It was the sound, softer than a sigh, of royal tears.

TWENTY-ONE

LONDON

That same morning in London, in a small stone chamber filled with tables and herbs and burning torches, Belpathian Grem stood waiting. He cast his eye about the room, a maddening display of animal carcasses, deadly plants, thick books, loose papers, and magnifying glasses.

Without warning, John Dee burst into the room.

"Let me see it, let me see it, let me see it!" he shouted.

He was dressed in a strange purple garment and an elaborate black hat. A white ruffled collar framed his gray beard, but his eyes were a child's, wild with wonder as he took the manuscript from Grem's hand.

They made a strange pair, the mystic mage and the weird king. Grem was unwashed, still dressed in his knotted black clothes and bedecked with dried flowers. His normally spotless boots were city-worn, and smelled of London streets. His shaved head was a stark contrast to Dee's elaborate hat.

Dee was turning page after page of the wondrous manuscript.

"I only saw this once, you know," Dee said to Grem without looking up. "Rudolf let me hold it. I never wanted anything so much in my life."

"And now you have it," Grem said, "thanks to the King of the Weird Folk."

Dee glanced up. "Yes. King of the Weird Folk. Ah. You do know that I've seen you perform. On the stage. You're quite a gifted fool."

Grem's gaze did not waver.

"Right," said Grem, "but which is the ruse and which the truth?"

Dee paused. "I hadn't considered that. Good. Good trick, either way."

And he returned to his manuscript, hungry eyes devouring every letter and picture.

"What does it say, this book?" Grem ventured. "If you don't mind my asking."

Dee looked up once more, grinning, eyes alive with joy.

"I have absolutely no idea," he said.

Fancy that, thought Grem, me knowing something that the smartest man in England does not.

"Not a single one of these plants is known to me," Dee went on, "and I know all the plants of the earth. And these drawings of naked women in tubs and tubes? What could they mean? And look: a star chart! Is this not the most mysterious thing you have ever seen?"

Grem looked down at it, unmoved.

"I have seen so many strange things in this life," he told Dee, "that my ability to distinguish *awe* from *yawn* has been disabled, as it depends on such a paltry thing as an arrangement of vowels. I am left to wonder at nothing."

Dee lost his smile.

"Then you have my sympathies, sir," he said curtly. "Your life is devoid of any genuine joy."

"Not quite," Grem corrected. "I will be quite happy indeed when you cross my palm with the sum agreed upon."

Dee paused, sighed, and reached into a pocket in his arcane robe. He produced a rounded leather pouch.

"There, sir," he told Grem, "and I pray for your soul."

"Thank you, sir," Grem responded, "and I believe I will count your money before I leave."

The sun was going down behind the western horizon when Marlowe walked his horse over London Bridge. He remembered crossing the bridge with Lopez on his first trip to visit Walsingham, a lifetime ago.

Where was Lopez? What was more important than uncovering the plot against the Queen? Only then did it occur to him that Lopez had been his instructor in the art of poison, and Leonora Beak was clearly an adept at that art. She had wielded powders and potions the way a man might use a sword, and to equal effect. Was there a connection between the two? Had they only pretended to be strangers when they'd met at the Bell?

Puzzling out such thoughts, Marlowe arrived, through the secret back entrance, at the door to one of Walsingham's small conference rooms. Two familiar guards stood grimly watching him approach.

Before he was close enough to address them, young Leviticus appeared out of the shadows. He was dressed for court, a silver suit and black shoes, the heels nearly five inches, giving the boy a bit of extra height.

"Mr. Marlowe," he whispered. "You are not expected."

"I have in my possession something that Lord Walsingham must see immediately." Marlowe kept walking.

"I would like very much to tell you something before you go in there," Leviticus whispered more urgently.

Marlowe slowed and stared at the boy. "What is it?"

"Since your revelation to me that I may be the son of John Dee's new wife," the boy answered, "I have been observing Dee with great care. I think you should know something that no one else knows: he has purchased a manuscript from a fairy king!"

Marlowe stopped walking. "Why do you say this?"

"Because I've seen it all! Seen the fairy, and the manuscript. It is more wondrous than you can possibly imagine, with fairy writing and strange pictures of naked women!"

"And you have told no one?"

"I fear that John Dee may use the manuscript and its magic," Leviticus told Marlowe, "against me, or my mother—the woman I think is my mother."

"Do you know where the manuscript is now?"

"I do."

Leviticus was about to go on but Marlowe began walking again.

"Tell no one," he said to the boy. "I must speak with Walsingham on another matter, but I think it is related to your discovery. When the time is right, will you take me to the place where the manuscript is hidden?"

Leviticus nodded, eyes wide.

"Good." Marlowe stopped several feet from the guards at the door.

Leviticus instinctively took the horse's reins but otherwise did not budge.

"I have urgent need of Lord Walsingham," Marlowe said to both of the guards.

One nodded. "You're to go in. You may sit. His Lordship will be a while in coming."

With that the door swung open.

Marlowe glanced at Leviticus.

"Thank you for taking care of the horse," he told the boy. "I will see you before I leave."

Leviticus nodded solemnly and was off, leading the horse behind him.

An hour later Marlowe was jolted from his seat in Walsingham's conference room by a sudden sweep of the door.

Walsingham strode in, a small cup in his hand. His robe was black, as was his cap, and he was decked in his chain of office, the insignia of the Secretary to the Queen.

"Why are you here?" he demanded to know. "Who is watching Mary?"

Marlowe took a breath. "I am here because I have astonishing information, and your man Drake is watching Mary!"

Walsingham set down his cup and glared at Marlowe.

"Do you imagine that yours is a tone one takes with the Secretary to the Queen?"

"The matter is urgent!" Marlowe answered. "Invasion through the Netherlands within two weeks, Mary's liberation two days hence, and armies sympathetic to Mary's cause in Lancaster, Derby, and Stafford! I must show you this missive!"

Walsingham's face contorted. "Do you mean to say that you have a *new* communication between Babington and Mary?"

"Yes!" Marlowe insisted.

He reached into his doublet, produced two folded sheets of paper, and thrust them toward Walsingham.

"So soon," Walsingham muttered.

"I was able to gain Mary's confidence at once," Marlowe snipped. "The note on top is the coded message in Babington's hand, the second is my translation of it."

Walsingham read the translation quickly, then went over the original note very carefully.

"You left out the revelation that there is an assassin at court," Walsingham said softly, still staring at the page.

"My prayer is that you might know the identity of 'C. P.'"

Walsingham looked up.

"Charles Paget," he sighed. "You have heard me speak of him."

"Paget!" Marlowe realized. "He was involved in Throckmorton's attempt to murder the Queen."

"He vanished," Walsingham muttered, "but he had, as you know, an accomplice in court."

"Penelope," Marlowe said aloud before he could prevent the name from escaping his lips.

"Yes." Walsingham set the pages down on his desk. "One wonders if she might not have been so innocent as her words and demeanor protested."

"Why do you say that?" Marlowe asked.

"Because of her discontent with her husband, Robert Rich, and her simultaneous attentions from the poet Philip Sydney. She is a duplicitous woman by nature."

"Hating one man and being beloved of another is not an indication of duplicity," Marlowe protested. "It's the evidence of a passionate heart. You only speak this way because your daughter Frances is married to Sidney."

"And you only speak this way because you love Penelope."

"Penelope is no conspirator," Marlowe insisted.

"Because she is young and beautiful?" Walsingham shook his head. "Had we the time, I would argue that notion out of your head within the hour, but this business is of the utmost urgency. And so I must send you to Paget. I am told that he is in London as we speak. I will send word to Sir Amias that he is to double his guard at Chartley, and close the bridge across the moat. And how fares Queen Mary?"

"She is cold," Marlowe answered.

Walsingham's face betrayed the hint of a smile.

"There is another matter," Marlowe said quickly. "John Dee is in receipt of a coded communiqué from the Emperor Rudolf. I believe this means that John Dee is the assassin mentioned in Babington's note. He is at court and close to the Queen. He has access to many poisons, which subject has been greatly on my mind of late. And let us imagine that someone has discovered his wife's bastard son, Leviticus. Might that be used as leverage to encourage Dee?"

Walsingham nodded once. "I had considered that—all of it."

Of course you had, thought Marlowe; why else would you have set me on that path in the first place?

"Where is the communiqué?" Walsingham continued

"Here in Hampton Hall," Marlowe answered. "I believe it is hidden in Dee's laboratory, but as luck would have it, young Leviticus has knowledge of its exact location."

"Good. I will have Dee under constant surveillance from this moment forward. In the meantime, you must still meet with Paget. Under your continuing guise as a Catholic sympathizer to Mary's cause, you will needle from him the identity of the assassin—Dee or someone else."

Without another word, Walsingham strode toward the door.

Marlowe scrambled. "Where might I find Paget, then?"

Walsingham slowed but did not stop or turn around.

"I understand that he wears a distinctive red cap," he told Marlowe, "and is often found at the theatre."

TWENTY-TWO

The Curtain Theatre was crowded and noisy. Afternoon sun slanted perfectly, lighting the stage and warming the air. Marlowe was stunned to see no less than Edward Alleyn, the foremost actor of the day, take bare stage.

"There is beyond the Alps, a town of ancient fame," Alleyn began, "whose bright renown yet shines clear: Verona is its name. And there one Romeus, who was of race a Montague, upon whose tender chin, as yet, no manlike beard there grew, found Juliet, a Capulet by hap, whose beauty, shape, and comely grace, did so his heart entrap."

From there Lyly's play proceeded more or less in accord with Brooke's poem of the same name. And there was Ned Blank in the part of Romeus, upon whose chin, indeed, no manlike beard there grew.

Marlowe stood in the dirt and shadows at the back of the open theatre, along with a hundred other groundlings, his eyes searching the boxes that encircled them for a man in any sort of red hat. He considered going backstage, confronting Ned, but thought better of it. For all his faults and idiocy, Ned deserved this night: a chance to prove himself in a male role. How Ned had convinced Gelis to let him go—or how he'd escaped the Travelers' camp—was a puzzle not worth attention at the moment.

Marlowe turned his attention to the play, but only momentarily.

Alas, he thought, this play is as terrible as the poem had been. No good work of theatre will ever come of it.

The crowd at The Curtain was, as usual, wildly diverse: drooling drunken men, whores on holiday, children filching pockets, lovers stealing kisses. The boxes were filled with demi-royals and their impatient supplicants, willing to sit through anything on the chance that they might be taken to court the next day, or the day after that.

At last, in a box near the stage, Marlowe spotted a man in a red hat and pale green doublet, his beard too neatly trimmed, leaning forward, soaking in the language as if it were ale. He was not alone. Marlowe was not entirely surprised to recognize Thomas Morgan, dressed in dark blue with a patterned sash that made him foolish. Morgan had been in service to Lord Shrewsbury, Queen Mary's jailor before Paulet. Morgan's Catholic leanings soon encouraged Mary to use Morgan as her secretary and go-between. He was one of the reasons Mary's trust had been so easy for Marlowe to gain.

Good, thought Marlowe, making his way through the crowd toward the box. That will make it easier for me to engage them.

The first scene being over, Alleyn again took the stage as narrator. Marlowe was momentarily distracted by the beauty of Alleyn's voice, and his ability to transform mediocre words, spinning them into gold.

If I could convince him to be in *Dido*, Marlowe considered, that would put the play over. After I finish rewriting it, I should speak with him.

But further consideration of his own work was set aside as he drew near the box. Morgan noticed first, and alerted Paget.

Marlowe did not slow his pace, and kept his eyes directly on Morgan's.

Paget did his best to hide the fact that he'd drawn a dagger.

"I have news of a caged bird," Marlowe whispered as soon as he was close enough. "Yesterday I was at Chartley."

Paget stayed his hand for a moment.

"Our holy salvation was poisoned," Marlowe went on, clutching the rim of the low wall that separated the box seats from the standing ground. "I was there, and saved her life."

Let them check that story, Marlowe thought. They'll see it's true.

"No idea what you're talking about," Paget said, his lip curled. "And you're destroying my enjoyment of the play."

Without warning Marlowe hoisted himself over the gallery wall and landed in the box beside Morgan, his knife under Morgan's chin.

"I think the playwright has already succeeded in that," Marlowe told Paget.

Both men froze.

"Now if you'll put your blade away, Mr. Paget," Marlowe said softly, "I'll take a seat and tell you my news from Chartley. Or I can just slit Morgan's throat and be on my way. Alerting our true queen, Mary, of your obstinacy, of course."

"We've had no news at all from Chartley," Morgan objected, his breathing labored.

"I told you it happened yesterday." Marlowe shook his head. "You may hear of it tomorrow, or the next day. But that will be too late for our purposes. Time is our enemy. Walsingham knows."

The two men exchanged a glance.

"Walsingham knows what?" Paget asked.

"Well," Marlowe snapped, "I see I've come to the wrong men."

He turned to leave through the door of the box.

"Who are you?" Morgan demanded.

Marlowe turned, glaring at the men. "There will be no invasion through the Netherlands. Gérard has given up that secret, his elimination of William was in vain. Walsingham has already sent troops to Lancaster, Derby, and Stafford. Our only hope is to send in the assassin today, before Walsingham finds him out. But I could not find him myself this morning, and so I thank you, gentlemen, you have succeeded in destroying *all* our plans."

With a flourish, Marlowe turned to leave, hoping that the onslaught of information had sufficiently stunned his audience of two.

"Wait," a panicked Paget whispered harshly. "I know where Sidney is!"

Marlowe froze. He dared not turn around to face the men, afraid that his eyes would betray him.

"Is that a fact?" Marlowe answered, his back to the men.

"Where he always is, at this time of the afternoon," Morgan said eagerly. "In Lady Rich's London home."

Marlowe forced all emotion from his eyes, and turned about.

"Lord Rich is at Warwick, on the Avon River, you see," Paget said.

"And so, of course, Philip Sidney is with Penelope," Marlowe said coldly.

"She spurns his affection, they say," Morgan reported, "but he goes to her every day nonetheless. He'll be there now."

Marlowe lowered his chin. "You may just have saved our queen."

Not realizing what Marlowe truly meant, both men smiled.

Behind them on the stage, Ned was addressing the audience as dancers swirled behind him.

"Juliet," he said, his voice breaking, "does seem to pass the rest as far as Phoebus's shining beams do pass the brightness of a star!"

And on the other side of the stage, a boy only two years younger than Ned, in white makeup and a pale dress, his Juliet voice high and sweet, sang out: "At last my floating eyes have anchored fast on him, who for my sake does banish health and freedom from each limb."

Marlowe willed his legs to walk, his lungs to breathe. But his mind objected to every thought it had, and every image it saw. He did not care for Sidney, but he found it impossible to believe that Sidney would murder Elizabeth. Then, worse, he imagined Sidney and Penelope in each other's arms, swimming in a white sea of bedsheets and sunlight.

At last he stopped, leaned against a wall, and closed his eyes.

Even in broad daylight, life on the wrong side of the Thames was questionable. Cutpurses wended through the crowded streets. Drunken men with clubs and daggers lumbered from one libation to the next. Whores with blood-red lips and missing teeth cajoled each man who came their way.

But Marlowe felt safer there, a hundred feet from the theatre, than in the finer climes at court, or in the home of Sir Robert Rich, where treachery wore a better disguise.

He knew the Rich household; he'd passed it a dozen times whenever he was in London, hoping to catch a glimpse of Penelope. He never had.

He knew he must hurry, and yet he found it impossible to move.

Philip Sidney could not possibly be an assassin in favor of Queen Mary.

It must be someone masquerading as Sidney. That was it. Someone had deceived Paget and Morgan.

But Penelope would know. She would not be deceived. That would mean she was a party to the plot, somehow. She had not learned her lesson. She still thought it possible to revenge herself against Elizabeth.

Rash, unthinking madness propelled Marlowe forward, through the crowd. He knew he must report to Walsingham at once, but he wasn't going to do it. As he rushed toward the bridge, he whispered a silent prayer: let me find an imposter in Rich's house.

Across the bridge, through tamer streets, in the direction of Hampton Court, but not too near it, he soon found himself in front of the home he had seen so many times before.

Still seized by an unnatural absence of logic, he pounded on the door.

A startled, indignant servant answered, scowling.

Marlowe pushed past him, bursting into the hall.

"I have an urgent message for Philip Sidney," he snapped.

The servant, dressed in black, lifted his chin and sneered, "Sir Philip is not here."

"The message is from Walsingham," Marlowe answered, his eyes narrow.

The servant was momentarily mute.

"Which is Lady Penelope's bedchamber?" Marlowe demanded.

And to give his demand meaning, he drew his dagger.

The servant's face went white. "Top of the stair, turn right, third door on the left. But she's not there!"

Marlowe raced up the stairs, not sheathing his blade. His heart pounded as he opened the door and pushed it in.

Empty.

Marlowe spun around and ran down the stairs.

"Where is she?" he shouted.

"In the garden," the servant answered, pointing. "It's past the kitchen."

Down the stairs, through the house, instinct and smell leading him to the kitchen, Marlowe plunged past cooks and startled maids, out the door to the kitchen garden, though a rounded iron gate into the more formal area.

There, on a stone bench, sat Penelope. Kneeling beside her was a man, his back to Marlowe. In a flash, Marlowe knew what to do.

When Penelope saw Marlowe racing toward her, she shrieked and stood.

The man turned his head.

An instant later there was a rapier in the man's hand and he was standing in front of Penelope.

Marlowe stopped short, breathing hard, his face red.

"Sidney," he whispered.

"Marlowe?" Sidney answered. "Christopher Marlowe?"

"I have been begging Philip to leave me," Penelope piped, "but he will not, no matter what I say."

"She fears the brute Rich," Sidney growled defensively. "She loves me."

"I do not!" she protested.

"She loves me," Marlowe gasped between breaths, bent slightly at the waist.

Sidney lowered his rapier slightly.

"Is—is that true?"

"I love him more than *you*," she said.

"Will you give me a moment?" Marlowe asked Sidney. "I've just run all the way from The Curtain and I'm a bit out of breath."

"Is it still *Romeus and Juliet*?" Sidney asked, lowering his blade completely.

Marlowe nodded.

"Terrible," Sidney complained.

"Ghastly," Marlowe agreed.

"Why have you run here?" Penelope wanted to know.

Marlowe drew in a deep breath and stood upright.

"I was there with Paget and Morgan," he said carefully, watching Sidney's eyes.

Sidney did not move or speak.

Marlowe let the silence be his ally. It only took a moment for Penelope to break.

"He knows!" she whispered to Sidney. "And he's Walsingham's man. He's the one who found me out at court, before."

"Are Paget and Morgan dead?" Sidney asked slowly.

"Not unless the second act killed them," Marlowe said. "They were alive when I left the theatre. I ran here to bring you an urgent message from them."

"Really." Sidney glared. It wasn't a question.

"Mary has been poisoned at Chartley," Marlowe said quickly. "You will hear that news shortly, I am certain. I saved her. But our plans must be accelerated. Time is our enemy."

"You attempt to convince me that you are not Walsingham's man," Sidney said.

"I am Walsingham's man," Marlowe told him, "in order that I might serve our true Queen Mary."

Here's the tipping point, Marlowe thought. If Sidney is not the assassin, now is when he will attempt to take me to Walsingham as a traitor.

Sidney sat down on the bench. Penelope backed away, looking back and forth between Sidney and Marlowe.

In that moment Marlowe tried to understand why he had been so rash, why he'd raced straightaway to confront Sidney.

Had he done it because he was truly in love with Penelope? Or had he wanted to prove to himself that Sidney could not possibly be the murderer? Or had he simply wanted to conclude the matter of the Queen's assassin so that he might return to a more personal task: finding Leonora's murderer?

Before any decisive answer presented itself, Sidney spoke.

"You and I, Marlowe, should repair to the nearest public house and drink." He turned to Penelope. "Would you, my love, send to our man at Chartley with great haste to see if what Mr. Marlowe has told us is, in fact, true?"

"No need to go that far," Marlowe called out. "Just ask any of your people inside Hampton Court what news has come from Chartley this day. That way you and I won't have to spend all night and tomorrow in a pub. I need sleep, not drink."

Penelope answered before Sidney could stop her.

"I'll speak with Daphne within the hour," she promised. "She knows everything."

Marlowe stared at Penelope's face. Words from one of Sidney's sonnets about her came into his head: "Stella's image, wrought by Love's own self . . . not only shines but sings."

"There," Marlowe said, at last sheathing his blade.

"No matter what you say," a stunned Sidney said, "I need a drink."

"Well, maybe just one," Marlowe allowed. "Where shall we go?"

"The White Gull," Sidney sighed. "It's near The Theatre, and dark."

"I'll send my man Tolbert to see you there the moment I hear anything," Penelope said quickly. "Now go, both of you!"

Marlowe and Sidney exchanged glances that were at least partially sympathetic.

Ten minutes later, they were sitting in a corner of The White Gull, ale in hand, leaning forward and speaking low. The entire place was only forty square feet, and lit by a single torch above the bar. There were a dozen other men in the place, mostly alone, all drinking. No food was offered, but the ale was stronger than most, and flavored with ivy and juniper.

An hour later, Sidney had finished ten tankards of the stuff.

"You must understand that I do what I do for her," Sidney whispered harshly.

"Whereas my Catholic father encourages my actions," Marlowe said in complete honesty.

The best lies, Lopez always said, are the ones that are also true.

Sidney's head drooped. "I am desolate."

"Yes," Marlowe commiserated. "Penelope has that effect."

"She doesn't love Rich."

"No," Marlowe agreed, "she hates him. And the Queen forced the marriage."

"That's right," Sidney agreed, his voice already slurred by the strong drink. "That's right!"

Marlowe pretended to sip, and then set his mug down. His brain raced.

"Can we discuss the new plan," he said to Sidney. "That way, when you discover that I have told you the truth, we will not have wasted this time?"

"The new plan?" Sidney asked, looking up.

"Well, we don't have time to wait for your original attack, do we?"

"I suppose not." Sidney gulped his brew. "My audience is over a week away, though I have already sent her the manuscript."

Instinct, calculation, and guesswork collided in Marlowe's brain, and he heard himself say, "You have presented Her Majesty with—what was it, your manuscript?"

"A new version of my masque, *The Lady of May,* rededicated to Elizabeth." Sidney's voice sounded hopeless. "To be performed for her in early autumn, or sooner, I had hoped. That's what we were to discuss in my audience with her."

"You have been driven to distraction by Penelope Rich," Marlowe said grimly. "And you ignore your own wife, a brave and wild companion."

"Frances," Sidney choked. "She has no feeling for me whatsoever."

"No?" Marlowe could not prevent a slight smile touching his lips. "Small wonder. Lord Walsingham secured the marriage, not Cupid."

"I haven't seen Frances since May," Sidney went on miserably.

An entire play broke out in Marlowe's mind. He watched images of Frances at the bottom of a cell in Malta, naked in a tub on a ship, sleeping in a field in France—a hundred other scenes of her as they fought their way back to England. And his yearning for her company suddenly threatened to overwhelm him.

Then, without warning, he realized that the face he saw in the visions was shifting. Frances's face became Leonora's.

With a sudden start he realized that he did not love Frances, or Leonora. Not in any romantic way. He loved them both as he would a man. He loved their boldness, their bravery, their skill—he loved the spirit of the person, not the face, or the form.

He was jolted from his realization by Sidney's drunken voice.

"What occupies you so completely?" Sidney asked. "Your face is a map of confusion and—I cannot tell what else."

"Something has just happened to me," Marlowe answered in wonder.

"What is it?" Sidney leaned forward.

"I think I am becoming a man, a true man. I may not be a boy any longer."

Sidney shook his head a little, trying to clear it.

"What?" he mumbled.

"I said—"

Before Marlowe could finish, he saw Penelope's servant, Tolbert, slip through the front door and cast an eye about. It took a moment for his eyes to adjust to the darkness, but he found the corner table at last, and steered for it.

He arrived at the table, clearly uncomfortable.

"I am to say only this: it is true." He clearly hated his role as carrier pigeon.

Sidney waved his arm grandly. "I already knew that. Marlowe and I have become bond kinsmen."

"Please tell Penelope to do nothing further," Marlowe instructed Tolbert. "It's too dangerous for her. She is to stay in her home. Yes?"

Tolbert nodded curtly.

Sidney looked up. "Will you take her a message from me as well?"

"Be off," Marlowe entreated Tolbert. "Sir Philip is in his cups."

One look told Tolbert that Sir Philip was, indeed, beyond his capacity. Without another word, Tolbert turned and sped away.

"Tell her I love her!" Sidney cried out.

A few of the men in the pub laughed. All the rest hung their heads; one nodded profoundly.

Marlowe stood up.

"We must get you to safety," he whispered to Sidney.

Helping Sidney to his feet, Marlowe steered toward the front door.

"Where are we going?" Sidney managed to ask.

"I know a certain hidden room at Hampton Court," Marlowe answered. "No harm will come to you there."

Some lies, Marlowe thought, are, in fact, the *opposite* of the truth.

But Sidney nodded, agreeing to go, and leaned on Marlowe as if he were leaning on his last true friend.

At The Curtain Theatre, the sun had gone and the show was over. Paget and Morgan sat whispering to each other as the last of the crowd dissipated. Ned Blank, in his street clothes, his face washed of makeup, ambled toward their box. When they saw him coming they stopped talking.

"Well?" Ned asked.

Morgan sipped in a breath.

"I thought you were quite believable as a man," Paget smirked.

"Bite my bollocks," Ned responded politely.

"We've had a visitor," Morgan said softly.

"Sorry?" Ned responded.

"Christopher Marlowe," Paget added.

"Christ!" Ned exploded. "That bastard will ruin my career yet!"

"You misunderstand," Morgan said. "He's just come from Chartley. He saved Mary's life. He's one of us."

"Says who?" a voice from the shadows called out.

Everyone turned in the direction of the commanding voice, and the rotund, slovenly figure of Thomas Kyd ambled into the fading light beside the box.

"Well, well," Ned sneered. "Come to steal a few lines from Lyly, have you?"

"I came to see your debut as a man, Ned," Kyd answered grandly. "I'm sorry I missed it."

"Got here too late for the show, did you?" Ned asked. "Was it an extra ale or a little boy that kept you?"

"Oh you misunderstand," Kyd said, smiling. "I saw the whole show, the whole wretched show—I'm still waiting for your debut as a man."

Ned growled and drew a small silver dagger.

Kyd's smile widened. "You know better than to point that thing at me, *boy.* I'll cut off your hand."

The last of the crowd was gone. Kyd drew nearer.

"Now, you were saying," Kyd went on, "that Marlowe saved Mary's life?"

Paget and Morgan nodded.

"He told us," Morgan said.

"If he says so," Kyd allowed, "then it's true. In general he's a great one for truth. But if he did save Mary's life I can assure you that he did it in service to Walsingham. He's not one of us. Not even a little bit."

"Why would he save Mary's life," Ned began, irritated beyond reason, "if he's not on our side? If she's dead, that's an end to it!"

"He saved her life, imbecile, to gain her confidence so that he might ferret out conspirators. You didn't tell him anything, did you?"

Kyd eyed Morgan and Paget.

"Nothing he didn't already know," Paget said indignantly.

"Christ." Kyd rubbed his eyes. "What did you say?"

"We just—we just told him where Sidney was," Morgan stammered.

Kyd froze for a moment. The smile left his lips.

"Gentlemen," he said to Paget and Morgan, "I no longer care what you know or say about my private life. You cannot hurt me now, I see that. You're too stupid to know what to do. So I divorce myself from you *and* your cause as of this moment. Ned, you're my witness. I no longer have anything to do with this affair. If these idiots don't realize they've been duped by a college boy, they won't have much sway any more. And so: adieu."

With that Kyd turned very delicately and vanished, once again, into the shadows.

Marlowe stood in Walsingham's smaller office, shifting his weight impatiently from one leg to the other. He felt he'd been waiting for hours, though only moments had passed.

Sidney was in a nearby closet, a small room with no tables or chairs. Incapable of staying on his feet, he'd sunk to the floor, his head rolled backward. Marlowe found a guard to stay at that door, and then sent word for Walsingham.

At last Walsingham burst into the room. His aspect was more disheveled than Marlowe had ever seen it.

"Why do you have Philip Sidney in a guarded room?" he demanded.

"Impossible though it may be to believe," Marlowe answered carefully, "Philip Sidney is the assassin."

Walsingham shook his head. "You have been misinformed."

"Paget and Morgan gave him away," Marlowe said firmly. "Then Penelope Rich confirmed it. And finally, Sidney himself admitted it to me. He has an audience with Her Majesty in a few days. He says he wants to persuade our queen to allow the presentation of a revised version of some masque written in her honor. He may have intended to work his treachery then, during this audience, or he may have planned to somehow incorporate murder into the masque."

Walsingham closed his eyes.

"I am rarely surprised," Walsingham admitted. "How is it that I have not seen this?"

"Because," Marlowe answered without thinking, "Sidney's is an irrational motive. His *mind* did not make this decision, it was made with another organ, and for a reason without politics or reason. It was made in a world much different from your own."

"You said that Penelope confirmed his treachery." Walsingham nodded. "You found him with her."

"I did."

"And you are certain of what you are telling me."

"I am. He's very drunk, in the closet nearby. Shall I bring him in?"

Walsingham sat. "No. Let me think."

"I am eager to return to the task of finding Leonora's murderer," Marlowe said.

Walsingham smiled ever so slightly. "I thought you said that she was murdered by Ned Blank."

"But you knew that wasn't true."

"Yes, I did."

"May I not leave all this to you, then?" Marlowe was unable to hide his impatience. "You have all the things that you wanted: firm proof of Babington's part in the plot, knowledge of the invasion, and now you even have the assassin in a small, guarded room right next door. Let me go."

"If only it were that simple," Walsingham lamented. "You have no idea of the reticence Her Majesty exhibits with regard to her favorites. And Sidney—he is a great poet and she loves him. I cannot simply do away with him. Not here in London, at any rate."

Marlowe could see the gears whirring in the spymaster's mind.

"Yes, not in London," Walsingham said at length. "You must return to the Netherlands."

"No!" Marlowe snapped.

Walsingham eyed Marlowe as he might glare at an unruly child. "As you know, the death of William the Silent has encouraged Spanish forces in that region, and the war there rages more violently than ever. You go to Zutphen. You take Sidney with you. You join our forces there against the Spanish troops. And then Philip Sidney will, alas, be killed in battle there."

"I suppose that's possible," Marlowe said hesitantly, "but Sidney's a great swordsman, and a brilliant man at arms. His better chances lie in survival, even victory."

"You misunderstand," Walsingham said softly. "You will see to it that he is killed. A pistol shot from behind."

Marlowe froze. His heart began to pound.

"I would never," Marlowe began.

"He means to kill the Queen!"

"He is your daughter's husband!" Marlowe countered. "For her sake alone, I would never murder Philip Sidney!"

"What did you imagine was the purpose of the Surety Act? Why do you suppose it was given to you? So that you would kill when necessity dictated. And Philip Sidney needs to die for his vile treason!"

"I—I can't do it." Marlowe shook his head. "You know that I can kill a man when he tries to kill me—"

"His intent is to kill the *Queen*!"

"But to shoot a man in the back," Marlowe began, sweat breaking at his hairline.

"Then Lopez will do it," Walsingham interrupted angrily. "He is there in Zutphen, under cover. Take Sidney to him, tell him what to do. You will watch the assassin carefully until then. Don't allow him to escape, do you understand? You will leave tomorrow, you and Sidney. Off to war. It is my command."

Without another word Walsingham rose and left the room.

A guard came in immediately.

"Food, bath, and bed," the guard said simply, "this way."

Stunned, all Marlowe could do was follow, straining to understand what had just transpired.

TWENTY-THREE

Marlowe's gray stone bedchamber at Hampton Court was small. Windowless, it held only a bed, a small table, and a chamberpot. He had bathed and eaten in another part of the Hall, and then a guard had taken him to the small room. Laid out on the bed was a soldier's uniform without insignia. Marlowe sat on the edge of that bed, staring at the suspicious uniform.

When the door scraped open he was stunned to see a familiar figure in the doorway.

"Frances?"

Frances Walsingham—now Frances *Sidney*—stood frozen, lit only by the single taper on the small table by Marlowe's bed. Her eyes were red and her face was sallow. She was wearing a simple blue dress, and her hair was down.

"May I speak with you?" she asked, her voice barely above a whisper.

A thousand images seared through his mind. He saw Frances dressed as a man when he'd rescued her from Malta, wielding a rapier better than any man could. He saw her sleeping in the French countryside, and riding next to him through wild forests. He saw the moment she bid him farewell, the moment when he thought he would never see her again. All in the blink of an eye.

"I've had a revelation about you," he said, standing up. "I realized that I loved you primarily for your fire, the force of your life."

"I don't understand," she said, frozen in the doorframe.

"Nor do I," he admitted. "Come in."

"I will not. I've only come to tell you that I know my father's plan—"

"Listen," Marlowe interrupted, "you have nothing to fear; I told Lord Walsingham that I could not kill Sidney."

"I know my father's plan and I endorse it," she continued as if Marlowe had not spoken. "Philip Sidney is in love with another woman, a vacuous puppet who tried to murder our Queen; and now he would commit the same unimaginable crime—for her sake. If I could dress as a man once more and go with you to Zutphen, I would kill him myself."

Marlowe stared, unable to talk.

"I have brought you a gift." Her voice was ice.

She held out a small package, something wrapped in purple damask and tied with a golden rope. Marlowe moved closer and took it.

"Thank you, Frances," he began. "I don't know what to—"

"Don't thank me," she snapped impatiently. "Open it."

He did, untying the rope and unfolding the damask. That fine fabric was wrapped around a wheel-lock pistol.

"That is one of the firearms used to kill William the Silent. Don't bother asking me how I obtained it. Only use it now to kill my husband. Will you swear?"

Marlowe stared down at the weapon.

"Frances," he said at length, "I understand that your heart is broken—"

"You really are an idiot," she interrupted again. "I'm not asking you to take my revenge. I'm asking you to eliminate a traitor, a man who would plunge our nation into chaos. And I'm asking you to use this particular weapon for Philip Sidney's sake. I want you to show it to him before you fire, explain its provenance. He will appreciate the grim poetry of it. Don't you think?"

Marlowe looked deeply into her eyes.

"I have no wish to do as Philip Sidney has done," he began, "and murder for the sake of a woman I love."

She shook her head. "You don't love me," she insisted. "You

love—*love.* And the more impossible that love is, the better you love it. You and I can never be together, so I am a safe object of your ardor. Safer still: a woman who is dead."

Marlowe's head pounded and his eyes betrayed his surprise.

"Yes," Frances went on, "I know about my sister—my half sister. Leonora was, by all accounts, a brave woman."

"A remarkable person of any gender," Marlowe managed to answer. "But I do not love her, and never did. I confess I have, foolishly, just realized that she was your sister. I—I should have seen the resemblance."

Frances glanced downward. "She looked like me?"

"A little. But the resemblance was more in spirit than in flesh."

She met his eyes. "You said you loved her fire."

He drew in a deep breath. "I did."

"Marlowe, take this pistol," Frances said, a hint of desperation in her voice. "Hide it away. Use it when the time is right. Not for my sake. You must do it for—you understand the grander scheme."

Without another word or glance, she was gone.

Marlowe looked down at the pistol once again. All he could think about was that she had called him *Marlowe*—not *Kit.*

In another room, Philip Sidney lay sleeping in a much more elaborate bed. It was nearly eighty feet square. The bed was large enough for five people, and covered in fine white silk and satin. There was a private closet for the chamberpot, a dozen chairs, and a separate dining area. A fire blazed in the hearth, and several windows admitted the moon's clear light. The stones in all the walls were obscured by elaborate tapestries depicting pastoral scenes from Edmund Spencer's *The Shepheardes Calender,* commissioned by Philip for the room. It was the room in which he slept with his wife, Frances Walsingham.

She stood over him, watching him snore, trying to think if there had ever been a time when she cared for him at all.

Beside him on the bed was a uniform exactly like the one on Marlowe's poorer bed.

After a moment she planted her feet, took hold of the coverlet upon which her husband lay, and pulled with all her might. She had done it many times before. He began to slide and then to topple, off the bed and onto the floor.

He shivered, opened his eyes for a second, mumbled incoherently, and then fell back to sleep.

Frances dropped the covers over him and stepped around to the other side of the bed.

As she undressed, she prayed: When he is dead, when Marlowe has killed him, let him stay silent. Let him not haunt me the way my half sister has haunted Kit.

Backstage at The Curtain Theatre, Thomas Kyd sat at a dressing table by candlelight, staring at himself in the looking glass.

Ned entered so softly that his feet made no din, but not so softly that Kyd did not pull out his dagger and turn around, smiling.

"I thought you'd gone for the night," Kyd said.

"I was worried about you."

"I doubt that." Kyd kept his dagger where Ned could see it.

"Look," Ned began, "you've got us both in a stew of shite. These fobs, Maggot and Poison, they'll be the death of us. Both."

"Morgan and Paget. They can only tell an idiot's tale, filled with sound and fury, signifying exactly nothing."

"Good line," Ned admitted, "but it don't get us clear of the danger, you and me."

"What would you suggest, Ned?"

"Tour of the provinces. Rouse Lord Strange's Men; take a cart, imitate the Gypsies, and get our dicks out of London. We'll do your stupid Hamlet play."

"You'd go back to playing Ophelia?"

"No," Ned railed.

"Well you can't play Hamlet!"

"I was thinking Ophelia's brother."

"What's this really about, Ned?" Kyd put away his knife.

"Marlowe," Ned said simply. "He'd just as soon give me up for a murder I ain't done: the woman what nearly broke my back."

"No," Kyd assured him. "Marlowe wants the truth. He's not interested in you if you didn't do it."

"Still, I'm afraid of him."

Kyd stood. "As am I. Let's find a cart. We'll go to Stratford first. They love me there."

"There's just one more thing we have to do before we leave London," Ned allowed casually.

"Christ," Kyd muttered, "tell me about it when I have drink in my hand."

With that Kyd lumbered out the stage door; Ned followed after.

In a paneled room at Hampton Court, lit with a dozen candles, Walsingham stood tapping his foot, staring at a door at the far end of the chamber, willing it to open. His skullcap was too tight. His eyes were red from lack of sleep. And the entirety of his patience had vanished.

At last the door flew open and Elizabeth sailed in.

"This is quite a late hour for a chat," she sniped.

"I have incontrovertible proof," he responded, without the usual ceremony.

The Queen was momentarily taken aback by her spymaster's abrupt tone.

"Mary conspires with Babington to murder you, invade England, and take the throne."

He knew that hammering the Queen with such a blunt presentation would irritate her, but he knew it would also stress the urgency of the matter.

The Queen took a moment to compose her response.

"Proof?" she asked curtly.

Walsingham held out Marlowe's letters, the original and the decoded copy.

"In Babington's own hand," he said, "addressed to Mary."

She glanced at the pages. "Marlowe obtained this information."

He nodded.

"So quickly." The Queen sat in the only chair in the room, a sturdy wooden one with high rounded sides and no back.

"Meaning that communication between Babington and Mary has been ongoing." Walsingham lowered the papers.

"Yes." Her voice was strangely forlorn.

"It's more than enough to execute them all."

"No." Elizabeth stared into space. "I will not order the death of my cousin."

"Once removed," Walsingham sniffed.

"I won't do it!" The Queen roared quite suddenly.

"Your Majesty," Walsingham began.

"But arrest Babington, and all his cronies," she interrupted. "Is John Dee involved?"

"I think not."

"That manuscript he acquired from Rudolf?"

"Thus far a mystery," Walsingham admitted, "but I have arranged to acquire it."

"You will make Mary's dungeon more secure."

"Already so ordered."

"Have you discovered the particulars of this newest assassination attempt?"

Walsingham looked down. "I have assigned Marlowe to take care of the matter. He's going to Zutphen to assist Dr. Lopez. We think the assassin will be there."

It wasn't quite a lie.

"Good." She stood. "Oh. Has Marlowe discovered the actual murderer of your—of the girl Leonora Beak?"

"Alas. But he is eager to return to that task."

"*Eager*," she said, rolling the word around in her mouth. "Does he fall in love with every woman he meets?"

"So far as I am able to determine," Walsingham answered, "yes."

The Queen turned to leave. "Well. That's what young men are wont to do, is it not?"

"I fear I cannot remember that far back," Walsingham sighed.

The Queen paused a moment. "Nor I," she said softly, "tonight."

TWENTY-FOUR

AT SEA

Marlowe stood on the deck of Her Majesty's ship *White Bear,* feeling foolish in his ill-fitting uniform, watching the sun come up. It was an old full-rigged, forty-gun ship in need of rebuilding, but it was steady and perfect for the short voyage to Monster.

He was glad to have left from London instead of retracing his path from the Bell Inn to Mersea, even though it meant a slightly longer time on the ocean. He hated the water, but he feared what dreams might come to him the other way, what ghosts might rise up, taunting him for leaving a murder unsolved. He struggled to align himself with Walsingham's wishes. His brain understood that the Queen was more important than anyone else, but his heart refused to agree.

As the waves rolled, he kept his mind on Sidney, and as far away from Leonora as he could manage. Mostly he wondered what sort of love would entice a man to kill a queen. He might betray a friend, or tell a lie to gain a woman's heart. But what good was a heart that wanted murder?

Then he thought of Lopez. Even as the doctor was training him to kill, he counseled Marlowe against killing.

"Blood will always want more blood," the doctor often said. "And if you ever find killing easy, you will know you have thrown away your compass."

Further reflection was interrupted by Sidney, staggering toward him.

"Christ!" he complained. "My head!"

"You drank prodigiously," Marlowe told him.

"And I slept on the floor," he railed. "That cow Frances shoved me off my own bed!"

Marlowe smiled. If Sidney would only continue speaking in that manner about Frances, killing him would be easier.

Sidney made it to the rail where Marlowe stood and stared down at the sea. Marlowe marveled at the fact that he did not vomit. Marlowe had already done so three times. Some men were made for the salt, and some weren't.

"We must speak carefully," Marlowe whispered, only a little theatrically. "No one on board this ship must know our true goal."

Sidney nodded wisely.

"I'll find a way to thank you, Marlowe," he said. "Getting me out of London has probably saved my life."

Marlowe looked away.

"And the guise of joining Her Majesty's troops," Sidney went on, "is brilliant. It gets us to the Netherlands, and the safety of King Philip's protection."

"The logistics may be a bit daunting," Marlowe warned. "We may actually have to join the battle on the English side of the line, at first."

"Of course," Sidney agreed.

At that Marlowe looked up, stared at the side of Sidney's face, and wondered at the torment that lived in such a poet's brain, that he could kill a queen, destroy a nation, and wreck his life for someone who would never love him.

"You know that Penelope is not in love with you," he said to Sidney.

"Not yet," Sidney answered confidently. "But she will be. My poetry is a lever that can lift the world; it will have enough power to win her heart."

Marlowe stared.

Will I ever hold myself in such high esteem, he wondered.

Sidney stared out across the waves.

"I love the sea," he boomed. "Don't you?"

Marlowe was seized by the sudden recollection of nearly drowning in the Great Stour River that ran through the center of Canterbury where he was born.

"As a boy I fell into a river and died," he told Sidney. "Someone dragged me out and brought me back to life. Since that time, all water looks like death to me. So: no. I do not love the sea. Although I sense a metaphor hidden somewhere here: drowning in love, love and death—something."

Sidney nodded enthusiastically. "Good, good; I like it. You should keep working. You might have something."

Sidney was drowning in his own love, Marlowe realized, and didn't know it.

In no time at all the coast of the Netherlands presented itself, and a few hours after that, the ship set in at Monster.

Marlowe willed his brain away from memories of his last visit to that port, and instead concentrated on the mundane particulars: horses, food, directions.

He and Sidney were on their way quickly, fake orders in pocket, fake mission in mind. It would be a hard riding to get to Zutphen by the next day, and Marlowe did not relish the prospect of conversation with Sidney.

But Sidney would not be silent. The first two hours were consumed by his elegiac meanderings concerning the joys of Penelope's face, uninterrupted by a single syllable from Marlowe.

But as the next hours dragged on, Marlowe realized what a purging, almost purifying effect Sidney's monologue was having. It was like eating too much of a favorite food. He found he was sick of Penelope, which was a blessing. And he was beginning to find it in his heart to kill Sidney if only just to make him stop talking.

When evening drew near, they paused in Utrecht to eat.

Utrecht was a lovely, sophisticated town of wide streets and bustling business, very favorable to anyone in the uniform of England. The setting sun fired everything with gold.

A small inn near the outer edge of town seemed inviting, and so they stopped. The horses were taken, and they strode into the crowded public room. Many of the people there turned to see the strangers. Sidney smiled; some smiled back.

Marlowe saw the table he wanted, in a safe corner, back to two walls, good view of the entire room, and headed for it.

Sidney, grinning, followed a little too eagerly, and kicked a leg of the first table he encountered.

"*Idioot*," a man at the table muttered.

"Sorry," Sidney said, still smiling.

"*Jij bent de reden waarom Willem is dood*," the man growled, beginning to stand.

Marlowe turned.

"Wait," he called out. "Wait. We are not the cause of William's death. Blame Philip, and Spain."

"*Wat?*"

"*Spanje is defect*," Marlowe answered.

"You speak Dutch," Sidney marveled. "What's he saying?"

"*Spanje?*" the man roared, coming to a full stand.

"*Je dronken*," another man at the table said to his friend.

"*Dronken?*" the man railed.

"We're about to get into a fight with a drunken Dutchman," Marlowe sighed.

"Oh."

Sidney drew his rapier at once, flailed its point quickly against the drunk's chest and stomach, slicing up his doublet without drawing much blood. Then he scooped the tip of his blade neatly into the hilt of the drunk's sword, pulled hard, and sent the man's rapier flying upward into the air.

Marlowe took a single step to his right and caught the blade by the handle. He flourished it, thrust into empty space once, and nodded.

"Nice sword," he said. "*Mooi zwaard*."

The drunk blinked, then looked down at his torn clothing. His friend at the table stared up at him.

"*Zeggen dank u en gaan zitten*," he advised his companion.

"Yes," Marlowe agreed, "say thank you and have a seat."

The drunk swallowed and sat. "*Dank u.*"

Sidney turned to Marlowe.

"You really are good at Dutch," he said. "I'm so impressed."

"I'm famished," Marlowe answered, sheathing his blade.

Then he glanced once more at the Dutch rapier, shook his head at its owner, and strode to the table where he sat.

"I'm giving this back to you," Marlowe said to the cringing drunk, "but if you draw it again, I'll kill you. Understand?"

The man stared.

"*Ik zal je te vermoorden,*" Marlowe repeated.

The man stared down at his sword and nodded.

"You *have* to teach me some of the language," Sidney said, following Marlowe to the corner table.

But all Marlowe could think about was how calmly, even joyfully, Sidney had dealt with the would-be assailant, how easily he'd taken the man's sword away. And how difficult it might be to kill a man with those talents.

Hours later, just as the sun was setting, a small inn on the outskirts of Zutphen came into view. Past a slope and into a grove of downy birch trees, they slowed their horses.

"We're supposed to meet our contact down there," Marlowe said softly, inclining his head in the direction of the inn. "That public house."

"Who is it?" Sidney whispered. "Do you know him?"

"Our contact?" Marlowe responded. "Yes. I know him."

He gently spurred his horse forward. Sidney followed.

There was a small rail to the side of inn where several other horses were secured. They headed for it.

Just as they pulled up to the rail: gunshots.

Marlowe was off his horse and running before the second volley sounded. Racing for the door, rapier out, he stopped short when a familiar figure in red burst out.

Dr. Lopez glanced at Marlowe, shook his head quickly, and then ran the opposite direction, toward a thicker grove of trees.

Marlowe stood very still.

Seconds later three men flew from the inn, weapons drawn, chasing after Lopez.

Marlowe was startled by a soft voice behind him.

"I hope that wasn't our man," Sidney whispered.

"I have no idea what just happened," Marlowe answered. "We ought to find food and lodging elsewhere. This place seems a little busy."

"Agreed," Sidney said as he watched the men running into the darker woods.

They turned as one and walked quickly back toward their horses, but slowed their pace when they saw a dark-skinned young boy holding the reins to both of their mounts.

"Those horses belong to us, boy," Sidney called out before Marlowe could speak.

"And yet," the boy said in English, "I hold the reins."

With that several dozen men, all oddly dressed in carnival rags and mummers' costumes, appeared from around the corner of the inn. In the last rays of pale sunlight they were more a vision than a reality.

"I know Gelis," Marlowe said simply, putting his rapier away. "And so do you."

"And is there any other name you want to tell me?" the boy asked.

"I suppose that would be *Belpathian Grem,*" Marlowe sighed.

"Who in God's name are these apparitions?" Sidney asked, his weapon still out.

"Our friends," Marlowe answered warily, "at least for the moment."

"Come along," the boy said, turning and leading the horses into the woods. "This way."

The other men stood staring, as if they could not move.

"I'm not going with them," Sidney objected.

Marlowe reached over and lowered Sidney's rapier with his hand. "Yes, you are."

With that Marlowe followed the boy with the horses.

Sidney stood for a moment longer, shaking his head. Then he sheathed his sword and went along.

Not far into the woods, the smell of smoke assailed the air. Then: food.

Marlowe picked up his pace and caught up with the boy and the horses.

"Is that *marmitako* I smell?" he asked the boy.

The boy stopped.

"How would you know that?" he asked.

Marlowe turned to Sidney. "You're in for a treat. They're cooking a Basque fish stew: potatoes, onions, tomatoes, and peppers, unbelievably delicious."

"You've had it before?" the boy wanted to know.

"I have," Marlowe answered, picking up his pace. "Beside the names of Gelis and Grem, I should have mentioned Argi."

The boy stopped dead still.

"You know Argi!" he cried.

"He took me to Malta a while ago," Marlowe explained, still walking. "He's a good and true friend. And possibly the best rifle shot I've ever seen."

"Best there is," the boy insisted, moving forward once more. "He is my uncle's second cousin. Famous."

"Yes," Marlowe agreed distractedly, "walk faster."

They arrived at camp and were greeted with cautious civility. Nine festooned Travelers' carts were arranged in neatly staggered parallels. Smoke rose from the central fire, and its orange light gave the encampment a dreamlike glow. There was only one man in evidence, bent over the fire.

Marlowe went immediately to the cooking pot.

"He says he's had Argi's *marmitako*," the boy told the rotund man dressed in green.

The man was sitting on a small ornate stool, stirring the pot with a long wooden spoon.

"Some of the best food I've ever tasted," Marlowe said, staring into the pot.

"Second-rate slop compared to mine," the man in green responded in a Scots accent.

"You know Gelis," Marlowe said before he thought better of it.

The man looked up at Marlowe.

"Gelis is the reason I'm here." He said. "The rest is with King Grem. We come on your behalf."

"Why?"

The man shook his head. "Gelis owes you, Grem likes you, we hate the Spanish, the Dutch were kind to us, William the Silent was lenient with Travelers, the fishing's good in these rivers this time of year. Take your pick."

Sidney caught up and stood beside Marlowe.

"What in the name of all hell is happening here?" he asked.

"Too much to explain on an empty stomach," Marlowe told him. "But these people are here to help us."

Without a word the man in green reached for a large wooden bowl, spooned it full of stew, and held it out.

Marlowe grabbed it and sipped, burning his lips and tongue.

"Well?" the man in green asked.

"Too hot to tell," Marlowe said, looking around for a place to sit. "You're a strange amalgamation of characters, here. Some are Basque, some are Grem's men, obviously from their dress. You're with Gelis and his family. Are there other Scots with you?"

The man looked away. "You're asking that because you fear it's many a Scot would support Queen Mary. But Mary's a Catholic, you see. And the Inquisition were no friend to Travelers like me. Not never."

Sidney stiffened.

"But Travelers keep their own customs," Marlowe said quickly. "They have no specific beliefs."

The man in green looked between Sidney and Marlowe, read Sidney's discomfort and Marlowe's warning, and nodded.

"We keep to old ways," is all he would say.

"You have *got* to try this stew, Sidney," Marlowe said quickly.

After a moment, Sidney's stomach commanded his brain, and he accepted a bowl of *marmitako*.

Several other well-wrought stools were presented. Marlowe and Sidney sat around the fire with several other men, slurping the stew without talking.

At last Marlowe set his bowl on the ground.

"All right," he called out good-naturedly, "you win. This is better than Argi's; just don't tell him I said so!"

The men around the fire laughed.

"Yes, excellent!" Sidney pronounced. "Now. What are we all waiting for?"

Everyone looked at him.

"Well, I can tell we're waiting for something," he went on.

Without warning a red shadow emerged from behind one of the nearby carts with a flourish of the crimson cape.

"You're waiting for me, Sir Philip," Lopez said clearly, striding toward the fire. "And here I am."

TWENTY-FIVE

The moon was high by the time Lopez concluded his discourse on the battle outside Zutphen.

"The fighting began when William was assassinated and chaos prevailed." Lopez sighed. "Now we deal in small skirmishes. I fear a greater battle is yet to come. Sometime next autumn, I imagine."

"There would be no battle at all," Sidney railed, "if Elizabeth had not taken the Netherlands under her protection, sent infantry and cavalry to the Low Countries, and made Dudley the Governor-General of the Netherlands! *That's* what started all this, not William the Silent!"

Marlowe put his hand on Sidney's arm.

The rest of the men around the fire stared motionlessly.

"We are here at the Queen's behest to do her work against the Spanish," Marlowe said solemnly. "And we will give full measure."

Sidney glanced around at the circle, realized he'd spoken rashly, and gained control.

"Of course," he said contritely. "We give full measure."

Lopez stood. "And now, Marlowe, will you walk with me? I have news from your father."

Marlowe nodded, eyed Sidney pointedly, and followed Lopez out of the circle of light and into the more moonlit woods.

"I'm very glad to see you," Marlowe enthused as soon as they were out of earshot of the rest. "Do you know that Leonora Beak has been murdered? And do you have any experience of a man called Belpathian Grem? And did you know that John Dee is in league with conspirators against the Queen? Also—"

"Marlowe," Lopez interrupted softly. "I was sad to hear the news about Miss Beak, there is no such person as Belpathian Grem, and John Dee is a foolish scholar, nothing more. Tell me why you and Sidney are here."

"That news from Walsingham has not yet arrived?"

Lopez stared into Marlowe's eyes.

"All right," Marlowe sighed. "You'll never believe it, but Philip Sidney, possibly our greatest poet, is also our greatest traitor. He has contrived to murder our Queen. He's the assassin in this plot."

Lopez did not change expression one iota.

"Penelope Rich," he said softly.

"Yes." Marlowe shook his head. "I've brought Sidney here on Walsingham's instructions. Sidney thinks that we're going to fight with you, and then, when we can slip away, meet with the Spanish and escape. In fact, my actual directive is to kill him."

Lopez nodded. "And make it seem he's been killed in the fighting."

"Yes." Marlowe reached into his pouch. "And his wife, Frances, gave me this to accomplish the task."

He produced the wheel-lock pistol.

"Odd pistol," Lopez mused.

"It's one of the two that killed William the Silent," Marlowe told him.

Lopez offered a rare smile. "Sir Philip will appreciate the poetry."

Marlowe nodded. "That's what Frances said. But I'm not certain I can do it—kill such a man."

"It's easy to kill a man who's trying to kill you," Lopez commiserated. "Instinct and training do most of the work. But this—it's cold-blooded, calculated."

"Yes, and lose a great poet."

"The poetry won't die when you kill the man."

"Yes, I won't kill what he's written so far," Marlowe agreed, "but I keep imagining the work to come, his future poems. Those I would be murdering."

"Is a poem worth a queen?" Lopez asked quietly.

The fact that Marlowe did not answer immediately gave both men pause.

So Marlowe changed the subject.

"I must confess that I am primarily consumed by a desire to find the man who murdered Leonora Beak," he said, staring into the darker woods. "You may have been the last man to see her alive. Do you have any small fact or observation that might aid me in my investigation?"

"It seems a decade ago," Lopez sighed. "Let me see."

And Lopez cast his mind back to his last moments at the Bell Inn.

Leonora Beak sat in her father's room at the Bell Inn, reading. Lopez stood beside her sleeping father. Downstairs they could hear the ordinary noise of the place, dishes rattling, lowered voices, the clank of a tankard on a wooden tabletop.

"He is much improved," Lopez announced.

Leonora looked up from her book. "He opened his eyes a while ago, and knew who I was."

"Good sign; he'll be up and about in a few days," Lopez concluded. "That means I must be on my way. As I have told you, Walsingham's message to me was explicit. I am to rally with Her Majesty's troops near Zutphen, further inland than Delft."

"Delft," she growled. "Don't remind me."

"In some way it is a blessing that your father lies here," Lopez told her. "It occupies your present mind so that you do not dwell on the past."

She sighed. "If only that were true."

"Well," Lopez said, heading for the door, "I must say farewell."

She stood. "And I must thank you, Doctor. You saved my father's life."

Lopez inclined his head politely, but did not stop walking.

"I know that I must bide my time here with my father," she said softly, "but I would rather be with Marlowe."

"Your father needs you," Lopez said in the doorway. "Read your book."

"What's all the noise downstairs?" she asked absently.

"Travelers, strangers—I haven't seen these new men before. They're just hungry, standing around in the kitchen."

"God." She yawned. "I understand that, I'm famished."

"I'll send someone up," Lopez told her, "but I must be on my way."

"If you see Marlowe," she began.

"I won't," Lopez said from the doorway, his back to Leonora. "Not for a while, anyway."

Lopez suddenly stopped his story and cast his eye about the Dutch woods. "Soft."

Before he could speak further, the woods around them exploded: orange fire and screaming men roared at them from all directions.

"Spanish troops!" Lopez said, drawing his rapier.

Marlowe turned his back to the doctor's and drew his rapier and dagger.

The soldiers were difficult to see by the light of the moon, but they were firing pistols, giving away their locations.

"Ten!" Marlowe shouted.

"A dozen!" Lopez corrected.

The first Spanish soldier ran at Marlowe. Marlowe turned sideways, took a step backward, and sliced the man's jugular vein. The soldier plummeted to the ground at the doctor's feet.

Lopez, in turn, ducked low and leapt forward, rapier point stretched far out in front of him, and struck another attacker in the gut. That man's rifle went off before he fell to the ground, moaning.

Lopez grabbed the rifle by its hot barrel and used the butt as a club, bashing it hard against another soldier's skull; the wood cracked.

Three men rushed Marlowe. Marlowe whirled. His rapier's tip cut each assailant on the face, slowing them all. Marlowe crashed to the ground, rolled, and bowled over two of the wounded men, his dagger then neatly slicing through each man's Achilles tendon. The third man, standing over Marlowe, had a pistol. It was pointed directly at Marlowe's head.

The Spaniard grinned, cocked his pistol, and then fainted dead away.

Marlowe was on his feet.

The third Spaniard had not, in fact, fainted. Sidney had killed him; stabbed him through the heart from behind.

"That was close," Sidney said happily.

"I don't know," Marlowe answered. "Spanish soldiers aren't really known for their marksmanship."

Sidney grinned. "You're welcome."

Then from behind another Spanish soldier thrust his blade, a clumsy larger weapon, in the direction of Sidney's neck.

Marlowe kicked forward with his rapier high, as if to stab Sidney in the head, missing his ear by the width of an atom, and parried the Spaniard's attack.

Leaping past Sidney, Marlowe engaged the soldier, an older man with several visible scars.

"*Apuñalar a un hombre por la espalda?*" Marlowe asked, taunting his opponent.

"*Un ojo por un ojo,*" the man answered. "He stab my friend in the back, I stab him in the back."

Marlowe glanced back at the dead man who had just tried to shoot him.

"I see your point."

The man smiled and held up the point of his sword. "Good, I'm glad you do."

"Well I wouldn't like to kill a man who speaks English and quotes the Old Testament," Marlowe said, walking around the man, "but if you keep pointing that ridiculous antique at me, I'll have to."

The man turned to keep facing Marlowe. "*Entendido.*"

Without warning the man sliced backhanded at Marlowe's rapier from below, and cut the rapier in half.

Marlowe stared at what was left of his blade.

"Toledo steel," the man said, glancing at his sword.

"I take back my insult," Marlowe said amiably. "It's a great weapon."

With that Marlowe cocked his arm and threw his dagger into the Spaniard's sword arm. It stuck there, and the man dropped his formidable blade.

Marlowe raced forward, kicked the man's kneecap, dislocating it, and then shoved his bulk against the man, knocking him to the ground. He picked up the soldier's sword and in an instant had its point at the man's throat.

"Your neck will cut more easily than my rapier did," Marlowe warned.

"I didn't even see your arm move," the soldier said in wonder, staring at the dagger stuck in his forearm.

The rest of the Travelers were in the woods by then, and the Spanish soldiers were quickly subdued. Most were killed, but three, including the man with the scars, were kept alive.

Lopez had those three tied and thrown to the ground near the cooking fire. Sidney and several of the Travelers sat around; the rest were on guard in the woods.

"How did you know where we were?" he asked in English.

The man with the scars answered immediately. "I didn't know anything, I just went where I was told. They say: go here, kill these, and so I do."

"A good soldier," Lopez said.

"For almost twenty years," the man said without a hint of pride.

"Why is your English so good?" Marlowe asked.

"I was in Queen Mary's guard for a time," he said, "in the employ of Nicolas Durand de Villegaignon, a commander of the Knights of Malta."

Marlowe glanced at Lopez. "Yes, I'm familiar with that order."

"It was expected of a few of us that we learn the language." The man struggled a bit in his bonds. "My knee is in much pain."

"Answer the rest of my questions," Lopez promised, "and I'll set the kneecap right."

"Ask quickly, then," the man said, "before I am to faint away; it really hurts."

"Where are the rest of your troops?" Lopez asked.

"Is that your question?" the man countered. "We're everywhere. There are very few places near Zutphen where we are not!"

"How many?"

"Don't know. Thousands."

"He's exaggerating," One of the Traveling men said. "We'd know if there were thousands. And we would have been prepared for this pitiful attack tonight."

"Yes," Lopez went on. "Why did you attack us? Us in particular?"

The man groaned. "I told you: they say 'go here, kill these' and we do."

"No idea why you were sent to wipe out an encampment of Traveling People who have absolutely nothing to do with our political disagreements."

"Well," the man allowed, "if I had to guess, I would say that it might have something to do with the famous Dr. Lopez or the poet Philip Sidney."

Marlowe stared down at the man. "So you *do* know more than you're saying."

"Fix my knee," the man groaned, "and I may be able to say more."

"How on earth did he know I'd be here?" Sidney asked, standing.

"As in days of old," the Spaniard said, laughing, "your coming was foretold."

And then he fainted dead away.

"This is far worse than I had imagined," Lopez said, mostly to himself. "Thousands of troops, and dangerous intelligence."

"No, but I mean: how would they know I was coming?" Sidney asked again.

"Penelope," Marlowe said coldly.

"No." Sidney shook his head and stepped closer to Marlowe, so that only he could hear. "She had no idea where I was going. Also, I love her, but she's hardly bright enough to gather such intelligence on her own. No, it was Paget, or Morgan."

Marlowe nodded.

How much did the Travelers know about the intrigue afoot? Lopez would only have told them the bare essentials. But had they discovered more? He wasn't certain how much he could say in front of them.

"I wonder why," one of the Travelers asked pointedly, "the most famous poet in England is in our little camp here in the Netherlands. Will you write an elegy about us?"

Without a word, Sidney drew his rapier and jumped several feet in the air, landing directing in front of the man who'd spoken. He tipped his rapier upward, knocking off the man's hat, and then he stuck the point of his rapier into the man's pistol holster.

Before the man could react, he found Sidney's dagger at his throat.

"I am here, my friend, because I am the greatest swordsman in England," Sidney said, leaning very close to the man's face, "as well as her finest wordsmith."

"It's true," Marlowe added casually. "Sir Philip came here to fight. And he's not bad, would you say?"

The Traveler didn't blink, staring back into Sidney's eyes.

"Not bad," he said, "for a poet."

"Would you challenge me?" Sidney asked a little too shrilly. "Would you question my abilities with a sword?"

"No," the man answered steadily. "I challenge your abilities as a poet—a real poet. How much do you know about *bertsos*?"

"Careful, Sidney." Marlowe grinned. "*Bertsos* are Basque improvised lyrics, lightning fast, with extemporaneous music. Devilish, intricate—and beautiful."

"Ah!" Sidney put his blades away at once. "A *real* challenge. What accompaniment?"

"None," the man said.

Sidney locked eyes with him. "Tell me your name."

"Egun," the man answered proudly.

"Good, I am Philip. Show me how to begin."

"Shall we sing in French or Spanish?" Egun asked.

"I'm better at French."

"Spanish it is!" Egun shouted, and the other Travelers laughed.

"Keep in mind that this is a double improvisation," Marlowe explained to Sidney. "You invent the melody as well as the verse as you sing. There are a variety of rhythmic structures, but my opinion, so far as I understand it, is that you should choose the 'small of eight,' "

"*Zortziko txiki*," Egun said, nodding.

"The first contains seven syllables," Marlowe went on, "followed by six syllables in the next line. A little like a couplet, but the rhyme is in the seven-syllable lines. You have four such couplets, or eight lines in all."

"And if you cannot find a rhyme," Egun added, "is called a *poto*."

"A point against the man who failed," Sidney said excitedly, "I understand. Since I'm new to it, you start."

"Fair," Egun admitted.

He stepped closer to the fire. The orange under-lighting gave him an eerie presence. His clothes were ornate, a little like Belpathian Grem's followers: necklaces, small items tied to his shirt, golden earrings, one in each lobe. His face was smooth, shaved, but his eyes gave away his age and his face was flushed with confidence as he began to sing.

His voice was high and clear, and the men around the fire were silent. Sidney listened with his entire body, soaking in the words and music.

And when it was his turn, Sidney improvised a variation of the melody Egun had used, and composed a short verse about the battle they'd all just won, even managing to use Marlowe's name. All in Spanish.

The men around the fire all applauded, including Egun.

But the contest went on. The melodies grew more intricate, and the verses more subtle until Sidney burst out laughing and conceded Egun's superiority.

Everyone roared approval as Egun embraced Sidney.

Marlowe applauded, staring at Sidney. How could he possibly kill such a man?

TWENTY-SIX

LONDON

At Hampton Court, in the middle of the night, Leviticus stole down the black stone hallway toward John Dee's laboratory. He knew that Dee was asleep because he'd just peeked into the old man's room and seen him in bed, snoring, a book collapsed on his chest.

Leviticus had dressed himself in his best black doublet and gold trousers for this espionage, because he wanted to go directly to Walsingham's small office, the one closest to the spymaster's bedchamber, as soon as he'd stolen his prize.

The laboratory was a frightening place. Skulls and dead animals and poison plants and potions all lay everywhere, in no order, and the moonlight slanting through the high openings at the top of the western wall only emphasized the air of terror.

The boy hesitated at the doorway. He needed more light but did not dare to risk a torch. He cast his eye about for a candle, but found none. Slowly he crept into the vault, eyes flashing everywhere at once.

A human skeleton dangled from a post, and seemed to be staring right at him. A sudden noise clattered in a far corner, and he jumped backward, nearly flying from the room.

A second later he heard the telltale muttering of rats.

Following one of the moonbeams, his eyes soon fell on a taper on a table at the far end of the room. He inched forward. More noise in the corner froze him for a moment. He was relieved to see a tinderbox near the taper and in moments had it lit.

Relieved by the flame's warmer glow, he surveyed the chamber.

In an opposite corner there was a large standing desk, old wood and steel bracing, and on that desk there was an open volume.

Leviticus moved carefully through the maze of tables, boxes, and random piles of herbs until he arrived at the desk. He stared down at the page to which the volume was opened and felt an odd surge of—something he'd never felt before, nor could explain. The images on the page were of naked women, sitting or standing in tubs. The tubs were connected by tubes or conduits, and each smiling woman wore a diadem.

Unable to make sense of the words, the boy stared at the pictures, not daring to touch the manuscript, afraid of what power it might have.

When, at last, his discomfort at standing in the laboratory overcame his reticence to take the manuscript, he slammed the volume closed, took it under one arm, and blew out the taper.

After his eyes adjusted to the moonlight once more, he carefully made his way back to the door and slipped out.

Walsingham would be able to read the language. Walsingham would explain it all. He might even confirm what Christopher Marlowe had told him: that his mother was indeed Jane Fromond, John Dee's new wife.

In the forest just outside London, the moon was going down. Gelis climbed into his covered cart, newly painted in green and gold. He woke his wife and child silently. His wife sat up in her quilted covers, rubbing her eyes; the boy turned over and went back to sleep.

"It's time we were on our way," Gelis whispered to his wife in Gaelic.

"Now?" She blinked. "Has something happened?"

"We've done our duty to Leonora Beak," he hedged, "and more. That's all. I don't like being so close to London."

"Nor do I," she agreed, "but that's not the reason you want to leave in the middle of the night."

"It's not the middle of the night," he argued. "The sun will be up in an hour."

She shook her head. "What is it, husband?"

His shoulders sank. "I fear very little in this life."

She put her hand on his leg. "You are the bravest Traveling man I know."

"But I am afraid of the Weird King." He avoided her eyes.

She leaned closer to him. "As am I, Gelis."

"As am I," the boy squeaked from beneath his covers.

"You want to be gone from him," said Gelis's wife.

"I do," he answered. "Not for what he might do to us, but for what he might do in the larger world. He'll bring strange forces to bear upon those around him. I feel it. I have no wish to be punished for his odd ways, or tainted by the mystic damage he might do."

"He has a strange power," she agreed. "We *should* leave now."

The boy rolled out of the covers and jumped up.

"So let's get started."

Gelis beamed. "I love you both, you know."

"You'd love a donkey if it agreed with you, Father," the boy said, patting Gelis on the shoulder as he slipped out of the cart.

"Where does he get that sort of an attitude?" Gelis asked his wife.

She looked away, raising her eyebrows. "I wonder."

As dawn drew back night's black curtain, Ned Blank awoke in his hammock, a paltry bed strung between two posts behind a dockside pub. He rubbed his eyes, and then his belly.

A shilling and a pence could get him a dozen eggs, and he knew he could eat them all. With the money he'd earned in the theatre and the ten shillings he'd pinched from Paget's purse, he could eat his fill, still have ale, and be quite content.

Swinging his feet onto the ground, he stretched.

"Beautiful morning," he said to the huge wharf rat nearby.

The rat lumbered off quite lazily as Ned took down his rope hammock and packed it into his shoulder bag. He was still dressed in his Romeus doublet and bright green stockings. He'd managed to get most of the makeup off his face, and his back was feeling much better. Money in his pocket, a good night's sleep, a starring role, and the promise of a great breakfast: things were looking up.

He sniffed and decided to walk around to the front door of the pub, just as if he were an ordinary patron, instead of slipping in the back through the kitchen. The sun on the Thames made the river golden and, for an instant, everything in the world was beautiful.

Ned shoved through the doorway and into the pub. It was not quite empty. A single serving man, no doubt the proprietor of the establishment, eyed Ned as he entered. Sitting behind the bar, he was dressed in drab brown with a soiled apron, and a weary frown. Another man was asleep at a table in the corner. Two women were talking to each other in low, grumbling tones. Ned took them for street whores at the end of a long night's work. He steered for a table as far away from them as he could manage, and sat down.

"Eggs, as many as you have, any style, a bit of mutton if it's not too old, and ale." He held up his fat purse to the serving man.

The man's eyes opened a bit wider.

"The eggs is boiled, the mutton's last night, and the ale is juniper, eh?"

"Perfect," Ned agreed. "Six eggs."

"That'll make it a shilling with everything," the man warned.

Ned smacked a shilling on the table at once and lifted his chin. "And I may want more eggs than that."

"Yes, sir," the man said, standing up at once.

Sir, thought Ned, grinning. Never been called *that* before.

The two women had taken notice of Ned's show, and were looking his way.

"Don't bother," Ned said to them sternly. "I'm an actor."

They both rolled their eyes and went back to complaining to each other.

Ned leaned back, idly running lines in his head as he often did in the morning, just to keep his memory crisp. He was so absorbed he barely noticed the two men who entered the place and stood in the doorway. Until one of them called out to him.

"Are you Ned Blank?"

Ned licked his lips. "What?"

"Are you the actor Ned Blank?"

The men were dressed in dark blue uniforms that bore a patch, a flourish of red above a helmet and a solid red horizontal bar. It looked to be a family crest, possibly a royal one.

"Who?" Ned snapped, exaggerating his irritation.

One of the drunken women spoke up. "He says he's an actor!"

"I am," Ned said indignantly. "Name of Burbage—greatest actor of the age."

The men moved silently toward him. One of them said, "I see."

"I'm trying to have a nice little breakfast," Ned complained. "And I'm famished for it. Do you mind?"

The guards moved quickly, on to each side of Ned's chair.

"Come along with us," one said, grabbing Ned under the arm.

"I will not!" Ned objected as the second guard took his other elbow.

"I've seen Burbage," the first man said. "You're half his age. And, incidentally, I also saw you as Ophelia in Kyd's *Hamlet.* You were quite brilliant."

They dragged him up from the table and toward the door.

"Here!" The proprietor shouted emerging from the kitchen. "What about them eggs!"

"Where are you taking me?" Ned moaned.

"Hampton Court, I'm afraid," the guard said almost apologetically. "See Lord Walsingham."

"Bleeding Christ," Ned muttered. "Why?"

"Paget, Morgan, and Kyd," the other guard answered harshly.

"Oh." Ned's courage gave out, and he allowed himself to be dragged along.

As they muscled through the door the owner shouted again, "What about this food?"

"He's left a shilling on the table," the first guard said.

"My Ophelia was good, wasn't it?" Ned said to him softly.

"I'm not ashamed to admit that I cried when you were dead."

"Well," Ned said, hobbling along between the two larger men, "that's something."

In the Queen's bedchamber, as Her Majesty sat before an array of mirrors, Blanche Parry stood nearby, holding several papers. Blanche was in a blue and gold dress with a high white collar. The Queen was still in her purple morning robe.

Blanche and Elizabeth had known each other for fifty years; Blanche was Chief Gentlewoman of the Privy Chamber, one of the very few who controlled access to the Queen. She was also in charge of the Queen's personal papers and presents given to the Queen; passed sensitive intelligence to her, and supervised the care of the royal ferret.

But it was not espionage or animal husbandry that brought her to the Queen that morning.

"You may recall the masque, your Majesty," Blanche said to the back of the Queen's head. "A woman comes to you whilst you are walking in a garden. She wants you to choose between her daughter's two suitors."

Elizabeth turned. "And her daughter is the Lady of May, I remember now. It was such a charming masque. Entangling theatre and reality in such a manner—where did the play begin and life end? I actually judged each suitor's talents, yes?"

Blanche barely took notice of the fact that the Queen had not used the royal "we."

"Yes." Blanche smiled, consulting the papers she was holding. "A crowd of people gathers: six foresters and six shepherds, including the suitors and the Lady of May. Something else happens and then the suitors begin their singing competition. You judge who sings the best, and the play continues according to which man you choose."

"Yes, yes," the Queen said, "the play has no determined ending, it entirely depends on my decision. I was delighted."

"You were," Blanche confirmed.

"And you say that Sidney has rewritten some parts? That is why he petitions for a showing of the masque here at court?"

"It says here," Blanche answered, again consulting her papers, "that new songs have been invented, and a secondary argument between a school teacher and shepherd has been added."

"How exciting," Elizabeth said calmly, turning back to her mirrors once more. "Let's have it. Sometime soon, don't you think?"

"It shall be arranged, Your Majesty," Blanche said, bowing only slightly, and backing away toward the door of the bedchamber.

"Does Sidney still love Penelope?" the Queen asked just as Blanche opened the door to leave.

"Oh," Blanche answered, sighing, "who can say what is in the hearts of young men?"

"I'm more worried about Penelope's brain," the Queen said, "than I am about Philip Sidney's heart."

Blanche inclined her head. "Are we certain that there actually *is* a brain in that lovely head?"

Elizabeth laughed softly as Blanche closed the door.

TWENTY-SEVEN

ZUTPHEN, THE NETHERLANDS

Marlowe woke up screaming. The other men around the fire sat up. Lopez stood over him.

Marlowe looked up at the doctor.

"I dreamed that the Bell Inn was filled with wild swine," Marlowe said, gasping, "and Leonora was drowning in blood, calling my name."

Lopez nodded. "The dead are never silent; although very few can hear them cry."

"God in heaven," Marlowe sat up.

"Leonora Beak?" the singer Egun asked, propping himself up on one elbow. "The one who helped Gelis and his family?"

Marlowe stared, regaining his composure. "Did you know her?"

"Gelis told me about her—and you," Egun said. "She calls out to you because her spirit is unsettled."

"Yes." Marlowe nodded.

"So why are you here," Egun asked, "instead of in England, finding revenge on the one who killed her?"

Marlowe stared into the fire. "I was told to come here."

"I was told to fight the English, but here I am with you," Egun countered. "I was told to fear God, but I only fear God's men here on earth. I was told—"

"I understand," Marlowe interrupted, standing.

He began to pace around the fire.

"Once you conclude your work here," Lopez suggested calmly, "you are free to return to England to pursue your murder investigations, am I correct?"

Marlowe nodded, still pacing.

"Then you should get on with your work here in Zutphen." Lopez stood.

Marlowe turned his eyes to the eastern horizon. A sliver of silver cracked between the earth and the sky. Dawn was at hand.

"We'll join the fighting today, then," he said.

"Good," Egun said, lying back down. "I'm going back to sleep until then. Wake me up when it's time to kill Spaniards."

He was snoring a minute later.

But Marlowe was wide awake. He drew Lopez a few feet away from the circle of men and whispered low.

"You understand what I have been told to do," he said to Lopez, "but how can I do it?"

Lopez nodded. "Pull the hammer back, take aim, squeeze the trigger."

"You know that's not what I meant."

"This is not a philosophical question," Lopez chided. "You make the matter too complicated with all your thinking: future poems, tangled love affairs, sympathetic understanding. Do the job. Pull the trigger."

Marlowe lowered his voice so that it was barely audible. "The man saved my life in the woods only a few hours ago!"

Lopez shook his head. "Sometimes I forget how young you are."

"This has nothing to do with my age," Marlowe railed. "I'm talking about a debt, a blood debt."

Lopez bit his upper lip for a moment. "You cared for Leonora Beak."

"She was second only to you in valor," he answered immediately, "and as brave a traveling companion."

"She saved your life."

"Probably several times," Marlowe said.

"Then you owe her a blood debt too," Lopez told him.

"I do."

"There is only one obstacle between you and the repayment of that debt. And the elimination of that obstacle is also your duty to your Queen."

Marlowe glanced in Sidney's direction. He was sleeping peacefully, curled up on his side, his face illuminated by the fire. It was the face of a cherub.

"How can treachery live in such a vessel?" Marlowe wondered.

Lopez stared at Sidney. "Satan has the power to assume a pleasing shape."

"But can the devil write the way that man does?"

Lopez offered a wan smile.

"Oh, my friend. The devil has written most of the great poetry of humankind."

The sun littered the horizon with splinters of gold, and several larks began to sing. A mourning dove, then a woodpecker, and then small wrens—all joined in.

It was morning.

Several hours later, on the banks of the River Berkel, the odd conglomeration of Travelers, Basque rebels, English poets, and a single Portuguese Jew lay on the ground, surveying a small encampment of Spaniards just across the water.

The sun was behind them, and the Spaniards were just waking up.

"This is the small group," Lopez whispered close to Marlowe's ear, "that brought Gérard into the Netherlands. Half of them are spies, all of them are vicious mercenaries, better fighting men than the ordinary Spanish troops. If we can eliminate them, the English cause will be greatly advanced."

Marlowe nodded. "This is a very strange war."

"It's gone on for nearly twenty years," Lopez agreed, "and little sign of an end in sight."

"Let's get on with it!" Sidney whispered harshly.

He lay on his belly on the other side of Marlowe.

Only twenty minutes earlier Marlowe had taken Sidney aside and told him the fabricated plan: Marlowe and Sidney would first engage in battle, then lose themselves in the fray, slip away from the fighting, and meet one of the spies from the Spanish camp. From there they would be spirited away, eventually back to Scotland, Castle Moil, where Mary's agents would relate the next phase of operations.

It was barely plausible, but Sidney wanted to believe it, and so he did. The fact that Marlowe had peppered his story with references to Penelope, even hinting that she might actually be waiting at Castle Moil, fueled Sidney's faith.

Lopez held up his hand. The men readied themselves. Marlowe checked the inflated lamb's bladder that Egun had given him, checked it for the third time.

"I hate the water," he muttered underneath his breath.

"I know," Lopez said. "The lamb's bladder will keep you afloat, high in the water. Don't worry."

"I'll float until some Spanish scab shoots an arrow through this thing!" Marlowe snapped nervously.

"The sun is still low," Lopez said, "and in their eyes. They probably won't see us at all, and they certainly won't be expecting an attack from the riverbank."

"Because to attack them from the riverbank," Marlowe said, "you would have to be insane."

"Exactly."

Lopez lowered his arm, and all the men slowly crawled toward the river.

Marlowe tried to occupy his mind with other thoughts: roast quail, random lines of poetry, Penelope's thighs.

In no time at all he was in the water, slowly pushing toward the far shore. He was astonished at how little noise two dozen men were making. His fears ebbed. Lopez was by his side, his pistols were dry on his back, and the water wasn't half as cold as he'd imagined. Moments later his feet felt the slimy river bottom, the beginning of the shore, and his heart slowed a little.

No one in the Spanish camp had seen them.

When all of Lopez's men arrived at the edge of the bank, bending low behind the tall grass on the bank, Lopez crawled forward onto the land, dragging his flotation device with him. One by one each man followed.

"Eliminate the muskets and musketeers first," Lopez whispered to Marlowe. "Pass that along."

Marlowe whispered to Sidney, Sidney told Egun, and in seconds each man understood.

Without another word Lopez leapt up, sword in one hand, pistol in the other, and roared incoherently, raging toward the camp.

The rest of the men were up, shrieking like tortured souls, and the battle was joined.

The small encampment was haphazardly littered along the bank: two small tents, one larger, sleeping soldiers under blankets on the ground, and several smoky fires. Only a few of the soldiers were up and about. A lean young man, shirtless, carrying water back for morning cooking, was the first to die.

Marlowe and Lopez charged together toward the largest tent, assuming that the occupant was the commander of the small force. But before they could get close enough to find out for certain, a tall man with a black mustache and a musket in each hand emerged through the opening and fired.

One of the musket balls tore through the morning air between Marlowe and Lopez and hit Egun in the side. The other rifle killed a boy of twelve, armed with a handmade knife.

A second later two men leapt from behind a smaller tent. Both landed on Lopez and sent him tumbling. Marlowe's rapier caught one of the soldiers in his knife hand before a third Spaniard came up from behind and stabbed Marlowe in his already-wounded arm just below the elbow.

Marlowe whirled around. His attacker was a boy of fifteen years or so, chin forward, teeth bared, face filled with insensate rage—someone too young to know that he could die.

Marlowe flicked his rapier against the boy's blade and smiled.

The boy lunged, roaring.

Marlowe stepped aside and the boy stumbled forward, stabbing air.

Marlowe cut the boy's side as he flew by, and hit him in the back of the head with the hilt of his dagger.

The boy skidded across the ground, losing his rapier. Marlowe jumped and landed on the boy's sword, snapping it at the hilt.

The boy rolled over on his back to reveal a pistol in his hand, cocked and pointed at Marlowe's chest. Marlowe kicked it out of his hand and the gun went off, showering the boy with powder and sparks.

Marlowe was about to say something to the boy when he saw that Lopez was still on the ground, wrestling with his two assailants. Marlowe glanced back at the boy, shrugged, and stabbed him in the heart.

Then he flew to Lopez, kicking one of the Spanish attackers in the ribs. That man yelped and rolled away. A second later Marlowe saw why Lopez was still on the ground: he had a dagger sticking out of his chest.

Marlowe stomped down hard on the second Spaniard's foot, then bent down and sliced his throat, shoving him aside.

"Get up!" he commanded Lopez.

"Lung," Lopez gasped. "Collapsed. Can't breathe."

Marlowe, ignoring the battle around him, sheathed his rapier and dagger and helped Lopez up. Lopez threw his arm around Marlowe's shoulders, holding out his rapier on the other side.

"The large tent," Lopez managed to say.

Marlowe nodded and they headed in that direction.

Halfway there two more Spaniards appeared out of nowhere, howling and flailing odd-looking sabers.

Marlowe drew his dagger once more, took it by the point, and flicked it underhand, sent it into the neck of the closest Spaniard. At the same time Lopez, still holding onto Marlowe, flashed his rapier high, then downward in a half-circle, coming up under the other man's sword hand and cutting his wrist. Then he stabbed the man in his gut. Blood exploded from the wounds. Both men went down.

"Tent," Lopez insisted.

They staggered together the several yards toward the tent, and fell inward through the opening, both crashing to the ground.

Marlowe was up again at once, blade to the door. Lopez got up more slowly and managed to get to the cot in the otherwise empty tent.

"I can't pull this damned knife out of me," Lopez wheezed. "It's the only thing stopping up the wound. But I have to get it out of my lung."

Marlowe backed toward Lopez, shifting his rapier to his left hand. His blood was up and his senses heightened. He took hold of the low corner of the doctor's crimson cloak and held it to the wound, then grasped the handle of the knife in his friend's chest. He waggled the blade as gently as he could. Lopez sipped his breath, but made no sound. Marlowe inched the blade up a little.

"There?" he asked Lopez, his eyes still on the door to the tent.

"Just—just a little more."

Marlowe eased the knife up a quarter of an inch more.

"There, I think," the doctor said.

"You need a surgeon. Sew up that wound. But what about the lung."

"The lung heals very quickly." Lopez winced. "And I can sew up the wound myself. Get back out there."

"I'm not leaving you."

"You have to, Chris," Lopez said softly. "You have to win this skirmish, and in that winning must lose Philip Sidney."

Marlowe stood for a moment, speechless and uncertain, but he knew that Lopez was right.

Without another word Marlowe flew from the tent, feeling the wheel-lock pistol's handle pressing into his back. The first thing he saw was Egun, back against one of the smaller tents, holding off a large Spanish soldier who was spitting and cursing and slicing back and forth with another of the odd sabers.

Marlowe raced toward them, lunged, and stabbed the Spaniard with his rapier, withdrew, and stabbed again, deep. The man turned toward Marlowe, no life in his eyes, and continued to fight, slashing empty air. Marlowe stepped aside to let the man fall.

"You've been shot," Marlowe said to Egun.

"Not bad," Egun said, but his teeth were clenched.

"Go to the large tent. Lopez is in there. He's wounded. You could help him, and he you."

Without waiting for a reply Marlowe dashed away, looking for Sidney. The ground was strewn with bodies, mostly Spanish soldiers. The air was filled with curses and prayers and smoke.

Marlowe caught sight of Sidney at the riverside, fending off three attackers. Marlowe rushed forward, catching Sidney's eye.

"I could use a hand," Sidney called out happily.

Marlowe ran, arrived, stabbed one of the soldiers in the back of the thigh. That one turned, pulled out a pistol, and took aim.

Marlowe pressed, stabbed the man again in the belly, but the man refused to die. Instead he fell forward onto Marlowe; they both went down and began to roll, wrestling and grunting.

Sidney was having an easier time with the two remaining soldiers, and Marlowe knew that the man on top of him was about to pass out. Kneeing the Spaniard in his privates, knocking the pistol away, Marlowe gained the upper position. He glanced at Sidney, who had his back to Marlowe.

Marlowe drew the wheel-lock pistol from the holster on his back, looked down at the weakening Spaniard, and put his finger to his lips. The Spaniard squinted uncomprehendingly. Marlowe held his breath, took aim, and pulled the trigger.

A second later Philip Sidney went down.

Marlowe dropped the pistol next to the Spaniard, jumped up, and ran toward the startled Spanish soldiers standing over Sidney. He dispatched the first Spaniard with a single thrust to the chest. The second turned, and Marlowe cut his throat with the tip of his rapier. It wasn't enough to kill the man, but he was bleeding and crying out—he'd soon be dead.

Marlowe looked down. The pistol shot had caught Sidney in the thigh. It was a gaping wound, and had shattered the bone. But Sidney was alive.

He blinked up at Marlowe.

"You've saved my life," Sidney said, shaking from the pain. "That damned Spaniard shot me, and his friends would have finished me off if it hadn't been for you. I am in your debt, Kit Marlowe."

And then Philip Sidney passed out.

An hour later the fighting had ended. All the Spaniards were dead.

In the big tent, Egun's wound was patched, Lopez was wheezing in his sleep, and Sidney pitched forward on the ground, writhing in pain.

A few of the Travelers looked at Sidney's wound. They shook their heads. The bullet had gone through the flesh, shattered the bone, and blasted the muscle to tatters. There was no repairing it. He would lose the leg, or die.

"It'll be gangrene very soon," one of the Scots Travelers said softly.

Another man nodded. "Maggots."

The others agreed. It wouldn't be long before the flies overtook the corpses. They only had to collect the maggots, place them in Sidney's wound, and allow the creatures to consume the dead tissue, leaving the living alone. It was the common cure, and it would work. But a good portion of the thigh was gone. Sidney would never use the leg again.

Marlowe paced back and forth in front of the tent, his face red and drenched in sweat.

One of the Scots emerged and put his hand on Marlowe's shoulder.

"You did what you could," he said to Marlowe. "Lopez is strong. He'll be fine. Egun too. And you saved Sidney's life. You should rest a while. The battle's over."

But Marlowe's brain was still battling, at war with itself.

"Is Lopez awake?" Marlowe asked distractedly.

The man shook his head.

From inside the tent another Traveler called out, "We need water in here!"

Without thinking Marlowe cast his eye about, found a large cooking pan, grabbed it, and ran to the river. Moments later he was back with the water, bursting into the tent.

Lopez was still unconscious. Marlowe went directly to Sidney.

"Here, Philip," he said. "Drink this."

"Give it to Egun first," he said, straining to keep his voice calm. "His need is greater than mine."

Everyone in the tent looked at Sidney with such reverence then that Marlowe couldn't move.

One of the men took the pan and handed it to Egun, who drained half of it and then handed it back.

"Give the rest to Sidney for God's sake!"

Sidney was handed the pan; he gulped the rest of the water down, gasping. Then he looked about the tent.

"Might I have a word with Marlowe in private?" he asked.

The men all nodded, heading for the tent flap at once.

Even Egun stood. "I'll be giving you your privacy, Sir Philip."

Before Sidney could object, Egun stumbled toward the door and the other men helped him out.

When they were gone, Philip lay back down on his pallet.

"Our friends," he began, whispering, "the agents we were to meet here: they're dead, I suppose."

"They are," Marlowe answered.

"Well." Sidney closed his eyes. "That's it then. I can't go to Spain without them, and I dare not return to England. If only the man who wounded me had been a better shot. I wouldn't be in this fix."

"Philip," Marlowe began.

"Listen," Sidney interrupted. "I know Penelope doesn't love me. I know that. And I know I've done a foolish thing—several foolish things. What is love, that it makes us lose our wit and will and every noble notion? I've slaughtered all my better angels on the shabby altar of this false love."

"The heart never heeds the brain," Marlowe said.

"My brain," Sidney groaned, thrashing. "I have no idea what's in it now. I have set in motion a thing that cannot be undone, a man who will not be stopped, and I do not know what is right, or if I should stop it. But listen to me now! Penelope is no more in league with the Spanish than am I."

"I know," Marlowe said gently. "She only resents being forced to marry Robert Rich."

Sidney writhed for a moment gasping, then went on. "No, you misunderstand me! Penelope has been provoked to rash behavior by entreaty and threat from her brother!"

Marlowe swallowed. "Robert Devereux is involved in this attempt to kill the Queen?"

Sidney nodded, wincing. "God! My head is on fire!"

Sidney's eyes closed and he dropped into unconsciousness. Marlowe touched Sidney's forehead. It was burning.

A soft voice in the tent said, "If only the man who wounded him had been a better shot."

Marlowe turned. Lopez was up on one elbow, shaking his head.

"Yes," Marlowe whispered, dropping his head.

"Troubling news about Devereux," the doctor said softly.

Marlowe could only shake his head and wonder what madness was at work.

Lopez sipped a breath. "What did Sidney mean when he said he'd set things in motion?"

"Not certain." Marlowe stood and took a deep breath. "But I believe that he has orchestrated the Queen's murder during the performance of a theatrical distraction at Hampton Court—and soon."

"Do you know the details?" Lopez whispered more urgently.

"A few of them. If I were in London I could find out more."

"Does Walsingham know about this?"

Marlowe nodded. "But he may think that the plan is foiled since

Sidney is removed from the scene. My fear now is that Sidney has assigned the task to—to others. The plan is still in force."

"Then you must go," Lopez said, sitting up. "You must return to England now!"

Marlowe glanced down at the sleeping Sidney.

"What about him?"

"Leave him to me," Lopez said. "It may be in our best interest to keep silent about his wound at the moment."

"I don't understand."

"If the other conspirators believe that Sidney escaped to Spain, or is at least alive and fighting in the Netherlands, they will continue with their plans, and you may discover the entire nest of vermin."

"You'll tend his wound."

"I will," Lopez said. "But he will die. It's only a matter of when—and when we release the news that he has died. I may wait for some time to do that, but at least until you have accomplished your work."

Marlowe clenched his jaw. "I would prefer that he didn't suffer."

"And I would prefer that he hadn't betrayed our Queen," Lopez answered.

Before Marlowe could respond, Egun peeked into the tent.

"We really ought to go back across the river," he said. "The men are feeling exposed here. The Spanish will send other troops here, they think."

"They're right," Lopez agreed, swinging his feet over the side of the cot.

"Can Sidney be moved?" Egun asked.

"We'll have to move him, won't we?" Lopez reached out for Marlowe. Marlowe took hold of him and helped him toward the door.

Egun signaled and several men came in, took up Sidney's pallet, and hoisted him, still sleeping, between them.

"When we are back to our encampment on the other side of Zutphen," Egun said to Marlowe, "I'll have a moment to thank you properly for saving my life, and Sidney's. We'll have some outstanding French wine tonight!"

"Mr. Marlowe won't have time for celebration," Lopez interjected. "He's heading back to London this morning."

Egun stared at Lopez, but knew better than to question his pronouncement. If Lopez said that Marlowe was going, then Marlowe would be gone.

TWENTY-EIGHT

LONDON

Marlowe was more tired than he had ever been in his life. His horse walked slowly past the woods outside of London where the Travelers' camp had been. They were gone, and not a trace of the encampment could be found.

The sun was down but the sky was aflame over the western horizon. A full moon, pale as a ghost, tried, and failed, to illuminate the night.

The prospect of reporting to Walsingham that he had failed to kill Sidney, just as he'd failed to save William the Silent, was an iron stone in his stomach. The thought of saying the name *Robert Devereux* to Walsingham in the same sentence as the phrase *murder the Queen* made Marlowe's head swim. So, as London Bridge came into view, he considered stopping his horse and finding the nearest public house.

But Walsingham would know. Walsingham knew everything. Except that the Queen's newest lover—everyone knew that she and Devereux shared a bed—was part of a plan to have her killed in her own home.

Shoreditch streets swelled with noisy rabble. Not so far from Marlowe's side of the bridge lay The Curtain Theatre. Would Ned still be there? Would it be worth a quick diversion to stop by? Question the boy again? To what end? It was unlikely that he knew anything about Devereux.

Once again deciding that Walsingham had eyes everywhere, and would already know that Marlowe had returned to the city,

Marlowe took a deep breath and headed across the bridge toward Hampton Court.

As he rode he tried to force his brain to assemble the pieces of a puzzle that would make clear the roots of betrayal. What sort of person would profess love for someone, and then plot their murder? What sort of person would lie about love?

But as he rode his head refused to form answers, and his eyes began to close. He fell into half-slumber, still astride his horse. And in that dreamlike state he roamed his wild memory more than the streets of London.

He was a boy drowning in the Great Stour River near his home. And as death wrapped his cloak around his sinking body, Marlowe saw, quite clearly, the faces of angels. They had no features, not like human faces. They were made of light and longing: they begged the boy to come along with them. But just as Marlowe was about to ride their radiance to some other place, a rough hand took hold of his shirt, snatched him back from incomprehensible beauty, and made him vomit water.

Marlowe's eyes snapped open.

He was awake, lost on a strange London street, and shaken by a bizarre realization. He had always supposed that his death experience had liberated him from a fear of dying. Now he was suddenly seized by the certain knowledge that he resented being alive. He was filled with indignant anger at life. Knowing what lay beyond it made all the world a shabby place, a theatrical set, peopled with ridiculous actors, men who forgot their lines and staggered on, women who lied as easily as they drew breath.

Just then his horse nudged a man carrying two sacks of grain.

"Watch where the hell you're going, you bleeding pustule!" the man growled.

Marlowe looked down at him. With a single flick of his dagger he could cut the man's throat and ride on. Few on the street would know what had happened; none would care. Marlowe fingered the handle of his knife.

But just as he was about to draw out his blade, he smiled.

"Apologies, friend," he told the man. "Here. Sling your sacks on the front of my saddle and let me hoist you up behind. We'll carry you."

The man stared upward. His face was a diverting entertainment filled with confusion, exhaustion, suspicion, and need.

Without waiting for a response Marlowe took up one of the sacks of grain and put in front of him, on the horse's neck. The man hesitated, then handed the other over. Marlowe took it, secured it, and then offered his hand. In seconds the man was riding on the back of Marlowe's horse, unable to find the words he wanted to say.

"Now," Marlowe said, not looking back, "Where are we going?"

The man mumbled incoherently, and then cleared his throat. "The White Gull," he said, "just two streets up and one over."

"Ah." Marlowe urged his horse forward. "As luck would have it, I know the place."

"Do you mind my asking your name, sir?" the man asked softly. "I'd like to know what name to include in my prayers tonight."

Marlowe smiled. "I am in great need of prayer, friend," he said. "It's Marlowe."

"Marlowe," the man repeated. "You're not from London—too much manners."

"Canterbury," Marlowe acknowledged. "Although I'm a student in Cambridge, Christ College, just now."

The man nodded sagely. "Student."

"You work at The White Gull, then?" Marlowe went on amiably.

"Worse," the man lamented. "I own it."

"My condolences to any man who makes a living dependent on the peregrinations of a whimsical public."

"Amen to that," the man groaned.

In no time they stopped at the door of the man's public house.

"You'll come in," the man said, sliding off Marlowe's horse. "You'll have ale and food on the house."

"Alas I am called hence," Marlowe said, handing down one of the sacks. "But I'll come back soon, I promise you. And I'll pay."

"Well," the man shrugged, taking up both sacks, "I don't like to argue. But I do expect to see you tomorrow morning, Mr. Marlowe."

With that he was gone into the small, noisy pub.

Marlowe turned his horse once again toward Hampton Hall feeling strangely refreshed. If he had not been so exhausted, he might have been suspicious instead.

The courtyard outside his usual entrance to Hampton's hidden side, where Walsingham's outer office lay, was unusually crowded. Three armed men stood near the bench where Marlowe often sat. The usual two guards were at the familiar door, but their weapons were drawn, and they were unusually attentive.

As Marlowe walked his horse closer, Leviticus came racing out to meet him.

"Mr. Marlowe! So much has happened! I don't know where to begin."

The boy took the reins from Marlowe, panting.

"Begin at the beginning," Marlowe advised.

"Well," Leviticus said, nodding, "arrests have been made in suspicion of a plot against the Queen!"

"Who has been arrested?"

"Actors! The brilliant Ophelia, and that fat old Thomas Kyd."

Marlowe froze "Where are they?"

"In the Tower! And there's more!"

Marlowe shook his head. "No. Sorry. I've got to go speak with Walsingham at once."

"No, but wait 'til you hear!" The boy grabbed Marlowe's elbow. "I found the manuscript, the one that was in John Dee's laboratory."

"Good," Marlowe said distractedly.

"And I think you might have been right about my mother." Leviticus lowered his voice. "I think that John Dee's new wife is she."

Marlowe patted the boy on the shoulder. "Good. I'm glad that you've been making progress, and I'm proud of you for finding John Dee's manuscript."

Leviticus blinked. "You're proud of me?"

Marlowe smiled. "I am. But I must go now."

With that he was off, racing to the door where guards stood at attention.

As they saw Marlowe coming, one stood aside and the other opened the door.

"You're expected," he said.

Of course I am, Marlowe thought.

In short order he stood in Walsingham's small office: littered table, one chair, ten candles. He didn't have time to be impatient; Walsingham appeared almost at once, dressed in black robes and a blue skullcap.

"Ned Blank and Thomas Kyd should not be in the Tower," he snapped before Walsingham had a chance to speak.

Walsingham's eyes flashed. "You forget yourself."

"No," Marlowe pressed. "You've arrested the wrong people. Kyd's an idiot in his personal affairs, but never a traitor to his country. And I'm afraid I misled you with regard to Ned Blank. He did not, most *emphatically* did not kill Leonora Beak, and you know it."

Walsingham looked Marlowe up and down. Marlowe's cheap uniform was stained and torn. His face was smeared with grime, his hair a wild tangle. His ruined boots were caked with mud and blood and dried river slime.

"You're a shambles, Marlowe."

"Yes," he agreed, "but I am in earnest: Ned Blank did not kill—"

"I know!" Walsingham interrupted. "You must calm yourself. That boy is not the murderer. Kyd is only being held. Everything is well in hand."

Marlowe took a deep breath. "Are Ned and Kyd in the Tower?"

"Yes," Walsingham admitted, "but not for long. I needed to keep them out of mischief, and to send a message to the real conspirators. I know that these actors are dupes."

Marlowe's shoulders relaxed, dropped an inch.

"What about Paget and Morgan?" he asked.

"Thus far elusive," Walsingham answered. "We think they have slipped out of England, likely gone to Spain."

"But at least not here in London, wreaking havoc," Marlowe acknowledged. "Good."

"Now," Walsingham went on. "What news from the Netherlands?"

"Ah." Marlowe closed his eyes. "Well. Philip Sidney is mortally wounded. But not dead. Lopez thinks it best to keep him alive as long as this current plot continues in order to ferret out the entire nest of vermin."

Walsingham inclined his head. "Good. Your idea? I mean to say: you shot Sidney with the pistol my daughter gave you?"

"I did," Marlowe answered, only a little surprised that the old man knew about the pistol. "It was done during a small skirmish near Zutphen. Lopez was wounded as well."

"And Lopez will treat Sidney while he keeps him under surveillance." Walsingham nodded. "This is excellent. Control his communication with the other traitors, keep Her Majesty unaware that her favorite poet nearly killed her, and of course Lopez can finish him off there in Zutphen when the time comes, when the Queen realizes what treachery has been afoot."

Marlowe was sickened for a moment by the icy manner with which Walsingham approached the death of so great a man.

Walsingham saw Marlowe's face.

"You disapprove," Walsingham sniffed. "But you must understand that the Queen chooses favorites and will hear nothing evil about them until the weight of that evil is so great that it breaks the bond of affection. She will not condemn Mary, who has plotted for years to kill her, without more proof of Mary's betrayal. And so she would never believe that Sidney could harm her. She thinks that I am grossly suspicious and see shadows in sunlight. But there are shadows everywhere. At the moment her—*favorite* is Robert Devereux, the Earl of Essex, but I believe you and I both know that he, more than poor, simple Penelope, is to blame for the disease of this current plot."

"Yes," Marlowe said, even as he marveled at Walsingham's breadth of knowledge. "I have no idea how you know this, but it is confirmed by Sidney: Robert Devereux is behind Penelope—and so also behind Sidney—in the threat of death. But I don't understand how that can be."

"Robert Devereux is ambitious," Walsingham said bitterly. "He is vain and greedy—but he is also a brilliant general and a remarkable man of letters. He wants—more. And he does not realize that Spain is, in fact, the author of the piece in which he is only a player. Spain uses the Catholic Church, Queen Mary, and the petty rivalries of our own court, all to its hideous advantage."

"But surely this plot has been foiled," Marlowe began. "Sidney is lame, Penelope discovered, Mary in prison, Babington unmasked, and the rest of the conspirators scattered or fled."

"Yes." Walsingham sat, his face contorted with worry. "Two things yet weigh heavily on my mind."

"Sir," Marlowe interjected impatiently, "I believe I have done my duty and more. I am genuinely eager to return to my pursuit of Leonora's murderer. You know it was not Ned Blank."

Walsingham looked up. "But do you have any other suspects?"

"No," Marlowe admitted, "but I have an odd itch at the back of my brain. Were I not exhausted, distracted, and heartsick, I feel that things would be much clearer in my mind. Which is why I beg you to release me from these courtly matters, now that they are primarily satisfied, so that I may bring all my concentration to bear on finding Leonora's killer."

His voice had grown quite loud; without meaning to, Marlowe's insistence had become very impassioned.

Walsingham met Marlowe's volume, if not spirit. "Do you imagine that I am not as anxious as you to find my other daughter's murderer? But we must put off this more personal matter until the greater threat has been extinguished!"

"What greater threat!" Marlowe shouted. "The plot is ruined, the danger is gone!"

"No!" Walsingham rose, banging the table with both hands.

Shocked, Marlowe took a moment to regain his composure.

"What in God's name remains to be done?" he asked slowly, shaking his head.

Walsingham's eyes pierced Marlowe's. "The Queen will shortly see a masque in the gardens, *The Lady of May*. By Philip Sidney. It may be an instrument of assassination, as you told me it would be."

Marlowe's ire evaporated. "No. Prevent its presentation."

"But Sidney won't be here to carry out his grotesque intention."

"He told me something," Marlowe said, taking a step toward Walsingham. "His last words to me were that he had set in motion something that could not be undone, a single man. That is the primary reason I raced to London after our battle in Zutphen, to warn you about this very thing. I forgot myself momentarily. I—I am weary and sick at heart."

"You forgot yourself. Well." Walsingham nodded. "But as to the theatre, his masque, there are others involved, others unknown to us. Not just one man."

Marlowe thought for a moment. "I am afraid that may be true. Who is to present the masque? What troupe?"

"An amalgam of Lord Strange's Men and bit players from The Curtain, I have been told."

Marlowe frowned. "Does that include Kyd or Ned Blank?"

"We shall see. They are to be let out of the Tower specifically so that you might watch them; see if they are a part of this business."

"Then I say again," Marlowe went on, ignoring the old man's tone, "have the presentation cancelled. Why take the risk?"

"If only it were that simple." Walsingham shrugged. "I cannot forbid the piece without explaining why. And I cannot, at the moment, tell the Queen about Philip Sidney, for reasons we have just discussed."

Marlowe's mind raced. "Are you suggesting that we must play his foul scene to its completion?"

"Yes, Marlowe," Walsingham said. "You must join your abilities at rapier and dagger with your skills as a thespian. You must be a part of the masque."

"Discover if the plot is, in fact, still in force," Marlowe agreed reluctantly, "and stay its hand."

"Yes."

"No. I've made such a mess of everything: William's death, Leonora's death, Sidney's death."

Walsingham looked down. "Everything has gone more or less according to plan."

"I don't want to know what that means," Marlowe said, staring.

"It means, at the moment, that you must be a part of the masque," Walsingham repeated. "In fact, it's been arranged. You are to go to a place called The White Gull. You have recently met its owner, I believe. I cannot be certain, but I believe that the players for Sidney's masque are to gather there. But have a care—that particular intelligence is not entirely reliable."

Marlowe felt the weight of unanswered questions threaten to capsize him. He was drowning. He felt, as he had before, the sensation that Walsingham was God, and knew everything.

"I did, in fact, meet the owner of that place," Marlowe said slowly. "Quite by chance, or so it seemed."

Walsingham saw Marlowe's distress. "I placed the man, his name is Went, in your path as soon as you entered the city," he said. "He is in my employ. He has told me that actors sometimes accumulate in his establishment, mostly to complain about acting. It seems a good place to start."

Marlowe surrendered; gave up the notion of figuring out the larger picture of the Queen's spymaster and chose, instead, to concentrate on the moment at hand.

"But you said there were two things weighing on your mind," he said to Walsingham wearily.

"Ah!" The old man opened a drawer. "Yes. It's this damned manuscript that the boy found in John Dee's laboratory."

He tossed the odd manuscript; it landed with a thud on the desk.

"Have you deciphered it?" Marlowe asked.

"No." Walsingham stared at the thing as if it were a dead animal. "No one can. And I find the drawings very disturbing."

Marlowe nodded, only glancing at the volume. "Who has seen it?"

"Burghley, the Queen, and most of all my secretary, Thomas Phelipps, the most expert code breaker in the world. Even he could make no sense of this vile tome."

"May I?" Marlowe asked, not waiting for an answer.

He picked up the volume and flipped through its pages. As he did he asked, "What does John Dee think this is?"

"We have not questioned him about it yet."

"Doesn't that seem in order?"

Walsingham nodded. "But we did not want to tip our hand."

"Is it possible that this is, in fact, a mystical volume? An angelic device?" Marlowe's eyes drank in the odd images and impossible words.

Then, on a certain page, Marlowe stopped. He held it close to his face and inhaled. He stared and his eyes grew wider.

"What is it?" Walsingham asked.

Marlowe shook his head. "This page," he whispered. "I should have realized."

"What *is* it, Marlowe?" Walsingham insisted.

Marlowe looked up. "Sometimes the stars align, and we suddenly see all things so clearly. I must refresh myself, find better clothes, and seek out Lord Strange's men."

Walsingham glared. "Are you going to tell me what you're doing?"

"No." Marlowe smiled. "I've failed you until now. Let me make amends."

"You know something."

"I know almost everything." Marlowe's smile grew.

Walsingham remained very still. "How?"

"One instant of intuition is, apparently, worth months of plodding and worry. I have what I believe to be the answer to, as I say, nearly everything."

Walsingham hesitated.

"Go, then," he said at length. "Finish this business."

Marlowe nodded and backed toward the door. "I will. And very soon."

TWENTY-NINE

Marlowe, bathed and dressed in new black clothes, rapier and dagger cleaned of blood, boots cleared of mud, strode toward The Curtain Theatre. He'd slept the best he had in a month, and he was famished.

Only a little lost, he turned down a certain street and suddenly saw, up ahead, The White Gull, a hard golden beam of sunlight crowning it as if it were a cathedral.

He steered through the crowded streets and into the dark public room. The place was packed but sedate, a quieter morning than most. The second Marlowe entered, the innkeeper spotted him.

"Mr. Marlowe!" he sang out.

Marlowe instantly felt exposed. Several heads turned his way, and Marlowe knew he recognized one of them. Will Kempe belonged to Leicester's Men, their finest clown. He was portly but muscular, jolly but stern, dressed slightly better than the rest of the men, in a quilted green doublet with a fine felt hat.

Kempe lifted his chin a bit, and Marlowe nodded, but the innkeeper prevented any further interaction. He rushed to Marlowe's side.

"Mr. Marlowe!" the innkeeper said again. "The only true gentleman left in London!"

The man dragged Marlowe to a place near the bar, shoved a tankard of ale into Marlowe's hand, and leaned his head toward Marlowe's ear.

"On the house and no argument. And these men have gathered here of a purpose."

Marlowe nodded. "Many thanks," he said and drank half the tankard. "I'll be wanting a bit of something to break my fast—and that I will pay for. No argument."

The man beamed and spoke so that the whole place could hear. "What did I just say? The only true gentleman."

And he was off, into the kitchen.

Marlowe turned around quickly to survey the crowd. He caught most of them staring at him. He saluted the room with his tankard. Something was very odd about this assemblage. Marlowe knew that his entrance had been a bit noteworthy, but these men were watching him with more than casual interest. The entire room seemed charged.

Marlowe leaned back against the bar, calculating how many men he would have to fight on his way to the exit. A bold moment was in order. So.

"Kempe," Marlowe said loudly, "I thought you were in Leicester House, cavorting."

Kempe took a drink. "Lord Leicester has gone to the Low Countries, to fight in the war against the Spanish. I am momentarily unemployed."

"Leicester has gone to the Netherlands?" Marlowe set his tankard down on the bar behind him. "Do you know where?"

"Town of Zutphen," Kempe grunted. "Took me with him when he first went, but I was only to be a carrier pigeon for his winsome nephew."

Marlowe forced himself to remain placid, his face unmoved.

"You were to bring messages back to London from Philip Sidney?" He asked.

"Yes." Kempe stared. "But Sidney never showed up. Leicester had letters for Sidney's wife, but I thought it best to deliver them to Lady Leicester instead of Sidney's wife."

Marlowe kept his eyes steady. "Why would you do such a thing?"

"Sidney's wife is in Hampton Court," Kempe said evenly. "It's a place littered with spies, you see, and I have no desire to fall into such company or such intrigues, as some other actors have, of late."

"You mean Ned Blank and Kyd, in the Tower," Marlowe said.

"Aye," Kempe agreed, "and more. I have just returned to London, as a matter of fact, and delivered the letters; heard the news. Dangerous times for an actor."

"Dangerous and unemployed," Marlowe observed. "Ingredients for mischief."

"As luck would have it," Kempe went on, "I *may* have secured a bit of work for myself and several others."

"I suppose you mean Sidney's masque," Marlowe interrupted. "I know about it; I have been instructed to fix the script."

It was not too bold a lie, and why not shoot straight for the heart? If these weren't the men assembled to discuss working on the masque, no harm done. If they were, Marlowe would appear not only in the know, but in control to some extent.

Kempe maintained his emotionless exterior, but several of the other men shifted uncomfortably in their seats.

"Instructed by Sidney?" Kempe asked.

There's a pregnant question, Marlowe thought. How much does he know about Sidney?

"Philip Sidney, too, is in Zutphen, as you are aware," Marlowe began. "I have only just returned from battle there. That battle is probably the reason Sidney could not speak with you directly."

"How did the battle fare?" Kempe asked with only a modicum of interest. "And Sidney?"

"Well: we won. Sidney's concern, as far as I was able to determine, was more for women than for fighting—or for theatre."

One of the men chuckled. "Always has been."

And most in the pub relaxed.

But Kempe pressed. "What did Sidney say about our play?"

"He has rededicated it to the Queen," Marlowe began, "and, I believe, the ending is quite different from the previous incarnation."

There it was. If these men were involved in the plot to kill Elizabeth, they would understand that the end of the play would also mean the end of the Queen. Marlowe tried to watch every face, read each expression.

The man who had laughed spoke up. "Do you know what parts we are to play?"

"That's up to the other man," Kempe snapped. "The one who's organized us here."

Marlowe did his best not to betray confusion. What *other man*?

But everyone else in the place nodded, somewhat solemnly, and Marlowe knew better than to press that issue.

Luckily, Went the innkeeper appeared from the kitchen bringing Marlowe food and drink.

"This is the gentleman," Went announced to everyone, "who picked me up on his horse, carried my sacks of grain—and him a stranger to me."

"Some of us know Mr. Marlowe," Kempe said.

Just then Marlowe spied a face he recognized. It was the boy who had played the part of Anna in his ill-fated presentation of *Dido* at The Pickerel Inn. That seemed a hundred years ago. What was his name?

He tried to look away, but Marlowe smiled and said to him, "I never did give you your fee for helping me with that monster of a piece in Cambridge, did I?"

"Kyd payed me, sir," the boy squeaked.

"He did? Good. I must remember to thank him."

"If he survives the Tower," Kempe said under his breath.

"Kyd's in the Tower." Marlowe shook his head; feigned amazement.

"You've been away," Kempe said as Marlowe sat down. "Something's afoot at The Curtain. Kyd's taken, as well as poor old Ned Blank."

"Do we know why?" Marlowe asked.

Went set down the food and drink in front of Marlowe and stood by, waiting to hear Kempe's response.

"I would imagine someone caught them cavorting," Kempe said softly.

Others nodded.

"Thomas Kyd is my friend," Marlowe said plainly. "Whatever else he is, he's the finest poet of our day, and does not deserve such treatment."

Everyone nodded.

"Ned's the one what showed me how," the boy who played Anna lamented. "A mentor to me."

"Well." Marlowe lifted his tankard. "Their health, then. And let them out of that damned prison."

Everyone assented. Marlowe picked up his plate, still standing with his back to the bar, and dug into his food.

"But we've assembled here of a purpose," he said to Kempe, his mouth full.

"Aye." Kempe nodded. "We're to get our parts, and the lines, and a bit of added instruction from our progenitor. But then you'd have the script with you, would you not?"

"I would not," Marlowe answered. "I was to get it from Sidney's wife, Frances Walsingham, tomorrow."

Kempe sat back. "I was told that another woman had it."

Marlowe nodded. "Penelope Rich."

Kempe stared, eyes steady. "Is your appearance here is a bit coincidental, or did you know about this meeting?"

Marlowe shook his head, still eating vigorously. "Went offered me a free meal. What poet ever turned that down? And, in truth, this place has a reputation for actors."

"And you say you've just been in the Lowlands?"

"I was there," Marlowe affirmed, "killing Spaniards—while you were playing carrier pigeon."

Marlowe's voice and demeanor had not changed even though his attitude had. It took Kempe a moment to realize he'd been insulted.

"Listen, *boy*," Kempe bristled, "I was riding little ponies like you when you were sucking your mother's teat."

Marlowe set down his tankard. "I don't care to hear about your amorous adventures with ponies. And as to my mother's anatomy—"

Without another breath Marlowe tossed his plate aside, drew his dagger, and strode to Kempe's table. Before Kempe could rise, the point of Marlowe's blade was pressed just under Kempe's ample chin. A single tear of blood grew there, like a droplet of red rain.

"It would be a great loss to the London theatre if you were unable to speak your lines," Marlowe said softly. "But if I push this knife a little harder, it'll push through the fat and slice your tongue. And there goes your diction."

Kempe was very still. "Your reputation for being quarrelsome is well founded, I see," he allowed. "They say you killed a fellow student at Cambridge just because you didn't like the color of his codpiece."

"Ah, you mean Walter Pygott." Marlowe nodded. "He was a bully and he deserved what he got."

No need to explain that he hadn't died at Marlowe's hand. It was good to have a reputation as a rash brawler. And overreacting to Kempe's insult had very neatly changed the subject from Sidney and the Netherlands—a subject too risky to pursue.

"Well, I'm not certain I deserve this blade at my gullet," Kempe said, "but now that I think of it, it may have been some other breast at which you have sucked. You have a reputation with les femmes as well, do you not?"

Marlowe pressed the point just a little. "Reputation is a false imposition; got without merit; lost without cause. I prefer the observation of deeds over the idle gossip of fishwives, street whores, and actors. So I will say this: though your reputation is that of our nation's finest clown, I have seen you act. And my observation is this: every good thing ever said about you has not done you justice. You are ten times the actor they say you are, and more. You are a man of true greatness. And so I completely forgive you reference to my mother's teat—especially as I am so very familiar with that part of your own mother. There."

The dagger was gone and Marlowe offered his hand, grinning.

The entire crowd burst into applause and laughter, including Went and Kempe.

"Ah, well said!" Kempe shouted. "With that golden tongue, you couldn't be nearly as bad a poet as they say!"

Marlowe sat back down, still smiling. "I don't know—ask that boy there. He was recently in a play of mine that nearly got us both killed, it was just that bad."

"It's true," the boy told everyone, laughing harder. "In Cambridge."

Everyone roared again.

There, thought Marlowe. My scene was well played. I am one of them now.

Midmorning on the road to the Bell Inn, Gelis slowed the horse, and his cart creaked to a halt. His wife was asleep in the back; his son was on the seat beside him.

The boy looked up at his father.

"Why did you stop?" he asked.

"I'm not quite certain," Gelis answered absently. "Something is not right."

Growling, his wife called from inside the cart, "Why have we stopped? Have we arrived at the Bell?"

"He says something's not right," the boy answered.

"I am vexed by my debt to Leonora Beak," Gelis mumbled.

"It's paid!" she cried.

"There's something more afoot," Gelis insisted.

"I'm hot," the boy complained. "Could we at least get out of the sun?"

Gelis sniffed and then urged the horse forward toward a stand of trees up ahead. As he did he wondered at his uneasiness.

"Something's troubling my brain," he said to no one in particular.

"It's probably just rattling around in that big empty skull you call a head," his wife answered. "Maybe your brain's come loose, eh?"

"It's about Lord Grem."

His wife instantly poked her head out from the cart, between her husband and her son.

"I've asked you not to speak the name of the Weird King," she admonished. "Did I tell you that he come into the kitchen when I was cooking and made some odd pronouncements over the food?"

Gelis turned to his wife. "Odd pronouncements?"

"He says, 'I hear you've had business with one Christopher Marlowe.' And I says, 'No business.' And he says, 'But Gelis knows him.' And I says, 'No.' And he says, 'That is not what was told to me.' And I says, 'Well.' But then, it was only a little later that he and his band of hooligans was shooting at us on the road. I think he was spying on us from the Bell to London, nearabouts."

"That's the Weird Folk," said the boy. "They know things others don't."

The cart stopped again.

"You spoke with Grem at the Bell Inn?" Gelis asked.

"Aye," she affirmed.

"Why wouldn't you tell me that before now?"

She raised her eyebrows. "Didn't like to worry you. It was strange there at the inn, and the red doctor was there, and the innkeeper wounded. Then the wild girl Leonora shows up—who knows what's on her mind. I kept it to myself."

"Why?"

"I keep things to myself!" she snapped. "You worry too much!"

"You do worry," the boy agreed.

"Shut it," Gelis said gently.

"I'd feel better if we was headed back to Scotland," the wife said, disappearing back into the cart. "Don't care to go to the Netherlands. Don't like the Dutch Travelers. They're too clean."

It was noon in London when Kyd and Ned Blank stumbled out of their cells in the Tower of London. No word of explanation for the release was offered, and none asked. They both walked as fast as they could out into the sunlight and tried very hard not to look anyone in the eye.

"Bugger a bung hole," Ned swore once they were a few blocks from the Tower. "What in the name of Christ happened to us?"

"Were you questioned?" Kyd asked, walking faster than Ned.

"Not one single whisper the whole time. You?"

"I spent all my time shivering and praying," Kyd admitted.

"This was all about that mess you got me into," Ned scolded, "puffing off to the Netherlands and cooking up trouble."

Kyd stopped and put his hand on Ned's shoulder.

"I'm sorry, Ned," Kyd said earnestly.

Ned turned to see Kyd's face, a mask of contrition. "Sorry? Take your hand from my shoulder and your influence from my life."

He shook free and raced away, disappearing into the crowd.

Kyd stood in the street, crowd shoving past him.

After a moment a young, red-faced man in brown apprentice clothes bumped into Kyd. The boy was carrying twenty or so tin pots.

"Move!" the boy screamed.

"Wrong man, wrong day, wrong tone," Kyd said loudly.

Then he spun around and shoved his dagger into the boy's gut—three times. As the boy fell, Kyd grabbed a pot.

Boy and pots clattered to the ground, but Kyd was already down the block, pot under one arm, steering for the nearest pub or the nearest fight, whichever came first.

At that same moment, Marlowe stood at Robert Rich's door, pounding on it. After a moment the familiar servant appeared.

"Ah," the man said with unabashed disdain, "Mr. Marlowe again."

"Lady Penelope," Marlowe snapped, devoid of manners.

"In the garden. If you will allow me—"

Without waiting for guidance, Marlowe brushed past the servant and ran.

"I know the way," he called.

Racing through the house and out into the garden, as he had before, he found Penelope sitting on the same bench, dressed all in gold, staring into a looking glass and whispering to herself.

"Penelope," he said, slowing to a quick walk as he approached her.

She turned. She smiled. "Marlowe."

"Sir Philip left a certain manuscript with you," Marlowe said, all business. "It's a masque, *The Lady of May*. You know the one I mean."

"Marlowe," she repeated. "Where is Philip?"

"Still in the Netherlands. I am to realize his play for the Queen."

"So abrupt." She seemed hurt.

But that was one of her tricks. She pouted as if it were her profession. She would feign a wound, her victim would attend to it, and she would have him.

"I must have the most recent rewrites today," Marlowe continued coldly, "in order to rehearse the company. The performance is only days hence."

Penelope lowered her voice. "And the play's the thing wherein you'll—"

"Yes, so Kyd says in another play," Marlowe interrupted. "The deed will be done near the end of the piece. As planned."

All guesswork on Marlowe's part, but how else would a good piece of theatre operate? Save the climax for the end, build to it, and then, just before the thing was over: catharsis—in this case, the death of a queen.

"I have it in a hidden place, of course," she whispered. "In my bedchamber."

"I'll wait here in the garden while you fetch it," Marlowe said at once.

She looked away. "There was a time when you would have raced me to my bed."

"When I was a child I behaved as a child," Marlowe answered. "When I became a man, I put away childish things."

"That's all I am now," she moaned, "a childish thing?"

Marlowe's gaze was stern. "You know what is at stake in this matter."

"That's a man for you," she protested as she stood up. "When intrigue walks in the door, love flies out the window."

"The script," Marlowe insisted.

"I shall fetch it as instructed," she said, brushing by, not looking at him, "and return with all haste."

"Penelope," Marlowe sighed. "Robert Rich is the envy of every other man in London. You are his jewel."

She stopped but did not look back.

"A jewel is a hard thing," she said softly. "It may cut glass. It must also sparkle whenever a light is shown upon it, whether or not it feels like shining. A jewel is a possession, Kit. Nothing more."

With that she swept across the garden walk and into the house.

THIRTY

That afternoon at The Curtain Theatre, dozens of actors had gathered, in costume, to rehearse Sidney's newly revised piece called *The Lady of May.* Marlowe examined the assembled from a place in the shadows, but the makeup and costuming hid all true identity. So he plunged into the afternoon's slanting light and began.

"I have the new lines," he announced as he took the stage.

The theatre was empty save for the actors who were all on stage. The light would fade in an hour or so. The work must happen quickly.

The group fell silent as Marlowe cast his eye about, looking for any familiar face under rouge and powder and wig.

When one of the men dressed as a shepherd came forward into the light, Marlowe saw that he was Kempe.

"We were given our roles by the master of the revel," Kempe said, "after you left The White Gull to fetch the script. I am to play the chief shepherd and to have a brief moment of cavorting, juggling, and a bit of abandoned dance."

Marlowe nodded. "Where is he, the master of the revel?"

Kempe looked about then smiled. "He's here."

Marlowe stiffened. "Where?"

"He prefers to remain in character," Kempe said, grinning.

Several of the others laughed.

From the back of the crowd a voice boomed, "He doesn't trust you, Kit."

Kyd, dressed as a forester, barged his way through the crowd.

"You're out of your cell," Marlowe observed casually, hiding his surprise.

"And in need of coin," Kyd affirmed. "Else I would not be seen dead in this obscene, ill-fitting costume."

The rags were indeed poorly constructed: a loose leather vest festooned with the carcasses of birds, and a hat two sizes too small that was tied to a ridiculous green wig.

"Well," Marlowe sniffed. "You're sober. That's something."

Best not to indulge in familiarity. There was no telling what Kyd was really doing amongst the cast.

"I'll be drunk soon enough," he replied.

"Now tell me, pray," Marlowe continued, "why the master of the revel would not trust me, and why he would not stand where I stand to instruct the cast?"

"Our master mistrusts you for three reasons," Kyd answered. "He fears you may be here to steal lines from Sidney. He knows that you left Sidney in the Lowlands. And he wonders if you did not betray me to Walsingham, who put me in the Tower."

Marlowe smiled. "These seem more your fears than anyone else's. I therefore posit that you are the master of this piece."

"Well," Kyd laughed, "you may *posit* what you will—the rest of us know better."

Marlowe cast his eye about. "Then why listen to me at all?"

The boy who had been in Marlowe's ill-fated *Dido* piped up. "Well, you have the lines, you see."

Why would the master of the piece not show himself to Marlowe? Or was Kyd lying? Was he actually the force behind the play's presentation to the Queen? Best to play along for the moment. It wouldn't have been the first time that the man guiding the play had hidden himself in the cast. Kyd did it all the time in his own plays.

"Very well," he sighed. "We have five other foresters, five other shepherds beside Kempe. Can you gather together here?"

Marlowe indicated a spot stage right. Men began to move.

"But we begin with the supplicant. Who is to play that part?"

A thin older man in a drab gray dress approached. Marlowe handed him a page.

"You first approach the Queen," Marlowe told the man. "We will be in the gardens at Hampton Court, as you know."

"Yes," the man said softly, his voice like a woman's. "My daughter, the Lady of May, has two suitors."

"I am the Lady of May," the boy who had played in *Dido* volunteered.

"And where are the suitors, Therion and Espilus?" Marlowe asked.

Two men appeared at once from the back of the crowd. Both wore half-masks and bright doublets.

"Do we need the masks?" Marlowe asked casually. "There is no mention of them in the lines."

"Our master suggested it," Kyd answered. "The Queen is to choose between them based solely on their singing abilities—not on beauty."

Best to go along, Marlowe thought.

"Good idea." He looked down at the pages Penelope had given him. "And where is the argumentative schoolmaster, Rombus?"

"Here!" A man in faded black raised his hand.

"I assume that Kyd is the forester called Rixus. Here are your lines." He held out several pages.

Kyd nodded and took the paper.

"And Kempe, you are his adversary in debate, the shepherd Dorcas?"

Kempe stepped closer and took his pages.

"Well, it's fairly straightforward," Marlowe announces, "as I'm sure you know: Supplicant asks Queen to decide which suitor is best for her daughter, the Queen of May. After debate and dance the two suitors sing. The Queen chooses the winner. The ending of the play proceeds according to Her Majesty's choice at the moment, and we all take our money and get drunk. Have I missed anything?"

"Musicians?" Kempe asked.

"I have only been charged with attending to the lines," Marlowe answered, only a little pointedly. "Our hidden master of the piece would know where the musicians are."

Silence prevailed.

At last the boy who had been in *Dido* suggested, in a small voice, "I play the lute."

Marlowe smiled. "There must be a band of musicians, and you are to be a shepherdess, by your costume. You must be in the dances and the chorus of singers."

"Right," he said quickly. "I was only—"

"The musicians have been secured," Kyd interrupted. "No less than our John Bull will assemble them on the date in question."

John Bull was the organist at Hereford Cathedral, and had composed music for several of Kyd's plays. More importantly, Marlowe remembered seeing him near Walsingham's office. Was Bull working for Walsingham?

Suddenly, as Marlowe cast his eye about the theatre, everyone was suspect. If Philip Sidney could plot assassination and Thomas Kyd betray his country, no one was beyond suspicion.

But all Marlowe said was, "John Bull? Good. An excellent musician."

It was unclear, from simply reading the newly revised script, how the assassination was to take place. The supplicant approached the Queen first, and would have immediate access to the royal person. But, as previously thought out, Sidney would never kill the play before he killed the Queen. No. The murder would come near the end of the piece, in one of three places. There was a new dance just before the Queen was to announce her choice of suitors, inserted in order to give Her Majesty time to consider her choices. Cavorting dancers would come close enough, and with enough frenzy, that one of them might easily do the deed. And finally, once the choice had been made, the winner of the singing competition, the chosen suitor, would approach the Queen for a royal blessing. He would be near enough to stab Her Majesty. But Marlowe ruled out that possibility as well. It was uncertain who the Queen would choose. She might choose either suitor. It would not be likely that both were involved in the plot: two assassins were too clever by half, and Sidney had said that only one man was involved. Marlowe was convinced that all the actors, save one, were innocent; knew nothing of the plot. Only one was there to kill a queen and destroy a country. It would be the hidden master of the revel, disguised as one of the dancers. He was certain of it. And it would likely be one of the men disguised as a woman: more makeup, more places to conceal a weapon, and less suspicion.

Marlowe shook his head and wondered at the folly of letting the play proceed. Was Walsingham mad? Why not cancel the play and obviate any possibility of royal harm? It seemed insane.

"Well?" Kyd snorted at length.

"Yes," said Marlowe, raising several pages in front of him, "let's begin."

The sun was down behind the Bell Inn when Master Beak, the innkeeper, awoke with a start. He sat up, gasping.

The baker, who had fallen asleep in the chair nearby, sat up. "What is it?"

The innkeeper's eyes were wide. "I saw my Leonora, plain as day. She was standing at my bedside, smiling. She told me her time was at hand."

"Her time was at hand?" The baker rubbed his eyes. "She's dead, my friend. Her time has come and gone. Do you not remember that we set her off on the River Rib?"

"I know that," the innkeeper continued. "She meant that she was to be reckoned. I don't know how I knew that, but I did."

"Reckoned?"

The innkeeper threw his legs over the side of the bed. "Her death will be justified; her killer caught."

"I see." The baker stood. "You look better. Want some sup?"

The innkeeper stood. "I do. I'm suddenly famished. I think my wound has healed."

"Your color's back," the baker said, heading for the door, "and that's the truth."

The innkeeper stood. His legs were steady. He followed the baker out of the room and down the stairs.

"It's not the first time I've had a dream like that," he told the baker. "When me and my good wife, rest her soul, realized that we could not have bairns of our own, I dreamed that a royal coach pulled up to the inn and left a basket of cabbages at our door. Dreamed it over and over again for weeks. And then one day, what do you think happened?"

"Boiled cabbage?" the baker yawned.

"Idiot," the innkeeper said. "A royal coach *did* manifest, and out comes two high-born ladies-in-waiting with a basket. And it were no cabbage in it, but our Leonora, pink and squalling."

The baker, halfway down the stairs, stopped and turned.

"I always wondered about that," he said. "Your wife was not at all pregnant on Tuesday, and Leonora born on Wednesday. Wondered how you managed that. But a royal coach?"

"No idea how it happened," the innkeeper said, his hand on the bannister. "I mean, you know that Her Majesty stops here aught in a while, and favors us. But as to where the baby come from, it's a mystery. And I don't care. We raised her up and made her our own—she's not my flesh but she is my daughter."

"But she was Walsingham's spy," the baker muttered, continuing down the stair. "Wouldn't it be something if *he's* the father?"

The innkeeper laughed so hard he almost took a tumble.

"Sir Francis Walsingham the father of our Leonora?" he finally managed to ask, gasping for breath. "Can you ever imagine that old man pumping away at his missus?"

"I never met the man," the baker said, laughing along.

"Nor I," the innkeeper admitted, "but you hear enough about him to let you know he's a thinker not a tinker, if you catch my meaning."

"Aye," the baker said, arriving at the bottom of the stairs. "Now what's to eat?"

"That lamb pie you made the other night was good," the innkeeper said enthusiastically.

"So it was, but we have our dear departed Mrs. Pennington to thank for it. The recipe was hers—and none like it anywhere else in England."

"Amen to that," the innkeeper agreed softly.

They both ambled toward the kitchen.

The night was moonless over Zutphen as Philip Sidney lay moaning in his cot beside the Travelers' fire.

"Is there any more you can do for him?" Egun whispered to Dr. Lopez. "He is suffering the tortures of the damned."

"He won't allow me to remove the leg," Lopez said calmly. "He's going to die. It's just a question of when."

Egun nodded. "I know."

Sidney turned onto his side, eyes closed, and began to whisper, quite coherently, "Come, sleep, the certain knot of peace . . . the balm of woe the poor man's wealth, the prisoner's release . . . shield me from the fierce darts despair doth throw."

"What's that?" Egun asked Sidney.

"It's a poem," Lopez answered. "It's one of his sonnets."

"Is he asking for death?" Egun asked softly.

"I suppose so," Lopez acknowledged.

"Should we give it to him?"

"Only God may give him peace," Lopez answered firmly.

"Penelope could give me peace," Sidney said.

Lopez and Egun turned to see Sidney's eyes wide, filled with tears.

"Penelope could lay her cooling hand on this burning brow," Sidney went on, "and change this moment from despair to bliss. Will you bring her to me?"

"You're in the Netherlands," Egun told him. "She is in England."

"I am in the Netherlands? So far from home?"

Egun turned to Lopez. "God help him."

"I dreamed a dream just now," Sidney muttered. "It woke me. I was on the battlefield. I was just about to die at the hand of some Spaniard, when Frances, my wife, appeared from behind a tree—not a real tree, a set piece on a stage, in a play. And she shot me with a pistol. She wanted me dead."

"Why would your wife wish you dead?" Lopez asked deliberately.

"Frances was forced to marry me," Sidney answered bitterly, "just as Penelope was forced to marry Rich. The Queen believes she is God, and can command a heart; tell it what to love."

"But you will soon have your revenge," Lopez said, leaning close to Sidney, "will you not?"

Sidney lifted himself from his cot a bit, raging deliriously. "I will, by God! And here's the jest: it will be revenge carried out by a thespian, in a large play within a smaller play. Then, in the new order of things that will follow, Penelope will be mine, as I am hers."

Egun leaned forward as well. "What's he saying?"

Lopez turned to Egun. "No idea. Fever dreams. The mad delusions of pain."

Egun nodded. "Well, God help him; I say it again."

With that Sidney sank once more into unconsciousness.

Lopez stood and stretched. "Is there more of that fish stew? I'm famished, and it was unsurpassed."

Egun leaned back. "It's gone. But I do have some wood pigeons. They're stuffed with apples we found close by. Very nice."

"I'll have ten," Lopez said heartily. "And that drink you gave me the other night, what's it called?"

"Patxaran?"

"Elixir of God. What is it?"

"It's made from the berries of blackthorn shrub," Egun answered. "Very strong—good kick."

"But I tasted coffee and cinnamon and anisette."

"All there," Egun said heartily. "You have a good tongue, my friend. I have plenty in my cart."

Egun headed for his rolling home; Lopez gazed up at the stars.

Neither man noticed that Philip Sidney had stopped breathing.

THIRTY-ONE

The best garden at Hampton Court was perfect the next morning, scrubbed, pruned, sporting new plantings just for the occasion: a masque in honor of the Queen. Musicians had been assembled, all of them dressed in gold. They were to be a mixed consort: cornets, sackbuts, shawms, recorders, and flutes, but also viols, krummhorns, a lute, a viola da gamba, a small harp, and a portative organ at which John Bull sat, speaking softly to the rest of the musicians.

Fifty-seven courtiers had assembled since dawn for an opportunity to stand close to the Queen. They were arrayed in subtle variations of blue and red, silk and lace. Everyone was sweating, pretending to ignore the late summer heat, nearing the noon hour.

A grouping of Queen's chairs—one large for Her Majesty, seven smaller for her ladies-in-waiting—had been arranged in front of an open lawn. The Queen had specifically asked that her ladies be seated around her. Speculation was that one of the ladies was pregnant, but most of the actors believed that the Queen was attempting to create a more theatrical experience for herself, an audience of which to be a part.

Close to the "audience" seating, and a little behind, there was a large blue tent set, and tables were laden with a great meal. Cooks and servants stood by. Wine had been poured, dogs lounged.

There were sheep grazing on the grass, and actors pretending to be shepherds attended them. Everyone else involved in the play was hidden behind several walls of shrubbery. They'd been waiting for two hours.

Marlowe stood near the musicians, hair combed, clothes clean, hatless. The morning sun burned his forehead and stabbed his eyes. He was trying to go over all the lines, but no matter which way he turned, the pages were difficult to read.

He looked up from them, wondering where the guards were. Not even the Queen's personal bodyguards were in evidence. And Walsingham's men were nowhere to be seen. Marlowe shook his head. The entire affair was madness. It even occurred to him, under the bright eye of the sun, that Walsingham was a part of the plot to kill the Queen. Why else would he allow so dangerous a game?

Just as he was beginning to believe that fantasy, John Bull blared a single chord on the organ; the musicians fell silent for an instant and then exploded in a blaring fanfare.

The Queen appeared from around one of the hedges, dressed in purple and gold, surrounded by her ladies, all of them dressed in pristine white dresses to honor this new dedication of Sidney's work—and to allow Her Majesty to stand out.

They entered laughing, and the music raised the spirit of the moment. Courtiers bowed, each shifting subtly toward the Queen's chair.

Still no sight of Walsingham, or his men.

The music reached its peak, held like a rising wave, then broke, and silence reigned.

From behind a bank of late-blooming roses, the supplicant appeared. The thin older actor had become a fat country housewife, bowing as she approached the Queen.

"Oh most fair Lady," he began, not daring to look at the Queen directly, "hear the complaint of me, poor wretch, as deeply plunged in misery. One only daughter I have, in whom I had placed all my hope. She is oppressed with two suitors, both loving her, both equally liked of her. Each are at this present in some controversy, and hope for your sweet guidance here."

Then he froze. He stared. Silence once again stilled the air. He had forgotten his line.

"I can no longer stay," Marlowe whispered loudly.

"I can no longer stay," the actor bellowed loudly, much to the giggling delight of the ladies-in-waiting, and many of the courtiers.

Before the supplicant could do further damage, Kyd, as Rixus the forester, roared around the corner of one of the hedges, and Kempe, Dorcas the shepherd, appeared from another, each with entourage in tow.

Rombus the tiresome schoolmaster delivered his foolish lines, duly chastised by the lovely Lady of May, and the singing competition between the two suitors began.

Marlowe moved away from the musicians once the songs began. The two masked suitors would never interrupt their music to ask for a line. Marlowe did his best to seem at ease, casually moving toward the Queen. No one took notice.

Espilus sang, "Two thousand sheep I have as white as milk, though not so white as is thy lovely face. The pasture rich, the wool as soft as silk, all this I give, let me possess thy grace."

Therion countered, "Two thousand deer in wildest woods I have, them can I take, but you I cannot hold: he is not poor who can his freedom save, bound but to you no wealth but you I would."

Marlowe was momentarily distracted by Therion's abuse of melody, his cracking voice. And his rhymes were not as solid as the ones Espilus sang. He glanced down at the script. The lines were correct. That was odd.

But the music continued and Marlowe's eye was caught by the sight of Thomas Kyd slipping behind the bushes. Kempe was still on the green, encouraging his shepherd cohort.

Marlowe edged slowly around the perimeter of the entertainment, unnoticed, and ended up behind a long row of low hedges. He was forced to duck low and move awkwardly, but he was able to come, at last, to where Kyd had secreted himself. Seated on the ground, back to Marlowe, he was fiddling with something in his lap.

Marlowe came up silently, drew his dagger, and then thrust forward, the tip of his blade at Kyd's back, set to destroy a kidney.

"Hello, Kit," Kyd whispered calmly. "Enjoying the show."

"What's that you have there?" Marlowe pressed the point of his knife ever-so-slightly.

Kyd half-turned his head, then held up his hand, offering Marlowe a small silver flask.

"You didn't think I could get through this shite without being a little drunk, did you?"

Marlowe let go his breath.

"God, no," he told Kyd. "Nor I."

Marlowe took the flask, drank heartily, and handed it back to Kyd.

"You and I have unfinished business, you know," Marlowe said, sheathing his knife.

"For example," Kyd said, finishing the flask, "I would like to know if you're responsible for my recent visit to the Tower."

"I'm not the one who got caught fondling little boys and then writing about it; and what else—oh, yes—betraying his country."

"So you don't consider yourself responsible?"

"I'm *not* responsible. I was in the Netherlands when it happened, fighting for my country."

Kyd shrugged. "If it means anything to you, the 'little boy' in question was Ned Blank, and he was well paid."

"Then maybe it was Ned who betrayed you."

Kyd turned. "I thought of that. But he was in the Tower too, you see."

The music stopped. The singing competition was finished.

Kyd leaned forward and got to his feet, with some effort.

"Got to get back out there," he panted, "and argue with Kempe. Go hold the book, I think I remember everything, but I'm a little drunk."

And away he went, out into the yard behind the group of foresters.

Marlowe worked his way back behind the low hedge and appeared just in time to hold up the pages again. Kempe as Dorcas had already begun.

"Now all the blessings of mine old granddame light upon thy

shoulders, Espilus, for this honeycomb singing of thine; all the bells in the town could not have sung better!"

Kyd lumbered forward, shoving his way through the foresters, roaring, "Oh Midas, why art thou not alive now to lend thine ears to this drivel? If yonder great Gentlewoman be as wise as she is fair, Therion thou shalt have the prize!"

Rombus the tiresome schoolmaster broke in with a few newly inserted lines.

"Come, musicians, play, leave naught to chance!" he called. "Forester and shepherd alike, come hither; dance! Give our Lady world enough and time to weigh these suitors, and to know Her mind."

With that John Bull called the tune, a Volt, the only dance wherein the performers were allowed to embrace. The melody was in three-quarter time, and energetic. The male dancers grabbed the "females" and lifted them high overhead.

Forester lads danced with shepherdesses. Shepherd boys danced with hunter girls. Couples whirled and flew into the air. Taken as a whole, the dance was a cacophony of color, human fireworks exploding with ever more raucous shouting. The music increased in volume and tempo, and Marlowe watched as the dancers moved ever-so-slightly toward the royal chair.

He moved closer trying to watch each individual dancer. That proved impossible. He tried to see the whole pattern, see if he might determine what part of the overall design was concealing the danger. Someone in that mass of spinning reds and greens was inching toward the Queen, a weapon in his hand.

Was it a knife? Or, as he suddenly recalled, could it be some manner of poisonous powder, the way Leonora had bested her attackers? A pistol would be too risky. The dancing was wild, the pistol shot might not remain in its barrel. And a gun would be more difficult to conceal, as would a sword. Powdered poison might go anywhere in the frenzy. No. It would be a knife.

That determined, Marlowe moved closer to the dancers, straining his eyes for a flash of silver; the twitch of a hand in the wrong direction.

The Queen was smiling, whispering to one of her ladies-in-waiting, not aware of the encroaching mob.

Where were her guards? Where was Walsingham?

Marlowe tossed his pages to the ground and strode toward the lead dancers, those closest to the Queen. But the group turned and twisted, a human gyre, so that no one man was ever in the forefront for long. The murder must be timed to the music!

Marlowe stopped where he was, only several yards from the Queen, and a little behind her. He gave his attention to the music. The drums beat a little faster. Instruments added every eight measures. Stringed instruments had begun, then recorders and flutes were added. Now low brass supported the melody. Then high brass pressed forward, piercing the air, stabbing the sky with high, clear notes.

The dancers were shouting, clapping, stomping. The ladies gasped. John Bull roared and the musicians stood up. The dance was coming to its full crescendo.

Marlowe suddenly raced forward, hand on the hilt of his rapier, set to thrust his body between the assailing crowd and the seated Queen.

And then the music exploded in its final chord, the dancers screamed, and all fell to the grassy floor, laughing, rolling, panting. The Queen nodded, smiling. The ladies-in-waiting applauded. The musicians bowed low. The Queen lifted her chin in the direction of John Bull, who dropped his head and touched one knee to the ground before sitting back down, followed by the rest of the consort.

The dance was over.

Blood pounded in Marlowe's ears. His hand was still on his sword. He was glad that he was out of the Queen's line of sight. He knew his face was red. And just as he was beginning to wonder how he could have been so mistaken, the Queen stood.

Everybody rose.

"We have considered these suitors," she began, her voice lilting. "The choice is clear, the decision obvious. Both suitors come forth."

With that she turned and one of the ladies handed her a garland. The Queen took it and held it high.

Therion and Espilus came forward. Only then did Marlowe notice that Espilus walked with a slight limp. Espilus had sung perfectly, far better than Therion. Espilus was the all-too-obvious winner. And Espilus had his hand in his pocket.

The Queen took a breath to speak. Both suitors stood before her, less than a foot away. Marlowe flew through the air, drawing his rapier, and landed at the Queen's left side, the point of his sword cutting through the poor costume Espilus wore, just where his heart would be.

The Queen dropped the garland and stepped back three steps, almost a dance, and her ladies-in-waiting surrounded her. Several had little daggers in their hands.

Before anyone could speak, Marlowe tore the masks from both suitors. Therion, whose singing had been so pitiful, was Ned Blank, face drained of blood, shivering. The better singer, the winner of the competition, and the Queen's would-be assassin, was none other than Belpathian Grem, leering and shaking his head.

"This man," Marlowe shouted, "is known as Belpathian Grem, King of the Weird Folk, and he was about to murder our Queen!"

Marlowe reached into Grem's pocket and produced a short dagger; tossed it to the ground.

Ned fainted.

From behind the hedges to the Queen's right, two dozen guards appeared, weapons drawn. Most were royal guards, but the three who led were wearing the markings of Walsingham's personal force.

And from the tent behind the Queen where the meal had been set, Walsingham himself emerged, pistol in hand.

"I could have killed you in your sleep," Grem whispered to Marlowe.

"And I could have believed that you were real," Marlowe answered.

"But here we are: you're about to be very uncomfortable, and then very dead. I, on the other hand, am about to return to college."

Walsingham drew up close beside Marlowe. He stared at Grem as he handed his pistol to a guard. The Queen shoved her ladies aside and stepped forward. She cast her eye about at all the guards, and then at Walsingham.

"You knew this would happen?" she demanded of Walsingham.

"Yes," he said calmly.

"You *knew*?"

"Your Majesty," he went on, "may I suggest that we retire to our conference room, where you might allow me to apprise you—"

"Insupportable!" the Queen roared. "Placing the royal person in such jeopardy is treason, Francis! Do you understand me?"

"Marlowe was here," Walsingham began. "I knew he would—"

"Your Majesty *must* know that I protested this folly from the beginning," Marlowe broke in urgently. "I vigorously opposed this mad plan."

"He did indeed, Your Highness," Walsingham affirmed. "But I knew he would not fail me. And there were other measures."

Walsingham flicked his hand and three archers appeared, arrows knocked. One had been in the tent with Walsingham, one behind the hedges with the guards, and one was hidden among the foresters on the lawn.

"They were about to let go their arrows," Walsingham said. "Their orders were to kill anyone who approached you. Except Marlowe. Both of these 'suitors' were about to be eliminated. Both."

The Queen held her breath. She looked around, squinting at the archers.

"Is that David Locke?" she asked, staring at the archer dressed as a forester.

"It is," Walsingham said. "You know that he is the best man in Europe with a bow and arrow."

"He is," she agreed, then turned to Marlowe. "But I have forgot myself. Christopher Marlowe, I believe you have just saved our life."

Marlowe dropped to one knee, unable to speak.

"Silent?" she asked softly. "That's a bit out of character for you."

He looked up. "Been rather a trying few days for me, Your Majesty."

"I would imagine." She glared at Walsingham. "We will go now to the conference room, as you suggested. Marlowe too. I have more to say."

"As you wish, Your Highness," Walsingham answered, bowing slightly,

"Get up, Marlowe," the Queen said. "The grass is wet."

With that the Queen turned, her ladies again surrounded her, and the women moved en masse toward the palace.

Marlowe stood. He turned to face Grem.

"Oh," he told the actor casually, "I almost forgot."

In the blink of an eye Marlowe's rapier lashed out. He stabbed Grem in the thigh, the side, and the forearm before anyone could move. Grem howled and dropped.

"That's for Leonora!" Marlowe snarled.

Walsingham's face contorted in rare surprise.

"This thing killed Leonora Beak?" he asked Marlowe.

"He did," Marlowe said, struggling to regain his composure.

Grem looked up, his eyes wild, filled with terror and defiance.

"She made a gurgling sound," he said, staring at Marlowe, "and then sexual noises, like the apex of lovemaking. You know the sound, I'm sure."

Marlowe raised his rapier once more, but Walsingham knocked it aside with his gloved hand.

"He must be alive," Walsingham insisted. "We must learn the particulars of his part in the larger plot. I have need of his testimony. Withdraw. Your Queen would speak with you. Marlowe."

Marlowe stood frozen. Walsingham nodded to one of his guards. The guards took hold of Grem and drew him up.

"He goes to the Tower," Walsingham instructed. "You know which room."

The guard glanced down at Ned, still unconscious on the ground. "What about this one?"

"Back to his cell. Await my instructions."

With that Ned's limp body was carried away, dragged behind the limping King of the Weird Folk. Marlowe watched them disappear around the corner of a building. All he could think was, "Poor Ned."

THIRTY-TWO

The consultation room in Hampton Hall was cold. Gray tapestries were only partially illuminated; three candles could not give much light. Marlowe stood alone in the room, close to a table and chairs, shivering. He knew that he was shaking from an evil concoction of unexpressed rage, bitter confusion, and complete exhaustion. He'd been standing in the room for nearly an hour when the door burst open and Walsingham rushed in.

The old man's face was red, and his breathing was labored.

"Her Majesty will attend us soon," he panted, "but I would have a word with you before she arrives. Sit."

Walsingham collapsed into a chair and indicated that Marlowe should also sit.

Straining to seem calm and casual, Marlowe sat, hiding his shaking hands under the table.

"I will explain to you something I dared not say to Her Majesty," Walsingham began, not looking at Marlowe, "but it must be said quickly, before she arrives."

Marlowe nodded, unable to fathom the spymaster's thoughts.

"Our Queen," Walsingham began slowly, "as I may have mentioned, has certain affinities which, I believe, cloud her judgment and impede action. For example, she favors the poet Philip Sidney, and so would never believe that this mad appendage of the Babington Plot was the product of Sir Philip's brain. Do you understand?

"No," Marlowe answered simply.

"Sidney plotted to kill the Queen," Walsingham snapped. "Unless she had seen it with her own eyes, she would not have believed it.

I *had* to make her see the treachery. This ridiculous masque had to be played out."

"And did it work?"

Walsingham nodded. "Yes. So your assault on Philip is now officially sanctioned."

It took a moment for Marlowe to realize that Walsingham was talking about the Act for the Surety of the Queen's Person, the newly signed law giving Marlowe the legal right to kill to protect the Queen. In addition to saving their monarch's life, Walsingham had assured that Marlowe could not be prosecuted for Sidney's death.

"And when I showed Her Majesty the letters you acquired at Chartley, those written between Babington and Mary," Walsingham went on, "she agreed, at last, to prosecute Mary for treason. That intimate communication was the last nail in Mary's coffin."

The full measure of what had been done slowly dawned in Marlowe's brain. It hadn't been enough to talk endlessly to the Queen about threats or possibilities, or even assassinations in other lands. Showing the Queen the point of Belpathian Grem's dagger had done more, in a single moment, than years of persuasive chatter: it had signed Sidney's death warrant, destroyed the Babington Plot, and assured the end of Mary, Queen of Scots.

Marlowe exhaled weeks' worth of tension.

"Well," he said, "I could have told you that showing is better than telling. It's a lesson I've learned from the theatre: it doesn't matter how beautiful the poetry of seduction is, the audience is waiting for the kiss."

"Indeed," Walsingham agreed.

"And how does Penelope fare in this business?" Marlowe asked.

"She is consigned to her unhappy marriage," Walsingham said. "Punishment enough—for the moment."

"Meaning you have other uses for her," Marlowe observed.

Walsingham smiled. "You really are learning, Marlowe."

"Or am I just more cynical?"

Walsingham looked away. "Well. Now tell me about the actor,

the so-called *Belpathian Grem*. He has already admitted to murdering Leonora. How did you know? How did it happen?"

"Several stars aligned," Marlowe began. "First, I fought with Grem, in the street, over the odd manuscript he delivered to John Dee. When we fought I thought I noticed a bit of a limp. It had already been determined that Leonora's murderer limped. Next, when I was able to examine the manuscript in your office, I found, on a certain page, the very distinctive smell of Mrs. Pennington's lamb stew—none like it anywhere in England. That made me believe that Leonora had discovered the text when Grem had been at the Bell Inn. Suspicion or curiosity provoked her to take it and examine it as she sat by her ailing father's bedside. She was eating the stew when Grem strangled her. Most of the lamb spilled onto the floor, some onto the manuscript, which proved that it had been at the Bell and suggested that it had been in Leonora's hand when she died. Then, today, just as I realized that one of suitors in the masque was to be the murderer in the plot, I saw that man limp, knew it was Grem, and was nearly certain that he'd done Leonora's murder."

"Clever thinking," Walsingham noted, "but slim evidence."

"Yes," Marlowe admitted, "but a few pricks with my rapier and the demon confessed, did he not?"

"He did," Walsingham said, "but he did not say why."

"We may question him on that subject," Marlowe answered, "but I believe he killed Leonora because his nature is base."

"Marlowe," Walsingham began.

"I mean," Marlowe interrupted, "that he assumes everyone in the world suffers his faults. He believes that human beings are, at heart, base."

Walsingham shook his head. "I'm not certain I understand."

"I believe that Leonora found the odd manuscript at the Bell Inn, I don't know how, and was merely curious. You have to admit it is a captivating manuscript. She took it to examine it. Grem realized it was missing and thought Leonora had stolen it, even thought she would try to sell it. Because that's what he would do. He told me as much when we fought in the street and he took the manuscript away from me."

"That loathsome thing," Walsingham mumbled.

"Where is it now?"

"Dee has it. No one can decipher it, not even Dee. He still believes it is an angelic text, and will reveal metaphysical secrets."

"You don't believe that," Marlowe observed. "You still think it might be a coded message from the conspirators."

"No," Walsingham sighed. "I now believe that it is an enigma unrelated to these recent events, except that, if your suppositions are correct, it was instrumental in the death of Leonora Beak."

Marlowe looked away. "I say again, sir: she was among the noblest persons I have ever met."

Walsingham nodded.

Suddenly the door to the chamber opened and two guards swept in, followed immediately by the Queen. Marlowe shot from his seat and bowed. Walsingham rose more slowly.

Glancing up, Marlowe could see that the Queen was angry and exhausted, her face contorted and her eyes were red.

"I know what you did!" she shouted, losing all decorum.

Marlowe licked his lips, not knowing what to say.

But Walsingham spoke up.

"It was done in service to the Queen," he said slowly.

"Damn it, I know!" She slid sideways into the chair at the head of the table. "Sit down!"

Walsingham sat. Marlowe didn't.

"Sit down, Mr. Marlowe," the Queen said again, only a little gentler.

Marlowe sank slowly into his chair.

"We know it was not your plan," she said to him softly. "Lord Walsingham takes a liberty as easily as you take a risk. We owe him a scolding. We owe you our life."

Marlowe raised his head and blinked. There she was, silver tiara hovering over hennaed hair. Her dress was black and gold, her collar white and stiff. Her face was wounded by sorrow. Marlowe, in a sudden onslaught of empathy, thought what a terrible thing it must be to rule a nation.

"You did it to shock us," she went on to Walsingham, "as you also recently did in telling us that William the Silent was dead when he was not."

"Yes," Walsingham said without a trace of remorse, "but, you see, William *is* dead. Now."

"You put us in peril to prove a point!" she snarled.

"Yes," he said again, very calmly, "but, you see, you are *not* dead."

"Thanks to Marlowe!" she answered, louder than before.

"And if Marlowe had failed, there were archers and soldiers and armed ladies-in-waiting—not to mention spells pronounced by John Dee and prayers offered to God. You were well protected. And now you believe me, you see the danger, you know your enemies."

The Queen's lips pinched together. Then she whispered, "Yes."

"Mary will at last stand trial?" Walsingham asked.

The Queen nodded. "Collect all evidence. Set the trial for October of next year. Fotheringhay Castle in Northamptonshire. Assemble as many lords and bishops and earls as you think necessary. It must be done with all consideration."

"And Sidney?" Walsingham pressed.

She closed her eyes. "Let him die a hero's death in the Netherlands. Wait until that same time, next October, to make his death known. We leave the actual particulars to you."

Marlowe shifted in his seat, extremely uncomfortable in the presence of such decisions.

"Yes, Marlowe, We know your distress. You are here so that a grateful Queen may acknowledge your valor. You annum is increased, your house in London improved—though I am told you are never there—and your father's financial matters will be settled. You have only to say what more can be done."

Marlowe swallowed. "Nothing, Your Majesty—I," he began.

"Stop it, Marlowe," Walsingham snapped impatiently. "Tell Her Majesty what more she may do!"

"Improvements to the Bell Inn for the sake of Leonora Beak?" he suggested softly.

"Yes," the Queen said at once.

"Kyd's release from charges in this matter," Marlowe went on, looking at Walsingham. "You know he is not a traitor."

"Done," Walsingham agreed.

"And there is a boy here at court," Marlowe concluded, "who ought to be recognized by his mother."

"Leviticus," Walsingham told the Queen.

"Oh. Who is his mother?" she asked.

"John Dee's new wife, Majesty," Walsingham answered.

The Queen took a breath, but decided not to pursue the matter. "You'll attend to this, Lord Walsingham."

"Yes," he answered.

"Then only this remains." The Queen rose. "Approach."

Marlowe hesitated, then stepped toward her.

"You are henceforth chief among my hidden agents," she said, "by this token."

She handed Marlowe a small box.

"It is a sapphire ring," she went on. "Sapphire to cure melancholy. It also bears an inscription that may prove useful in future endeavors."

Marlowe bowed. "I scarcely know what to say."

"Silence is the perfect herald of joy," Walsingham said quickly. "Go now. You need your rest."

Marlowe backed away from the table, still trying, in vain, to think of the right thing to say.

The guards opened the door and before he knew it, Marlowe found himself alone in the darkened hall. In sudden need of strong drink, he opened the box and moved toward the sconce on the wall. The ring was simple, elegant: a gold band with a single sapphire. He held it up to the light and squinted. He could barely make out the inscription, but when he did, he gasped. It said, "Exempt from all law." And after that phrase was the Queen's signet mark.

Inside the room, the Queen closed her eyes. "What a long day this has been."

"But a fruitful one, in the end," Walsingham noted. "This most recent plot against your life is defeated and your cousin is, at last, condemned. You may rest easy."

"If only I could," she sighed. "Betrayed by a poet for the sake of a girl who doesn't fancy her husband—so sordid, so common. The political treachery of a Spanish king or religious objections of a Catholic rival, these motives have at least the stain of nobility. But if I am destroyed by an unhappy housewife, what will history say of me?"

Walsingham's voice softened. "Nothing will destroy you. I will not allow it."

The Queen smiled and opened her eyes. "You will not ever allow death to come for me?"

"Not until his time is due," Walsingham sniffed. "And even then I stand at the door, sword in hand."

"Death delights in swords," she answered, standing. "I fear weariness more than steel."

Walsingham was on his feet. "If Lopez were here he might offer a sleep remedy."

"Will you see what John Dee can cook up in his odd little laboratory?" She took several steps toward the door, then turned around. "What is that manuscript he bought from Rudolf?"

"No one knows."

"Let me have a look," she said, and moved forward again.

The guards opened the door. One stepped into the empty hallway.

"Majesty," Walsingham said tentatively.

She stopped. "Yes?"

"What inscription was placed on the ring you gave Marlowe?"

Though her back was to Walsingham, he knew she was smiling.

"So I have, at last, proof that you do not know everything that happens in this house."

And with that she was gone.

THIRTY-THREE

The White Gull was crowded and noisy and Marlowe thought it would be just the place to go unnoticed. He sat in the corner, in the shadows, watching the room. Actors, thieves, whores, sailors, and clergymen all roiled the room with laughter and argument. Marlowe finished his third ale, longing for Gelis's Water of Life. Just as he was about to order another ale, the young boy who had played in *Dido*, and the Queen of May—what was his name?—stood on a chair close to the fireplace and began to sing.

His voice was high and clear and Marlowe recognized the tune, "The White Hare of Howden."

"She's faster than the black," he sang, "and she's bonnier than the brown, and there's not a dog in England that'll ever bring her down."

Something tickled Marlowe's memory. After a moment he realized that the last time he'd heard the song was in Buntingford, near the Bell Inn. He recalled the scene, the warm late-summer day that seemed so long ago. Amber sunlight turned the fields to gold and someone was singing "The White Hare." After a moment, others joined in.

Then, in The White Gull, everyone sang, and the room was filled with the beauty of the white hare that escaped all capture, that could never be brought down.

Marlowe's addled brain struggled for a moment with the metaphor. The white hare was England; no plot could destroy it. Or was it the Queen, whom Marlowe would protect from all harm?

In the end he decided that the image was more personal to him, at least at that moment. The white hare was Leonora's spirit that, because it was ethereal, could never be extinguished.

But before he could pursue that thought, the singing boy caught sight of Marlowe, smiled, and concluded his song. Without hesitation he began to speak.

"Is this the wood that grew in Carthage plains, and now toils in the watery billows? Oh cursed tree, had thou but wit or sense thou wouldst have leapt from the sailors' hands! And yet I blame thee not; thou art but wood. Break his oars! *These* were the instruments that launched him away from me. Instead of oars, let us use hands, and swim to Italy where my heart lies."

The place was silent.

Then, "Aye," whispered one of the sailors, wiping his eyes.

Marlowe sat frozen.

The boy looked around, enjoying his command of the room.

"These are the words of one Christopher Marlowe," he said, "in a play about Dido, the Queen of Carthage; the same Christopher Marlowe who this very day saved the life of our Queen, in her gardens, as many of you in this place will bear witness."

The boy looked toward Marlowe, about to acknowledge him, but Marlowe slumped down further into the shadows and shook his head slightly.

"I know not where he is tonight," the boy went on seamlessly, "doubtless in some grand, royal company. But raise your cups, gentlemen, and drink to our finest poet, and the salvation of our country."

The place roared. Marlowe stood to remain inconspicuous. He drank and nodded to the boy, who smiled back.

I should really learn his name, Marlowe thought. He's better than Ned Blank, and has youth on his side.

Thomas Kyd crashed drunkenly around his rooms, packing. He was at once astonished that he had not been arrested and outraged that he felt afraid.

"Tour of the provinces," he grumbled out loud. "Ned was right. Get out of London."

A sudden knock on the door sobered him. He froze.

"Open the door," a voice whispered.

Kyd didn't move. The voice was neither commanding nor desperate. It was a simple request.

Another knock, and a calm insistence: "I know you're in there."

Kyd moved carefully to the door. He drew his dagger and took hold of the handle. Keeping the door in between him and the visitor, he opened the door and peeked out.

A stranger stood in the dimly lit hallway.

"What is it?" Kyd growled.

"I want to learn what you know about the theatre," the stranger said, standing in the doorway.

He was a young man, perhaps twenty. His manner of dress was odd, Travelers' clothes with theatrical touches, bits of shell and feathers and dried flowers all tied to his pale doublet by bits of colored ribbon. He wore no hat and sported the bare beginnings of a beard. He had no weapon in his hand, and only a dagger at this waist. He smiled.

"I don't understand," Kyd said, lowering his knife.

"I'll explain," the young man said. "You are the greatest playwright of our day. Your plays are perfect. I write. I want to write better. I want you to help me."

Kyd stared. "You're a bold sort," he said, sheathing his blade.

"So I've been told."

"Well." Kyd stepped aside.

The young man strode into the room. "You're packing to leave."

"I am," Kyd affirmed, going to his bag. "Thinking of a tour of the provinces, assembling Lord Strange's Men. Get out of London."

"Perfect," the visitor said. "I've just lost my company—we've traveled all over Europe, and we were a very bizarre crew. Masquerading as Traveling People."

Kyd tried not to react, but he put his hand on the hilt of his knife again. "And what company was that? Who was your master?"

"We had no master," the visitor said, "but we were employed by a strange man of great repute."

"His name?"

"Belpathian Grem."

Kyd nodded slowly. "And—let me see—why have you left his company?"

"I have not. His company has left me. Grem is arrested and the rest of us scattered."

"Were you at Hampton Court this morning?"

"I was."

"You were one of Belpathian Grem's men."

"Yes."

Kyd looked up then, stared into the man's eyes.

"I was one of your foresters," the visitor went on. "I've followed you all day, since the shabby business in the garden."

Kyd moved so suddenly that the visitor had no time to react. The point of Kyd's knife cut the visitor's doublet and pressed into the flesh of his stomach.

The visitor smiled.

"I have only to lean forward," Kyd said, "and you'd be gutted."

"You should read my play before you kill me," the visitor said calmly. "Plenty of time for murder afterward if you don't like the poetry."

"You're not here to take me in?" Kyd blinked. "You're not from Walsingham or Marlowe?"

"Who?"

Kyd paused a moment, then retracted his knife. "You are a very curious creature."

"Yes," the visitor said impatiently, "but will you read my play or not?"

Kyd sighed. "I'm leaving London."

"I'll come with you. My play is good. And I'm a great cook."

Kyd shook his head.

"All right," he told the visitor, "what's the play about?"

"It is a revenge drama!"

Kyd shrugged. "People in London like that sort of thing these days. You say you can cook?"

"A favorite of my previous company was a delectable badger and swan," he answered. "Both are on the fire at once, the swan closer to the coals, the badger over it so that the fat from the badger will baste the swan. And the meats, combined, are matchless."

"It does sound good," Kyd mumbled. "I have no idea why, but I am somehow taken with you, boy."

"I'll help you pack."

"If we hurry," Kyd said, "we'll catch many of Lord Strange's Men at The White Gull. They'll be drunk, and therefore amenable to your company as well as my tour."

"What plays will you tour?" the visitor asked, stuffing Kyd's things into the bag on the bed.

"*Hamlet,*" he grunted.

"And maybe my play," the stranger suggested.

"You are a bold wag," Kyd smiled. "Yes, if it's any good, we shall do your play. What's your name?"

"Will," the stranger said, closing up Kyd's bag. "From Stratford."

Kyd clapped the stranger on the back.

"Well, then, Will," he said, steering them both for the door, "let us throw ourselves into the night, thence to lower us into the questionable pools of theatre."

"And off we go," Will said cheerfully, following Kyd out the door and closing it behind him.

Night closed around Marlowe the way a nearby raven swallowed a seed. The streets were empty and the moon was high as he ambled, drunk and exhausted, toward The Curtain Theatre. As he walked, he composed and then abandoned snatches of old tunes in new ways. Twice he heard noises behind him and spun around, only to realize that he had imagined them.

When he arrived at last to the theatre, illuminated by the moon, he stumbled in and stared at the stage, unable to think how the characters who played there were any different from the men and women he'd known since meeting Leonora Beak at the Bell Inn.

Suddenly a noise from on stage startled him momentarily sober and he called out, "Who's there?"

He drew his dagger.

A round old man emerged from the shadows, taper in hand. He was dressed in brown, his beard was white, and his skin was ruddy and hale. He smiled.

"It's only Dim, sir," he answered. "Caretaker of the theatre. Who's there?"

Marlowe sheathed his knife. He recognized the man.

"Christopher Marlowe," he answered grandly, owing to his descent again into drunkenness.

"Mr. Marlowe," Dim said warmly. "What are you doing here at this hour?"

"Don't know," Marlowe answered, sitting down on the ground.

Dim came to the lip of the stage and sat, placing the taper beside him.

"Whose theatre is this, Dim?" Marlowe mumbled.

"Mine, sir," he answered, "at this time of night."

"Yours indeed," Marlowe agreed. "You command the stage."

"It was said you were sent to the Netherlands."

"Several times." Marlowe nodded. "I was mad to go."

"Well, you've recovered your wits, they say. Or if you have not, it is no great matter."

"Why is it no great matter?" Marlowe looked up.

"In England, in these days, sir, who can tell the mad from the sane?"

"There's the truth," Marlowe agreed. "You seem a wise man, Dim."

"A wise man's son, more like," Dim demurred.

"You may be able to tell me something." Marlowe struggled with his thoughts a moment, and then resumed. "How is it that great affection for a beautiful woman can lead a man to treachery and treason?"

Dim considered for a moment, then said, "As a beautiful maiden may bear a hunchback child, so might a great love engender evil deeds. We never know the fruits of our labor whilst we are at work—only after. Who can know the outcome of love before the first kiss? And after that kiss, it's too late. Sometimes the heart's a lock. A single kiss can click it and a fate is sealed."

"There is a greatness in these words." Marlowe stared up at the man. "You are a poet and a philosopher, Dim."

"And you, I fear, are very drunk, Mr. Marlowe."

"And I will tell you why." Marlowe struggled to his feet and staggered to the stage, right next to Dim.

"I failed to save William the Silent from assassination, I failed to keep Leonora Beak from a useless death, and I nearly allowed our Queen to be killed because I could not see things as they were."

"But, as it's been said to me, the Queen is alive, and the murderer is apprehended. You are a hero."

"I am, in fact, an idiot." Marlowe went to gesture grandly, lost his balance, and fell to the ground.

Dim hopped from the stage and helped Marlowe up.

"Why don't I take you backstage," Dim said gently, "and you can fall into one of the actors' cots, get a good night's sleep. I'll watch over you."

"Sleep," Marlowe moaned, but could say no more.

Dim supported Marlowe as they stumbled around the stage and into the dressing quarters. Marlowe sank into the nearest cot, fell back, and began at once to snore. Dim covered him with a purple satin cape, part of a king's costume.

Then Dim tiptoed back to the front of the stage to retrieve his taper. As he did he whispered, "Where are you?"

The nameless boy who had praised Marlowe in The White Gull, and who had played in *Dido* in Cambridge, crawled out from underneath the stage.

"You followed him here from Hampton Court?" Dim asked.

"No," the boy said. "I was told to wait for him at The White Gull, and sure enough, there he came. I followed him from there. Made a bit of noise, I'm afraid—the streets are treacherous-dark—but he never saw me. I'm sure of it."

"Good." Dim drew out a blank page and a tip of pointed charcoal from his pockets. "One last thing for you tonight. I want you to deliver this note."

Dim began to write. "C. M. at Curtain as you predicted. Drunk and divulging sensitive intelligence. Dangerous. Suggest elimination. Await your directive."

He folded the note three times and handed it to the boy.

"Take this to your friend Leviticus at Hampton," Dim instructed, "and tell him to give it to Walsingham. Got it?"

"Of course," the boy said, tucking the note into his boot.

"Have a care with that note," Dim warned. "Charcoal smudges."

The boy glared at Dim. "If it is too smudged," he said indignantly, "I'll just tell Leviticus what it said."

"You can read?" Dim asked, failing to hide his surprise.

"Christ," the boy muttered. "Yes I can read."

Dim nodded. "Well, I ought not to be astonished. Your older brother can read too, this I know. You're as clever as he."

"The difference is," the boy said, heading for the theatre exit, "that Ned always gets caught, and I never do."

With that he disappeared into the moon-made shadows, out the door and into the night.

HISTORICAL PERSONAGES AND SALIENT FACTS

1. Christopher Marlowe was born in Canterbury 1564. He attended Christ Church Cambridge, wrote poetry and plays (notably *Dr. Faustus, Dido, The Jew of Malta, Tamburlaine*), and was allegedly killed in a tavern brawl in 1593. However, so many conspiracy theories exist about that event that the truth remains elusive.
2. Thomas Kyd (1558–1594) was, in 1585, London's greatest playwright. Author of *The Spanish Tragedy,* he also probably wrote versions of *Hamlet, King Lear,* and dozens of other plays long before those stories were used by Shakespeare. In 1593 he was taken to the Tower of London and tortured, owing to treasonous and blasphemous writings found in his rooms. He said they were actually written by Marlowe. He emerged from prison a broken man, and died less than a year later, his greater efforts vanishing into obscurity.
3. Dr. Rodrigo Lopez (1525–1594) served as physician-in-chief to Queen Elizabeth beginning in 1581. He held that lofty post until just before he was executed in 1594 for plotting to poison the Queen. A Portuguese Jew, he is the only royal doctor in English history to be so executed. He was Marlowe's Jew of Malta and Shakespeare's Shylock.
4. Sir Francis Walsingham (1532–1590) was Queen Elizabeth's principal secretary from 1573 until his death. He is the man for whom the term *spymaster* was invented.

5. Balthasar Gérard (1557–1584) was a professional French assassin and the murderer of Dutch independence leader William of Orange, also called William the Silent. Already a Roman Catholic admirer of King Philip II of Spain, Gérard was tempted by Philip's offered reward of 25,000 crowns to anyone who would kill William. While Gérard succeeded in that task, he was immediately apprehended and his torture was unusually brutal, even by Elizabethan standards. First he was lashed with a whip, then his back was smeared with honey and a goat was ushered in to lick the honey. (Goats apparently have tongues that are abnormally rough.) When the goat wouldn't touch the body, Gérard was hanged by his arms and a three-hundred-pound weight was tied to each of his big toes. Most creatively of all, he was given shoes made of uncured dog skin and then his feet were set near a fire. The dog skin cured, shrank, and slowly crushed the assassin's feet to rubble. Then his skin was torn off and his armpits were branded. Sizzling bacon fat was poured over his head. There was more of the same for days. (The Dutch declared that they had learned a few techniques from the Spanish Inquisition.)
6. William the Silent (1533–1584) was the prime mover of the Dutch revolt against the Spanish, engendering the Eighty Years' War. (That conflict eventually resolved itself in the complete independence of the Netherlands in 1648.) Because of his rebellion against the Spanish King Philip II, William was declared an outlaw in 1580. He was assassinated by Balthasar Gérard in Delft in 1584. Tourists can still see bullet holes made that day in the wall at his palace, the product of wheel-lock pistols.
7. Robert Armin (1563–1615) was the leading comic actor in the troupe most associated with William Shakespeare (after Will Kempe parted ways with Shakespeare). Armin also wrote comedies, including a play called *A Nest*

of Ninnies. His work greatly improved the nature of comic roles, changing them from idiot servants to wittier characters, a more sophisticated lot. As his renown grew, many provincial actors copied his style, even claiming to be the man, giving rise to the notion that he was capable of being in many places at the same time.

8. Sir Philip Sidney (1554–1586) was one of England's leading poets in Elizabeth's court. Also a scholar, soldier, and deadly swordsman, his great works include a grouping of sonnets called *Astrophel and Stella,* which lament his unrequited love for Penelope Rich. He perished in the Netherlands from a gunshot wound in his thigh while fighting in the Eighty Years' War.
9. Penelope Rich (née Devereux), later Penelope Blount, Countess of Devonshire (1563–1607) was an English noblewoman in the court of Elizabeth and the sister of Robert Devereux. She was the inspiration for *Astrophel and Stella,* a sonnet sequence written by Philip Sidney. She was unhappily married to Robert Rich (later 1st Earl of Warwick) and when that marriage ended she wed her very public paramour Charles Blount, 1st Earl of Devonshire.
10. Frances Walsingham (1567–1633) was the daughter of Francis Walsingham, Secretary of State for Elizabeth I. She became the wife of Sir Philip Sidney at age sixteen. When he died she married Robert Devereux, 2nd Earl of Essex, Queen Elizabeth's favorite. After Devereux was executed for plotting against the Queen, Frances married her longtime lover Richard Burke, 4th Earl of Clanricarde, and went to live in Ireland.
11. Charles Paget (1546–1612) was a Roman Catholic conspirator, involved in the Babington Plot to assassinate Queen Elizabeth.
12. Thomas Morgan (1546–1606) was a spy for Mary, Queen of Scots, also involved in the Babington Plot. He was

captured and placed in the Tower of London for three years before his exile to France.

13. Anthony Babington (1561–1586) plotted the assassination of Elizabeth, conspiring with the imprisoned Mary, Queen of Scots. The Babington Plot eventually led to Mary's execution. Babington's involvement with the plot was reported to Walsingham, and Babington was taken to the Tower of London. Babington offered Elizabeth £1,000 for his pardon. He was rejected and publicly executed. Parts of his body were strewn all over England as a warning to those who thought they might succeed in a plot against the Queen.
14. Mary Stuart (1542–1587) was Queen of Scotland from 1542 until 1567. In 1586, after particulars of the Babington Plot emerged publicly, Mary was arrested. Walsingham had deliberately arranged for Mary's letters to be smuggled out of her confinement at Chartley. Mary was misled into thinking her letters were secure, while in reality they were deciphered and read by Walsingham. The letters made it clear that Mary was deeply involved in the attempted assassination of Elizabeth. She was executed in 1587, but it took more than a single blow to remove her head. The first missed her neck and struck her in the back of her head. The second failed to completely cut the neck, leaving her head hanging by small bit of muscle. The frantic executioner cut through that using his axe; thereafter he held Mary's head high and called out, somewhat ambiguously, "God save the Queen!"
15. Scottish Travelers, sometimes called, in Elizabethan times, Gypsies or tinkers, continue to be a widely diverse and unconnected group of itinerant people, variously calling themselves Gypsies, Travelers in Scotland: Indigenous Highland Travelers, Funfair Travelers, or Showmen, Romanichals (a subset of the Romani people),

and Lowland Gypsies. Contemporarily the word *Gypsy* is out of favor. Interestingly that word is a Middle English declension of the word *Egyptians,* suggesting the origins of all Traveling People and bringing to mind the so-called Lost Tribes of Israel, though there is absolutely no proof of that connection.

16. *The Lady of May* is a pastoral one-act play by Sir Philip Sidney. It's interesting for its allegorical content relating to Queen Elizabeth I, for whom it was first performed. The Queen herself was asked to mediate the outcome of the masque, judging which woodland suitor would win the hand of the country maiden.
17. The odd manuscript referred to in the book is real and was actually in the library of John Dee during his time in Elizabeth's court. Often called the most mysterious manuscript in the world, it's comprised of at least two hundred and forty pages and carbon-dated to around 1400. It's contemporarily known as the *Voynich Manuscript,* so named for Wilfrid Voynich, a Polish book dealer who purchased it in 1912. It's an illustrated codex of some sort, handwritten in a completely unknown language. The drawings are as described in the novel. The entire work has been examined by the world's greatest cryptographers, including the code-breakers of WWII, and, more recently, by computer analysis. At this writing it remains undeciphered, a complete enigma. The original now resides in Yale University's Beinecke Rare Book and Manuscript Library (MS 408). It may be examined (and it's worth a look) online at: beinecke.library.yale.edu/collections/highlights/voynich-manuscript